RADIANCE

Book Three of The Watchers Chronicle

Evan Braun
and Clint Byars

THE LAW OF RADIANCE
Book Three of The Watchers Chronicle

This is a work of fiction. Names, characters, places and incidents either are the product of the authors' imagination or are used fictitiously, and any resemblance to actual persons, living or dead, businesses, companies, events, or locales is entirely coincidental.

Word Alive Press
131 Cordite Road, Winnipeg, MB R3W 1S1
www.wordalivepress.ca

WORD ALIVE
—P R E S S—

ISBN 978-1-4866-0913-0

Cataloguing in Publication information may be obtained through Library and Archives Canada.

www.thebookofcreation.net
www.facebook.com/thebookofcreation
sherwoodbrighton@gmail.com

Cover illustration by Bradford M. Gyselman (http://occamite.com).

ACKNOWLEDGEMENTS

Writing these books has been an unprecedented experience. As always, I must first acknowledge Clint Byars, with whom I began this great endeavor almost ten years ago. What a great ten years!

The act of writing a book is, at the end of the day, solitary work, but a crew of dedicated and insightful critique partners and proofreaders has collaborated with me to produce this book. Leigh Galbreath's careful ministrations have elevated many aspects of the series. And I wouldn't have gotten through this final volume without the attention of Tom Buller, Sherry Peters, Gerald Brandt, Troy Unrau, and Rob Riddell. Grazie. I must also gratefully acknowledge the rock-solid support of my immediate family.

I would like to take a moment to thank a number of specific fans and advocates who have kept me going in good times and bad, in ways too numerous to mention. Thank you so much to Joey, Liz, Colette, Frank, Jen, Angus, Samantha, Rory, Louise, Sylvia, Roxanne, Brenda, Maureen, Nancy, Jan, and many others for your kindness, compassion, and fervor. As the saying goes, a little bit of love goes a long way. (And a lot of love goes even farther!)

—E.B.

CONTENTS

PROLOGUE

New York, New York
TWENTY-NINE YEARS AGO

R adiance." The professor's voice carried through the small classroom as he paused in his blackboard scribblings. He turned to face the dozen students enthroned on uncomfortable metal stools trapped behind long, blacktopped tables. "The power of God has been described in so many different contexts that I can't begin to treat them exhaustively. All we have time for is a brief survey. Bear in mind that I'm not talking about purely *spiritual* power. Yes, all theological studies are inherently spiritual; what I mean is that this kind of power isn't the indistinct, hazy power of prayer we often associate with God. It's real and active and substantial. Tangible. Pragmatic. And this word—radiance—is a key term, the English translation of a profound Hebrew concept: *zohar.* You're going to hear that word a lot in this class."

Ira Binyamin put down his pencil, its once-sharp point worn down to a useless nub, and massaged his wrist. Already the instructor,

Rabbi Roth, had filled four blackboard panels. The rabbi plucked up a felt eraser and enthusiastically rubbed clean the first board, without a thought to any slow copyist who might not yet have gotten through its hastily scrawled words.

"The *Zohar* is a collection of twenty-three texts central to Jewish belief," Roth continued, an unbroken line of chalk streaming out behind his left hand. "These are commentaries on the Torah, on its more mystical elements. The writer of the *Zohar*—if there is a central voice, which is often disputed—takes on cosmogony and religious psychology, the nature of God, the origin of the universe, its complex causal structure, the composition of the human soul, and the byzantine relationships between energy and mankind."

Roth wiped another panel clean and Ira sped up his note-taking for fear of being left behind. He scribbled down the words so fast that he barely registered Roth's voice.

"The texts didn't surface in any form until the thirteenth century, though they're said to have been written during the Second Temple period and passed down rabbi to rabbi until reaching a Jewish writer in Spain, Moses de Leon. De Leon identified the original author as Shimon bar Yochair, though it's no surprise that skeptical Hebrew scholars suggest de Leon wrote it himself and invented its more ancient origin."

Ira threw down his pencil, giving up as Roth's eraser flew over a paragraph he hadn't gotten to yet. The pencil clattered against the black ceramic tabletop, drawing a look of ire from a pair of Hasidic students in the front row. The taller one averted his eyes, but the second angrily flicked his dangling side braid of dark brown hair.

Ira picked up the pencil… then set it down again.

The *Zohar* didn't interest him. His passion lay in the Torah itself, no more and no less, memorized from childhood and put into practice as diligently as any devout Jew was able. The esoteric teachings, and the reams of Talmudic law that seemed to bury his family's religious life, were too much to bear. They seemed full of contradiction, so much of which didn't pass his most fundamental, albeit self-centered, spiritual litmus test—it didn't *sound* like divine inspiration.

"It all comes back to radiance," Roth said loudly, piercing Ira's mental insulation. He sat upright and refocused on the rabbi, who stepped away from the blackboard and turned his animated face on the class. "These texts purport to reveal the radiance of Jehovah, for those who seek meaningful and practical answers regarding the meaning of life, of existence, of all creation. Whether the *Zohar* is canonical is immaterial in the shadow of these possibilities."

Ira picked up his pencil, turned the page of his notebook, and wrote one sentence:

WHAT ARE THE POSSIBILITIES?

He sighed, staring at those letters. At thirty-eight, his life had gone precisely nowhere. From the age of twelve, his father had set him on the rabbinic path—not a personal choice so much as a family one. He had met his responsibilities, lived the expectations of the Binyamin name. He couldn't be faulted.

Nor can I be credited.

Ira looked up at the sound of stool legs scraping against hard floor tiles. Class was over, by all accounts. As students crowded the door, he closed the cover of his notebook and tossed it into the worn leather bag next to his feet.

"Rabbi Binyamin, could I have a word?"

Ira turned to the end of the row, only now appreciating that Roth had taken up position there. Going by the instructor's smooth features, he couldn't have been past his sixties—his father's age.

"Of course." Ira approached the end of the row. "Is something the matter?"

Roth hoisted himself agilely onto the edge of the tabletop. "We don't get many like you."

"Like me?"

"Students in mid-life." Roth gestured for the empty stool across from him. "May I ask what you thought of today's lecture?"

Ira hesitated, once again letting his bag drop to the floor. He didn't say anything for many seconds. The silence stretched on for an embarrassingly long time, yet Roth maintained his patient demeanor.

"I enjoyed it." Ira groaned inwardly at his word choice. Enjoyed. This was rabbinic seminary, intended for serious students, not entertainment. "Sorry, that's wrong."

Roth let loose a disarming smile. "It's not wrong to enjoy yourself."

"Of course not. I meant to say that the lecture intrigued me."

"I didn't mean to make you uncomfortable, Ira. You don't mind if I call you that, do you?"

Ira wasn't sure why Roth would have bothered to know his name, but he nodded anyway.

"Your file caught my attention." Roth hopped off the table and made his way back to the front of the classroom. He collected his study materials, pushing them into a single stack of pages. "This isn't your first time through seminary. Are you auditing?"

"I am."

"Well, you just lied to me about finding the lecture intriguing." Roth said this without missing a beat. "Since all your studies are elective, I'm not sure why you chose this class. Why are you here?"

The actual reason—*"I find myself between synagogues, and bored with life"*—didn't feel appropriate. He had spent the last five years teaching at a synagogue in Stamford. He'd been prepared to spend a lifetime there, if they would have him. They wouldn't, it turned out, and it was just as well. He was no longer content to officiate weddings and funerals and deliver sermons during the High Holidays. Never again would he play politics with the powerful men and women of his spiritual community, to tailor the advice and wisdom he dispensed in the hopes of maintaining a job.

Being a rabbi is not a job, he reminded himself. *It's a calling. A way of life.*

"It's complicated," Ira said, hoping Roth wouldn't ask more of him.

"Yes, I can see that."

Ira accompanied Roth to the classroom door, then held it open for the older man. "I didn't lie earlier," he said. "I am intrigued, to an extent."

"I'm hosting a gathering this evening at my home," Roth said as they entered the corridor. "I'd like to invite you to join us."

"Will other students be there?"

"No, no." Roth began to walk, and Ira hurried to keep up. "Just close friends and associates."

"I don't understand why you'd want me there."

A wide smile cracked Roth's face. "It would be rude to decline the invitation."

Roth stopped, having arrived at the convergence of several corridors. To their right, the bright light of midday pierced a wall of tinted windows. Snow flurries ravaged the sky, blowing into drifts around the building's main entrance. Three men in brightly colored parkas wielded shovels, clearing the front walk.

"Should we set a place for you?" Roth asked.

"I suppose so," Ira said, restraining his urge to fidget under the man's scrutiny.

Roth raised an eyebrow. "Is that a yes? My wife would be vexed if we had an empty seat at the table."

Ira looked toward the building's front door with longing. That snowstorm was several magnitudes more inviting than the rabbi's offer. "Surely you wouldn't invite me just to even out the seating arrangements—"

"It was a joke, Ira."

"Yes, okay." Ira met this strange man's gaze. "You've certainly piqued my curiosity."

"Well, if I couldn't get the same reaction in the classroom, I'll take it now."

Roth reached into his pocket and pulled out a scrap of paper; Ira thought it might have been ripped off the corner of a pack of chewing gum. It even smelled slightly of spearmint. Roth produced a pen from his lapel and scribbled down an address.

"I'll see you at seven. Looking forward to it."

"Same here," Ira said as he watched Roth walk down another corridor. He wasn't sure he meant it.

The wind howled and the snow piled up in the streets, making the drive back to Connecticut a nightmare. Halfway to the state line, Ira changed his mind and decided to stay in the city until his dinner appointment. He didn't want to drive through this mess more than once. He pulled into the left lane and turned at the next intersection, his wiper blades working overtime and his wheels churning through several inches of brown slurry.

Roth lived in a two-story redbrick home on the east side of Queens. As Ira wound along the wide street, he noted the neighborhood's quiet, suburban ambiance. Roth may not have been wealthy, but he certainly put Ira in his place. He pulled up to the curb, behind a line of three other cars.

More than two feet of snow had formed into hard-packed drifts around the driveway, but Ira bravely trudged through them, leaving knee-deep gashes in his wake. He gripped the handrail that guided him to the top of the home's front landing and stood for several long seconds with his hands in his pockets and chin dipped low into his collar.

He brought his hand up to the brass knocker, then lowered it, scowling at his argyle sweater and light blue jeans.

I can't wear these, he thought, suddenly trying hard to remember if Roth had mentioned anything about a dress code. Before he could scamper back to his car, the door sprang open. Shards of ice fell from the edges of the frame, dislodged from where water had frozen in the crevices.

A short woman with a shock of curly grey hair stared back at him. Her oversized glasses sank more than halfway down her dimpled cheeks, seemingly held aloft solely by her enormous smile.

"You must be Ira," she said, stepping out of the way. "Come in, come in. My husband is waiting for you."

Ira swept into the small entrance and closed the door behind him. He had to give the handle a solid heave to ensure it shut all the way. His own glasses fogged up without delay; he leaned over to unlace his shoes, feeling a twinge of embarrassment as he accidentally shook loose a cache of snow from the hollow of his pant leg. It settled onto the clear plastic floor mat and immediately began to transform into sludge.

Once his glasses thawed, he turned his attention back to the short woman.

"Aaron doesn't commonly invite strangers to dinner," she said. "You must be a very special young man."

Ira shuffled off his coat and placed it gently over her outstretched arm. He didn't suppose he qualified as a young man anymore, though from the perspective of Roth's wife, it might well have been an apt description.

She turned her back to him, fetched a hanger, and slipped the coat onto the closet's central dowel as a burst of laughter floated out from one of the rooms at the back of the house. Ira looked up sharply and took in his surroundings for the first time. To his right, two steps descended into an empty sitting room, its dusty cushions and tables looking as neglected as city ruins. Beyond, an arch led into a brightly lit room.

"This way," the woman said, crossing toward that arch and passing into the light.

Ira followed her into a modest kitchen bordered by dark cabinets and faded wallpaper. Three men stood on the far side of the room, leaning against a bright yellow countertop. Two of them were stooped, with strings of matted grey hair falling over their foreheads. They looked enough alike that Ira thought they might be related; their sunken blue eyes shone like gems, their cheeks pockmarked by deep craters. The third was a dapper young fellow in his forties. Chestnut-brown hair poured over the sides of his head in voluminous waves, fusing with the color of his tweed jacket; he loosened his necktie as his dark eyes made contact with Ira's.

Before greetings could be exchanged, Roth entered through a side door Ira had failed to notice until now. The instructor had dressed casually in jeans and a brown woolen sweater.

Roth took Ira's hand. "I'm so pleased to see you," he said, then turned to the three strangers. "Gentlemen, this is the man I told you about, Rabbi Binyamin. He'll be joining us from now on."

From now on? Ira thought.

Roth disappeared into the side room, and the other men followed. The instructor's wife busied herself by the kitchen sink making final preparations for dinner. The scent of roast chicken, with a hint of rosemary, spilled into the air when she opened the oven.

Ira stepped into a richly appointed dining room. Several impressionist-style paintings graced the wall in gilded frames. Ira wasn't enough of an art critic to discern their artistic merit, though they'd likely all been composed by the same artist. Six place settings divided the oak table.

Without waiting for invitations, the other men all chose seats. Ira hesitated before taking the open seat next to Roth. It almost seemed that the others had intentionally left it available.

Ira placed his hands on the varnished wooden armrests, the soft cushion yielding beneath him. The slightly worn table and chairs looked like antiques; even the burnished silverware was older than anything Ira was accustomed to.

"You look uncomfortable," Roth said quietly.

"Can I ask what I'm doing here?"

"I like you. Isn't that enough?" Roth looked up as his wife came into the room holding a glass bowl of steaming green beans. "Marianne, can you bring the wine?"

His wife nodded and returned to the kitchen. Within a few moments, all the food had made its way to the table, including the chicken, its golden brown gristle flashing under the glow of a light fixture that hung from the ceiling via a silver chain.

Roth intoned a short, to-the-point prayer, and a few moments later the various main dishes made their rounds left to right. Ira helped himself to a chicken leg and a large spoonful of mashed potatoes.

The two elderly guests turned out to be brothers, Moshe and Ezra Rosenbach, family friends visiting from Poland. The third man, introduced merely as David, was quiet most of the meal. Disengaged. Ira wondered about David's role in this cadre; he barely seemed friendly to the other men.

Ira listened unobtrusively to the lively dinner discussion between Roth and the Rosenbach brothers. They devoted a large amount of time to catching up on family happenings, and the rest went to theological ramblings running the gamut from traditional Judaism to some of the stranger notions Roth had begun to delve into in class.

After some time, Roth turned to regard Ira. "What do you make of all this?"

Ira hesitated. His preferred answer would have been impolite, yet he couldn't bring himself to lie. "I'm not well-versed enough to form an opinion."

To Ira's surprise, Roth laughed. "Ira, you are a pleasant enough fellow, but you have a tendency to equivocate."

"You've put me in a delicate position, Rabbi—"

"Please, call me Aaron."

Over the course of his short acquaintance with Aaron, Ira had grown desensitized to the feeling of being continuously caught off-guard. "Okay, Aaron. I have my doubts about Kabbalah, about this business with the *Zohar*. A lifetime of mainstream rabbinic education has taught me to distrust it."

"It's a cult." David put down his fork and turned to face Aaron eye to eye.

Ira looked across the table, surprised to have heard anything out of the silent man, never mind something so antagonistic.

"A cult," David repeated. "I'm disgusted to hear that you're pedaling this nonsense at the seminary level. You know what those people did to me?"

What people? Ira wondered. A hundred questions coursed through him, and a few came close to forcing themselves out his mouth before an unusually terse Aaron broke in.

"David, we've talked about this."

David locked eyes with Ira. "My father would have you believe there's some sort of mystical healing power in the *Zohar*. There's not."

So they're father and son.

"When I was diagnosed with cancer ten years ago, I visited a Kabbalah institute in Stockholm," David continued. "They sold me over two thousand dollars' worth of holy water and ancient Aramaic texts which I couldn't even read. They told me all I needed to do was scan the pages, meditate, and drink the water." He paused, visibly shaken.

"I *did* get better, but only months later after an intensive regimen of radiation therapy."

"For goodness sake, David, would you shut up for a minute?" Aaron placed his hands on the table, every zen molecule in his body evaporating like sweat on a hot summer day.

Marianne pushed her chair away from the table and quickly began clearing the dinner plates. Ira leaned back as his potatoes vanished before he had a chance to point out that he wasn't finished with them yet.

"David, you haven't listened to a word I've said." Aaron took several deep breaths, his calm exterior snapping back into place. "I don't claim to believe in all aspects of the *Zohar*, but it's an important part of Hebrew research that cannot be ignored. If anything, it's become ever more essential to study as it gains popularity."

"Would you agree that it's a cult?" David demanded.

Aaron stared at his son with a blank expression. "I'll agree if it appeases you."

Evidently, that was the wrong thing to say. David stood, threw his napkin down, and withdrew almost as quickly as Marianne had.

"Give my love to the grandchildren," Aaron said softly as David disappeared from view.

Ira kept his eyes downturned for the long, painful seconds that followed. He could practically hear his socks brushing against the carpet's thick fibers, the electric hum of the light overhead.

"I'm not sure you handled that as well as you could," Moshe Rosenbach said, reaching for his glass of wine. He took a careful sip.

"He doesn't understand." Aaron let out a long sigh. "Or rather, he won't let himself understand. Have I made mistakes? Have I been wrong about things? Yes, and I've admitted as much. He refuses to forgive."

"Forgiveness is one of the hardest things there is," Ezra said.

Aaron straightened his back and sat forward. "That was awkward, but it's just as well for you to have seen it."

It took Ira a few moments to realize Aaron had been speaking to him.

"I think I should go," Ira said.

"No, no. I won't have it." Aaron pushed aside his half-filled glass. "For twenty years, I was one of those cultists my son mentioned. I've changed my mind about most of it, but I still recognize there are important truths about the world to be taken from the Kabbalah teachings. David may never be comfortable with that. But I'm hoping you will be."

Ira wanted very much to stand up, leave this room, and never come back. "Why on earth would you care what I think?"

"Because you are unique among men." Aaron rubbed his chin, at a loss for words. "Ira, it's difficult to say without sounding crazy. I just ask you to cut me some slack. When I met you this morning, I was struck by—"

"Drop the pretentions," Moshe said quietly. "You weren't struck by anything. God spoke to you, just as he spoke to us. Ira, you've been recruited."

Ira opened his mouth to speak, though no words came out.

"I know how you feel," Aaron said nonchalantly.

"Do you?" Ira asked.

"I was once in your position. Moshe and Ezra delivered the same news to me, and I didn't take it well."

"But what have I been recruited to do? And by whom?"

Ezra chuckled as Marianne came back into the room carrying a tray of pastries. The men around the table reached for the small cakes. Marianne poured coffee. Ira watched the dinner theater play out, too flummoxed to participate.

"Recruited," Ira whispered, still trying to wrap his mind around it.

Aaron nodded. "For generations, men and women have been

chosen to guard the secrets of the deep. The ancient texts have great power. In the hands of the unenlightened, this power has the capacity to destroy. Many modern-day followers of Kabbalah search for answers in the ancient texts, such as the *Zohar* and the *Sefer Yetzirah*, claiming to look for God." He put up a finger. "But really, they're looking for the *power* of God. Some might call it the practical science by which Jehovah created the universe. When mankind wields these powers, they destroy themselves, even when they operate out of the purest intentions."

"Such as what happened at Babel," Ezra added, putting down a piece of cake. "And when the Watchers came to earth, as Enoch chronicled, they set out to instruct humanity in creation science, to teach them how to use it. The disastrous consequences of this are laid out in the Torah's flood account."

"And elsewhere," Moshe added.

Ira slid his chair back and stood up. "David was right. You sound like cultists."

"I know." Aaron, too, came to his feet. "You'll need to see proof."

Aaron made his way toward the door to the kitchen, and the Rosenbach brothers followed. Ira lingered in the dining room, deciding whether to join them. Everything he knew from a lifetime of rabbinic studies told him they were crazy—but Aaron had seemed to anticipate this. If Aaron offered proof, what could be lost by humoring him?

When he heard Aaron call his name, he stumbled into motion.

All four men gathered outside on a terrace behind the house, the glow from the kitchen window their only illumination. Beyond a row of roof-bearing white columns, Ira saw that the snow had tapered off. He hugged his sweater close to his chest as a gust of wind swept in from the yard.

"What are we doing here?" Ira asked.

Aaron walked to the edge of the terrace and then pressed his eyes closed in concentration. He held out both of his hands, palms up.

Shivering from the cold, Ira looked to Moshe and Ezra for an explanation, but the two men had closed their eyes as well. Frustrated, Ira looked up at the warm light pouring out of the window and wished he was back inside—or better yet, at home, in his own bed.

In his peripheral vision, he saw the glow of approaching headlights. Then it occurred to him that the street wasn't even visible from here. Ira turned, and for several long seconds he didn't understand what he was looking at: the glow didn't come from the street; it came from Aaron's hand.

Another gust carried a sheet of snow into Ira's face. He stiffened, expecting to be hit by a wall of cold, but instead warm air rushed over him in a mist.

Aaron raised his hands higher. They seemed to be consumed by fire.

"Stop it," Ira whispered, but the wind snatched his words away in a frenzy. He shouted louder. "Stop!"

Aaron batted his eyelids, then the light winked out. The man's muscles sagged, and then the rest of his body followed suit; he collapsed to his knees, his arms falling to his side.

Ira rushed to him. "Are you okay?"

Aaron opened his mouth, and Ira expected him to speak. Instead he let out a deep, blissful belly laugh. He laughed so hard that he quaked from head to toe.

"Of course he's okay," Moshe said, creeping up behind Ira and resting a hand on his shoulder.

"I've never been better." Aaron's eyes cracked open, and what Ira saw shook him to his core. The man's face shone—from ecstasy, from pride, from excitement, Ira didn't know what. "Do you understand now?"

"What was that?"

"Radiance," Aaron said. "The splendor of God, that which David can't understand. This power…" He gathered his remaining strength and got to his feet. Ezra took him by the hand. "Mankind *can* wield this power, if he discovers the technique. The knowledge, however, was never meant to be given to us."

"Then how did you discover it?" Ira said, still working to accept what he had seen.

If mankind can wield this power, then perhaps I could as well. He shuddered at the implication. Was that the reason Aaron had invited him here? To graduate him from the ranks of ordinary man to some kind of Superman?

"There are two methods, one that is safe and another which results in utter destruction to all who attempt it." Aaron walked slowly back toward the door. "The safe method is a relationship with the creator. The other was revealed to mankind by the Watchers many thousands of years ago. Teaching men and women to manipulate creation was the ultimate attack on the stability of creation itself."

Ira followed him into the house. As they walked through the kitchen, he saw Marianne cleansing the dining room of all evidence of dinner.

"Even the safe method is not truly free of danger," Moshe said as they approached the front sitting room. "Because we were never intended to wield this power, doing so means death. There is a time and place for all things, but Jehovah has not yet ordained his power for our use."

Ira turned to Aaron. "Then what you just did…"

"Has consequences." Aaron descended into the sitting room and steadied himself on the edge of a loveseat. "I only did it because I must, to demonstrate the truth. I won't live forever, Ira. My son refuses to accept the mantle of responsibility, but I believe Jehovah sent you to me. It takes constant vigilance to guard mankind from those who seek to unveil this power. But to guard against it, you must master it—and mastering it comes with a terrible cost."

Ira had so many questions. Too many to sift through, and in Aaron's depleted state he wasn't sure now was the time. But now *had* to be the time. How could he be expected to sleep on this?

"Not now, Ira," Aaron said, as though reading his mind. "The mission is urgent, but we cannot begin today."

"But if not today, when?"

Aaron's thin lips managed a smile. "Tomorrow."

ONE

Mount Khunjerab, Pakistan
JULY 28

W e're not alone," Ira said, drawing out the words. He searched the terrain from one side of his vision to the other, squinting as the midday sun hit his eyes. To his human senses, there was nothing amiss. The sky overhead and the land below. Boulders and patches of heavy brush dotting the slope. The land plunged toward a valley surrounded on three sides by the towering Karakorams, an impenetrable wall save the glacier trail they had just passed over. To his *other* sense—a sixth sense, a supernatural sense—he knew trouble was brewing.

Dario caught up to him, the lumbering form of Noam Sheply clinging blindly to the Italian man's shoulder. Sheply was a pitiful sight, a once intimidating man reduced to this shadow of his former self. His wide eyes saw nothing, yet they flared open, probing the darkness.

Perhaps it's just as well he's no longer dependent on sight, Ira thought, though he kept it to himself. The danger ahead lurked unseen.

His gaze fell on the hole in the ground in the middle of the valley, a manmade opening large enough to serve as an aircraft hangar. So not all the dangers were unseen.

Dario's expression was troubled, but before he could give voice to his fears, a resounding gunshot broke the stillness, echoing off distant mountains and boomeranging back to them. Somewhere off to his left, a flock of birds took flight.

Two more shots followed. Ira's hands flew to his chest, as though to confirm it was still intact. The shots had been fired into the air, he suspected. A warning.

In short order, Ira made out three people approaching from downslope—two men and a woman with fiery red curls. More gunmen flanked them to the rear, he realized, hearing the sound of their boots crunching over dry grass and cracked earth.

"We should have seen this coming, Ira," Dario said.

Ira sighed. "I did. We came anyway."

He considered disclosing the plan, just like he had considered disclosing it the previous night in the jeep. They had lain together across the reclined seats as crickets chirped, creating such a damned racket that sleep never came. He had sensed Dario's frustration; it was a powerful force, straining against the young man's skin almost as powerfully as in Brighton. Just as in so many matters, the knowledge of what was to come wouldn't have done anything but inflict harm. He had to find Brighton and bring him back. Everything depended on that.

"Welcome to Shamballa," the red-haired woman called to them, the wind snatching her words and flooding over them in a mighty gust. "We've been waiting for you all morning."

Ira looked over her and quickly assessed what he was dealing with. Her confidence and aggression were unnatural, in opposition to her otherwise gentle features. It wasn't really *her*, he realized. It was something else.

Aaron, this is where your path led me. We must not be too late. He turned his eyes heavenward and transmitted a silent prayer to his old friend.

"Where are Sherwood Brighton and Elisabeth Macfarlane?" Ira said, lowering his eyes back to the possessed woman. "I have come to retrieve them."

Her mouth cracked open and laughter escaped, her eyes crinkling in delight. "And we have come to retrieve you."

Ira turned just in time to catch sight of the three men behind them. He stiffened as one of those men nestled a rifle into the small of his back.

If only Brighton had been sensible, it wouldn't have come to this. But of course that had been his flaw all along. He had thought too highly of the young man, who surely had no concept of his own importance.

"Check them for weapons," the woman said.

One of the ambushers grinned as he discovered a hunting knife inside Dario's pocket. He slipped it out of its leather sheath and held it up, inspecting it under the light.

The woman joined them in another burst of laughter. "How much damage do you think you could have done with that?"

"Are you going to kill us?" Dario asked without flinching.

Perhaps it's best not to goad her, Ira wanted to say, but he never got the chance. She nodded at the man standing behind Sheply, and a moment later the blade's jagged edge was pressed against the blind man's throat.

"Don't move," Dario whispered to Sheply, whose first reaction was to squirm free. "They've got the knife."

Please don't let this be a mistake. Ira closed his eyes as events swirled around him. He imagined a river, a fast-flowing river, and waded through the shallows, his fingers gliding over the willowy tips of bulrushes and reeds. He had been here many times before, in times of crisis. It only took a moment to shut the world out and ground himself in the vision. The water pulled at him, gently at first and then stronger as he waded up to his waist, the cold water lapping against the sensitive skin of his lower stomach, seeping through his clothes.

"Behave yourself," the woman was saying, her voice floating to him through the thick, humid air above the river. "I could let this one bleed. Is that what you want?"

The current tugged at his legs and soon he found himself drifting out toward the center of the river, caught in the flow. The trees along the riverbank passed quicker and quicker, almost in a blur. He fought to keep his head above water. The water was so fast, so deep. More than usual. He struggled to exert control.

"You, old man, are a delicious prize."

Ira's eyes snapped open to find the woman staring at him with a cold, hard intensity.

"The Grigori have been hoping to possess you," the woman said.

"I have not come to assist the Grigori." Ira's eyes grounded him in the present moment, on the slope, the flanks of Mount Khunjerab all around him, but the vision was never far; the water still pulled him along.

"What you have come for is unimportant," the woman said. "You will do what is required, or your friends will die. We have many methods to aid us in eliciting cooperation, including substances to make one pliable to our needs."

Ira smiled as his feet dragged along the muddy river bottom, then dug in. "I have a stronger mind than most."

"You may be right, but it may not come to that. Another plan is in motion at this very moment. Sherwood Brighton is on the cusp of making the most important decision of his life, and we have taken steps to ensure his pliancy."

"Sherwood, too, has a stronger mind than you think," Ira said, but he wasn't sure he entirely believed it. Was it true? Did they have him? Had events progressed so far?

Damn it, Sherwood. All you had to do was trust me. We could have avoided this.

"How very self-assured for a man facing his doom." The woman lifted a single finger and Sheply cried out, blood trailing down from the wound and pooling in the hollow at the base of his neck.

Sheply whimpered and then cried in anguish. "Just kill me," he pleaded. "Get it over with."

"What are we waiting for?" Dario clearly had no patience for this, and perhaps not much empathy for Sheply. "Either let us go or finish it."

"You face two possible paths," the woman said, turning to face him. "In one, you are a prisoner, and in the other, you are dead. Are you so impatient for the end to come?"

The end, Ira thought. *How near to it we've come. And if Brighton has truly passed out of our hands, then we've arrived at it, full stop.*

"No," Ira said, his feet digging into the mud anew. He felt the course of the river, felt its various potentialities. He drew himself up, seeing the possibilities, and chose a path. The path. The only one remaining to him.

He sensed all eyes turning to him in surprise.

"There is another path."

He silently flexed his wrist, just as Aaron had taught him so many years ago, working his fingers slowly at first and then so aggressively that he felt like the joints would pop free of their constraints. Aaron had explained that the movements weren't required, but the action was helpful in stirring the accompanying electromagnetic force that lay dormant inside. His mind formed the complex string of calculations he had repeated every night for ten years with steadfast resolve, eventually coming to memorize that which he had once deemed too complicated for the human mind. Oh how he had underestimated the human mind, through no fault of his own; so few people understood their inborn capabilities.

As the equation snapped into focus, the numbers and figures in their proper places, he felt a pulse of energy deep in his gut, running outward through his chest, his arms, and landing in his palms, even his fingers. As they gyrated to the internal rhythm of his subconscious, blinding light radiated out from him. The warmth churned toward white-hot heat, enough to singe his fragile skin, blacken it, peel it back to expose muscle and bone; he gritted his teeth against the brain-melting pain that pounded through every fiber of his being, persuading himself that the physical harm was psychosomatic. If he concentrated, he could feel every electron rising and falling in its orbit, photons forming in accordance with everything he knew about quantum mechanics, blazing into the physical world in glorious streams of nonlocality.

Shrieks of torment erupted amidst the pain and ecstasy. When they had started, he couldn't say. He had only inhabited this heightened state once before, and on that occasion he had lost nearly an hour in the space of a minute. The heat was all-consuming.

"Ira, stop!"

He barely heard the shout through the maelstrom of wind that had kicked up around him. He lowered his arms slightly and pulled back on the source of heat inside him. All his focus went into the effort, imagining himself in the river, in control, and the light pulling back into his skin.

"Ira!"

Those voices wrenched at his consciousness, fighting for attention, distracting him. He built a wall around himself to shut them out—or at least tried to. His eyes gaped from the effort, but the flame would not be extinguished; he had fanned it too long. He tried clenching his fists, hoping to extinguish the energies now whipping so furiously.

One moment he was standing with arms outstretched, and the next he was flat on his back, wincing from where his shoulder blades had jammed into the rugged ground. All-encompassing yellow light lingered in the air as he raised his head, drawing in ragged breaths. He'd had the air knocked out of him.

The light soon faded just enough to reveal Dario's face pressed into his chest, a frenzied look in the young man's eyes. Ira turned his head and saw the razed corpses strewn amongst the grass.

You were supposed to stop them, not incinerate them.

"What have I done?" he whispered, the reality of the situation barely registering. "Oh Lord, what I done?"

Pops of gunfire broke through the roaring silence that surrounded him like a bubble, and with them the real world rushed in.

Screams rent the air and Dario's head whipped around to face the carnage. A splash of bright red blood hit Ira right between the eyes, and in the background, just out of focus, Noam Sheply collapsed. Blood streamed out from his throat to his exposed belly where bullets had gutted him like a fish.

Tears sprang to his eyes. It wasn't supposed to happen like this.

Sherwood, why have you been such a fool? But then another voice, another perspective. *If he was a fool, he wasn't the only one.*

"Dario," Ira shouted to be heard above the gunfire.

Dario didn't answer. He grabbed Ira by the shirt and hauled him backwards.

"Dario, what are you doing?"

With one final lurch, Dario pulled him to the relative safety provided by a boulder whose sharp point stuck out of the ground just high enough to shield them.

"What's happening?" Ira asked.

Dario turned on him with frenzied eyes. "Ira, how can you ask that?"

"Tell me. I lost control."

"Lost control?" Dario's face turned red. He was livid. "Is that what you call it? Everyone's dead, Ira. Including Sheply."

Ira's heart broke to hear it. He'd harbored no sympathy for Noam Sheply, but he had certainly never intended to cause him harm. But for the others? Well, they had barely been people. Possessed by the Nephilim. They hadn't been themselves.

But they were people, underneath it all. You didn't give them a chance.

Ira shook his head, tried to think clearly. "They were going to kill us."

"But what about Brighton and Elisabeth?"

Another round of bullets sailed through the air. Chunks of the boulder they hid behind shattered loose, pebbles spraying the ground.

"Clearly they're not *all* dead," Ira said.

Dario nodded. "Someone's firing at us from downslope. Short of flaying them with another burst of that light, I'm not sure how we're going to get out of this."

"I'm not doing that again."

The look on Dario's face betrayed relief and disappointment. "It may be the only option."

You don't understand, he wanted to say. *You don't understand what it did to me. To focus it. To control it.*

The gunfire had stopped, and that could only mean two things. Either whoever held those guns had fled, leaving them in blessed peace, or more likely, they were at this moment advancing on his and Dario's position.

"But we have to do something," Ira said after a few moments.

"After what you just did, I doubt these people would be able to contain you."

Ira propped himself up. "Perhaps, perhaps not. The forces in this valley have powers of their own."

"Who are they, Ira? Are there aliens here, like Carter and Marilyn believe?"

"In a manner of speaking."

"Damn it, I'm sick and tired—"

Ira put a finger to his lips. "Now's not the time. Perhaps I've held my cards too close, and if so I've paid a price. For now, we need a plan."

"I say we run like hell."

"We won't make it far."

Ira closed his eyes again and summoned the river. Its water, not quite as cool and refreshing as he was accustomed to, flowed over him in a torrent. But he maintained control, his feet grasping the bottom and finding purchase. He visualized the branching flow of the delta, identified the path most suitable to their needs, and channeled the water toward it. The waters changed direction, and…

His eyes peeked open just as Dario was about to launch into another round of protests. He snaked his hand out and clenched Dario's wrist.

A moment later, the air sizzled around them and the mountains popped out of existence.

TWO

Mount Khunjerab, Pakistan
JULY 28

Raff Lagati sat alone in his apartment—his *room*. It would take some time before he grew used to calling this home. If he ever did. He hadn't lived in such austere conditions in decades. The room's four bare walls, painted a bland creamy yellow, loomed silently, pressing in from all sides. A psychological torment more than a physical one. Who had selected that awful color? He didn't think this particular paint swatch had crossed his desk.

His only company was two economical pieces of furniture, including the small cushioned chair he sat on. A twin bed had been wedged into the corner; he didn't need to look at it to know it would be uncomfortable. It was a question of standards.

This is what they've chosen for me, he reminded himself. *They chose it for a reason.*

They, of course, were the Grigori. The Watchers. The adepts. They went by many names, but none did justice to the experience of meeting them in person.

For years, he had spoken to them from the safety of his home, through meditation. He summoned the thrill he'd felt on approaching the shimmering walls of Shamballa for the first time, the thrill of communing with the Grigori directly. He also summoned their disappointment upon learning he didn't have what they needed, though he had promised to obtain it for them. Three years from the making of that promise, he found himself in this new, humble abode. One of his own making. He had commissioned these apartments, or at least refurbished them from the raw, empty spaces they had been, though he hadn't imagined one day living in one.

He tried to tell himself this windowless chamber wasn't so different from some of the rooms in his home in Switzerland, much of which was entombed in a mountainside.

A knock at the door roused him. If it had been Semyaza or Azazel, they would never have bothered to announce their presence. As much veneration as he felt for the Grigori, he had to admit some small relief at not facing them again so soon after his latest lesson vis-à-vis Barakel.

"Who is it?" he asked authoritatively. His tone was perhaps no longer appropriate for his station. That would be a hard habit to shake.

"It's Antoinette."

Lagati brushed the copper-plated square next to the door, hearing the door open behind him as he returned to his chair. He sat down, facing Antoinette Patenaude. The full-figured brunette, middle-aged and striking, entered the room with her hands clasped behind her back. She appraised the room, her slanted gaze wandering over its stark ornamentation. He took a moment to admire her. She wasn't the beauty she'd been in her twenties; along the way she'd exchanged physical perfection for wit, for cunning, for sharp intelligence. An admirable exchange. This woman was superior to the one he had known fifteen years earlier. He longed to stand, to run his fingers over her prominent cheekbones, over the delicate epicanthic folds of her eyes. He restrained himself.

"So this is where they put you." She sat on the edge of the bed. Where else was she going to sit? "People have been wondering all afternoon what became of you. A few thought you were dead."

He raised an eyebrow. "Dead?"

"All we knew is that from the moment the Grigori appeared, you disappeared." Antoinette patted the edge of the bed. "Come, join me. I feared the worst."

Lagati lifted himself from the chair and joined her. As soon as he sat, she lay back. She really was one of a kind. If he had ever decided to marry, he would have asked her; she knew this, which is why she stayed. What they had was as good as marriage, or at least as good as they were likely to experience in this lifetime. That was the curse of wealth, of success. How difficult it was to trust in blind romanticism.

"Do we have time?" he asked, gazing into her eyes. She was only half-Japanese, but all those Asian genetics were concentrated in the face. The rest of her was all French—insolent and prideful when the situation called for it, and full of false humility when it didn't.

Well, that was too harsh an assessment.

"No, actually," she said, arching her thin eyebrows. "Aren't you going to ask how I found you?"

"How did you find me?"

Her eyes crinkled as she laughed. "I asked."

"Who?"

"Who do you think? One of the Grigori was in the hangar. I don't know his name."

"I see. He spoke to you." Lagati couldn't help feeling a bit incredulous, but he shouldn't have. From the start of this project, he had been the only one to speak with the Grigori. He acknowledged a pang of jealousy. "You should be careful. I've told you how dangerous they are."

Antoinette traced a tender patch of skin over his left kidney where Azazel had once kicked him. He no longer felt pain in that spot, but he flinched anyway.

"Stories are going around," she said. "I wanted to confirm them."

"Tell me."

"There's talk of an incident on the surface."

He straightened up. "What kind of incident?"

"A battle, if you can believe it. All kinds of gunfire… and other displays of power. Something about a blinding light. Do you know anything about it?"

Lagati stood up and paced as far as the opposite wall. He rested his hands on the back of the chair. "When did this happen?"

"Wow. You really aren't in charge anymore, are you?"

"Answer my question."

She drew her knees up. "Noon, give or take."

He slumped back into the chair. How unsettling to be out of the loop in such a critical moment.

"This is the first I'm hearing about it," he said. "I spoke to Semyaza nearly an hour ago, and he didn't say a word. Not about this, anyway."

"What did you talk about?"

Lagati laid out the whole uncomfortable exchange, taking several minutes to recap the Barakel lesson. "They're putting Barakel back in captivity for the role he played during the pre-Flood rebellion. You should have seen the terror in Barakel's eyes. The moral was clear: we are subject to them now. We'll have to watch ourselves."

"Are you scared?"

That was a complicated question, which made it all the more important to provide as precise an answer as possible. His instinct was to say no; he didn't fear the Grigori, but he respected them and knew their capabilities. But what was the difference between fear and this definition of respect? He would take more time later to analyze the margins.

"Yes," he answered honestly. "But I still believe in what we're doing, if that's what you're asking."

Antoinette sat forward. "There's a clean-up crew heading out to the scene of the incident."

He had been about to explain that Semyaza had given him an assignment: to catalogue the cargo coming off the ships. "What are they cleaning up?" he asked instead.

"The Grigori didn't say. I'd sure like to find out." She stood up, taking his hand in hers. "Unless you have something better to do."

Lagati stood again, thinking at first that he should somehow prepare to leave. But what was there to prepare? He had nothing but the clothes on his back.

They emerged from the room in lockstep. The corridor, like the entirety of the underground base, had been blasted from the bedrock many thousands of years ago, and its craggy walls had an unfinished look. The passage followed a gentle curve to the left, its long span interspersed by hundreds of identical doors. If they were to continue walking, the circular corridor would eventually land them right where they had started, though the revolution would require them to hike nearly four kilometers.

They took up a brisk pace, exchanging nods and pleasantries with the few people they passed along the way. Many exhibited surprise at seeing him, but he never stopped long enough to explain himself. It gave him pleasure to force them into speculation.

When they came into the hangar, Lagati preceding Antoinette by the merest step, he was surprised to find the cavernous space mostly empty. A part of him had been working under the assumption the bulk of the staff would be here. Instead only a small group—ten people, by his quick count—gathered around the one and only spacecraft in its usual berth, its burnished hull shining like a beacon under the bright strips of glow-rock overhead.

Turel, one of the Grigori, loomed over the group. He was obviously the one in charge. Lagati had only interacted with him once before.

"You are not assigned to this activity," Turel said in a low, inflec-
tionless tone.

Lagati drew himself up. "I wish to volunteer."

Turel regarded him for several long moments before turning
away in indifference. He didn't even reply as he went back to briefing
the group on what they were about to do. Lagati barely had a minute
to get up to speed before everyone hightailed it toward the door with
Turel in the lead. Antoinette took a flashlight given to her by a col-
league, then took him by the arm and steered him in the group's wake,
another position in which he was unaccustomed to finding himself.

The sun wasn't up by the time they ascended to the surface,
though the sky had already turned a hundred shades of blue over the
eastern peaks.

"It's good to see you, sir." This from Amir Balasubramian, his dark
brown skin barely visible under the beam of Antoinette's flashlight.

"I'm not sure you should call me that anymore," Lagati said, trying to sound comfortable with it. "The chain of command has
changed in the last few hours."

Amir shrugged. "You want us to call you by your name?"

"Yes."

"Your first name?"

Lagati hesitated. He had difficulty imagining these people referring to him that way. Nobody called him Raff except Antoinette, and
even that intimacy had taken nearly a decade to develop.

"Call me Lagati," he told the aerospace engineer.

Only now did Lagati notice the shovel in Amir's hand. In fact, all
the men and women of their group seemed to be carrying one.

"What are the shovels for?" Lagati asked.

"We'll soon find out." Amir's gaze was fixed on Turel's back, the

Grigori's powerful shoulders straining against the confines of his shirt. Perhaps Amir was considering how long it would take their leader to snap off each of their arms and legs like so many branches of a tree.

They walked in silence, the only exception the swish of their shoes through grass, the normally sunburnt blades moistened by light dew. As the day broke, Lagati felt more than saw the others staring at him; each person only stared for a few moments, but the effect, when magnified by ten, felt continuous. He had grown accustomed to people staring at him—that was the price of fame and fortune—but this attention could be attributed to a more unnerving reason. Should he say something? Stop the group and address it, as he had done with Amir? Did they deserve an explanation? Did they require one? Would he be able to develop a working relationship with any of them in the wake of having commanded them for so long?

He arrived at answers quickly, as was his habit. He didn't need to say anything; the news would spread like a virus. People only ever deserved what they got, and he didn't owe them anything. It was the old karmic principle in action, delivering to people what they attracted. And that which someone received was often precisely that which he or she required; the real question was whether they had ever known what they required in the first place.

He did, however, feel doubt about establishing relationships with these people. He didn't care for them in the manner of friends; his only interest in their well-being was of a cold, professional caliber. He supposed many would condemn him for his very practical stance.

The way he handled this personal crisis would be a test of character. This elicited a smile. Was it possible such a test was the underlying reason for the Grigori's treatment of him thus far?

Yes, he decided. It was possible.

The fell field was sprinkled with lavender flowers sprouting up between cracks in the arid rock. To his right, the Khunjerab glacier swept down the saddle out of view, avoiding this hidden alpine valley on account of a high ridge to the east. The sun lofted above it, illuminating a sprawling disc of blackened rock and burnt and twisted scrub near the path.

Lagati recoiled at the smell as they approached. All the others in the party reacted, except Turel. If the Grigori detected the putrid scent of scorched human flesh, he gave no indication. Like all the Grigori whom Lagati had encountered, Turel exercised great self-control.

It soon became clear what this clean-up operation was meant to accomplish. The half-dozen black husks, all that remained of the victims of this fire, barely resembled people. Lagati stepped up to one of these mounds and leaned over it, its slumped shoulders right at eye level. A spherical piece had broken off and rolled onto the ground—a head that resembled an oblong lump of coal. The flesh was burnt to a crisp, except for a rancid white substance at its center which oozed out like melted ice cream.

"Over here!"

Lagati stood, and along with Antoinette and Amir he walked toward the young woman who had shouted. She hunched over a body half-hidden behind the remains of a shrub, its once verdant branches now a mass of thistles. For whatever reason, the body hadn't been burned like the others.

Lagati smiled again—a bizarre reaction to a dead body, but he couldn't help himself; he had despised this man. Noam Sheply stared up with blind, cloudy eyes, his forehead more exposed than Lagati remembered, the poor man's hair having burned away, leaving the scalp unblemished. A deep cut in this throat indicated he had died from a nicked carotid.

"He used to work for me." Lagati brushed the mixture of human and plant remains from the knees of his workpants. "His name was Noam Sheply."

Antoinette saw his smile and thus didn't offer any condolences.

"What happened here?" Amir asked.

Turel stood in the center of the blackened mounds, his voice carrying over the slope with minimal effort. "We suffered an attack."

Well, that much is plain, Lagati thought.

"I sent these people," Lagati whispered to Antoinette, trying to keep his voice from reaching Turel. "Or at least I authorized their assignment. We knew Ira Binyamin was coming this way, along with Sheply and another young man. I never knew his name. Ohia wanted to go out and greet them, prevent them from interfering with my meeting with Brighton."

"How many did Ohia take with him?" Antoinette asked.

Lagati counted the human remains. "Five, I think. And there was backup to follow at a distance."

Antoinette looked surprised. "Was it necessary to send so many?"

"I've told you about Ira."

"But he's in his sixties, Raff."

Lagati gestured to the mounds of burnt flesh. "In his sixties and capable of this."

"You can't be serious."

Lagati counted again. "I count seven bodies, Sheply plus the six men I sent. Including Ohia."

"You can't be certain who's who. You'd have to run tests on the remains."

"I don't need to run tests. Ira isn't among the dead, and Sheply wasn't burned. I'm willing to bet Ira's male companion wasn't burned, either, and I don't see him around here. That means he and Ira escaped, and by extension they must be responsible. The only other person who could have started the blaze is Ohia, and that doesn't make much sense. I think Sheply was preserved because the fire was targeting my men."

Antoinette put a hand on his shoulder, but he shrugged it off. She knew he didn't care for public displays of affection.

"Fire doesn't work that way," she said. "It burns indiscriminately."

"Not this kind of fire."

Lagati felt another, gruffer touch on his shoulder and turned just as Turel thrust a shovel into his hand. He was a Grigori of little words, it seemed, for he only grunted. Lagati saw that the others were stabbing the tips of their shovels at the mounds.

He hefted the shovel and approached the nearest one. He summoned all his frustration and channeled it into the hilt of the shovel, ramming it into the mound. Half a foot of powdery skin and bone sloughed off, leaving behind more of that goopy white liquid. It spilled free and ran in a steep river to the parched earth.

"Level them," Turel said.

It took an hour to scatter the remains, though the blackened circle of land all around them would likely endure for some time, a testament to what had occurred.

Where did you go, Ira?

THREE

New York, New York
JULY 28

The air distorted, exploding in Dario's ears like the first bursts of microwave popcorn. He hadn't even had time to close his eyes; one minute he was surrounded by the mountains and the next a tall brick façade. Night had fallen and police sirens wailed. Or perhaps they were ambulances?

Dario turned in a slow circle, examining his environment. He and Ira stood on a sidewalk on the edge of a darkened square. The brick façade belonged to a ten-story apartment block, one of many identical structures.

He looked Ira in the eye, not all that surprised to find the old man at peace with the madness he had wrought.

"What the hell kind of plan is this?" And then the obvious question: "Where are we?" And then the even more obvious question: "How did we get here?"

Ira took Dario by the arm and began walking up the street, setting a brisk pace. Dario stumbled after him for a few steps, then jerked free. He hurried to catch up, for Ira didn't miss a beat.

"Ira, hold on!" He came alongside the old man, alarmed at how fast Ira could move. "Didn't you just say you were going to be more open-handed with information?"

Ira slowed to a walk, then an amble, and then stopped altogether.

"You're right," Ira said, breathing heavily. "Instinct, you see."

"Would it be so hard to explain yourself?" Dario surveyed the neighborhood, its urban character illuminated by flickering pools of street light. A breeze pushed bits of trash over the cracked pavement where they eventually nestled into the refuge of a parked minivan's long shadow. Looking in either direction, Dario saw that the street went on and on. Wherever they were, it was a sizeable city.

The slew of questions advanced to the tip of Dario's tongue, then dissipated as a series of clues came into focus. That parked van had a New York license plate. All the street signs were in English. An American flag flew in the second-story window of an adjacent apartment block.

"We're in America."

Ira nodded as he began walking again, this time at a more relaxed pace. "New York, to be specific."

Dario had never visited New York before, though his younger brother had lived there—*here*, he reminded himself—for a few years. Several cousins had been born and raised here; he had never met them.

His most troubling association with New York was that Rhea had raved about her many visits to the city during her teenage years. She'd called it her favorite place, citing its pizza and architecture. He smiled, remembering the conversation in her cramped tent at the base of the Tiahuanaco ruins. She'd described the pizza with an almost religious zeal, in his mind a too-thick, too-cheesy, toppings-heaving abomination that bore no resemblance to its Italian namesake.

Yet he suddenly felt a craving for it. In honor of his fallen comrade.

"You're wondering how we got here," Ira said.

"My god, you've read my mind."

Ira disregarded the sarcasm. "The old texts would call it 'translation.' Moving from one place to another instantaneously. It's a rare skill. Hard to master."

Dario could make no room for skepticism anymore, as these New York apartment buildings attested. He had been *there*, and now he was *here*. It wasn't some abstract phenomenon; it had happened.

The shock still hadn't settled in as they came to a glass storefront. A clock on the wall of the darkened coffee shop showed the time as 2:48. A sports car roared past, its nocturnal driver shouting a random obscenity out the rolled-down window. Heavy bass thudded in the pit of Dario's stomach as the car disappeared into this dense metropolitan milieu.

He felt a pang of fear, though the more he analyzed the emotion the slighter he found it, considering the terror they had just escaped. Had he been afraid they would be robbed?

Go ahead, Dario thought. *Take my wallet and its dwindling supply of Pakistani rupees.*

"I can't believe it's still here," Ira said, nose to the glass. "My friend lived across the street, and we spent hours sitting in this coffee shop. It was halfway between my house in Connecticut and the seminary."

Dario only half-listened, the noise from that sports car's stereo still pounding in his head. "It's the middle of the night and we're not exactly in the best neighborhood, Ira. Did you bring us here for a reason?"

"It was on my mind, I guess. I think that's how translation works."

"You think?"

"Well, this was my first time. Seems you have to be in a desperate place for all the mechanics to come together." Ira cocked his head, genuinely apologetic. "That's the best explanation I can offer right now."

"Maybe we could continue this conversation somewhere else."

Ira stepped away from the window. "In fact, I have just the place."

They walked three long blocks to the nearest subway station, at which point they stared in confusion at the map's twisting maze of colored routes. Dario's only experience with metros was from Rome, whose simple two-line system was almost rural by comparison, and which certainly didn't run at three o'clock in the morning.

After a mere twenty minutes, they boarded Line 6 and journeyed south from the Bronx toward Manhattan. Ira didn't say where they were going.

Sometime later, they ascended into the Upper East Side. Full-bodied oak trees lined the sidewalks, creating a canopy overhead. Stone-fronted townhouses, abutted by small but surprisingly green terraces, stretched for blocks, a far cry from the dingy street they'd landed on only an hour earlier.

The townhouse they arrived at was three stories, with its front door a half-story below street level. Dario followed Ira down into the tight space and waited as the rabbi rang the bell. They seemed to wait an eternity, and Dario wondered if the occupants would risk answering their door in the dead of night.

Ira jammed his thumb into the ringer five times. Was the bell even connected to anything? Sure enough, after the fifth ring, the door cracked just wide enough for a pair of suspicious eyes to peek out. One hand held the door open; Dario imagined the other held a loaded gun just out of sight.

No words were exchanged. Perhaps none were necessary. Over the course of five seconds, the look on the homeowner's face morphed from apprehension to affection, and for each arc of this transformation the door swung a bit wider. The man sported wide shoulders and a powerful upper body for his age; he must have been an athlete. Despite his commanding physical presence, his brown eyes were as soft as a puppy's. These two were very old friends. The sudden relaxation of their body language gave it away.

Ira made the first move, and soon the two men embraced. Dario was surprised to see a tear fall from their host's eyes, distorting through the thick lens of his glasses.

After Ira, Dario stepped inside. He shuffled out of his shoes and left them on the tiled floor next to the straw doormat.

"This way," their host said, climbing the stairs.

Dario minded his step as he mounted the wooden slats, each stained in the middle from a century of heavy use. They ended up in a sitting room on the third floor with a view toward the urban jungle of Central Park. The streets encompassing it were quiet and dark, as asleep as the woman in the bedroom across the hall. Their host had gently closed the glass-paned sitting room door to avoid waking her.

Ira sat in a chair facing away from the window. "Dario, I'd like to introduce you to Lawrence Hoffman. He's the friend I told you about, the one I used to meet in the coffee shop."

"Everyone thought you died, Ira," Lawrence said as he took a seat. Dario did the same. "Over and over, I've reflected on the events of our final evening together in Fair Haven. You were on your way to meet Raff Lagati, and just as suddenly you went off the grid. No sightings, no word. The people from your synagogue were beside themselves."

"Then you remember what was at stake," Ira said.

"Lagati needed help translating the original *Sefer Yetzirah*." Lawrence clasped his hands. "Impossible as it may sound."

"Indeed, it was a lie. He didn't have the original, but he wanted my help searching for it. The source of all creation science, written by Jehovah's own hand, stolen from heaven and brought to the earth during the rebellion."

Dario's head spun as Ira told the tale of all that had transpired during that initial mission. The shape of the story was similar to the one Ira had related in Shiskat, but Ira now went into greater detail. Exquisite detail, everything from their harried escape from Egypt to a trip to the bottom of the ocean. Two weeks ago, he wouldn't have believed a word of it. Now? Well!

Lawrence appeared no less amazed, especially when Ira got to the part where he absconded with the Book.

"What do you mean you 'returned' it?" Lawrence asked. "Returned it where? To whom?"

Ira looked away. "I think you know."

"Yes, I *think* I know, but what you're suggesting—" Lawrence broke off, his breath snatched away. "It's biblical in scope."

"I tend to believe everything is biblical in scope," Ira deadpanned.

Lawrence wouldn't be distracted. "I think you're saying that you returned the book to God. That you..." He couldn't say it. He couldn't seem to get it out. "Ira, are you saying you visited heaven?"

"Yes."

There it was, such a bald answer, so straightforward, spoken without hesitation, without second thought. So un-Ira-like. Whatever his history with Lawrence, Ira felt more comfortable in his presence than anyone else Dario had seen him with.

"I came back because we were too late," Ira continued. "The Book of Creation had been removed from the world, but the knowledge it contained was... absorbed... by another, quite by accident. Sherwood Brighton glimpsed the text of the book, and it was contained in his memory. I suspected that the Watchers—better to call them the Grigori—were luring him, and unfortunately that suspicion proved correct. For all I know, they have captured Brighton. With access to his memories, it's only a matter of time before they find a way out of their restraints."

"So the Grigori are real..."

"Of course they're real," Ira snapped. "Lawrence, you've taught from the sacred texts. You know what they say."

Lawrence leaned forward. "Yes, Ira, I know what they say. I had doubts! Doesn't everyone? Reading something in an ancient text doesn't make it literal truth."

"It does," Dario said. Even he was surprised to have spoken up. "I don't know anything of the ancient texts, except that I grew up going to Mass. I don't know any more about the Grigori than Ira has told me, yet I've seen things that are impossible to deny. Ira has real power."

"Power, huh?" Lawrence's eyes turned up to study the ceiling. "Those texts warn against the use of power."

"For good reason," Ira said. "But when the power is applied through relationship with the creator… well, that counts for something."

Dario yawned, much wider and louder than he'd anticipated. It drew the older men's attention.

"You should get some rest," Lawrence said.

"No thanks." Ira stood up and walked to the window. "I'm feeling jetlagged."

Did the term jetlag apply to their situation? There sure hadn't been a jet.

Lawrence showed Dario to a spare bedroom on the second floor. He sat on the edge of the bed and yawned again, three times in quick succession.

"There's an adjoining bathroom." Lawrence pointed toward an unassuming door next to an antique wardrobe. "I'm not sure what Ira has in mind, but you're free to stay as long as you like. After what you've been through, I imagine you could stand some peace. This may be New York, but I think you'd be surprised how quiet it can get up here."

Dario lay back and listened to the occasional emergency siren or throttling engine. After a while, none of it registered. He could have fallen asleep anywhere.

FOUR

New York, New York

JULY 29

Ira stood in front of the window hours after Dario and Lawrence had gone to bed. Over and over he closed his eyes, planted his feet in the river, and attempted to translate to Southampton. He had to believe the Grigori would soon be free. In the pit of his stomach, he knew the worst had already happened. Which meant there was much to do, much to plan, and before he could begin he needed help. Specifically, Trevor's help.

But no amount of effort worked. He tried so hard that his eyes turned bloodshot and the joints of his fingers ached from repeated clenching.

"You can't force it," Aaron had told him the day after that fateful night in Queens. "That's your first lesson. You can't push water down a river; the river has a force all its own. The radiance of God works the same way."

Ira sagged in frustration at his inability to make it happen. At

Mount Khunjerab, it had worked exactly the way Aaron had taught him. He'd followed every step, remembered every nuance, yet this time nothing happened.

Ira dragged one of the chairs so that it faced the window; it took an initial shove to force the wooden legs out of the carpet grooves they had rested in for untold years. He fell into it, feeling discouraged.

He awoke with a start when Lawrence tapped the back of his chair.

"Good morning." Lawrence wore a navy blue robe, its decorative tassels tied across his ample waistline. He sat on the window ledge. "Your friend Dario is still asleep. He was exhausted."

Ira rubbed the dried rheum from his eyes. "He's a good kid. I pray he'll be able to avoid what's to come."

"And just what is that, Ira?"

"If the Grigori are free, we're in for a fight."

"Would Jehovah let that happen?"

Ira hesitated, taken aback to hear Lawrence say that. "I didn't think you were so naïve."

"Come now!"

"I mean it, Lawrence. Jehovah doesn't sovereignly act on this world; everything he accomplishes, he accomplishes through people. If people fail to act, nothing happens. Which is why *we* need to fight. Without our intervention, the Grigori will overwhelm us all."

"This is a very different world from the one they left six thousand years ago," Lawrence said. "You may not be giving our modern civilization enough credit."

Ira hadn't been so amused in ages. "You're talking about technology, but this is bigger than airplanes and nuclear energy. You should have seen the scope of the power I manifested in those mountains. I couldn't control it."

"That scares me."

"Perhaps for good reason." Ira stood up. "With this power…"

He stopped himself. With this power, he should have been able to find Trevor, yet he couldn't. It wasn't just that he couldn't translate there; he couldn't even visualize the place. Normally he could slip into his memory and find any detail, focus on anything he chose, but Trevor's home was as slippery as wet tile. Why couldn't he remember it?

I wrote down the address, he recalled. This, at least, stood out clearly in his mind. Aaron had ripped a blank page from a book in his study and jotted it down in red ink. He'd told Ira to keep it safe.

"I need to use your car," Ira said.

"I don't own one."

"You don't? Why on earth?"

"I live in the heart of Manhattan. What would I need a car for?"

Ira circled around the chair. "I just assumed. You had a car when you drove up to Fair Haven."

"I can give you the number of a rental place." Lawrence left the room and came back a minute later with his phone. "Where are you going?"

"Home to Syracuse. There's something I need there."

"What is it?"

"An address." Ira hoped his friend wouldn't press him for details.

Lawrence cocked his head, giving that some thought. He opened his mouth, perhaps to ask another question. "What about Dario?"

"If you don't mind, it might be a good idea for him to stay put."

"Yes, that's fine."

Lawrence handed the phone to Ira, the number for the rental agency already cued up. He paused before making the call.

"Lawrence, I'll need to make the reservation in your name. I don't have a credit card or any ID."

"Of course you don't." Lawrence took back the phone and dialed. A few minutes later, he had secured Ira a subcompact for two days. "I'll go get the car myself. Hold tight."

For the next hour, Ira found himself with little to do except sit and ponder his situation. He felt tempted to give translation another try, but why work himself up? Perhaps Trevor's place was protected somehow, so people couldn't just appear in and out of it without warning.

Before Ira departed, with Dario still snoring happily beneath the sheets, Lawrence stocked the car with bottled water and snacks. He even insisted that Ira take a few hundred dollars in cash.

The two men stood at the front door and embraced.

"I'm worried about you," Lawrence said. "You may be right that the fight falls on mankind's shoulders, but does it have to be you?"

"For thirty years, I've known it might come to this. I've been recruited, Lawrence."

Ira walked to the door without looking back. He couldn't be dissuaded, and Lawrence, as much as Ira loved and respected his friend, was only making things more difficult.

Navigating Manhattan in a car was nightmarish, and he breathed a sigh of relief when he crossed the Hudson, traveling east along the interstate. Fifteen miles later, the sprawling suburbs gave way to the first signs of countryside.

It took five hours to reach Syracuse. He drove up his home street, admiring the view of Onondaga Lake, then parked the car and glanced at the house he had lived in for almost ten years. It had never been his first choice—it was far too large—but the place had been owned by Temple Emmanuel, his synagogue. With the lake in the background and groves of hemlocks peppering the front and back yards, at least Ira had never been short of quiet places to meditate.

As he swung himself out of the car, the home's front door opened unexpectedly. He froze, lowering himself behind the car to avoid being seen. It had been a year and a half since his disappearance, so it should have come as no surprise that other people lived here now.

The synagogue might have the address, Ira thought as he got back into the car. The synagogue had owned the house, so maybe they had also appropriated Ira's old possessions.

Ira drove through a fast food takeout window, securing a late-afternoon snack, then got back on the main highway and steered his rental car into the heart of Syracuse.

From a parking spot across the square, he watched the front doors of Temple Emmanuel. The wide sandstone arch across the entry allowed for deep shadows, and nobody crossed through them from the time he arrived until 8:30, when the sun finally dipped below the buildings of downtown. He waited another two and a half hours, exercising an abundance of patience. If anyone lingered inside, they wouldn't stay much later.

A few minutes before 11:00, a car inched its way out of the alley behind the building. Before merging onto the street, however, it stopped. A woman in khaki pants and a blue t-shirt got out of the car and hurried back toward the back door.

Janene! He instantly recognized his former assistant. *What are you doing here so late? Go home already.*

He grew ever more impatient as the car remained idle in the entrance to the alley. His stomach growled as the minutes ticked by. If she'd left on schedule, he could have been in and out by now. What was she doing?

At last, a few minutes to midnight, she reappeared carrying two boxes stacked on top of each other. She piled them into the trunk of her car, got into the driver's seat, and pulled away. Ira watched as her taillights took a corner two or three blocks up the street.

He jumped out of the car and hurried toward the alley, prepared to commit a crime. Breaking and entering. He stopped in front of a steel door set in a concrete wall, hoping and praying his old access code would still work. He flipped open the plastic flap on the electronic keypad and stared at the glowing red buttons.

Here goes nothing.

After punching in his six-digit code, the lights flashed off. Ira's breath caught in the long second that followed.

Then—green.

He grasped the handle and yanked open the heavy door. He entered, waiting for the door to close before fumbling for the light switch.

So much time had passed since he'd graced these back halls, yet how little they had changed. The round table around which he'd shared so many cups of coffee with the office staff. The four chairs with faded red cushions and spindly legs. The ceiling fan with one broken blade. Walking into this room felt like stepping backward in time.

He feared he wasted too much time admiring these details—time he couldn't afford after Janene's late departure. He approached the main hallway. At the end, a door just slightly taller than the others gaped open, edged by dark wooden moldings. His old office.

Ira held himself in check and turned first into the filing room, dominated by a row of five taupe cabinets. He opened the first drawer and browsed its tabs, not even sure what he was looking for. His personnel records would be a good place to start.

This turned out to be a dead end, so he searched instead for records about the house itself. At least this avenue of investigation yielded some information, though not the kind he had hoped for. He found rental agreements going back ten years, along with all the property's financial records.

Several hours passed, and he got no closer to an answer. He soon gave up, making sure he left the filing room just as he'd left it.

Ira expected his former office to have been redecorated, but instead he found it unchanged. It remained his personal sanctuary. Either his successor hadn't left his mark or hadn't taken over the office at all.

For old times' sake, he took his customary spot behind the desk, sinking into the chair's worn leather. It felt good. Comfortable.

A host of memories came back to him, but none as strongly as the last time he'd been in the office. Mr. Wendell—he'd never learned the man's first name—had invaded his world, forcing him out of what had been shaping up to be a relaxed semi-retirement. There had been days here at Temple Emmanuel when he'd almost forgotten Aaron's lessons, almost forgotten his responsibilities.

How satisfying it had been to watch as Dario broke that chair over Wendell's head in the Pakistani restaurant. Only one hour after Brighton had betrayed him in the worst way, Dario had made him so proud. Wasn't it surprising that such pride radiated forth from an act of violence? Wendell had crumpled in balletic form. Ira shouldn't have derived such satisfaction from this, but Wendell had been the worst kind of pest, and pests were best dealt with by means of a quick swat.

"That's not very charitable," a familiar voice said from the couch.

Ira himself nearly crumpled from the shock of hearing it. A tall man with short, dark hair reclined the full length of the couch. He couldn't have been older than thirty, maybe as young as twenty. His voice was higher and fuller than Ira remembered, but it was unmistakable.

Aaron Roth's eyes sparkled. And why shouldn't they? It wasn't every day a man had the chance to return to the body of his prime. Ira stood in awe at how much this version of Aaron looked like his grandson David.

"Aaron!" he exclaimed, feeling no need to hide his surprise. "You're looking well."

"Death is the most remarkable condition I've ever experienced," Aaron said, looking down and inspecting his slender frame. "It's a shame the human body diminishes as it does. No one should have to endure it."

"Yes, I'd heard you died."

"We all die. Nothing special about that." Aaron stood up, trying out his new legs. He bounced on them a few times, laughing broadly. "I could run a marathon, you know that?"

"Nothing's stopping you," Ira remarked, catching the first flashes of morning light around the edges of the office's shuttered window.

"Well, that's not entirely true. I have some urgent business to attend to."

"Take a seat then."

"I'd rather stand. This body is something else." Aaron approached the desk. "What you've done, Ira, didn't go unnoticed. You drew a lot of power. That power wasn't intended to be used this way."

"If you know that much, then you must also know I didn't have much choice. They had taken Brighton."

"I know. And despite your display of fireworks, they managed to turn him. Got a peek inside his head."

Ira's heart sank. "Then the Grigori are free."

"Yes, but I'm not sure that's the worst of it."

"Not the worst of it? Aaron, you know what they did the last time. The entire human population was nearly wiped out as a result of—"

"As a result of exactly the kind of thing you're doing now," Aaron said, finishing the thought. "You've crossed a dangerous line. Many have crossed it before. Have you not learned from their examples?"

Ira stood up and walked to the window. It wouldn't be wise to stay too long. "There have been no examples in recent memory."

"But it's exactly what we have been charged with preventing!"

Ira turned back to look at Aaron, surprised at the vehemence in the man's voice. "I knew the risks."

"You knew, but you didn't heed. There will be consequences."

"I understand."

Perhaps all this passion was taking its toll on Aaron, for the man sat back down on the couch, tired, looking a bit more like his older self. "I met Sherwood Brighton. He came to see me."

"Yes, I know."

"You were right about his importance. He is destined for big things."

Ira had always believed this was the case, but in light of recent developments so much of what he thought he'd known had been called into question. "Even now?"

"Now more than ever, Ira. It's not the first time history has turned on the fate of a single individual."

"I helped him as much as I could, though he refused to see that." A surge of frustration welled up inside Ira, almost overwhelming his sense of control. He had done so much for Brighton, and none of it had ever been acknowledged. "Just two weeks ago, Trevor intervened in his escape from England. He was never alone, not ever."

Insistent knocking from somewhere outside the office made Ira turn his head. If only Aaron had picked a more opportune time for this otherworldly visit, he could have gotten out in time. It was hard not to feel anger at his former mentor, who he felt hadn't prepared him for the future as well as he could have. Aaron had always been a cipher, especially in the years leading up to their falling out. Aaron claimed not to hold grudges, but then why hadn't he reached out to Ira sooner? Why had a crisis been necessary to bring them back together?

More noise from the offices. A door opening. Feet pounding on the floor. Ira even thought he heard the word *police*.

"I've got to get out of here," Ira said.

Aaron held a finger to his lips. He reached into his pants pocket and produced a slip of yellowed paper between his thumb and forefinger. Though folded, a stroke of red ink stuck out, having pooled into the crease.

That's it. The address.

Aaron laid it on the edge of Ira's desk, smiling all the while.

Ira got to his feet and approached the door, listening for more footsteps, trying to make out what the voices were saying. They were definitely police.

He turned, ready to take Aaron by the arm and force him to

leave—but Aaron was already gone. Ira seethed, standing alone in the center of the large office. He wondered if he could break the office window and get out that way; certainly he'd gotten out of worse scrapes.

He pushed both his hands out in front of him and steadied himself, imagining the river. It *had* to work. He needed it to. He waded out from the shallows as quick he could, the deeper course of the river exerting its usual pull. And there—the ground. The muddy ground, and below it stones, and below it clay, and below it solid earth.

You can do it. You have to do it.

Light from his palms, a gentle ripple in the air, and then a sound akin to boiling water. With a loud pop coinciding with the opening of the office door, the walls blew away. Just as suddenly, he found himself back in Lawrence's sitting room, a startled woman looking up from her chair in open-mouthed astonishment, a cup of coffee halfway to her lips.

"My apologies," he said to Lawrence's wife. "I suppose that was rude of me."

FIVE

Mount Khunjerab, Pakistan
JULY 30

Sherwood Brighton had never been prone to claustrophobia. Nonetheless, these last two days spent in nocturnal servitude had frequently been panic-inducing. In his hours—the hours he controlled—he often sat in his small apartment with nothing to do. The headaches he incurred from such uncharacteristic idleness, or from attempting to sleep in the middle of the day from the exhaustion of his body being put to work all night, threatened to drive him mad. This wasn't living! His sudden uselessness after months of running around with the fate of the world on his shoulders struck him with terrible force.

He wanted to go outside and breathe the fresh mountain air, but Abranel wouldn't let him, thus triggering a second and far worse form of claustrophobia. He was no longer alone in his own head. The creature whispered to him constantly. He didn't want to engage, and over and over he resolved not to.

For the past two weeks, he had existed in a deluded state, though he hadn't possessed the insight to appreciate it. Ira had never been his problem. Though the rabbi had failed in spectacular ways, he had tried to steer Brighton clear of this mess. No, Ira couldn't be blamed. Brighton had to accept that he alone was not responsible for his situation.

You're a terrible decision-maker, he told himself.

"Yes, you are," Abranel agreed. He had a knack for confirming the worst parts of Brighton. *"You should never have let me in. Deep down, you knew better."*

The relationship was frustratingly one-sided. Abranel knew everything about Brighton, yet Brighton knew next to nothing about Abranel, who was able to keep his memories outside Brighton's reach.

He blinked, only now realizing that he wasn't in the apartment anymore. This happened sometimes; he would retreat into his own headspace, allowing the world to flow by.

Abranel could take control at any moment, and had demonstrated the technique a dozen times. One minute, Brighton would be going about his life, and then he'd feel pressure in some distant and pitiful environ of his mind and discover his legs or arms moving seemingly of their own accord. Abranel had places to be, usually at night, and none of it involved Brighton's input.

He blinked again, finding that he sat on a wooden crate in the middle of a large room he had never seen before. He didn't remember how he'd gotten here, but that wasn't unusual. Sometimes it was easier to stop paying attention. When it came to Abranel, Brighton had no leverage.

Brighton decided to stand, and felt surprise when he found he was able to do it.

"Stand if you want," Abranel whispered. *"It doesn't concern me."*

And the moment it did concern him, Abranel would step in. He didn't need permission.

Most of the rooms in this facility were small enough to drive

Brighton to distraction, except the hangar, cavernous in the extreme, and the chamber deep underground with the metallic barrier. Shamballa, they called it. This current room, however, was nearly as large. Brighton felt amazed he hadn't been here yet; between his and Abranel's wanderings, he thought he'd been just about everywhere.

High walls sloped toward a domed ceiling some fifty feet above his head. It reminded him of the inside of an abandoned grain silo he had once visited during an autumn trip to Canada. As an eight-year-old, he and his cousins had hiked more than a mile through recently levelled cropland to reach the decrepit structure, its rusted tin-sheeted walls weathered from decades of exposure to the extreme prairie climate. That silo couldn't have been more than twenty feet from top to bottom, but to his young eyes it had seemed never-ending. Strong winds had whistled and slapped the structure, generating a sonorous, feminine wail that sunk into his bones and remained there throughout his adult life.

A row of tall-backed stone chairs were stacked into the far side of the chamber—and these he recognized. They were the same sort of chairs he had seen on his visit to Shamballa, except they had been positioned in a circle. The Grigori had sat in them. The chairs themselves, fashioned from granite, looked impossibly heavy.

"Indeed, too heavy for our current servants," Abranel said. "There was a time when I could have lifted such a chair with one hand."

Then the pressure, and Brighton resigned himself to his fate. Abranel walked closer to the chairs and pushed against one of them experimentally. Regardless of who was in charge of his brain, his body wasn't up to the challenge of moving them.

Abranel stormed out of the room. As they passed through various corridors, it became clear that Abranel would be using his arms and legs for the foreseeable future. So Brighton tuned out. The only window of interest that afternoon occurred when Abranel visited the hangar, gathered a team of workers, and departed behind the wheel of a low-riding forklift. Brighton thought it made for an amusing vignette. He had noted countless anachronisms in the last two days, but riding a forklift through these ancient stone tunnels was by far the drollest. The pleasant thrum of the motor vibrated up through the seat, the feel of the steering wheel's hard plastic gripped in his hands.

Once back inside the silo-like chamber, Abranel set to the task of moving the heavy stone chairs and arranging them in a circle. When the task was done, the forklift back in the hangar where it belonged, Abranel deposited him in his apartment. This was the last place he wanted to be, so he returned to the corridors and walked with no particular destination in mind.

He didn't get far before his feet began to ache, followed by the muscles in his lower legs and thighs; Abranel had used him up. It was a strange sensation to wake as if from a long sleep, brimming with psychological energy, only to remember that one's physical energy had already been spent. On another day, he might have resigned himself to sleep, but today the growing rage in his gut lent him a second wind.

*   *   *

Overnight, one of the four spacecraft returned. Lagati strode into the hangar just as the pilot was settling the ship into its berth, its running lights splashing the wall with patterns of red and blue. Next he heard the familiar working of gears and the bottom of the ship dropped out, lowering to the ground. A dozen chrome-covered crates had been lashed to the inside of the hull.

The compartment atop the ship slid open and the pilot settled on the lip of the elongated saucer, dangling his or her legs over the side. When the helmet came off, Lagati saw it was a woman; she had been known as Sharon upon first arrival, though her body had since been

appropriated by a Nephilim. After a spate of initial accidents, everyone had realized humans weren't equipped to handle the vessels, at
least not without a great deal more time to learn their controls. The
shortcut had been to assign the spirits. They'd been sidelined for centuries and been only too enthusiastic to see action again.

Sharon jumped to the floor, an intimidating distance but one she
confronted without the merest hesitation. Lagati couldn't remember this
spirit's name, so he contented himself with thinking of her as Sharon.

"How was the trip?" His voice echoed in the enormous chamber.

Sharon walked around the back of the ship to the cargo hold.

Lagati joined her, stepping close enough to the nearest crate to
run his finger along its smooth edge. "I take it you didn't encounter
any problems."

Footsteps at the entrance stole their attention. Turel marched in,
drew himself to his full statuesque height, and made his way toward
them. Sharon closed the distance.

Lagati didn't know what he had expected, but the fervid embrace
between the two wasn't it. Turel picked her up in his big, thick arms
and held her tightly to his chest. Lagati took a few steps closer and
realized that she was crying.

He's her father, Lagati realized. These disembodied Nephilim spirits were the long-dead sons and daughters of the Grigori, so with both
parties in tight quarters Lagati was surprised he hadn't heard about
more of these reunions.

Outside of a general wrathfulness over the ordeal they'd been put
through, Lagati didn't attribute much emotion to the Grigori. Perhaps
that was why the display of familial affection surprised him. Ordinarily
the Grigori behaved so coldly in every respect.

Realizing that the room had fallen silent, he turned and found both
Grigori and Nephilim had moved their reunion out of the hangar.

Lagati approached the chrome crates, stacked neatly upon the ship's lowered cargo hold. He grabbed onto one of the hold's struts and hoisted himself up. There was only a narrow space between the crates, loaded three high, each one shaped like an oversized coffin. None of them had labels, which would complicate the cataloguing assignment Semyaza had given him.

The first few shipments had contained items of archaeological interest. Emery Wörtlich would have pissed himself at the collection Lagati's people had amassed, including books and ancient tablets, stone carvings, golden trinkets, tools of surprisingly sophisticated metalwork. Even better, some crates had contained the mummified remains of animal/human hybrids. The leading-edge genetic manipulation performed during the pre-Flood era was staggering in its scale and complexity. Once, years ago, Lagati had been amazed at the human/avian skull that to this day sat in repose at his Switzerland estate. That skull now seemed no more unique than a single grain of sand in all the Sahara.

He ran his hands along the impenetrable chrome top, free of imperfection in the same way the Shamballa barrier had been. Skilled hands had crafted it—likely Nephilim hands. To get inside, he would need a specialized tool his people had devised over a year ago. After months of trying to open the crates with every combination of guile and force they could conceive, they'd stumbled on the solution almost by accident; a pulse of concentrated hydrogen gas into any point along the crack between the lid and body of the crate released the lid. An elegant locking mechanism, tricky to ascertain and yet convenient in the sense that hydrogen was the most plentiful substance in the universe. The science behind the lock still hadn't been explained, but Amir had theorized that trace amounts of lithium bonded to the undersides of the lids, indicating a neutrino reaction.

Loud voices preceded the arrival of a line of workers, decked in blue coveralls. When they saw him standing atop the ladder, they stopped talking. A sign of respect.

A surge of gratification rose up from Lagati's gut. It felt good to be acknowledged with some measure of fear. At least these people remembered who he was and his substantial capabilities.

Within a few minutes, they set to work transferring the crates off the ship and onto long flatbed trolleys. A storeroom three doors down had been converted into a storage area for the crates. Already a sizable number had been deposited here, with more on the way.

"Sir," a voice called.

A young man Lagati didn't recognize broke away from the others. He held his hands together in front of his chest in an awkward display of nerves.

"Yes?"

"I was wondering if you had any updates on the missing ship." The man shifted from one foot to another in a steady rhythm, rocking from side to side like a human demonstration of perpetual motion.

"The missing ship." This was the first he was hearing of it.

"Yes, sir."

God, it felt good to be addressed that way again. "What missing ship?"

The man stopped rocking. "I apologize, I didn't realize—"

Lagati's frustration rose in him anew. "You didn't realize I'm not in the loop."

He nodded as he turned to leave.

"No." Lagati reached out and grasped the man by the shoulder, stopping him in his tracks. "You don't say a thing like that and walk away. Explain yourself. Tell me about this missing ship."

"We were tracking Number Three on its descent last night."

"Did it burn up in the atmosphere?"

"No, sir. It had already reached low orbit and levelled off on an eastward trajectory over the north Pacific."

Lagati regarded the ship in front of them. Number Two, based on its markings. These ships were made of the strongest alloys Lagati was familiar with, so he had a hard time believing anything could bring it down.

"Who was the pilot?" Lagati asked.

"Rajesh. Sorry, I mean Dr. Goyal."

They were interrupted by Turel's quiet return. Lagati didn't see the Grigori until he had arrived at the main group, who had unloaded two of the crates onto their trolley.

Lagati set his eyes on Turel. "Could I have a word?"

The Grigori pivoted toward him and proffered a withering stare. "What do you want?"

"I've been told Number Three went missing over the Pacific. What do you know about that?"

Turel stood as immovable as a block of granite. "The situation doesn't concern you. You have other responsibilities." He gestured to the crates.

"I don't need a reminder of my responsibilities."

Lagati didn't wait for a reply. He headed straight for the exit, ignoring crate duty. A missing ship was more important, and he wouldn't tolerate being left out of a development of this magnitude.

He practically ran through the corridors. It only took a couple of minutes to access the second level, along a corner of the facility that housed some of the more executive areas. Several offices overlooked the hangar, including the one he had once occupied. He slowed to a walk, evened out his breathing, and took the final turn of the corridor.

As though by sheer coincidence, Sherwood Brighton stood just outside the office door. Lagati couldn't begin to guess what he was doing there. Brighton had served a great and noble purpose, but now that the Grigori were freed he wasn't of much use.

The door opened and Semyaza appeared, his tall frame filling the doorway. He wore a dark brown robe that looked to Lagati like poorly tailored pajamas.

Why had Brighton been summoned, and not Lagati? Nearly two days had passed, and Semyaza hadn't reached out to him once.

As Semyaza ushered Brighton inside, Lagati thought he detected a mocking smile on the Grigori leader's face.

SIX

Mount Khunjerab, Pakistan
JULY 30

Brighton wouldn't have come were it not for Abranel forcing the issue. He acknowledged being curious at Semyaza's summons—it was impossible not to be at least curious—but it was too soon to be in the same room with the monster.

I am not afraid.

"You are."

Abranel's all-knowing voice grated. The truth was like a knife, its serrated edge slicing through his consciousness as though through soft butter. Not enough time had passed. Maybe no length of time would ever prove sufficient. Semyaza had killed him as utterly as if he'd put a bullet in his heart. In fact, he wanted to die.

"You think I'd let you go?" Abranel asked, sweetly.

And that was the worst part. The only relief he could hope for was the eventual organic failures of old age. Never before had he regretted his youth and excellent health, but there was a first time for everything.

"Come in and sit down," Semyaza said, maneuvering his lithe frame around his desk, its metallic surface gleaming under the fluorescents pouring in through the window, presenting an elevated view of the hangar.

Abranel sat.

"My business is with Brighton." Semyaza leaned forward, resting his upper body on his knuckles. "Quickly, grandson. Don't make me wait."

Brighton's consciousness burst forward like water breaching a dam.

"How are you feeling?" Semyaza asked coolly.

In an act of defiance, Brighton didn't reply. He couldn't imagine this creature had any genuine interest in his well-being.

Semyaza cracked a thin smile. "I appreciate this little display of mettle," he emphasized *little*, "but it's a pointless exercise. At any rate, I could instruct Abranel to assume primacy, and he'd relate to me every thought in your head. Is that how you want to spend these precious minutes of control?"

"You lied to me."

"Of course I lied!" The Grigori swept his brown robe aside and lowered himself into a chair built from hard wooden planks. "You would have done the same."

"Would I?"

"Yes, you would have. If you'd been imprisoned for six thousand years by a cruel and vindictive rival who desired only to inflict eternal suffering, and a lie would have brought that torture to an end, not just for you but for hundreds of fellow prisoners, then yes, you would have done the same. Do you understand me, Mr. Brighton?"

Again, no answer.

"Abranel, does he understand me?"

Pressure.

"Yes," Abranel said, using Brighton's own mouth to betray him.

"Good. Now give him back."

And sure enough, Brighton was back. "Haven't you already gotten what you need from me?" he asked. "I've given you everything. Literally everything."

"Come now, that's very dramatic."

"You could kill me."

Semyaza chuckled. "Oh, you'd like that. Tell me how you feel."

"Why do you care how I feel?"

"You may find this hard to believe, but I'm grateful. Because of you, I'm here, in the flesh. You claim that you've given me everything, and I agree that I owe you everything."

"Then perhaps—"

The Grigori raised a single finger. "Only to a point, Mr. Brighton. Now is not the time for requests."

"In that case, I feel… exhausted."

"That's a common side effect at the start of inhabitation. You'll grow accustomed to the cycles over time. You probably feel the need to exert yourself when your inhabitant has already expended your physical resources. My advice is to sleep when your body demands it and pay attention at all times, even when you're not in control. It will preserve your sanity." Semyaza pursed his lips. "Another thing, Mr. Brighton. Inhabitancy is not parasitic; it's a relationship. Like all relationships, if you treat the other party well, he will treat you well in turn. There's no reason to suffer unduly. In fact, this base is full of people who have volunteered for the experience. It may seem right now like Abranel has all the power, all the advantage, but in truth you have much to gain. Abranel is thousands of years old. You can learn a great deal from him."

Brighton clenched the armrests of his chair. "Abranel has not been particularly forthcoming."

"Then endear yourself to him. Abranel is a gentle soul. Give him time and he will come around."

Brighton smiled despite himself. Gentle soul!

"You are skeptical." Semyaza sat forward and folded his long fingers into a tight fist. "I am in a position to appreciate the truth of Abranel. He's my grandson, and I know him better than you, though you may soon overtake me in that arena. The lifetime we have known each other is nothing compared to the glory of inhabitation. You and he are one."

"There are things he won't tell me."

"Remember, there are things he doesn't know."

"Of course. But perhaps I could take advantage of your gratitude and get some answers."

"A fair exchange." Semyaza uncoiled his fingers again and splayed them. "Ask me anything."

"Won't you lie?"

"But I already have what I need from you. What would be my motivation?"

"To this one, a lie is its own reward."

Brighton almost laughed. *Semyaza, do you know what your grandson thinks of you?*

It didn't appear so.

"Emery Wörtlich died in Tubuai," Brighton said. "Elisabeth and I were drawn here under false pretenses, thinking he would be waiting for us. That much was a lie. What of the rest?"

"I'd prefer to address specifics."

"Very well. You called yourself one of the Twenty. What does that mean?"

"It's an unimportant detail, I assure you."

"You said you'd answer my questions. Was that, too, a lie?"

"Of course not. I just can't imagine such tedium would interest you." He stood up and turned his back to Brighton, staring down into the hangar like a plantation owner inspecting his fields. "The Twenty are administrators, to borrow a human concept, and we are numbered."

"Numbered?" Brighton asked. "By importance?"

Semyaza curled his fingers again. "Not at all. The explanation of the order is too complicated for our time together. Ask another question."

"What number are you?"

"You are impertinent." The Grigori swallowed his frustration. "I am the first."

"Which means you're the leader, I take it."

Semyaza faced him. "You do not appreciate the breadth of responsibility conveyed by being first of the Twenty."

"Don't press the issue," Abranel whispered.

Brighton nodded, reveling in this feeling of control, however fleeting it might be. "It sounds as though your impatience exceeds your gratitude."

"Ridiculous."

Brighton waited for more, but nothing came. He moved on to his next question; he had so many. "Are you an alien?"

"We come from another world, very far from here. Everything I told you about our origins is true. We arrived as gardeners, to tend this planet and create a species to take after us. We infused in humanity the essence that makes us unique in the cosmos. We are creators, and thus so are you. Evidence of your creativities are manifold." He paused. "Next you will inquire after Jehovah, and on that subject you already have a full picture. He passes himself as the singular God of this world, but he is no more than a compatriot of ours. Everything he touches turns to ash. Every word out of his mouth oozes venom. He has spread his conceits from one corner of the globe to another. He was always prideful, but even the Twenty never imagined he would take his condescension so far. He has been interfering in your development for millennia. You find your role in recent events repugnant, but you should take satisfaction in what you're accomplishing toward bringing that monster to heel."

Brighton found himself wanting to believe it. He had never been fond of organized religion—or any other form. By the time he'd grown old enough to reject the fairy tales espoused by the Sunday school teacher at his parents' country church, he was able to see the degree to which faith had consumed his parents and most of the other adults in his life. They spoke constantly of the love of God and the essential goodness of belief, yet they did horrible things to each other.

Except for Ira.

He checked himself at this gut response. No, Ira had proven to be as hypocritical as all the others, if not worse. Surely the best argument against religion was the examples of the people who purported to follow it.

"You sound bitter."

I sound pragmatic, Brighton insisted.

Semyaza detected the inner dialogue. "Speaking with Abranel? Perhaps you're beginning to appreciate the joy of never again having to contend with loneliness."

"If anything, I've come to miss it," Brighton said. "I'd like to know more about the Book of Creation. How can it have been stored in my memory, yet I was unaware?"

"Humanity is cursed with imperfect recall," Semyaza explained. "It's a biological problem my people were never able to correct, though our efforts along those lines may soon resume. The memory works in complicated ways, and it is known to store vast quantities of information that are inaccessible to the average person. Every moment of a person's existence is stored, back to one's birth. It's a question of access."

"Ira Binyamin had a technique by which he could access his own memories."

"Not surprising. We've not perfected a universal solution, but individuals have found workarounds. Would you like help accessing your memories?"

Brighton hesitated. The truth was that he did want help with this, though he didn't want to accept it from the Grigori.

"I'll take that as a yes," Semyaza said. "I cannot devote the time, but Abranel is another story. I should warn you that it may not be possible, no matter the amount of effort you exert. As I said, it's fundamentally a biological problem. Not every human brain is created equal."

He couldn't tell whether that was a deliberate insult.

"Do you have any other questions?" Semyaza asked.

"I wish you'd just tell me what you want from me. You obviously called me here for a reason."

"We want you to participate."

"I am participating. Abranel spent all night moving chairs around, didn't you know?"

"That was Abranel. I'm referring to *you*."

Brighton looked at his feet, remembering how easy it was for them to betray him. To suddenly lurch up and carry him someplace he didn't want to be. "I guess that's up to Abranel. I don't control my own body."

"I have something in mind," Semyaza said, ignoring the remark. "I think the best thing for you right now would be to get some fresh air. Some time away from the base."

Brighton couldn't help it; a small bubble of hope rose up inside his gut.

"I see the prospect appeals to you."

"Of course it appeals to me, but why would you let me go?"

"If it was just you, naturally, I wouldn't think of it. Abranel provides the necessary insurance. You see? Yet another advantage of inhabitation." Semyaza swung himself back into his seat, steepling his fingers. "There's been a mishap with one of our crafts. It was carrying a load of cargo when it went off-radar. We believe the pilot may have been forced to make an emergency landing in North America, some-where far to the north. Considering the importance of what he car-ried, we need to recover it quickly. Both the cargo and the craft. It doesn't seem wise to send a conspicuous force, and I hear you're well-practiced at travelling covertly. What do you think?"

He felt skeptical, but he couldn't think of any reason to turn down the offer. Even Abranel's voice was silent, a rarity. The creature didn't seem to need sleep, and every moment he wasn't in full control he whispered like a stereo Brighton was powerless to mute.

Semyaza's voice barely registered as he launched into specifics. Brighton was too excited at the opportunity to escape this hellhole to pay them any mind.

*   *   *

If Brighton hadn't known where he was going, he might have missed the corridor entirely. Very little set it apart, except that the doors were a few feet closer together. These rooms might have been storage clos-ets, or even served as overflow apartments if the base's population ever exceeded capacity.

He counted the doors on the left. There were eight before the next intersection, and if he remembered correctly she was in the fourth. He pressed his thumb to the copper panel and waited for the door to open. It took a moment, but then the door slid aside to reveal a cramped anteroom barely large enough to fit a single person. He squeezed inside.

The door closed behind him and he waited, not sure what to do next. There was a second door, and it clearly wasn't going to open on its own accord. He looked down and spotted another of those thumb panels. He grazed it and the door opened obediently.

Brighton hadn't been sure what to expect, but he'd imagined something along the lines of his own apartment, only smaller—a dimly lit room with no windows and only minimal furniture. A room that would drive a person mad. Instead this space was spacious, longer than it was wide. Two couches faced each other with a wooden table between them, followed by a galley kitchen, and beyond it a bed.

The sheets moved, and Brighton stopped. Had he interrupted her sleep? The answer became apparent when Elisabeth Macfarlane sat up and made eye contact with him across the full length of the cell. Prison. Luxury apartment. Whatever it was.

She leapt up, and he saw she was wearing a short-sleeved tan shirt and no bottoms. Realizing the impropriety, she used the sheet to cover herself as she slipped on a pair of shorts that had been cast onto the carpet beside the bed.

"Sherwood, am I glad to see you," she said once she was dressed. She hurried through the galley kitchen, sidestepped the squat living room table, and gave him a hug. She held on for a long time, and Brighton didn't pull away. It felt good to see her again, to know she wasn't angry at him, didn't blame him for her circumstances. "They wouldn't tell me what happened to you."

"They're good at keeping secrets."

She finally stepped away, almost falling backward onto one of the couches. Brighton sat opposite her. Despite her apparent enthusiasm, it was an awkward reunion. The last time he'd seen her, she'd been little more than the Grigori's plaything, sobbing and fumbling blindly in the bizarre reality behind the Shamballa barrier.

"Have you been told anything?" Brighton asked. "Do you know what's been going on outside these four walls?"

"They bring me food, but no news."

"What's the last thing you remember?"

Elisabeth's eyes glazed over. She seemed to have lost all sense of time, confined to her attractively furnished cell; Brighton was often confined to the stark reality of his own mind, a fate far more piteous. She had gotten off easily and didn't realize it.

"I couldn't see." She stood and retreated to the kitchen. "The world went black, and I felt pain. I don't know how long it lasted. Minutes? Hours? Then I awoke in bed." She gestured behind her. "They told me you were safe and that you would come to me. How long has it been?"

"Two days."

"It felt longer."

"That's an understatement." Brighton let out a protracted sigh. "Still, I wanted to come earlier."

"What kept you?" She managed to compact two full days of resentment into that question.

How could he explain to her what had happened to him? How could he explain Abranel without sounding like a mental patient?

Pressure. Just the tiniest application of pressure.

"I wouldn't let him come," he heard his voice say. "There were more important things to do. Priorities that couldn't be ignored."

Like moving chairs, Brighton thought. *Damn it, Abranel. I could do this myself. You'll scare the crap out of her.*

Elisabeth stared for several long moments. Brighton could see in her eyes every stage of the process, from confusion to denial to acceptance. She didn't need someone to hold her hand. She had seen possession with her own eyes, back in Tiahuanaco. The dead girl. This was no different, except he wasn't dead.

Wasn't he?

That was a matter of some debate.

"How did this happen?" Elisabeth asked, approaching with tentative steps.

Abranel folded his hands in his lap, appearing as unthreatening as he could. Brighton felt the muscles on his face relax, releasing all the tension he himself held but Abranel didn't.

"Brighton gave himself over to me, and hence he is not always in control of where we go and what we do."

"So he's still in there."

"Of course. My general principle is to give over control of our shared body whenever possible. I'm no tyrant."

"Do you have a name?"

"I am Abranel. My father is Ornias, my grandfather Samhazai the Great."

If Abranel's face had sagged to the point of disregard, Elisabeth's had frozen into rigid, icy contours.

"If you're so gracious, kindly get out."

"Excuse me?" Abranel asked.

"Go."

Abranel grinned and then did as instructed. Brighton stretched his arms as though working the blood back into them. The switch was always a mild shock, from full paralysis to able-bodied in a split second. The human body wasn't designed to be put on and taken off like an overcoat.

"He's gone," Brighton breathed, staring at the carpet as a wave of nausea came over him. Tiny crumbs, as though flaked off the side of a French loaf, stared back at him. Obviously this prison catered, and the menu wasn't too shabby.

Elisabeth sat next to him, maintaining a respectful distance.

"How did this happen?" she asked for the second time. "Was it your choice?"

"Yes." He wanted to say it hadn't been, but yes, he had chosen this. In the pressure of that moment back in the pyramid, back in the presence of the Book, as the words of that ancient text had roared through him like water over the edge of Niagara, it had seem an inevitability. He had done what they wanted, what they needed. He hadn't realized…

He hadn't realized. Simple as that.

Elisabeth craned forward, leading with her chin, waiting for him to elaborate.

"Just yes?" Abranel asked. *"Is that all you can say for yourself?"*

"Yes," he said again. "It was a terrible mistake. I regret it now."

Elisabeth looked away. "Can you get me out of here?"

"I don't know. I doubt it."

She nodded, having expected that. Or maybe just feared it. Without looking at him, she walked to the kitchen. She stood with her back to him.

She can't look at me.

Abranel seemed to chuckle. He was always lighthearted when Brighton was at his lowest ebb. *"Do you blame her?"*

No. She's right to blame me.

"I'm going away," Brighton said. "There's a mission, and I've accepted it."

"So you're working for them now." Elisabeth turned just enough that he could see her in profile. She was much too old for him but handsome nonetheless. He could appreciate what Wörtlich had seen in her. She was one of the shrewdest people he'd ever met.

Brighton hesitated before answering. Was he working for them? Had he switched sides? No. He was doing everything he could to coexist with Abranel, and if that meant refocusing his priorities, then—

"You're talking to yourself. Talk to her. She's the one you have to answer to."

Startled at this keen observation, Brighton sat up. "I'm doing everything I can to get by. I don't know what else to do. I wish I could do more."

"Where are you going?"

"Someplace north. One of their ships has gone missing, and they want me to look for it."

"Why you?"

"I suspect it's not me they want."

"Abranel then." Her shoulders relaxed. In resignation. "When do you leave?"

"Soon."

She still wouldn't turn, wouldn't regard him. He felt as though she needed something from him. Rescue. It would be disingenuous to offer it, but what other way could he lift her spirits?

"If I can do anything to help you, I will." As he said it, he realized it was not enough. He was largely responsible for getting her into this. "I will do what I can."

It sounded so hollow.

She retreated to the edge of the bed and sat down. "You're only here as a courtesy. I don't figure into your plans."

That was the worst way of interpreting his current situation, but it was true.

"Goodbye, Elisabeth."

Perhaps she inclined her head in his direction, or perhaps it was just his imagination.

SEVEN

Provo, Utah
JULY 30

Henry's groans waned in concert with the daylight. Gayle Voss had awoken that morning to renewed hope, but then she walked into her husband's room and saw how much paler he'd gotten. His skin had taken on a sickly translucence such that she could make out each purple vein beneath his dry, papery flesh. From the first light of dawn, she knew this day would be his last.

Everything she understood about the passage from life to death suggested this should be a joyous occasion. Not an ending, but a passing from one form of existence to another. Henry's current body was not the body of the man she had met eleven years ago. His cells, his molecules and atoms, even those unknowable, seemingly irreducible substances which were infinitely tinier, had replaced themselves again and again in a constant cycle of renewal. She had married his eternal consciousness. Henry would never cease to be Henry, though she struggled to accept that he would cease to be anything she could readily *identify* as Henry.

As much joy as she should have felt, she felt an equal portion of sorrow. She didn't grieve for Henry; she grieved that she was too small to comprehend what was happening to him, the process that was consuming him.

In a brief moment of lucidity, they shared their last breakfast together. He hadn't the strength to eat, but he sipped a cup of tea. He asked her to stop medicating him against the pain, so this time it was truly only tea, nothing added. He didn't want her to numb the experience of death.

"We only get to do this once," he said, keeping his eyes open just long enough for her to see that his irises had shifted into yet another shade of blue she had no word for.

Henry required little attention during this deathwatch. They spoke on occasion, when he was able, enough for her to trust that he wasn't in as much pain as she feared. How regrettable that nobody could chronicle the journey he was embarking upon. There was so much for her to learn from him in these crucial hours, but the closer he approached the moment of death the less capable he was of expressing the experience in any meaningful way.

She opened the blinds and lit incense. She played music and spoke incantations over the room to calm his spirit—though really it was her spirit that needed peace; his had already found all he would ever need.

Gayle could not spend every waking moment by Henry's side, as much as she felt she needed to. It was so difficult conceptualizing a world without him in it. This precious remaining time had to be savored. But the deathwatch took its toll. She therefore took periodic breaks to take care of herself. She showered. She went for a short walk. She prepared dinner, even though she wasn't hungry. And throughout the day, her thoughts were consumed with the small but escalating realization that each activity she performed would be her last as a married woman. Tomorrow, she would awake to a cold new reality.

"I wonder what I shall become," he whispered as the noon hour passed and the sun began its slow fall toward the horizon.

Those proved to be his last words. He was too weak by late afternoon to open his mouth, never mind make any sound.

As the sun set, Gayle closed the curtains over the room's sole window and settled into the chair next to the bed. With her hand resting upon Henry's shuddering chest, and with tears of joint celebration and anguish flowing down her cheeks like a mighty river, he breathed his last.

*   *   *

Thirty-seven miles east of Provo, amidst the steep cliffs and troughs of the Wasatch Range, Gayle found the meadow where she and Henry had married. A windrow of river birch cut across the meadow, following the path of a burbling stream. She stood in their shadow, dressed in her wedding gown, and ran her hands against one tree's smooth reddish-brown, almost purple bark, striated by horizontal white creases.

She stepped back, judging which of these trees she and Henry had stood under. Only five people had been present that October afternoon—themselves, the priestess, and two witnesses. The whole affair had been beautiful but hastily arranged. They had been together only six months when Henry asked her to marry him, and they hadn't wanted to wait for the following spring to stage an outdoor wedding.

Yes, it had been this tree. She was certain.

Gayle moved back under its protective boughs, sunlight dancing all around her. She wore a wreath of white lilies in her hair, the long-stemmed flowers selected from the garden in their backyard. As she lowered herself at the base of the tree, the white silk of her dress draped over the lush, river-fed grass. She gazed across the meadow, waving at the silver car idling on the edge of the gravel road. The car doors opened and three friends emerged.

The friends sat cross-legged on the grass, arranged in a circle. Tomas placed a green box in the center of the sacred space and lifted the lid. The slight breeze disturbed Henry's ashes, but none of the grey flecks lifted high enough over the box's lip to escape.

They shared stories for over an hour. Tomas had known Henry the longest, having met him in college more than twenty years ago. Gayle had already heard most of these college-era tales, shared along with bottles of Sambuca during Christmas getaways. She had expected the storytelling, the memories, to cheer her up, but whenever Tomas got going Gayle was struck by the shortness of her time with Henry; they had only known each other a quarter of their lives, and the other thirty years now felt like wasted time.

"The wheel turns," Tomas said, finishing his improvised eulogy.

In fact, all three of these friends had known Henry longer than Gayle had. None of Gayle's friends had been able to get to Utah on such short notice.

Elisabeth should be here, she thought as Alice, their priestess, recounted her circumstances of first meeting Henry—at a Mormon temple, of all places. *Where have you gone, Elisabeth?*

"The wheel turns," Alice said softly.

Gayle tuned out as Jim spoke about the long hikes he and Henry had taken through these very mountains. He barely looked up from the piece of paper he had written his remarks on. She couldn't blame Jim for planning ahead; he was painfully shy and almost never spoke extemporaneously—but it hurt that he couldn't overcome his limitations to speak from the heart.

This was supposed to be a healing experience, for all involved, and Gayle had been certain that's what would happen. What a beautiful plan she had devised—storytelling, nature, gorgeous weather, the scene of their wedding—but none of it had gone as expected. Henry deserved more.

When Jim finished speaking, Alice put both her palms against the ground and pressed her weight against them. "The wheel turns," she intoned.

Gayle graciously excused herself from the circle. She swept through the tall grasses, coming to the edge of the stream and then turning to follow its course in a mindless daze. The trees and bushes thickened around her. Branches snatched at her arms and legs, leaving long pink abrasions on her skin.

Would Henry have appreciated this sendoff? It felt meaningless, like she had no real connection to this place. The grass and trees and sky and rock were just that—grass and trees and sky and rock. They had no shared consciousness, no sense of being, no memory of that special day so many years ago. Nature had no memory, no personality. It was just matter, seemingly random collections of atoms, their protons and electrons spinning in a tedious, motiveless pattern.

"Gayle, I sense something is the matter," Alice's voice called to her.

Gayle stopped, her feet mired in a patch of mud. Her husband had just died. Of course something was the matter!

She felt the priestess's hand on her shoulder, but she didn't turn. She stared at the stream, gushing downhill through the westward sloping valley, transporting fresh rainwater toward the great salt lakes of central Utah. The stream didn't know who Henry was, who she was, didn't care about anything. It ran downhill because of gravity's unremitting pull.

"It's time to scatter the ashes," Alice said.

Gayle sat down, not caring about the mud slopping up the sides of her dress. "Why did we come here?"

Alice leaned against one of those purple birch trees. "This place carries special significance to your relationship with Henry. Can't you feel it? Nature is so alive with memory."

Precisely what Gayle had expected her to say, and precisely what Gayle didn't want or need to hear. Such foolishness.

But it's not all foolishness, a small voice inside her purred. *Henry was killed because of that burst of nodal energy. Nature is alive, and it's being tampered with.*

Gayle lowered her head, trying to banish the emptiness engulfing her. Indeed, the energy had come from… somewhere out there. The Starseed people were coming alive. Perhaps they were set for an imminent return.

"What do you know of the Starseed people?" Gayle asked, looking Alice in the eye.

"I see. You believe they have something to do with Henry's death?"

"Henry was a channeler. He was among the first to detect the rise in nodal energy, and I'm certain it came from space. I'm not sure what to make of it except to pin it on the Starseed people."

Gayle reconsidered these words. She had always expressed belief in the Starseed people's existence, but she'd never contended with such powerful evidence. A part of her had harbored skepticism—skepticism that no longer made sense following Henry's death. *Something* had killed him, after all.

Alice didn't say anything right away. What could she say? She didn't know any more about the Starseed people than Gayle did. There wasn't much literature on the subject and everything they knew was more or less anecdotal.

"Let's scatter the ashes," Gayle said in resignation. "It's why we came."

She stood, slops of mud falling off the back of her ruined dress. It didn't matter. The grass and trees and sky and rock were just grass and trees and sky and rock—and the dress was just a dress, another collection of atomic particles not unlike any other.

Tomas and Jim waited for them by the wedding tree. The men's eyes expressed surprise at the condition of Gayle's dress, but she didn't care. Not now. She had to say goodbye and move on. There were things to do now, things that couldn't wait.

She needed to contact Elisabeth. Gayle didn't know how, but she knew Elisabeth was involved in all this. The energy was concentrated somewhere near Kashmir, and that's where Elisabeth had gone.

Jim picked up the box of ashes and handed it to Gayle. It felt light; how amazing that all one hundred and fifty pounds of her husband had been reduced to this. While the others watched in reverential silence, Gayle opened the lid and stared at the morass of grey powder.

"Let's return him to the world from which he came," Alice said beside her. "The wheel turns."

The wheel turns, the wheel turns, Gayle thought with irritation. Everything came back to that damned wheel. Supposedly it turned steadily on its nonexistent axle, rendering everything in the world both meaningless and pregnant with cosmic significance.

Gayle reached into the ash, shivering at the strangeness of it. She was touching him, but it wasn't *him.* Did he truly exist somewhere still, his consciousness merged with the universe, as he had believed?

She removed a handful of ash and held it over the fast-moving stream. She closed her eyes, opened her fingers, and felt the ash slip away. She blinked her eyes open, watching as the ash hit the water, instantly being absorbed by it. A second later, there was no evidence the ash had ever existed.

She took another handful and repeated the motion, then invited the others to do the same until the wooden box sat empty on the ground, discarded.

Someone is responsible, she reminded herself. *Starseed people or no, I will find them. Henry, you didn't die for nothing.*

EIGHT

New York, New York

JULY 30

Lawrence's wife had gone out of the house to avoid the raised voices hammering out of the kitchen.

"They often used to fight with each other," she said to Dario as she slipped her shoes over her stockings. "Not really angry, just with a lot of passion. This time, they're angry."

The intensity caught Dario off-guard, as Ira was usually the picture of serenity. He and Lawrence were at each other's throats. Once Lawrence's wife was out the door, Dario sat on the bottom of the stairs and listened.

The exchange had begun innocently, with a discussion of how they would retrieve the rental car from Syracuse; it had been placed under Lawrence's name, and he was naturally worried about its fate. Ira wouldn't translate back for it. "An abuse of power," he called such an effort. This led to a long debate about what qualified as an abuse of power, as Lawrence believed Ira had long ago drifted over that invisible line.

The argument escalated slowly but ended abruptly. Ira bounded out of the kitchen midsentence, squirting by Dario and hurrying up the stairs without giving him a second glance.

The house radiated silence after that, except for the occasional rush of water out of the kitchen tap and the clinking of plates.

Dario stuck his head in the kitchen and found Lawrence scouring the dishes with such furious concentration that Dario wouldn't have been surprised if one of them shattered under the pressure, raining shards of razor-sharp pottery into the soapy water. Dario wordlessly plucked up a towel and started to dry them. He stacked the plates neatly on the counter, watching as Lawrence unplugged the sink and the dirty water drained away. By the time the sink was empty, save a few patches of lingering suds, Lawrence was calm.

The sound of Ira's footsteps upstairs seemed to set him off all over again. This time, the rage only lasted as long as it took Lawrence to cross into the sitting room and fall into a leather recliner. Sweat beaded his forehead as though he'd just run a marathon.

Dario remained in the doorway, one foot in the sitting room and the other squarely on the kitchen hardwood.

"Come in," Lawrence said. "No point in just standing there."

Dario approached the loveseat by the window and perched on the edge of its soft, indulgent cushions. "That was quite the spat."

"Sorry about that."

More angry footsteps passed overhead, dislodging a tiny piece of plaster from the ceiling; it floated down in a puff of dust, landing on the lush carpet next to Dario's socked feet.

"It's a shame the only interactions you've witnessed between Ira and me have been bad ones," Lawrence said. "This isn't representative of the friendship we had. Ira isn't the same person he used to be. Neither am I, though. We all change over time into unrecognizable versions of ourselves."

"I've never seen Ira that way."

Lawrence planted his slippers on the floor and sat forward. "He has a temper if you press his buttons. He has a lot of patience, but when it runs out, it runs out abruptly." He stood up and walked into the kitchen. "Want anything?"

"I'm fine."

Lawrence came back with an orange juice and a need to unburden himself. "For years, Ira was all about preserving the knowledge of the *Zohar*, of the *Sefer Yetzirah*. I was skeptical. The idea that they contained the keys to magical powers? Rubbish. Fantasy theology. Ira has always been steadfast that the power of creation is within the grasp of humankind, but that it must be limited. Now he appears on my doorstep having literally transported himself halfway across the planet, *Star Trek* style. I don't know what that is, but it's not Judaism." He sank back into his chair. "What am I to make of it? What kind of God have I been serving all these decades? What does it even mean to be Jewish? I can't answer those questions, and it breaks my heart. It may even break my faith. What I do know is that Ira has had a serious change of heart. The power is real and he's using it. What about those consequences he used to warn about? Do they not apply to him?"

Dario remained silent. Too much history existed between these two men for him to get involved, and Dario had only known Ira a few days.

"I wonder if I should go talk to him," Dario said, realizing that the pacing upstairs had stopped.

Lawrence grunted. "And what would you say?"

A good question. If someone with decades of history with Ira couldn't get through to him, he didn't have a prayer.

"But you're right." Lawrence stood up again and walked toward the front entrance. He placed his hand against the banister and stared upwards. "Ira?"

The seconds ticked by, Lawrence's one-word query met with

stony silence.

"He must be ignoring me," Lawrence mumbled as Dario approached.

"That doesn't sound like the Ira I've gotten to know."

Lawrence raised an eyebrow but said nothing for a while. Instead he shifted his attention back to the stairs. "Ira, is everything all right?"

Dario counted the seconds as they passed, surprised when he reached double digits without a response.

"I'm going up." Lawrence climbed the steps slowly, pausing on the landing only for a moment before completing the journey to the second floor. It didn't take long for him to return to the top step—alone.

"He's gone, isn't he," Dario said.

It wasn't a question, though the open frustration in Lawrence's tired eyes nonetheless provided an answer.

*   *   *

Frustration seemed to do the trick. Ira stood on a cobblestone street under a bright midsummer sun, fresh off his argument with Lawrence, and realized that emotional urgency was the common factor in all three of his successful translations. Somehow the rage—the sheer volume of *need* inside him—impelled the process. He had to be provoked.

Ira blinked away the lingering cobwebs of irritation and surveyed his surroundings. Squat two-story buildings lined the street. A handful of children and their blue-collar parents walked along the sidewalks, barely wide enough to navigate two abreast. Horns blasted through the salt-tinged air, divulging the shipyards he knew occupied the shore of the Solent. He'd only been to Southampton once before, but he remembered it well, and it hadn't much changed.

The door to Celeste's pub was especially unchanged, the wood a bit worried around the edges, stained from salt and stone and dirt. He grasped the handle and yanked hard, squinting into the dim room. Only two men occupied it—they looked inebriated beyond the point of consciousness, their heads slumped next to empty pint-sized mugs, remnants of foam clinging to their rims.

The door slammed shut behind Ira loud enough for even the drunkest patron to jerk awake. Not for long, though.

A woman's head poked up from behind the bar.

"What can I get you?" Celeste Hodges asked, reflexively scrubbing the bar with a well-used rag even though Ira could see nothing there to clean. "We've got the usual. Not much to choose from, but what we've got is the good stuff. No one complains."

Ira sat upon one of the stools. It creaked under him. "I'm not thirsty."

"No one comes here who's not thirsty." Celeste was about to say more, but her mouth snapped closed the moment she got a good look at Ira. "Ah! No, I suppose you're not thirsty. Not for anything I could serve you. You'll be wanting to see Trevor, yeah?"

Ira nodded. "Yes. But it's nice to see you again, Celeste. You do remember me?"

"I always recognize Trevor's type." She tossed the rag into the bar sink. "But you. Yes, I remember. Name's Ira, yeah? From America? Is Trevor expecting you?"

"Not sure," Ira said. "I expect he might have had some forewarning."

Celeste angled her chin toward a staircase. "In the parlor. Upstairs. If he's not in, he will be soon."

He gave her a wink, then hopped off the stool and climbed the stairs, holding fast to the handrail. The steps were steep and the walls narrow on either side. Fortunately, he was as slim in his sixties as he'd been in his thirties. That's what happened when you spent your old age hiking through deserts and climbing glaciers.

Light poured into the parlor from two large windows. He settled into the deep grooves of a threadbare couch, but only after tossing aside a half-dozen orange and yellow throw pillows, cloudy puffs of wool squeezing through their frayed edges.

Trevor wasn't in, not that Ira minded. The last days and hours had passed in a blur. He closed his eyes and breathed in and out. He'd always been able to find a place of rest in his meditative river.

"Ira Binyamin, is it you?"

When Ira opened his eyes, Trevor stood before him—tall and lean and chiseled. His figure was the sort that romance novel illustrators had conjured since the early days of publishing. A perfect human specimen, which was only possible since Trevor was, of course, not human at all.

*   *   *

"He can't keep doing this." Lawrence stomped down the stairs, swung open the front door, and looked up and down the street. A futile gesture, carried out by instinct. If Ira had disappeared from the house, he certainly wouldn't have done so via the front door.

In any event, Lawrence was wrong; Ira *could* keep doing this, and probably would, as long and as often as he wanted. Neither of them could do much to stop him.

"He's playing God, that's what." Lawrence came back into the house, slamming the door behind him. Picture frames rattled on the walls.

"What can we do?"

"Not a damned thing."

Lawrence pulled out a handful of ice from the refrigerator and wrapped it in a dishcloth hanging from the oven door. He held the improvised cooling pack to his sweaty forehead.

"He could have gone anywhere." Lawrence moved the damp towel to the back of his neck, closing his eyes at the cool sensation.

"There's no limit to the range of his new ability."

"You mean he could translate anywhere on earth?"

Lawrence let out an unamused laugh. "Or beyond, honestly. Who knows?"

"Beyond earth? You mean the moon? Mars?"

"He's gone beyond earth before, but I don't think he was visiting other planets."

Dario caught the gist of what Lawrence meant, and it made him squirm. Despite a long relationship with the Catholic Church, Dario had never been too comfortable with the notions of heaven and hell.

"You look positively stricken," Lawrence said.

Dario sighed. "I suppose I am."

"Well, that makes two of us."

*   *   *

Ira had met Trevor twice before—once in this very parlor, fifteen years ago, and another time much earlier, at Aaron's house. Ira felt amazed that he had ever been confused about Trevor's identity. The Watchers were almost alien in appearance. Sure, they had eyes and ears, a nose, a mouth, and hair color that fell within the usual human spectrum, but these were surface similarities. Their skin was too smooth, contours too sharp, faces too proportionate, bodies too lithe yet muscled.

Ira stood up. Even drawing himself to his full height, he fell short of Trevor by several inches.

"Ira, we are long overdue for a conference."

"It's good to see you again," Ira said. "You haven't aged a day."

This was an inane observation, as the Watchers never aged. It was a human pleasantry. Trevor smiled graciously as though it had somehow been a compliment.

"I need your counsel," Ira said, sitting down again. "Developments have been proceeding apace."

"In Pakistan. Yes, I've felt it."

"I suspect the Grigori have been released." Ira lowered his voice. "Have you done anything? Do you have a plan?"

Trevor was quiet. "It's not my decision."

Ira felt the air go out of the room. "I've heard that philosophy before, yet there has to be—"

"Please understand, I cannot sanction your personal choices. You have your own agency, the freedom and responsibility to act of your own free will. This is your world, not mine."

"But surely you have a stake in it!"

"I can offer guidance, if you've come for that."

Ira clenched his jaw. Centuries of protecting the secrets of creation had come to this: a moment when it was necessary to come out into the open, to show their power and use it—judiciously—to ensure the future of the human race. If the Grigori were allowed to have their way in the world again, everything would be destroyed. What had been the point of his work, of the work of his predecessors, if Jehovah wouldn't fight for himself?

Trevor turned his back to Ira and looked out the window at the street below. A group of schoolchildren were riding over the cobblestone on bicycles. They couldn't have been more than seven or eight.

"Do you see those children?" Trevor asked. "They accept what their parents tell them and do what they're told. It's for their own good. They don't rail against it. Usually."

"And what is your point? Am I like a child?"

"You are not a child, my friend, though it would be better for everyone if you were."

What did that mean? Ira waited for Trevor to explain himself, but he remained tightlipped.

"I'm going to hold a meeting," Ira said, pressing forward. "I've heard what you said, but I can't accept it. The stakes are higher now than they've ever been, and you must understand that. Join us. Perhaps we can persuade you."

"And perhaps I can persuade you."

"I hope not." Ira stood up. "Come to Fair Haven, Vermont. There's a home in the countryside that belongs—well, used to belong—to Aaron Roth. You remember him?"

Trevor smiled. "I know the place you mean. When is this meeting?"

"In two days. At noon."

"I will be there," Trevor said. "But Ira, I fear you will not like what I have to say."

Ira turned and walked toward the stairwell. He had never been more sure of anything in his life—Trevor would change his mind. His kind had been brought to earth to watch over humanity, and the fate of humanity now hung in the balance.

NINE

Mount Khunjerab, Pakistan
JULY 30

Lagati thrust his fists against the storeroom's cool metallic door, leaving a line of tiny cuts across his left knuckles. He winced, then jammed his thumb against the copper panel. Nothing happened. Clearly, the Grigori had changed the permissions throughout the facility; Lagati should have been allowed access to any room he wanted. Especially this one, since they had assigned him to catalogue the crates inside it.

The best course of action would be to talk to Semyaza. Surely it had been an oversight. Did the Grigori make oversights? Unlikely.

Lagati retraced his footsteps from earlier that day, venturing to his former office. The corridor was deserted, like most of the base at this time of night. He pressed his finger to the door trigger, but again nothing happened. Not that he'd expected anything.

He leaned against the wall, reliving the frustration at having seen Sherwood Brighton ushered into Semyaza's office like a guest of honor. Lagati had been part of this enterprise for three years, and Brighton had been at Khunjerab for maybe three days.

It rankled.

Did Semyaza know how he felt? Did Semyaza care? He suspected the answer was yes to the first, and no to the second. Or perhaps no to both, which was somehow even worse.

Without putting much thought into where he was going, he began to walk—slowly at first, then more quickly. Frustration and bewilderment grew to overwhelming proportions, thudding against the confines of his brain in the form of the worst headache he had ever known.

His emotional control returned as he approached the Shamballa cavern. Those damned glow rocks lit the way, installed into the ceiling joints. Lagati still didn't understand the science behind them. They produced light without heat, and did so indefinitely; he presumed they had glowed without interruption for thousands of years. Antoinette and two chemists whose names he couldn't remember had dedicated themselves to studying the phenomenon for a full week before Lagati decided their expertise could be put to better use. Glow rocks had paled in comparison to the abandoned ships in the hangar.

"Why are we meeting in this abominable place?"

Lagati slowed down, listening. Voices drifted up from the lower chamber.

"This place will do." That plangent voice belonged to Semyaza. Lagati would have recognized it anywhere. "The barrier serves as a reminder of our purpose."

Lagati crept closer. His mind shouted at him to get the hell away, but his feet responded to a stronger instinct: he refused to be left out any longer. He would eavesdrop, risks be damned.

"Batraal," Semyaza said. "You have a report."

A higher-pitched voice took over, commanding attention. "Abranel is preparing to depart, and he will be watched to ensure our property is recovered. I'm confident he requires little supervision in this task."

Several voices replied at once, and Lagati couldn't discern what they were saying. Was this an argument? Discord between the Grigori? Perhaps they weren't as unified as they made themselves appear.

"Little supervision?" Azazel said, breaking through the tumult. "Abranel has given the host far too much leeway."

"Just enough, I think." Semyaza's rebuke was firm. "The host must feel an element of freedom in order to be compliant."

"Compliance is assured," Batraal's high-pitched voice observed. "Abranel sees to that."

Abranel, Lagati thought. The name didn't ring a bell, but he would have bet his right arm it was a reference to the creature inhabiting Brighton.

"Are we concerned about this morning's infiltration?" an unfamiliar voice asked.

"You refer to the man and woman who discovered us," Semyaza said. "They were quickly dealt with."

"But there will be others."

"We chose this place for its isolation." Azazel now. "But it's not as isolated as it was. People see our vessels in the skies and track us down. We must decide if our base remains viable."

A hush settled over the conversation for a time. Had they realized someone was listening in?

Lagati took a backward step, hoping the answer was no. *What am I doing? Azazel will kill me, and delight in the undertaking.*

He fled, moving only quickly enough to ensure both speed and silence. It took him a few minutes to reach the relative safety of the base corridors. When he reached his tiny apartment, he thumbed the door and flashed into its womb-like darkness. His heart beat wildly as he forced himself to relax, to restore calm.

They didn't hear you, he told himself between heaving breaths. *If they had, you wouldn't be here now. You're safe. You are in control of the situation.*

Once he had slowed his breathing enough to allow his other senses to kick in, he realized he wasn't alone. Slowly, anticipation replaced all his fear and panic. Antoinette's slightly honeyed scent made him feel safe.

Lagati sat on the edge of the bed, removed his shirt, and lay his head on the pillow. He closed his eyes, feeling her warm breath against the side of his neck. Sensing his presence even in the midst of sleep, she snuggled into him.

He rolled onto his side, mindful not to roll right off the edge of the twin bed. He propped his head up with his right hand and watched her sleep. Her chest rose and fell to a steady rhythm. Her olive complexion glowed in the dark apartment, pitch-black except for the pale blue light of a computer monitor.

Antoinette had been intoxicating even in their first meeting, though she had hated him. She'd been so richly, unbearably French. The faculty of the Paris-Sorbonne had invited him to speak to a group of top doctoral candidates, and Antoinette had listened from the back of the auditorium. He found out later she was a professor—not only that, but a member of the Council of Administration. Those unblinking Japanese eyes had watched him throughout his presentation, dripping with unconcealed disdain.

"You didn't agree with my thesis," he remarked when she followed him into one of the university's opulently appointed halls. He couldn't imagine what she found so offensive about him; all he'd done was highlight the struggles faced by the underclass and the accessibility of French education.

Antoinette had lifted her chin. "You come from a position of extreme privilege. Why should I consider any opinion you hold on the subject of free education?"

"I came from nothing," he reminded her. "You know nothing about me."

This didn't impress her. She was a stone.

A stone he'd become determined to crack. And here she was, fifteen years on, thoroughly split open. Laid bare.

She stirred, and for a moment he thought she would awaken. Instead she nuzzled into the crook of his arm and sighed. Her eyelids fluttered, and he thought she must be dreaming.

He exhaled, feeling her hair brush lazily against his forehead. He wouldn't sleep tonight, not after the mixture of frustration and terror and relief to which he'd been subjected.

Light poured into the room in a sudden stream, but only for a split-second before a huge, hulking mass lumbered into the open doorway. Lagati bolted upright, accidentally kicking Antoinette in the thigh. She let out a cry of surprise, then sat up. Her cry turned into a scream as all seven vertical feet of Azazel charged into the dark apartment.

Lagati didn't have time to negotiate. He felt Azazel's bear-like hands grip him by the shoulder and haul him out of bed. He hit the ground hard, his knee spasming. Before he could react, Azazel hoisted him into the air with one hand, his feet dangling a foot above the floor. Azazel held him in place and slapped him hard across the face. Lagati tried to protect himself by twisting away, but it only succeeded in enraging the Grigori.

Lagati cringed as Azazel dropped him like a sack of potatoes. He landed on the same knee as before; it throbbed now, but he didn't think anything was broken.

Yet.

"Get up." Azazel waited in the doorframe, towering over him. "Get up!"

Lagati did as he was told, silently. He wouldn't cry out. He would get through this. He would not die today.

He followed Azazel into the corridor, limping heavily. He cast a last, long gaze at Antoinette, who was mouthing silent words at him. Lagati squinted, trying to read those beautiful lips, but it was too dark and he couldn't afford to keep Azazel waiting.

The doors closed.

"You were listening to us," Azazel said, taking Lagati by the shoulder again. "We have allowed you too much freedom of movement. Turel should not have taken you on the clean-up crew. For that matter, he should have restricted your access to the hangar. Nothing there is any of your concern."

"But the cargo—"

"Yes, the cargo." Azazel's chiseled face wore a bemused expression, his emotions having softened more quickly than seemed natural. "That is where you must focus your energies. There is work to be done."

The Grigori proceeded down the corridor in long strides, Lagati limping along as fast as his legs could carry him. He only barely avoided being dragged along the floor. Fortunately, it was not a long walk to the storeroom door.

Inside, the lights zapped on as Lagati stumbled into the room and fell on his side. Unopened crates, their chrome lids shining under the overhead fluorescents, surrounded him on all sides.

"I didn't mean to—"

Azazel gestured to the nearest crates. "This is not a complicated business. You do what you are told or you will be replaced. You would have been replaced long ago, except Semyaza has a soft spot for you. He's grateful for what you have done for us. As for myself, I've gotten over my gratitude."

He delivered a swift kick to Lagati's gut, then turned on a dime and walked out.

Lagati groaned as he collected himself. He could barely stand, not after that last kick, so he settled for crawling to the base of the nearest crate and using it to leverage himself into a sitting position.

"Don't forget the lesson," Semyaza had told him not long ago. *"For every action, there is a consequence."*

Lagati drew a long, shuddering breath. For all he knew, Azazel was right; he would be dead were it not for Semyaza's leniency.

He wasn't sure how long he sat clutching himself in pain and exhaustion, but his ears soon perked at the sound of insistent knocking on the door. A relapse of agony swept through him at the fear that Azazel had come back to finish the job.

Except no, that made no sense. Azazel would never have knocked. Whoever stood outside the door didn't have access to the room. It had to be a human.

He had no way of opening the door without lurching across the room to the thumb panel, so he swallowed his dignity and did just that. He staggered slowly, walking near to the crates so he would have something to hold onto if his legs gave out.

The door careened open, revealing Antoinette's hourglass figure. She had dressed quickly and pulled her straight brown hair into a hasty ponytail, leaving behind disheveled strands clinging to her sweaty cheeks.

She gasped at the sight of him. He leaned his full weight against her as she struggled to keep him upright.

"I can't believe what he did to you." She lowered him to the floor and closed the door. "You should see a doctor."

"I'll be okay. It's not the first time he's done something like this. Besides, I provoked him. It's my own damned fault." He put a hand to his forehead. "I feel lightheaded. I don't suppose you brought water. Maybe something to eat?"

"I'll get you something."

"In a minute." He rested his hand on her lower leg. "Antoinette, I need you to do something for me."

"Anything, Raff."

"The Grigori aren't going to include me in their deliberations. I don't know what they're planning, but there's one man who does: Sherwood Brighton. Follow him."

She narrowed her eyes. "Is he going someplace?"

"I heard the Grigori mention that he's departing. Go after him, if you can. You know how to get out of here without being seen. We prepared for this contingency."

Antoinette took his hand off her leg and gave it an affectionate squeeze. "Let's go together. This is no place for us."

"I'm in no condition to hike through the mountains." He paused, allowing enough time for the reality of his predicament to settle in. "I can follow later, but Brighton is leaving soon. I need someone I trust to go after him, and frankly you're the only person I trust."

"What about you?"

Lagati gestured to the cargo. "I'll do what they want of me, for now. Whatever is in these crates, it's critical to their plans." He lowered his voice. "I got word this morning that one of the ships has gone missing, and I know for a fact it was full of cargo. My theory is that Brighton—or rather Abranel, as his spirit is called—has been tasked with recovering it. Do you understand what I'm asking of you?"

"Yes, I do. Are you sure I can't persuade you to come with me?"

Lagati chuckled, and immediately regretted it as pain blossomed in his gut. "You can persuade me, but I still wouldn't be able to make the trip. It's for the best if you go alone."

"How do we stay in touch?"

"See Wendell. He'll know what to do."

Antoinette leaned in and gave him a deep, probing kiss. He forced himself to turn his head, breaking away from it.

"Not now," he said. "I need you to hurry."

She nodded and stood up, but she didn't leave.

"I can take care of myself," he insisted.

Yeah, and look where that's gotten you.

Without another word, she left the storeroom. He closed his eyes, trying to burn this last glimpse of her into his memory.

TEN

Mount Khunjerab, Pakistan
JULY 31

This valley was a peculiarly desolate place, Brighton decided as Abranel adjusted his backpack and forced himself to climb yet another steep section of this endless trail. With grey cliffs to his right and the jagged Khunjerab glacier to his left, he had nothing to concentrate on except the excruciating push and pull on his legs as Abranel drove him onward.

They—a plural pronoun was the only way to encapsulate his new reality—soon crested the top of the pass, laying out yet another bleak vista. Four or five kilometers down the slope, the glacier discharged a stream into the Hunza River. The sun beat down on Brighton's shoulders, warm against his skin despite the cool chill in the air.

Can't we have a break? Brighton asked.

"You wanted fresh air, to get out into the world again," Abranel said aloud. It must have looked ridiculous, as though he were talking to himself. Fortunately, there wasn't anyone around to witness this absurdity. "Don't complain now that you have it."

This wasn't my idea. It was Semyaza's.

"You wanted it. You can lie to yourself, but you can't lie to me."

Brighton didn't respond, but he didn't need to think the words for Abranel to know them. He was out in the open, sure, but he wasn't free. In fact, the pain of Abranel's presence felt sharper than ever. This was no more than a cruel tease.

We're looking for a crashed ship, Brighton thought. *Do you know what kind of cargo it carried?*

"Yes."

Pitilessly, Abranel said nothing further.

I wish you'd tell me what we're looking for. Perhaps I could help.

"Enough already," Abranel said. "What a fool you are. If I feel like including you, I'll do it."

The words stung. Brighton shrunk back into the dark recesses of his thoughts. Such a strange experience to literally live in one's own head. The level of introspection he subjected himself to was unbearable.

They stopped briefly on the way down, ironically in the same natural hollow where he and Elisabeth had paused to sleep on their way over the saddle. Memories of that uncomfortable night flooded back. He had been possessed, propelled by a force he had believed was Emery Wörtlich.

Abranel laughed. "It was me, you know. Such a fool, such a fool. I met you at Stonehenge, then followed everywhere you went. You did exactly what the Grigori wanted."

They reached the bottom of the path three interminable hours later, and Brighton's shins and hamstrings burned. Even Abranel must have tired; Brighton noticed they had slowed their descent considerably near the end. They now faced a meadow of low grasses and shrubs, and beyond that the river and the highway, entwined like two strands of a rope.

"Take over for a while," Abranel told him as his control slipped away.

Brighton almost collapsed from the strain on his lower legs. He stumbled from the suddenness of the transition, wishing there was something to grab hold of. He gave in, falling to his knees and feeling the coarse, rocky earth in his dry hands, parched from long exposure to the high mountain air.

Why now? Brighton asked.

"I'm resting."

Did that mean Abranel could be overworked? Could extreme exertion be used to his advantage?

"I wouldn't count on it."

An SUV waited for them, parked on the rocky shoulder of the highway. As Brighton approached with painstaking steps, the window rolled down and a familiar face appeared.

"I should have known it would be you," Brighton said to Wendell.

Wendell unlocked the doors and Brighton climbed into the passenger seat. It felt amazing to take the weight off his overworked feet. He closed the door and leaned back, shutting his eyes and relishing the cool air that washed over him from the forward vents. The plush leather conformed to Brighton's body, a glorious cushion of bliss not to be taken for granted.

Wendell shifted the vehicle into drive and pulled onto the highway, cruising south.

"It's been a long time, Mr. Brighton."

"Indeed it has." Brighton turned to the driver and reacted with surprise at the man's injuries. A long cut angled from the bridge of his nose to the top of his forehead, a jagged line marked by a series of close stiches. He looked a bit like Frankenstein's monster. "What happened to you?"

Wendell kept his impassive eyes on the road. "I ran into some friends of yours. You travel with a dangerous crowd, Mr. Brighton."

"Did Ira take a knife to you?" Brighton deadpanned.

"A chair."

"That hardly seems likely."

Wendell ran a finger along the scar. "Believe it."

It must have been Dario, Brighton thought. *I knew there was a rea-*
son to like that kid.

Dario had been an innocent, and Brighton regretted whatever
outcome the man had been led to. But not Ira. Ira had come back with
his eyes wide open and deserved no sympathy. If he met some horrible end, it was only right and just.

"Do you want to know what happened to them?" Wendell asked.

"Yes, of course." Not caring about the outcome wasn't the same
as not wanting to know the nature of it. But if history was any indication, Wendell wouldn't reveal anything.

"Bodies were found in the valley. They were badly burned."

Brighton flinched as he recalled a blackened patch of land they'd
passed during the climb. "I think we walked by the spot where it happened."

"We?"

"Me and..." He considered whether there was any advantage in
keeping the existence of Abranel to himself. He decided there was
little point. "I have a companion now."

"Ah. The inhabitation." Wendell nodded as they approached the first
in a long series of switchbacks. "Personally, I wasn't interested. I passed."

He passed? Had that been an option? Perhaps Wendell was a
smarter man than he.

"Most people are," Abranel reminded him.

Shut up.

"They think Ira is dead," Wendell said, demonstrating remarkable
candidness. "No one knows for sure what happened."

"Why are you telling me this?"

Wendell shrugged. "You're one of us now. That creature inside you can exert total control, can't it? You'll do whatever Lagati wants you to do."

"I get the sense Lagati isn't in charge anymore."

This gave Wendell pause.

"Surely you must have considered that," Brighton said.

"Lagati set all this in motion. He's at the center of the storm."

"Perhaps." But Brighton didn't believe it. "I think this storm has been brewing long before your boss entered the picture. The forces in play are very old. And very angry."

They cruised through several small towns before falling into the line-up of cars waiting for the ferry in Shishkat. The blue-green lake provided a sharp contrast to the steep, dismal slopes diving into it on either side. The ferry came twenty long minutes later. They boarded it and remained in the SUV, eyes glued to the dreamlike scenery as they coasted down the gullet of the south-snaking lake; entire towns had been swallowed in its relentless backflow.

"Where are we going?" Brighton finally asked, astonished that he hadn't thought to ask earlier. "I assume we're meeting a plane some-where."

"At Gilgit. Two hours from here."

Brighton closed his eyes again, hoping to spend as much of that time asleep as possible, resting his weary bones. He awoke to find Wendell taking the turnoff from the Karakoram Highway to Gilgit. Brighton recognized the incongruous corn fields that marked the area. Mountains roared up into the sky all around, but here, at the conflu-ence of rivers, there was enough open space for a good-sized city.

They rolled through town, past one squat stone building after an-other encased by trees whose green boughs rejoiced in the height of summer. The streets were quiet, but some men and women criss-crossed the roads. Wendell had to be careful, for there were no official crossings; pedestrians walked where they wanted and expected cars to dodge them.

The airport's single runway cut through town in an indiscriminate swath, severing all roads except those on the fringes of the valley. Likely, this location had been the longest flat surface the city builders had been able to pin down. On the far side of the runway, concrete gave way to a soccer pitch; boys raced around it end to end, kicking a ball while spectators cheered from the sidelines. Despite the distance from home and differences in culture, life in Pakistan didn't always seem so different from the one he had left behind in America.

They parked in a graveled lot outside the small terminal. If he hadn't known better, Brighton might have mistaken the building for a large house. Its wide windows and white-pillared exterior gave it the look of a villa. An even smaller second story peeked out, and above it the square control tower presided.

The single security guard stepped aside and let them both through a gate leading directly to the runway. A mangled barbed wire fence separated the adjacent properties, many of them modest houses; Brighton wondered what it was like to have planes screaming just outside one's windows several times a day.

These thoughts flew right out of his overcrowded head when he caught sight of the plane taxiing toward them. Its sleek, blue-striped fuselage gleamed in the fading daylight—not the same jet Lagati had tasked to rescue them from Egypt. A man like Lagati might easily have a fleet of planes deployed around the world to respond to his every whim.

"I'll say this for Lagati," Brighton said under his breath. "He rides in style."

Obviously the beauty and excitement of Bentleys and private jets had long since lost their sizzle for Wendell, who approached the jet with all the pleasure of a ten-year-old being told to mow the lawn. The side of the jet cracked open and began a slow and graceful arc to the ground. Wendell stopped below the stairs and gestured for Brighton to enter ahead of him.

Brighton climbed halfway up before stopping. "Aren't you coming?"

"I have business here," Wendell replied, betraying no emotion.

"So I'm going alone." Brighton looked toward the cockpit window. "Except for the pilot, of course."

The chauffeur laughed. "Alone? Mr. Brighton, with that creature inside you, you will never be alone again."

ELEVEN

Macleay Island, Australia
AUGUST 1

The ferry from Redland Bay deposited Gayle Voss's lime-green Mazda on the shore of Macleay Island in the midst of a light drizzle. Beyond the parking area, a two-lane street twisted off through the mangrove forest, the trees' gnarled roots coiling over the swampy shoreline like boa constrictors. Mist spiraled over the ground, concealing the road's dividing line. She followed closely behind a rust-colored Escalade to maintain her position in the lane.

The High Central Road climbed north, a spine thrust through the heart of the island. She eventually came to a three-way junction at which the sweet Queenslander accent of her GPS suggested she take a right. This new road narrowed until it devolved into a gravel track, but then returned to pavement after crossing a rickety wooden bridge through a grove of swaying palm trees.

Her destination turned out to be a whitewashed house partially hidden behind a red-brick wall. A jeep rested on the driveway just inside the wall, effectively blocking the way in.

Not very friendly, she mused as she got out of the car, her sandaled feet squishing into moist ground. Perhaps she should have worn better footwear; it had been nearly seventy degrees when she left Brisbane, though it was much cooler now.

She opened the trunk and removed a grey hoodie from her suitcase. It fit snugly around her slim frame, doing little to keep out the chill.

Gayle stepped through the opening in the brick wall and steered around the jeep, treading through wet overgrown grass and keeping an eye out for snakes. She'd been warned snakes outnumbered people on these islands ten to one.

Flat, circular garden stones formed a connect-the-dots path to the door. The pitter of rain on the trees above made her look up; a drop landed on her forehead and rolled down the bridge of her nose. She brushed it away and knocked.

For the longest time, nothing happened, but eventually she heard the pounding of feet descending a flight of stairs. The door flung open and she found herself looking at a mostly bald man whose few remaining tendrils of white hair had been combed flat to his scalp. In his arms he held two white boxes.

"Gayle Voss?" He held the door open and she bustled in, slipping off her sandals. "I can't believe you're here. You must have had a long travel day."

"You have no idea."

"Come in, come in."

He took her on a circuitous route through the house, ending in a screened porch. The view of Moreton Bay's southern basin took her breath away. The sun was peeking through the clouds over the water, rays of yellow light descending from the heavens like searchlights. The sea lapped at the stilts holding this wing of the house aloft.

"It's not normally so rainy," he said in an Australian lilt. "Dead of winter, you understand. You should have come in January."

"The timing wasn't my choice."

"Yes, of course." He dropped the two boxes on a counter along the back wall, then extended his hand. "Max Holden. You said you're a friend of Elisabeth's?"

"I am," Gayle said, facing the window. The fresh air tasted wonderful, albeit more humid than she was used to. At this time of year, Provo could be dry as a bone.

"Well, like I said on the phone, I'm not sure I can help you find her, but I'll do what I can. She's a dear friend. Sit down."

As she found a place to sit, settling on a rocking chair with bright blue cushions, Max opened the doors to a refrigerator and carefully placed the two white boxes inside.

"You said something about her going missing?" he asked.

"She's not the only one. You worked with her at the archaeological institute in Cairo, is that right?"

He sat across from her. "Years ago, yes."

"You worked with Emery Wörtlich and Noam Sheply, too?"

"And our boss, Zahi Menefee."

"Of course. Elisabeth mentioned him once or twice. He's the only one still employed there." She waited for some kind of confirmation, but all she got was a look of cool curiosity. "The problem is that Wörtlich disappeared last year, near as I can tell." She paused. "Unless I miss my guess, Elisabeth and Sheply have gone missing as well. That's an awful coincidence, wouldn't you say?"

Max stiffened. "Noam Sheply is missing?"

"Do you know anything about that?"

"No," Max said, stretching out the word. "I'm not sure it constitutes a coincidence, but it's a terrible thing."

Gayle rocked silently in her chair. "Mr. Holden, I know you were one of the last people to see Emery Wörtlich alive."

If Max had seemed stiff before, he now looked like his spine had solidified into a steel bar off which his body hung like a scarecrow. "How could you know about that?"

"Elisabeth told me."

"And how could Elisabeth know?"

"Suffice it to say, she knows. I'd like you to tell me what happened when Emery Wörtlich visited you here a year and a half ago."

Max stood up again but looked like he might topple over. "I think you should stay for dinner. You don't mind, do you?"

"As long as your answers validate my coming here."

"Well, I can't promise that. But I can promise the most delicious blue swimmer crab you've ever tasted." He went back to the fridge and retrieved one of the white boxes he had deposited there. "Caught fresh this morning."

Max spent the next hour alone in the kitchen, and Gayle decided not to disturb him. She explored the house, finding three bedrooms and a downstairs family room that provided access to the dock. A small green-hulled fishing boat—barely more than a dingy—bobbed at the end of it, kept in place with thick cords of knotted rope. She chose a novel from a shelf of old books, most of their covers tattered at the edges, and settled into a flower-patterned armchair to read.

"Where is the rest of your family?" Gayle asked when she wandered back upstairs, drawn by the overpowering aroma of baked crab. "I saw some pictures downstairs. Do you have a wife and children?"

"The children are home in Sydney," Max explained, whisking the contents of a saucepan. "We spend most of the summer and fall here, but the grandchildren are all in school now. I'm retired, and I'm sorry to say my wife has passed away."

Gayle took a seat at the table. "My husband died, too. Two days ago."

Max turned sharply. "Two days! What on earth are you doing here then? I took months to grieve after my wife died."

"I don't have that luxury. You see, my husband was killed."

"You mean murdered?"

"I'm not sure what I mean," Gayle admitted. "Most people dismiss me as a quack, so this may not make sense to you, but hear me out. I'm very sensitive to nodal energy, and my husband was able to channel it. In small doses, anyway. A few days ago, a massive bombardment of energy hit Kashmir, spreading out through a network of ley lines that encircle the planet like the stitches on a soccer ball."

Max continued stirring the sauce. "I've heard of this before. I don't subscribe to it, but I'm familiar."

"Good. But understand that whether you believe it or not, this energy killed my husband."

"I don't mean to sound insensitive, but what does this have to do with me?"

"Elisabeth was in Kashmir."

Max took the saucepan off the heat. "Is that right?"

"I believe something's happened to her, and I also believe it involves your former colleagues in Cairo. I want you to tell me what you know of Emery Wörtlich, for starters."

"Dinner's almost ready," Max said.

He cracked open the oven, intensifying the smell—crab doused in butter with a savory combination of seasonings her nose couldn't readily identify. Was that rosemary?

A few minutes later, they were staring at each other over the small kitchen table, the platter of crab exhaling a pillar a steam. She didn't wait for pleasantries, instead using a large spoon to transport one of the crabs to her own plate. She tapped its hard shell appraisingly with an oyster fork.

"What you ask is impossible," Max explained as he broke off the crab legs and began worming his way into the thin but delectable ribbons of meat contained therein.

"Explain."

Max cracked the leg in half. "There are matters about which I've been sworn to secrecy, including the details of my final encounter with Emery Wörtlich. The parties involved would be very unhappy if I were to break their confidence. These are serious people, Gayle."

"My husband is dead, and you can help me get to the bottom of it."

He ate in silence as she put down her fork, having largely lost her appetite.

"Do you want me to beg?" she asked.

"I want nothing of the sort. But I have to think of myself."

"Listen, I already know you saw Emery Wörtlich before his disappearance. You wouldn't be giving away the secret."

Max hesitated. "There are other secrets."

She picked up the crab again, twisting the main body in half and pulling back the shell. "These serious people you mention, I believe they're more serious than you realize. But I don't think they're interested in you. Bigger fish to fry, you understand."

Max put down his utensils. "You wouldn't say that if you knew the names of the men involved."

"Try me."

Max chuckled. "Tell me about your husband."

"What do you want to know?"

"Anything you'd care to share. When I lost my wife, it helped to talk about her. To anyone who would listen. It's the only thing that kept me sane."

Gayle breathed in. "I don't really know how to talk about him."

"At the beginning, I think that's normal."

"Is it? Our friends certainly haven't had trouble. When we scattered his ashes, they told story after story—and I resented them for it. Resented them for knowing him better than I did, for knowing him longer. What am I now? Not a spouse. Not anything, really. Elisabeth is my only real friend, and she's missing, perhaps swallowed up by the same darkness that claimed my husband."

Gayle sagged in her chair, the crab dinner a very old memory.

"I'm alone, and I don't think I can be alone." Gayle looked up into Max's middle-aged eyes, bracketed by deep skin creases forged by age and apparent concern. "You have a family, a legacy. Children and grandchildren. People to keep you company in your grief. I don't have any of that. You can't understand what I'm going through. You can sympathize, but you can't *know*."

Thank god he didn't rush to comfort her. He allowed her to stew in silent anguish, and that's what she needed. It felt horrible, and lonely, but it also felt just a little bit good.

But it couldn't go on forever.

"My wife's name was Patricia," he said at last, after clearing his throat. "I loved her more than words can say."

For some reason, this angered her. She hadn't asked him to reciprocate, and it didn't make her feel better to hear about his wife. Their circumstances were nothing alike, past a few surface details. Henry hadn't just died; he'd been killed! And there would be no justice.

"It's not the same—"

Max raised a single finger, and this stopped her just long enough to evaluate her reaction. Where had all this rage come from? This man hadn't done anything to her; she was the one to have shown up on his doorstep.

"It's not about the length of time you love someone," he said. "Whether you loved your husband for twenty years or twenty days, love is love. You might have more memories if you spent your lives together, but would the intensity of your connection be stronger? Not in my experience. I could have worked in Egypt for decades. Did fieldwork draw me? Absolutely. But my family was more important. Being away from them left me homesick. Now that my wife's gone, I feel like I'll never be home ever again. Sure, I have children to remind me of her, but they're not replacements. Besides, they have their own lives. I'm an old man they see a few times a year."

He picked up his plate, the crab only barely touched, and carried it to the counter. Evidently, he had lost his appetite, too.

"I'm sorry," he said quietly, facing away from her. "Saying those things didn't help either of us."

He cleared the rest of the dishes, his ashen cheeks looking a bit more sunken than they had earlier. He eventually left her alone in the kitchen.

Gayle awkwardly pushed her chair back and stood. She had made herself miserable—a skill she had become quite adept at—but she hadn't intended to bring Max down with her. Her greatest guilt lay in the fact that she felt pleased on some depraved level that he was lonely, too.

She found him in the downstairs sitting room, surveying the water. The moment she came down the steps, he walked outside into the small, tall-grassed backyard. He must have heard her coming and wanted to be alone.

Screw that, she thought as she crossed the room and grasped the door handle. *I've come a long way for answers.*

Max strolled to the end of the dock and got down on his haunches, untying the rope around the fishing boat. "Want to go for a ride? It would help us get our minds off our own misery, at least for a little while."

Gayle stepped to the edge of the grass in bare feet. The rain had tapered off, giving way to sunny skies.

"Is it seaworthy?" she asked, appraising the craft.

Max jumped into the boat, all the while grasping the rope to prevent him from drifting away. "Of course it is. I've owned this boat for ten years."

She stepped onto the rickety boards of the dock. "Ten years, huh? Doesn't make me feel better."

"Get in."

It was a lovely evening for a boat ride, she had to give him that. The cool breeze lifted the hair off the back of her neck as he started the small outboard motor and steered them over the water's choppy surface. To the west, a tall wharf protruded from the water. To the east rose the houses of Brisbane's waterfront suburbs.

"Are we going to fish?" she asked, noticing all the gear on the floor.

"Seems to me you've been fishing all evening." He shaded his eyes from the setting sun. "Emery Wörtlich came to see me a year and a half ago, fresh off a huge find in Antarctica. He had found some sort of bone field under the ice, evidence that an ancient race of giants lived on the continent long before its discovery by European explorers."

"All Elisabeth told me was that he had a breakthrough. I don't think she knew what it was."

Max nodded. "I betrayed Emery by revealing his find to Noam Sheply, who was working for Raff Lagati. You must know of him."

"Of course." She wasn't surprised to hear such a famous name used in connection with all this chaos, but she was surprised Elisabeth had managed to somehow keep it secret from her.

"Anyway, Emery had a team and they went to some island in French Polynesia. The last time I spoke to Sheply, he didn't know what had become of them."

"I think Emery died there," Gayle said.

Max throttled the motor and the boat began to drift. "I don't see how you could know that."

"Elisabeth befriended one of the other men on Wörtlich's team, and he told her the whole story."

"Then you know more than I do," Max said.

Gayle got up from her seat and moved to the one directly opposite Max. "Elisabeth didn't share the details, and now I wish she had. Her life could depend on it. Fifteen years ago, you worked in Cairo with Wörtlich, Sheply, and Elisabeth. They're all gone now."

"And what do you think happened to them?"

"You tell me, Max. All I know is that Elisabeth went to Kashmir, and she didn't go alone."

Max rubbed his eyes in exhaustion. "I haven't seen Elisabeth since the old days, and Sheply only rarely. He would contact me when Lagati wanted something I could provide. It usually had something to do with hieroglyph analysis. Whatever Lagati was doing, he needed a lot of ancient writing translated."

"What was the writing about?"

"I never got a complete picture. The bits and pieces I examined told the story of a race of giants trying to escape a coming flood. The giant bones Wörtlich found in Antarctica seemed to corroborate this, but when I pressed Sheply for details he told me not to ask questions, and never to discuss what I had learned. I already told you about the threats."

"There had to be more."

"I swear to you, there's not. What happened to Sheply?"

"I contacted the Cairo Institute. He went on leave two weeks ago and hasn't been heard from since." Gayle brushed a hand through her hair. "Do you think someone is targeting your old team?"

This gave Max pause. His facial features slackened as he thought over the possibility.

"When's the last time you were contacted by Sheply?" Gayle asked.

"Almost a year. I assumed my involvement was finished now."

"I wouldn't be so sure. My first instinct was to fly to Kashmir and look for Elisabeth, but it's a big area—and it's not safe. I need help."

Max turned away and revved the motor again. He turned the tiller and the boat rolled to the left; they were headed back for shore.

"I can't go with you," Max called over the sound of the motor. "I don't want anything more to do with this. Perhaps you should speak to Zahi Menefee. He may know more about what's going on."

He didn't say another word until they brushed up against the dock. He jumped out of the boat and busied himself with the ropes. Gayle watched him expectantly, hoping for something more. Max didn't cooperate.

"I wish there was something I could do," he said.

She stepped into her sandals. "But there is."

"I'm too old for this game." He shook his head. "They'd kill me. They'll kill you, too."

Gayle could tell from his tone that he felt guilty, but he seemed resolved to cast her off. Catch and release.

"I really do wish you well," he said from the front step as she opened the door to her rental car. "I hope you find her."

No thanks to you, Gayle thought.

She pulled out, determined to channel her frustration into action. Max Holden was a sad and lonely man. She would not follow him down the same path.

TWELVE

Fair Haven, Vermont

AUGUST 1

A re you sure this is the right place?" Dario asked, his head hanging out the passenger window. The gravel road twisted through green hills, making it difficult to see farther than a half-kilometer into the countryside.

Lawrence ignored him, still angry at Ira's message to meet so far away. Just because Ira could cover vast distances in the blink of an eye didn't mean everyone could.

"As far as I know, Ira's original rental car is still collecting parking tickets on some street in Syracuse," Lawrence had mumbled somewhere around the Sarasota Springs bypass. "He asks me for a favor, and see what I get in return."

Talking about Ira set Lawrence off, but Dario couldn't avoid it. The rabbi was the only thing Dario and Lawrence—two-day-old acquaintances—had in common.

Lawrence pulled the car into a thickly treed private drive bisecting a sprawling grassy lawn. At the end of the road, the foliage opened to reveal a white colonial-era farmhouse with a wraparound porch.

"Have you been here before?" Dario asked.

"Once. That was a long time ago."

Dario's breath caught at the rustic beauty of this sanctuary, and he could understand why Ira had chosen it. Thick trees grew in organized rows everywhere he looked; those trees must have been at least a hundred years old. Their gnarled arms stretched in all directions, bending out of the shadows and rising to meet the sun.

"Come on," Lawrence said as he walked the path toward the house.

A tall man with grey in his tightly cropped beard met them on the porch. He'd been waiting in a porch swing, painted white but badly chipped from years of exposure to cold winters and humid summers. The man, well-groomed but portly and on the far side of middle age, wiped sweat from his cheeks as he came out from under the roof.

The man said nothing as they approached, but this didn't deter Lawrence, who clopped up the wooden steps and extended his hand.

"Good afternoon," Lawrence said. "We're friends of Ira Binyamin."

"I'm David Roth."

The two shook hands, then David acknowledged Dario with a nod.

"Funny," Lawrence said. "You're the second David Roth I've met. Can't be a coincidence."

"Must have been my son," David said. "He practically lived here the last few years. He was close to his grandfather."

David fell quiet. Abruptly so, in Dario's estimation, as though he had been about to continue. Dario guessed that this man was resentful of his son's relationship with his grandfather. The truth of it was written all over his face, the muscles around his thin mouth clenched in a way that implied years of bitterness and anxiety.

David led the way to the door and held it open for them.

"Is Ira here?" Dario asked.

"He will be soon." David entered, the door squealing on its hinges. "He told me to take you to the sitting room."

The sitting room could be found only by crossing through the kitchen. Its two windows peered out into an orchard that stretched up to the edge of the forest, bounded on two sides by a white fence that had seen better days. Bright yellow apples grew suspended from the branches, small and not yet ripened.

"Do you know how long he'll be?" Dario asked.

David shook his head and departed the way he had come.

Lawrence grunted. "Lately, Ira's done little else but keep people waiting. I wouldn't expect that to change anytime soon."

*   *   *

The river surged in such a vortex of sound and fury that Ira could barely contain it. His whole world had taken on this tumultuous aspect; everywhere he went, he felt on the edge of losing control. His interactions had turned heated in a way they never had before. So much opposition, and with it a host of support from the lesser voices shouting to be heard amidst the gale roaring in his ears. He had always exercised enormous discipline; every area of his life had been regulated. Restrained. His circumstances now rebelled against that. He'd been thrust into a role fraught with jeopardy and responsibility. What a horrible and awesome experience to hold the future in one's hands, to guide its course, to steer it away from calamity.

But he needed help to do it.

Trevor will come, he assured himself as he opened his eyes and felt the soft grass beneath his crossed legs. Trevor would help, or the world as they knew it would end. The situation was as uncomplicated as that. Trevor had power—and more importantly, he wasn't alone. Many beings like him wandered the earth. An army of them, if they chose to mobilize.

Ira put his weight against the thick trunk of a tree behind him and surveilled the orchard. A certain man from Nazareth had meditated in a garden much like this one just before he undertook his final charge, according to Christian texts. Had Jesus been the Christ? The notion swam upstream against every doctrine and custom Ira had been taught, yet he couldn't help but entertain some doubt. The giant in the pyramid on the Pacific floor had been awaiting restitution. But from whom? Something about the blood of the Hebrew Messiah.

He smiled to himself, amused that he had compared himself to Jesus Christ. The smile faded as he considered that the comparison might be apt. If Jesus had truly been Jehovah's son, he had faced head-on the fearful task of redeeming the world. Did Jehovah have in mind for Ira a task so different?

Trevor would come soon. He would take the burden from Ira's shoulders, carry the weight of responsibility, decide on a course of action. Ira had done enough; he'd travelled to another dimension, returned the Book of Creation. What more could he do?

Jehovah wouldn't see me, he reminded himself. *He wouldn't show himself.*

Ira remembered his last moments on earth before the shift. Thinking upon it now, he was struck by how effortless it had been, compared to the exertion he required now to translate from place to place. Traveling from one dimension to another had been easy. One moment he'd been on Tubuai, standing in the rutted road outside the motel he had shared with Brighton and Wörtlich. Brighton had gotten into a car, bound for the island's small airport, and Ira had watched it go.

That was the last thing he remembered. The next moment, he'd been somewhere else. A blink away, a blink into total and utter darkness. Nothingness. He hadn't been holding the Book of Creation, but it had shifted along with him, his only connection to reality.

While standing along that rutted road, Ira had *thought* about making the shift, but he hadn't exerted any effort toward accomplishing it. He hadn't known how to do it. He'd once asked Aaron if there was a known technique; it had to have been possible, since there were documented cases of humans translating to other realms. Enoch had passed freely between dimensions, if the Hebrew texts could be believed, which was why Semyaza and Azazel and the other Grigori had used him as a messenger, their only link to Jehovah.

"I hope you never find it necessary to travel that way," Aaron had told him.

Ever after, Ira had been obsessed with the notion of travelling between dimensions. When he eventually did discover the Book, he had known there was only one course of action. He couldn't destroy it, as Aaron had once suggested right here in Fair Haven. No, he had to return it to its maker. To Jehovah himself.

In the darkness of this unknown time and place, he'd had no sense of location, but the feel of the Book's parchment comforted him. The Book emitted an otherworldly glow, just enough light to reveal Ira's immediate vicinity: nothing but darkness in all directions.

The darkness had surprised him; he'd assumed the heavenly dimension would be filled with light. Scripture had certainly suggested it. Enoch's florid descriptions of heaven had flowed through Ira's imagination from an early age. Stones of crystal, a firmament of agitated stars and lightning, cherubim of fire amidst a stormy sky, structures as hot as fire and as cold as ice. Enoch had reported glorious mountains and rivers and deep valleys everywhere he looked. He'd witnessed grand forests of fruit-bearing trees, including the tree of knowledge alluded to in the Genesis account, the tree whose fruit had been sampled by the first humans of Jehovah's creation. Enoch had seen many things, and it had all blazed with radiance.

"The rules are different here," a voice called from out of the darkness.

Ira had held up the Book, hoping to glimpse the source of the voice. Was it a man? A woman?

"Who are you?" Ira asked. "Where is this place?"

A man appeared. He wore a thick brown beard, and that was all; as he approached, his nakedness became evident, though he exhibited no shame. His body was slim and well-proportioned.

Ira recognized him immediately. It was Enoch himself, whom Ira had glimpsed in a previous vision. His features were unmistakable.

"This is the realm of Jehovah." Enoch's dark, soulful eyes demanded Ira's full attention. "You can't perceive it the same way you perceive the world you come from. That's the first thing you must understand. Use your imagination, your creative instincts, to visualize heaven. Every individual perceives it in their own unique way. It's what makes this realm so magnificent."

Ira didn't know how long he remained silent, but it could have been five minutes or five years. Enoch's answer sank into his soul. It was difficult to understand, yet it didn't surprise Ira. So much of what he understood about Jehovah involved altered perception, using the human mind in creative ways. His way of visualizing the river, for example, required him to the world and its physical properties as a metaphor. There was no physical river, yet he could allow himself to be caught up in it.

"Yes, you have the general idea," Enoch said, reading his thoughts and parsing them as though Ira had spoken them aloud. "All of heaven works on the same principle. It begins as a blank slate, as you can see."

Enoch swept his hands wide, indicating the great darkness.

"You must not fear the darkness," he said. "But you may change it, if it disturbs you. For your whole life, you have visualized words in a book ascribed to me. Those words capture the majesty of this realm, but you must mold your own reality. It will be just as majestic, I assure you."

Dozens of images flashed through Ira's mind. The streets of New

York. The sprawling countryside outside Syracuse. Temple Emmanu-el. The seminary. Aaron's home. The estate in Fair Haven. The icy slopes of Antarctic glaciers. He saw them, felt them—the bitter cold and the warmth of a hot summer sun. Just as Enoch had written, as hot as fire and cold as ice. Everything was possible here, he realized. He could be anywhere, feel anything. He could form the world in his mind, then make it real.

The power of the opportunity proved overwhelming.

Enoch laughed, a deep and rich sound. "You'll get the hang of it."

"I brought the Book of Creation," Ira said, remembering why he had come. "I've come to return that which the fallen angels stole."

A long pause as Enoch walked around him in a wide circle. "Jeho-vah knows."

"Can I see him?"

"No."

That one word hit him like a nail to the wrist, grinding through bone and sinew. It carried such finality. It was the wrong answer.

"I will take the Book," Enoch said. "You are not meant to remain here. You must go back. You are needed."

He didn't want to return; he wanted to stay in this place, to study it, to soak it in. He wanted to learn more of this power to create, to take his thoughts and give them physicality. It would require medita-tion. And time.

Enoch took his hand—not the hand grasping the Book, but the other. "Time isn't real here, yet it passes quickly in your world. One of ours has already intervened to save your young friend."

"My young friend?" *Sherwood,* Ira realized. Who else could Enoch have meant? "Who intervened?"

"His name is Trevor. You've met."

All around them, the darkness shuddered. Jolted. A wide forested valley appeared from the void, Ira's feet already sinking into thick and lush grass that hadn't existed a moment before. Or rather, he hadn't perceived it. Perhaps it had always been there. In the distance rose snow-covered mountains, a line of seven peaks dominating the horizon. Light poured out into the world from the sky above them. This place had no sun, no single source of light; the light came from all around.

"You don't need time to learn," Enoch said. "The ability is already yours. You have been created with this purpose in mind. Do you understand?"

"I don't."

"A good place to start."

Enoch then grasped the Book, gently removing it from Ira's tight grip. Sadness enveloped Ira as it came out of his hand, but also relief at completing his mission. He had returned the Book, just as he'd purposed.

"You've done what you came for," Enoch said. "Go back, but take heed: the division between this realm and yours exists for a reason. Jehovah instituted it at the beginning of time. You must not exercise these creative powers in your physical world. Not if you can avoid it."

Ira had wanted to protest, but there was no opportunity. And no point. He exercised no control over his presence here; he had only breached the invisible barrier between realms at Jehovah's allowance. If he was to be sent back—

And then the world around him was snatched away. It blinked out of existence—or perhaps just out of perception, he reminded himself—as quickly as it had formed, replaced by a new kind of darkness. This darkness was more familiar. Stars danced across the clear night sky, fresh air flooded his nostrils, water lapped against a nearby shore. The lack of salt in the air told him it was a freshwater lake.

A series of loud noises had drawn him out of his meditative state. He then wandered up from the water and encountered a ramshackle hut, built from rotting wood and rain-soaked shingles. It had been falling apart for decades.

From it stumbled a young man. Ira's heart lurched in his chest as he realized this was Sherwood Brighton, in the flesh, swaying and exhausted. Tired and lost. Needing guidance.

The memory faded.

Ira gazed around the orchard outside the Fair Haven house. Gethsemane, in a way. Had Jesus, too, contemplated his failures before his final acts of redemption? No, Jesus hadn't ever failed. This was the most troubling aspect of the Christian narrative, the one that most caused him to question it. Ira found it impossible to imagine a man without fault. Despite enormous potential, mankind had evolved into such a despicable breed. Jehovah couldn't have intended this outcome.

So many failings, and so little time.

I failed Brighton. Ira's thoughts descended into resignation and regret, as they had many times throughout the unfortunate events of the drive up through the Karakorums. Brighton had eventually rejected him, and perhaps rightly so.

"Ira, I want to talk to you," a voice called.

Ira used the tree behind him to stand. He brought his hand up to shield his eyes from the sun just as David Roth appeared, marching through the orchard from the house.

"What is it, David?"

"The guests you mentioned have started to arrive. Two so far, a young man and an older man."

Even from such a meagre description, Ira could guess their identities: Dario and Lawrence. It was no surprise they were the first to arrive, but the others would join them soon enough.

Including Trevor. Trevor had to show up for any good to come of this council.

"Did you make them feel at home?" Ira asked.

David shrugged. "They're in the sitting room, waiting for you."

"Very well. I won't keep them waiting any longer."

THIRTEEN

Fair Haven, Vermont

AUGUST 1

As Ira came around the side of the house, he spotted an old grey station wagon kicking up a cloud of gravel as it rocketed down the private drive. Thick dust rose into the welcoming leafy boughs arching over the driveway. The car rolled to a stop, overshooting the edge of the driveway by a couple of feet. Its heavy front end stopped on the lawn, wheels pounding thousands of unlucky grass stems into the dirt.

"Watch where you're going!" David shouted.

A young man jumped out. He swept his brown hair to the side, combing through it with slender fingers, then pulled off the sunglasses covering his eyes. This carefree kid reminded Ira of Brighton—or at least, the Brighton he had first met before their adventures began, not the calloused and frustrated man he had left behind in Pakistan.

"Nice to meet you again, Rabbi," the young man said.

Ira lifted his eyes to give the man's face a closer inspection. Had they met before?

"You're David's son," Ira said, suddenly remembering. "Your name is David, too."

"But you can call me Junior. By the way, I brought a passenger."

Ira glanced back at the car just as Janene Kaplan closed the door behind her. Her straight brown hair fell in a single sheet past her shoulders, an austere style that made her look a little plain. She walked up to him and threw her arms around his shoulders, hugging him tightly.

"I knew you were alive," she whispered as she pulled away.

"I was worried you wouldn't believe the message I sent," Ira said. "It's been a long time."

"I heard you at the synagogue three nights ago. When I came in that morning, you were in your old office, talking to someone. I didn't recognize your voice at first, so I called the cops. I thought I was going crazy when it turned out there was no one in there!"

"I see. I wasn't nearly careful enough. That shouldn't have happened." The smile on her face fell the tiniest bit, and Ira knew this had been the wrong thing to say. "But if anyone was to eavesdrop, I'm glad it was you."

"In your message, you said we had something important to discuss."

Out of the corner of his eye, Ira saw the two Davids speaking together. The elder David seemed to be reprimanding the younger—an archetypal father-son moment if ever there was one.

"Have you met David Roth?" Ira asked, tugging on David's shirtsleeve. David turned his attention away from his son and focused on Janene.

"Yes, we've met," David said. "A couple of times."

"After you disappeared, Ira, I did some investigating of my own. I found Aaron, and met his son." Janene nodded toward Junior. "And his grandson, of course. I was with them at the hospital the day Aaron passed away."

"She's become a family friend," David affirmed.

"So what's this all about?" Janene asked. "Is it just the four of us?"

Ira shook his head. "There are two more people waiting inside, and a couple more are coming."

They had better, he added silently.

Janene climbed the stairs to the veranda, with both Davids a step behind. Ira followed them into the house, his thoughts a jumble.

*   *   *

"That's it, I'm not waiting any longer," Dario announced, standing up. The floorboards creaked beneath him. "I need to step out for some fresh air."

Lawrence had sunk into his chair like a lead weight. "Ira will get here when he gets here. Can't think of anything I could do to rush him."

Dario looked out at the orchards. It was a long way to the back fence, but he thought he saw someone moving through the trees.

"I think I see him."

"Ira, you mean," Lawrence said.

Dario pointed. "There. Do you see that? Someone's out there."

He located a back door off the sitting room and walked into the orchard. The trees had been planted in neat rows with a well-worn path forged straight through the center. At one of the larger trees, Dario stopped and inspected the apples nestled amidst its leafy limbs. He plucked one of the larger apples and held it in its hand—light, small, yellow with a greenish tinge. He raised it to his mouth and took a small bite. Sour. He tossed it to the ground.

"Ira, are you there?" Dario called. "I'm tired of all this mystery. Won't you tell us what's going on with you?"

Nobody answered, but he detected movement. He verged off the path into a denser copse of trees.

There, against the back fence, stood a man. He faced away from Dario, looking out into the forested hills behind the property.

"Ira?"

The man heard Dario's voice and turned. Dario immediately saw this couldn't be Ira; the man was far too young. Thirty, at the most. He sported close-cropped brown hair and observed Dario with bright, inquisitive eyes.

"Oh," Dario said. "I'm sorry. I mistook you for someone else."

The man nodded. "You just missed him."

"That seems to be Ira's pattern. People are always just missing him."

This man offered a warm smile. Who was he? The groundskeeper? Surely the acreage had to be looked after, and David Roth hadn't seemed to be the gardening type. Or perhaps this was the son Lawrence had mentioned. Yes, there was a resemblance around the eyes. The cheekbones, too.

Dario couldn't inquire, because the man walked away, treading the worn grass along the fence line. He didn't look back.

Dario sighed and turned his attention back to the house. He squinted; someone stood by the back door, waving.

Perhaps Ira had finally arrived.

*   *   *

Ira watched from the window as Dario trotted back to the house.

"What are you planning, Ira?" Lawrence asked.

Ira turned to face his old friend, shutting out the sound of David moving chairs from the kitchen and setting them in a circle. "I'm sorry for the way we left things. I was insensitive, but I hope you understand that I had things to do."

I'm sorry for the way we left things, he thought, replaying those bitter words. Over and over, he found himself repeating them. His life bespoke a pattern of betrayal through one after another of his most important relationships. First he'd sabotaged his friendship with Aaron, and only by the old man's unfathomable grace had the two ever reconciled. Was reconciliation even possible with Brighton?

The worst part was that every one of his betrayals had been justifiable in view of his larger purpose. Including this one.

"But where did you go?" Lawrence asked, sitting forward. "You just disappeared! You can't keep doing that. I would have been happy to be left out of all this, but you dragged me in. You're my friend, Ira. What's happened to you?"

Well, at least Lawrence still considered him a friend. That counted for something.

David dropped a wooden chair next to him and Ira sat, his back to the window. "I'll explain in a few minutes, once everyone has arrived."

This seemed to anger Lawrence. The man had wide, thick shoulders and an intimidating presence. If it came to a fight, Lawrence would clean Ira's clock, no question about it. He'd been a wrestler once, and he still looked capable of a chokehold or two.

The sound of a toilet flush echoed through the room, and a moment later Janene entered from the kitchen, wiping her palms on the side of her jeans. Junior had positioned himself near the kitchen door, and his father made a point of sitting a few chairs down, next to Lawrence.

"How many more are coming?" David asked.

Ira managed a quick count. David, Junior, Janene, Lawrence, Dario—the moment he thought Dario's name, the man entered through the back door and sat down.

"Two," Ira said, clasping his hands together.

"Should we wait?" David asked.

Ira nodded. "I'd like to."

David returned to the kitchen. "Anyone want tea?" he called behind him. "Water? Coffee? I have some orange juice…" They heard the sound of the refrigerator opening. "Sorry, out of juice. Just water and coffee."

Ira tuned out. What a trivial matter, these beverage orders. None of it mattered—not the tea and coffee, not the state of his friendships, not anything so long as the Grigori were free to wreak havoc.

He looked up at the clock on the wall. The minute hand had crept past the twelve. Four minutes late. Of course, it wasn't unreasonable for a person to be a few minutes late for an appointment, even an important one, but Trevor wasn't a *person*. If he was late, he must be making a point.

"Who are we waiting for?" Janene asked.

Ira felt wistful at her keen innocence. To her, this was just a meeting. An exciting one, a secret one, but a meeting nonetheless. To Ira, this was life and death. The end of the road. The culmination of a lifetime of commitment to an ancient principle. But there was danger in thinking of this as a mere principle; the menace Aaron had warned him about had finally taken form. This was the worst-case scenario, and it had quickened on Ira's watch. That made him responsible.

"Two people who are critical to our cause," Ira finally said, realizing Janene probably didn't have a clue what their cause entailed.

Five more minutes passed, and then ten.

"Let's get on with it," Lawrence said. "I don't have the inclination or patience to wait all day for these mystery guests."

Over the course of an hour, Ira laid out the events of the last month. By his own accounting, only five weeks had passed since Wendell had first appeared in his congregation at Temple Emmanuel with a message from Raff Lagati. Nearly two years had gone by for the others. That part of the story was hard to explain. But as difficult as it was to make them understand his apparent jump through time, nothing compared to the trial of getting them to believe what came next—translating from Pakistan to New York in the blink of an eye.

"The Grigori are loose," Ira concluded. "I've confirmed that they escaped their confinement and are planning to launch some sort of offensive in the coming days and weeks. We need to take preemptive action. The last time they were loose in the world, they bred themselves into local populations and taught knowledge and expertise far beyond the people's technological sophistication. It was nothing short of genetic and cultural warfare."

As expected, this took a long time to digest. Dario and Lawrence didn't need as much time to get up to speed, so they naturally were the first to ask questions. Janene's face had gone as slack as a puppet whose strings had been cut.

"Our technology today is very sophisticated," Lawrence pointed out. "Almost magical, really. It seems to me their old modus operandi won't work this time around."

"Is that an argument to do nothing?" Ira asked. Lawrence should have known better, or perhaps he was playing devil's advocate.

Lawrence bristled. "It's not that I'm advocating inaction, it's that I have no idea what to do. These matters are too immense, too weighty for our mortal hands. Who are we to be making such decisions? How could we even carry them out? The only weapon we have against them, we dare not use." He fixed Ira with a penetrating stare, but said no more.

"What weapon?" Janene asked. Then it clicked. "Oh. Does he mean your power to translate from place to place?"

Ira sighed at her endearing naiveté. "Yes and no, Janene. The power I access goes beyond any single application. It's the power of genesis, the same power Jehovah used to create the world."

Once again, Janene sat back in her chair, thunderstruck. Did she believe? Did she understand the stakes? He wouldn't have blamed her if she couldn't bring herself to believe *or* understand.

"He may be right that the power is our only weapon, but what a weapon!" Junior exclaimed. "Can you teach it to us?"

It was a young person's question. Ira had felt the same sense of selfish excitement in the early days of his training with Aaron, Moshe, and Ezra. Even in the face of their insistence that the power could not be wielded, Ira's heart had surged at the possibilities.

Now it was time to actualize them.

"I don't think teaching it would be a good idea," Ira said. "It takes decades of training and preparation. We have to strike fast."

"Then what can we do?" Junior asked.

That was a better question for Trevor. Ira felt empty in the face of it. If Trevor wouldn't help, what strategy could they employ? This all depended on how the Grigori proceeded. Would they infiltrate society subtly? Would they contact world leaders? Governments? Influential organizations? If so, could Ira get to them first? Perhaps he could poison the ground, as it were, so the Grigori's seed didn't sprout.

Before he could offer an answer to the question at hand—any answer would do—Ira heard the front door open. Everyone's head swiveled as one, a futile gesture since many walls separated the sitting room from the home's entrance. David stood and disappeared through the kitchen. Ira stood as well, his heart in his throat as he waited for his final guests to make their appearance.

*   *   *

The first of the new arrivals was a middle-aged woman, her face creased from years of hard labor and her head a mass of short, tightly wound auburn curls. Even before she opened her mouth, Dario knew she wasn't American—something about her bearing, working class and proud of it. From what he'd seen of this country, the working class weren't proud of their lot in life; they were either resigned to living off wealthy men's scraps or ambitious of accumulating wealth themselves, if only circumstances and good fortune would align.

"Good day, Rabbi," the woman said.

Dario turned his gaze to Ira. He said nothing for a long while. Dario thought it rude not to acknowledge the woman's greeting, but Ira seemed to play by his own social rubrics.

The English woman was eclipsed by her companion, who stepped into the room and instantly pulled all the attention to himself. His features were perfectly symmetrical, and he stood nearly tall enough to brush his head against the top of the doorframe.

"Ira," the man said in a low voice. "I came, as you asked."

Ira moved toward the newcomers, but even Dario could tell by the rabbi's stilted manner that he was fighting the urge to rush at them with wild abandon. Who were they, and why were they so important?

"Everyone, this is Trevor," Ira said. "And Celeste, of course."

Ira's behavior was so bizarre; he seemed to be waiting for them to do something, or say something. A long time passed in which nothing happened.

Ira finally took a step back, giving Trevor and Celeste enough room to enter and sit.

"Trevor, would you like to introduce yourself?" Ira asked, his voice pregnant with some sort of meaning Dario couldn't ferret out.

Trevor let loose a long-suffering sigh as he made eye contact with each guest. Dario felt a shiver go through him when the extraordinary man's eyes connected with his.

"I am one of them." Trevor faced Ira as he spoke. "I presume you've told them, Ira? About the Watchers?"

Dario gasped as he put the pieces together. He was one of *them*. A Watcher, the same as these so-called Grigori, the ones who had been loosed on the world.

Trevor seemed to sense his thoughts. "There is a contingent of us here on earth. We've been here for centuries, representatives of Jehovah." He paused, gazing straight at Dario with a thoughtful expression.

"Well, not representatives. We work in the shadows, offer assistance to mankind in quiet, unobtrusive ways. If we work according to our design, no one knows who we are. We prefer it that way."

"The time of your quiet, unobtrusive ways has come and gone," Ira said, standing in front of the windows. A bird flitted behind the glass.

Trevor shook his head. "You misunderstand our purpose, Ira. Despite recent developments, our work hasn't changed. We still operate behind the scenes."

"Do you have the same power as Ira?" This came from a young man Dario had noticed but not been introduced to.

"I suppose I do," Trevor said. "I'm not empowered to use it the way Ira would want."

Dario cast a glance at the English woman, Celeste. She was staring at the floor, pondering it, shifting her feet. She radiated discomfort.

"It just can't be," Ira said, clearly fighting to remain composed. "Why are you here if not to help us in our time of need?"

"I can encourage you," Trevor said. "I'm sorry, Ira, but I can't do what you're asking of me."

Trevor's tone sounded positive, upbeat, but there was no denying the rejection behind it.

"You haven't even heard what I'm proposing!" Ira's anger thrust out like a dagger.

"I know what's in your heart."

Ira turned his back on Trevor—on everyone in the room. His shoulders heaved, and he hunched forward. What did he feel? Rage, Dario thought. Ira was going to lose it. Dario instinctively grabbed hold of his wooden seat, bracing for what he suspected might come next. The last time Ira had unleashed his wrath, he had incinerated a half-dozen victims.

"Trevor, please."

Dario's head turned, surprised to hear Celeste speak again. She faced Trevor, resting her hands on the man's forearms.

"You can do something, yeah?" Celeste prodded. "Ira's right."

"You don't understand, Celeste."

Ira spun. "Have you considered that you're the one who doesn't understand? This could mean the end of all humanity."

In the ensuing silence, Dario considered the two sides in this confrontation. He understood where Ira was coming from. Dario had seen the danger firsthand, and also what Ira was capable of. Trevor, on the other hand, was just as capable, and knew what was going on. But he was impotent. Either he wanted to help but was restrained, or he was callous.

"Will you stop me?" Ira asked.

Trevor didn't hesitate. "No. You are free to make your own choices, of course."

Was that a tacit endorsement, or a forewarning of doom? Dario thought it was the latter.

Ira turned to Lawrence. "My friend, what do you say? Will you stand with me?"

Lawrence rose slowly, taking his time. "I don't think so."

"What was that?" Ira approached Lawrence and embraced his wide shoulders. "I must not have heard you right. We've talked about this."

"But you haven't listened to a word I've said."

Ira lowered his head. Dario could only imagine the frustration seething in his gut.

Despite his better instincts, Dario got to his feet. Everyone's eyes turned to him in surprise.

Sit down, you fool, he told himself.

"Ira has a point," Dario said in an unhurried tone, ignoring his inner voice. "I've seen the threat. I was with him in Pakistan, and I know what's going to happen if we do nothing. Ira may be the one with the power, but he can't do it alone."

He couldn't believe he'd said it, but he also felt proud. He'd been a tagalong up until now, but he couldn't stand by and deny what he'd witnessed. Ira took many missteps and alienated a lot of people, but he was committed to doing the right thing.

Ira's shoulders relaxed. "Thank you, Dario. What say the rest of you?"

David crossed the room to stand next to the young man who had spoken earlier. "My son and I rarely agree on much, but I think this will be the exception that proves the rule. My father was a private, secretive man, and I despised that about him for most of my life. But he always said the secrets should be preserved until such time as they needed to be used. That time is here. It's right now."

Ira approached the men and gave each a warm hug. When he let go, he faced Janene. "And you?"

"I'm just honored you asked me here," she said. "I'll help in any way I can, of course."

Trevor rose, as inconspicuous as a Christian in a den of lions. As he made his way out of the room, not saying a word, Celeste pulled at his shirtsleeve.

"Trevor, this isn't right," she pleaded. "Reconsider, for all our sakes."

Trevor made it to the door. "Celeste, I won't tell you what to do. If this is what you want, follow your heart."

Celeste planted her feet, watching as Trevor exited through the kitchen. She turned to Ira, her face wrought with confusion and devastation.

"It's just not like him," Celeste said.

Ira reached out to her and she took his hand. "Welcome, Celeste. I'm glad you've decided to stay." He twisted around to face Lawrence. "My friend, will you reconsider?"

Lawrence walked toward the door also. "I'm afraid not. Dario, are you coming? I won't come back for you."

Dario shook his head. "Thank you for everything, but no. I'm staying."

"Suit yourself."

An oddly flippant remark, yet Lawrence said it without a hint of reluctance. He didn't spare a backward glance as he left. A few moments later, the front door opened and banged shut.

Ira released Celeste's hand and took a backward step, just far enough to get a good look at those who remained. His expression changed so rapidly from one emotion to the next that Dario couldn't be sure what the man was feeling. Joy, at first. Then something akin to gratitude, followed by a stitching of his forehead—fear. Yes, he was definitely afraid.

As Dario watched Ira, standing with his back to the window, he found his attention drawn to the orchard—and a man standing in the midst of it, staring at the house. The groundskeeper.

Dario stiffened. The man wasn't staring at the house; it seemed as though he was looking right into Dario's soul.

FOURTEEN

Mount Khunjerab, Pakistan
AUGUST 1

Lagati hunched over his bowl of cereal, now little more than mush drifting overtop a brown sea of leftover milk. He stirred the tiny lumps of granola with his spoon, requiring only the slightest movement of his wrist—all he could manage without feeling stabs of pain in his left side. Standing and walking had become major issues as the swelling in his knee worsened. He probably should have tracked down someone with a medical degree to take a look and ensure no permanent damage had been inflicted. Lagati also knew there existed a supply of painkillers and other medications he could avail himself of, but doing so would mean admitting what had happened. It was easier to stay silent.

Today he'd left his apartment early in the morning, hoping no one would see him hobbling to the cafeteria suite. He hadn't gotten out before the breakfast rush, so he now felt compelled to remain at the table until the room cleared out. Losing a couple of hours was a small price to retain what little dignity remained to him, but if he didn't get to the storeroom and start working on the crates, Azazel might make another house call.

He missed Antoinette, and wondered where she was and what she was doing. He felt so alone without her; she'd been his only confidante. But it would have been selfish to have her stay, and impossible for him to go with her. Not in his current condition.

We'll see each other again when this nightmare is over, Lagati thought to himself as a group of three left the suite, leaving another half-dozen men and women. He couldn't resist eavesdropping on their conversations.

Your eavesdropping hasn't exactly paid off lately.

He shrugged off the thought and zeroed in on the discussion at the table behind him. It involved two men he'd seen on the clean-up crew three days before.

"They were both incinerated. I heard Turel gave the order. Good thing I wasn't there, or he might have made me do it."

"Who were they?"

"A husband and wife. Came down the mountain and stumbled across the base."

"That's going to happen more often with the ships coming and going. They aren't invisible, you know."

This must have been the same man and woman the Grigori had discussed during their conference the day before. The two men had a point. If the activity around the base continued, they were bound to draw more attention. Lagati knew rumors were already circulating in nearby villages—

"Lagati?" a man's voice called to him.

With some reluctance, he made eye contact with Amir, who had stopped next to the table. Amir leaned his long arms against one of the chair backs, blocking Lagati's view of the door.

"Do you need something?" Lagati asked.

"No, but I think you do." Amir pulled out the seat and sat down. "You haven't moved in over an hour, and one of my fellow engineers said you were seen limping through the corridors. You're hurt, aren't you?"

Lagati felt the urge to throttle the man and his damnable curiosity. All this effort would go to waste if rumors of his ill health circulated. He may as well have crawled through the base on his hands and knees begging for help.

"My business is my own," Lagati said, pushing his bowl aside.

"I'm concerned about you."

Was that true? Lagati barely knew Amir; when had they gotten so chummy? The simple answer was that they hadn't. If Amir harbored any feelings of friendship, they certainly weren't reciprocated.

Lagati didn't know how to respond. "Thank you for your concern" felt wrong, yet it was the appropriate response; Lagati didn't feel the least bit grateful, so he couldn't say it. He didn't care to lie for no particular reason. He'd told thousands of lies in his lifetime—he'd done it professionally—but they'd always served some a purpose. No matter how he sliced it, lying to Amir to save his feelings felt worse than pointless.

He might be able to get you medical attention, Lagati told himself. *He'd keep it quiet if you insisted.*

"Thank you for your concern," Lagati finally spat out after a long pause. "Maybe there is something you could do."

Thirty minutes later, Amir had left and returned. He planted himself across the table from Lagati and opened his palm to reveal two tiny yellow pills.

"What are they?" Lagati asked, his voice carrying in the now-empty cafeteria.

Amir placed the pills on the tabletop in front of Lagati, then stood up to get a glass of water from the serving station. "Cyclobenzaprine, a muscle relaxant. Wasn't sure what you needed, but if you've been tossed around a bit—"

Lagati locked eyes with him. Did he know what had happened?

"Sorry," Amir said quickly. "I'm just speculating."

Lagati swallowed both pills without even a glance at the water. "Hell, it's a good guess. Azazel doesn't like me very much. Never has."

Amir's round eyes grew even rounder.

"How long do these take?" Lagati tested his knee; it hurt just as badly as ever. "I mean, when will the pills kick in?"

"I have no idea. It's not my area."

Lagati offered a tight smile. "Right. You're an aerospace engineer, not a doctor."

Amir shrugged.

Lagati pushed back his chair just enough for him to swing his legs out from under the table. He grimaced, grabbed hold of the edge of the table, and tried to stand.

"You could wait a bit longer," Amir said.

Lagati drew himself up, standing still for several seconds. "Not much point, since everyone's gone. No one to see me now."

He took a few tentative steps. Perhaps the pills were kicking in, just a little. It might have been his imagination, but the pain seemed to have lessened. He felt just a touch lightheaded. A vaguely pleasant sensation.

"There's another way you might help," Lagati said as he picked his way toward the door. "I'm spending the afternoon in one of the storerooms, cataloguing the contents of the most recent shipment of crates. I'll need to unlock them."

"We keep several unlocking tools in the supply cupboard by the hangar."

"Could you get one and meet me in the storeroom?" Lagati clenched his jaw. It took so much effort to phrase it as a question—a request. He wondered if he would ever grow accustomed to it. Even more troubling, would he ever reclaim his former status?

Yes, he thought, reassuring himself on that second point. He didn't much care whether he grew accustomed to his current circumstances so long as they proved temporary.

Lagati stepped into the storeroom. Strips of fluorescent lighting traversed the ceiling, casting an even glow. The crates were stacked three high, forming a perimeter on three sides.

He stepped up to the nearest stack and grazed the chrome. He squinted to make out the thin, almost imperceptible line betraying the lid. It wouldn't budge without the assistance of the unlocking tools his people had devised.

The door opened behind him.

"Any idea what's in them?" Amir asked, coming to stand next to Lagati. The man rubbed his hand against the dark stubble on his pointed chin.

"More artifacts, I imagine."

Lagati actually believed there would be more to these crates than the trinkets and writings they'd unearthed from the others. Any archaeologist or historian would have killed to get their hands on those, but in the context of what these crates might contain? They paled in comparison. These crates were much larger, for one thing, and to him that suggested a more significant find.

"They look heavy. Think we might need some help." Amir's voice grew distant as he crossed the room.

Lagati turned just as Amir located a stepladder. The Indian man hoisted it by the center of its span and carried it to the first stack. Lagati stepped out of the way as Amir spread its legs.

"Here, let me." Lagati climbed the metallic steps, favoring his right side. He held himself steady as he reached the top. He placed a hand flat against the side of the topmost crate and pushed lightly against it, gauging its heft. The crate was solid, to be sure, but he also detected a slight give. "I don't think they're as heavy as they look. We may be able to get it down, but we'll need a second ladder."

"Right."

Amir left the room again.

Lagati stared at his warped reflection in the side of the crate, amazed that it might be possible to move it with just two pairs of hands. It looked like it weighed a ton, its case fashioned from solid metal.

Amir returned a couple of minutes later with a second ladder. Lagati descended and moved his ladder to the far side of the crate, Amir positioning his on the opposite end.

Lagati struggled to get a good grip on the bottom of the crate, working his fingers around the sharp corner in a way that protected his skin from injury. Balancing himself on the ladder while bearing his end of the crate wouldn't be easy.

Amir counted to three and slowly hoisted his corner into the air. It lifted without much difficulty.

"There can't be much in here," Amir mused as he settled the crate back down.

"I doubt any of these crates are empty. Not after the extreme effort taken to retrieve them."

"From where, exactly?"

Only a select few knew the secret location. The clique included himself, Antoinette, the pilots, and no one else. The ships had been commuting back and forth for a couple of years now. Lagati was proud of how successfully he had contained the secret.

"You know I won't answer that," Lagati said.

To his credit, Amir didn't press the matter.

For just an instant, Lagati considered letting it slip. Maybe it was the painkillers.

"Let's lift on three," Amir said.

Both men hoisted the lightweight crate into the air and took careful, coordinated steps down the ladder. Once on the third step, Lagati nearly lost his balance. Amir saw it just in time and waited; if he'd taken the next step, Lagati would have been forced to let go, sending the crate crashing to the floor.

They managed the rest of the way without incident. When the crate was safely down, Amir removed the wand-like unlocking tool from his pocket and got down on his haunches. He positioned the wand horizontally along the axis of the lid, placing its flattened edge onto the chrome. He pressed a button on the end of the device and waited two or three seconds.

Lagati shifted his feet impatiently, then jumped when the lid lurched a centimeter out of alignment.

"That should do it," Lagati said.

The gunmetal grey interior seemed to swallow up the room's light. Lagati peered hard into the shadows before he realized what he was looking at. He let out a low gasp but didn't pull away. Rather, he leaned in for a closer look.

The bottom of the crate was coated in fine powder, and nestled amidst it a collection of scattered bones, bronzed a dark russet from age and dry enough to leech the moisture from Lagati's mouth.

"Bones," Amir said.

Lagati felt a surge of annoyance at the obvious statement. "More importantly, human bones."

Amir shook his head. "Not an ordinary human. These bones are very large, don't you think?"

Lagati took a closer look and realized what he had taken for a rib might have actually come from the hand. He knew very little about basic anatomy.

"We can catalogue the contents later," Lagati said, turning back to the stacked crates. "Let's get the next one down."

They climbed back up their respective ladders. When Lagati

slipped his fingers around the corners of the crate, he realized this one was significantly heavier. He gripped tight and heaved, but even throwing his full weight behind the effort wouldn't move the crate.

"Whatever's in this one, it's more than a pile of old bones," Amir said, wiping a bead of sweat off his forehead.

Lagati climbed back to the ground. "We'll need the forklift."

"Looks like it." Amir stuffed his hands in his pocket and trotted out of the storeroom.

Lagati moved both ladders out of the way, clearing a path for Amir to drive the forklift through the wide doors to the stack.

"We may as well get them all down," Lagati called over the purr of the forklift's engine when Amir returned.

"Without a pallet to grab onto, we'll need to somehow push the crates onto the lift," Amir said. "Got any ideas?"

Lagati gave the problem further consideration. The crates were stacked evenly, without any significant ledges. Amir was right. The forklift wasn't going to be much help. They'd need some elbow grease.

Lagati signaled for Amir to cut the motor, and a moment later the storeroom lapsed back into cavernous silence.

"We'll have to recruit more help," Lagati said in resignation. The last thing he wanted was to surround himself with a bunch of near-strangers he didn't trust, but there didn't seem to be any way around it.

"Nothing's stopping us from taking a peek, is there?" Amir asked.

Lagati turned to stare at the brown-skinned engineer. Amir was right. They didn't need to lower the crate to the floor to get a look inside, to see why it was so much heavier.

"Agreed." Lagati shuffled toward the wall to retrieve his ladder, and Amir followed suit.

A minute later, the two men were perched just high enough to access the top of the crate. Without waiting to be told, Amir extracted the unlocking tool and again placed it horizontally along the seam.

A hiss of released air preceded a loud pop, and then the lid lurched, flying into the air a couple of inches and falling back. It was a more dramatic effect than with the first crate. Lagati exchanged a look of surprise with Amir, who took the lid from him and tried lowering it gently; midway down, he lost his grip and the lid clattered to the floor. Amir hurried to the ground to set the situation aright.

Lagati ignored him, instead casting his gaze into the darkened recesses of—

His breath caught and he felt the blood retreat from his hands. His grip loosened and he very nearly fell off the ladder, only stopping himself at the last moment by falling forward. Just as quickly, he reeled back, and this time he did lose his balance. He tried in vain to grab onto the ladder, but the move made the ladder tip sideways. Lagati lifted his head and protected it with his arms as he hit the ground. He let out a shout, then a moan as pain flashed across his chest.

"Damn it!"

Amir scrambled to his side. "Are you okay?"

"Yes, yes. I may have bruised a rib."

He sat up, wondering if in fact he'd *broken* a rib. He dusted off his shirt and waited a few moments for the room to come into focus. The sharp pain subsided, leaving behind only a grim, lingering reminder of the fall. No, he didn't think he'd broken anything, no thanks to his own inattention.

"What's in there?" Amir asked.

"See for yourself."

Amir obligingly clambered up and looked inside. The muscles in his face slackened as he turned away, assaulted by a fetid, antiseptic odor.

Lagati came to his feet, drawing steady breaths through his mouth.

"It's a body," Amir said as he backed down the ladder. His face was alight with a million questions. Lagati felt sympathetic to the man's plight; Amir didn't have the knowledge and experience to explain the unexplainable. Lagati was shocked by the discovery, too, but at least he knew where it had come from.

The Grigori have some explaining to do, Lagati mused. They had insisted that he transport this collection to earth, but they hadn't said anything about transporting biological material.

Once he'd regained his composure, Lagati returned to the top of the ladder, using one hand to pinch his nose. The body of this giant had indeed been bisected to fit inside the crate, and it was missing its bottom half. Its torso widened to enormous proportions, its bald head bulbous and misshapen, its arms folded tightly over each other such that its fingers seemed to grip its shoulders. Everywhere, the creature's skin was desiccated and cracked, like the broken surface of a saltpan.

"Not possible," Amir whispered.

"Quite possible, I'm afraid."

The man's eyes were wild, distressed. "But what is it?"

"A giant," Lagati reluctantly acknowledged. "Or at least, part of one. And older than dirt."

"I hate to ask a second time, but I must. Where did these crates come from?"

Lagati rubbed his chin as he descended. He quietly assisted in replacing the lid, trapping the pervasive smell. Amir couldn't be counted on to keep this discovery quiet unless he felt he'd been brought into the inner circle, or as near the inner circle as Lagati himself dwelled these days.

"The ships have been bringing back a range of cargo from a base on the moon," Lagati said, wanting to snatch the words back the instant he let them out. There was no turning back now. "Amir, this can't come as a surprise. You're an aerospace engineer. You knew these vessels were designed for space travel."

"I knew they were capable of some limited space travel, yes." Amir's shoulders heaved as his mind worked to reconcile at least a year and a half of confusion. "Still, to have all doubt removed. Why were there giants on the moon?"

"I suspect giants were everywhere." Lagati paused, glancing back at the crates. "And it seems we're not quite rid of them yet."

FIFTEEN

Kamchatka, Russia

AUGUST 1

"Do we have permission to fly through Chinese airspace?" Brighton slurred when he poked his head into the flight deck. The pilot, a jaded middle-aged man who barely paid attention to him, nodded. And that was it.

Not much for company, he thought as he stumbled back to the main cabin from his attempt to make conversation. The stumbling, he assured himself, was a result of turbulence. Nobody except a trained professional could walk smoothly through such a plane without a sway in their step.

Leather couches, their cushions alternating black and white, curved sinuously along both sides of the plane, with a long, low table between them, bolted to the deck. A small chandelier, wider than it was tall, hung from the ceiling, its faux crystals glittering in the sunlight coming through the windows. Along the rear wall waited a kitchenette. More to his interest, the liquor cabinet stared back at him, its translucent doors betraying a hint of tall, spindly bottles in a variety of thirst-inducing colors.

Already he had emptied a bottle of forty-year-old Glenfiddich. He'd only finished the job another traveler had started, as the bottle had been two-thirds drained by the time Brighton got his hands on it.

"I'm surprised you're letting me have my way," Brighton said as he sank into the welcoming embrace of one of the black cushions. He stared longingly at the bottle and the lowball glass beside it—the remnant of a pair of ice cubes melting into oblivion at its center, the cool water mingling with supple strains of leftover whisky, its dark honeyed color refracting off the glass's hard angles...

"What are you going to do, bring the plane down?" Abranel chuckled. *"You're as trapped on this plane as anywhere else. You have no control, only the illusion of it."*

Brighton responded by picking up the empty bottle and turning it lovingly in his hands. This bottle must have been worth a thousand dollars, but here it had been, opened and abandoned, as though waiting for him to rescue it. It had been thoughtful of Lagati to gift him with such a treat. For all Lagati's wickedness, he had shown remarkable generosity.

"He's not worth hating. Besides, the two of us are much more important to the Grigori than Raff Lagati. He sits in the base, hands tied. He's nothing more than a puppet."

The speaker above the couch crackled to life. "Prepare for landing, sir."

Brighton turned to look out the window behind him. They were flying over an austere, unwelcoming coastline. Choppy grey water rolled up stark beaches dotted with enormous boulders and tiny patches of vegetation. It looked cold.

"Where are we?" he whispered. He was finally starting to get used to talking to himself.

"I'm not sure."

"You mean Semyaza never told you where we were headed?"

"North America. I know little more than you do."

Brighton looked out the window again. "This isn't North America. We haven't been in the air long enough."

He struggled to his feet again, paused to orient himself, then headed back to the flight door. The pilot sat with his back to him, a dark headset accenting his bald white head.

"Sorry to disturb you, but I'd like to know where we are."

"Kamchatka," the pilot said without turning.

Brighton said the word to himself a couple of times, hoping the repetition would spark his memory. He'd become pretty good at geography these past two years, but he couldn't place this one.

"Sorry?" he said.

The pilot swiveled to face him. "Russia, Kamchatka peninsula. Could you take your seat, sir? We'll be on the ground in a few minutes."

"What are we doing here?"

"Refueling, sir."

Brighton backed out, shut the door, and returned to his seat. He looked around, wondering whether there was a place to buckle up. This was the part of a commercial flight when flight attendants would ensure everyone had lifted their tray tables and fastened their belts, but he was alone and the only seating were these two long couches and a pair of easy chairs.

He pushed back into the cool leather cushion and steeled himself.

The plane skirted a line of forested mountains. At last, a bright blue high-altitude lake came into view, nestled between two peaks. Judging by the path of descent, that was their destination. Indeed, a runway became visible next to the water. The only other sign of civilization was a two-story structure near the end of the runway, only a handful of narrow windows interrupting its concrete exterior.

Not exactly the Ritz.

As they jetted toward the runway, Brighton held on tight in anticipation of a hard landing. Instead it went smoothly. So smoothly, in fact, that Brighton barely felt the moment when the plane's wheels hit the tarmac.

Once they'd rolled to a final stop, Brighton remained in his seat, waiting for the pilot to emerge. Several long minutes passed before the flight door opened.

"You can come with me or wait here," the man said. "We'll be on our way as soon as possible."

"I think I'll stay." The skies outside had turned cloudy and big, wet drops hit the windowpanes. He didn't want to leave the comfort of the plane, especially for that pockmarked old building.

The pilot released the door and climbed outside. Cool air instantly floated in. Brighton moved back to the kitchenette. To the liquor cabinet.

"No matter how much you imbibe, I'll still be here. You can't get rid of me."

"I know," Brighton snapped.

"Even so, I won't allow it to continue. It's not good for either of us. Once we arrive, we'll have important business to take care of. I have neither the time nor inclination to let you wallow."

"So you do know where we're going."

"I have a notion."

Brighton waited, but Abranel didn't elaborate. And Brighton knew he wouldn't.

Abranel remained silent for several minutes, the duration of which was extremely uncomfortable. How strange to feel this lonely with two people sharing one brain. It seemed that when he longed for company, Abranel was nowhere to be found, and when he longed for solitude, Abranel was right there, chipping away at him with his metaphorical icepick. Either Abranel had a dreadful sense of timing, or a perfectly spiteful one.

Brighton knew that the moment he were to stand up to select something from the liquor cabinet, Abranel would take over and force him back down. So he remained still until he could no longer stand it.

"Semyaza talked about Ira's memory trick," Brighton finally said. "He said you could help me with that, to learn the technique."

"Are you sure that's something you want to do while you're under the influence?"

That stung. Brighton wanted to say, "I'm not under the influence of anything but curiosity." Abranel would know better, so instead he settled on, "I think I'm a pretty good judge of when I can and cannot have a serious conversation."

"No. I don't think you are." Nonetheless, Abranel indulged him. *"The biological brain is the most sophisticated data collection device in existence, and humanity's is the best. At least on this planet. Unfortunately, mankind's ability to access stored memory is poorly developed. So even though every memory is carefully stored, only a very small percentage of it is ever available for recollection. The Grigori have been working on this problem for millennia, long before Jehovah forced an end to it. At the time, they were close to a breakthrough. The timing of Jehovah's final attack was no accident, yet he took the Grigori's research and passed it off as his own, disseminating those advancements to a very select group of people. In fact, Ira Binyamin is the latest in an extremely long line of rabbis who were taught the ancient secrets. I can assist you in matching him. Even surpassing him. But it's important to realize that this is a difficult and lengthy process. Fortunately for you, the two of us will be spending a lifetime together, so we'll have all the time we need should you submit yourself to my lessons."*

Brighton would need some time to absorb this rush of information. He'd never expected Abranel to be so forthcoming. Perhaps he'd done it to throw Brighton off-balance.

Footsteps on the steps alerted Brighton to the pilot's return. The man stood in the doorway and drew the door up behind him.

"Are we ready to go?" Brighton asked.

"Yes, shortly."

"And are you ready to tell me where we're going?"

"I've just found out myself," the pilot said as he disappeared into the cockpit and closed the door behind him.

"Don't push it," Abranel said. *"The mission we're on is too important for Semyaza to reveal the details. The pilot requires the destination, so he has it. You, however, do not."*

Brighton stood up and slowly walked the length of the cabin, wanting to stretch his restless legs before takeoff. "I don't understand. What's the risk?"

"You would understand if you knew what we're hunting."

"Some kind of cargo," Brighton said. "That's all Semyaza told me."

"He has his reasons."

Such non-explanations had become the norm, but that didn't make them any less irritating. Still, Brighton knew better than to probe further.

As the plane sped down the runaway, Brighton resigned himself to his ignorance. Wherever they were going, they'd get there soon enough.

SIXTEEN

Mount Khunjerab, Pakistan
AUGUST 1

Lagati stood, arms folded, at the opening to a short, crescent-shaped corridor with doors spaced a few feet apart. There was no one in sight, he noted with bemusement. Apparently the Grigori had decided that maintaining a guard was a poor use of human resources; if Elisabeth Macfarlane, the only occupant of the detention area, hadn't managed to bust through her enclosure yet, she probably wasn't going to.

Or maybe they just didn't care about her.

He approached the fourth door on the left and triggered it, waiting until it slid open to reveal the small anteroom, barely large enough to fit a single person. Once inside, and the door closed behind him, he felt the walls pressing in. He sucked in a deep breath. He disliked confined spaces, though he acknowledged this one served a useful purpose.

He was about to enter unannounced when he realized courtesy would better suit his objective. He raised his arm and knocked three times in quick succession. Elisabeth didn't reply, despite the fact that Lagati knew he had struck the door loud enough to be heard on the other side.

Was she asleep? It was early evening, but she likely had no way of keeping track of the time. He might have gone to sleep himself under different circumstances. The cyclobenzaprine lingered in his system, gifting him with a slightly euphoric unsteadiness.

Lagati prepared to knock again.

"Yes?" she finally said before he had the chance to strike.

He lowered his hand. "May I come in?"

"You'll come in anyway. What does it matter to me?"

He smiled. Her pragmatism impressed him.

"You're early," she added.

This brought him up short. Surely she hadn't been expecting him; who had she mistaken him for?

"I'm coming in," he said, shelving the question for the time being.

He thumbed the door open, revealing a room lit only by a bedside on the far end of the apartment, twenty or thirty feet away. He squinted, adjusting to the soft ambience.

Elisabeth was nowhere to be seen.

One moment he stood in the doorway, and the next he was sprawled on the beige carpet, a sharp stinging sensation flaring up in his shin. He caught only a vague blur as a dark object crossed his vision and cracked him upside the head; the nerves behind his eyes throbbed as he tried to roll out of the attack, but he couldn't move fast enough.

"Stop it!" Lagati shouted. He jerked his knees up to meet his chest, a fetal position to protect himself. For a moment, he thought she would leave him be, but then he felt another thwack, this time to the back. He arched his spine and let out a strangled cry.

The danger of entering unarmed hadn't even occurred to him. Azazel's beating must have dulled his faculties.

Not sure how much more of these thrashings I can take, he thought as he waited for the next impact. But none came, and Lagati finally gathered his wits and rolled toward the wall. He nursed himself into a sitting position, feeling stabs of pain—now on both his left and right sides.

He focused in the dim light, trying to see toward the far end of the apartment. She'd gone into the anteroom. He would have tried to escape, too.

"Elisabeth," he wheezed. He tilted his head to peer through the open door. Elisabeth's back was to him. She stood facing the second door, her head hung in frustration. "You'll never get out that way."

She pounded at the thumb panel. The door didn't budge.

Elisabeth turned without warning and moved into the galley kitchen, pulling out one drawer after another and rifling through its contents. She moved with calculated poise, free of desperation despite the long hours she'd spent rotting in this luxurious cell. A cell, nonetheless.

"What are you looking for?" he asked.

No response.

"Elisabeth, when we designed this place we made sure not to include any obvious weapons." But surely, after several days in here, she already knew that.

He couldn't be sure if it was something he'd said, but Elisabeth turned and made eye contact with him for the first time. Her face registered surprise.

"You're not the usual…" She stopped, mouth open. "Holy mother, you're Raff Lagati."

Lagati felt a cough coming on. He covered his mouth with the back of his hand just in time to catch a splatter of blood. He wiped it off on his pant leg. "I take it you were expecting someone else."

"They bring food once a day." Elisabeth closed the drawer she'd been combing through and walked toward him. "You didn't bring food, did you?"

He managed a weak smile. "Sorry to disappoint."

"You're a damned liar."

"As you can see, I really didn't bring any food—"

"No," she said through her teeth. "I mean, you're a *liar*."

Lagati sighed. "Well, you've got me there."

Elisabeth returned to looking through the drawers.

"Now I know what Emery Wörtlich saw in you," he said, trying to rub the pain out of his shoulder. A futile effort. "Noam Sheply, too, if I recall correctly."

"What did Noam see in me?" Elisabeth asked absentmindedly.

"You have spirit. Tenacity."

She grunted as she pulled out a long serving spoon. "No weapons, you said?"

Lagati inched his back deeper into the immovable panels of the wall. "Well, I suppose you might have to get creative. You seem to be up to the task." A glance to the side revealed the unscrewed leg of a metal bedframe. That must have been what she'd used to hit him. "I only wonder, what's the point?"

"The point is obvious."

"You could hurt me," he conceded. "But will that get you what you want? You want to get out of here. Well, why do you think I came?"

"I don't know, but it wasn't to rescue me."

"Actually, that's precisely the reason."

Elisabeth turned to regard the spoon. Her face fell as she dropped it onto the counter. Perhaps it struck her as unsatisfactory for whatever task she had in mind.

"You've already admitted you're a liar," she said.

"True." Lagati shrugged. "I'm not lying about this, though."

"You're full of shit. You used me as a pawn to lure Brighton here. I know everything, including what you did to Brighton. He's possessed."

"That was his choice. I had nothing to do with it."

Not nothing, he silently corrected. *The drugs I provided certainly greased the wheel.*

"You had everything to do with it," Elisabeth insisted. "You're responsible for bringing us here, for imprisoning me. God only knows what you're planning next."

Frustration nearly overwhelmed him, and he struggled to contain it. How wrong she was. He was responsible for virtually nothing. The Grigori had reduced him to an archivist. He did as he was told, or they administered their unique and humiliating form of discipline.

Of course, Elisabeth could administer a striking amount of discipline of her own.

He raised his chin. "Could I have a moment to—"

"No, I don't think that's wise." She walked toward the bed, leaned over, and snatched up the bedframe's metal crossbar. It must have taken her a long time to get those screws loose without any tools. "And I think you should shut up."

"If you keep going, I may change my mind about rescuing you."

She crossed the apartment and wielded the four-foot steel rod only a few inches from his face. He eyed the weapon as it swung menacingly across his field of vision.

"You're not thinking clearly," he said.

Thwack!

The end of the crossbar clipped his shoulder on the way to punching a hole in the drywall. Already he could feel blood rising to the surface of his skin and soaking through his shirt.

"I'm thinking more clearly than I have in weeks." She lowered her eyes to meet his. "I've been living in a sort of trance, but now I'm going to get out of here, and you're going to help me. You'll do what I tell you, or you won't leave this room alive."

Would she really kill him? The look in her eyes was powerful, feral. He'd gotten far in life by knowing how to size a person up. Elisabeth Macfarlane appeared to be a woman of her word.

"First, you'll get up and open the outer door. I need your thumb-print," she said.

"And if I don't cooperate?"

"Your thumbprint will do the trick whether or not it's attached to the rest of your body."

The ominous sentence hung in the air. Lagati sighed. He wasn't about to lose a thumb today. "I will cooperate."

"Good."

He raised a finger, then lowered it protectively. "But I need you to listen to me, just for a moment. I have a proposal."

"What did listening to you ever get Emery? Or Brighton?"

Fair enough. "Not what they deserved perhaps, but everything I've done has had important reasons. I'd like to help you understand those reasons."

She closed her eyes and shook her head. "I don't want to hear this."

"I was telling the truth when I said I came to release you. I need your help. I need allies."

"What do you need allies for? And why me?"

It was now in his best interest to be forthcoming. "It's hard to find someone on base who's willing to take action against the Grigori, even action that's only *perceived* to go against them. And ever since Bright-on freed them, I've been forced to take a step back from my leadership role. The Grigori are calling the shots now. I need your help to find out what they're up to."

Blessedly, Elisabeth seemed to soften. She sat quietly on the couch as he outlined most of what he knew about the crates. He even told her about the lunar base; now that he'd told Amir, he couldn't see many drawbacks to sharing it with Elisabeth. Allies always felt valued when made privy to confidential information. It helped establish a bond of trust.

She barely seemed fazed when he went on to describe the giant body he and Amir had found.

"Brighton told me about the giant he met," Elisabeth said, her cold rage fading into a kind of reluctant acquiescence. "Mahaway."

Lagati straightened up, feeling the spot on his back where she'd hit him. Was it possible?

"You must be mistaken," he said, dismissing the possibility. "The giants have all been dead for thousands of years."

Elisabeth's face registered surprise, but only for a split second. "You're right. I must have misheard him."

But she hadn't misheard him. Why would she devise such an absurd story? Somehow it must have happened. Brighton had encountered a giant whose name was Mahaway. But when had this occurred? The man had been on the run for two years, and Lagati had only traced him for the final couple of months. The encounter could have taken place anywhere.

It still didn't make sense. How could a giant have survived so long, intact? The body in the crate had been dead for at least a thousand years. Probably longer.

He had to drop it. Elisabeth must have known she'd made a mistake by mentioning Mahaway. She wouldn't say another word now. Not unless she was compelled.

"I have a hard time believing you don't know what the Grigori are up to," Elisabeth said, changing the subject. "You've been plotting to set them free. Do you expect me to accept that you did it blindly?"

"Not blindly. I know their goals, but not their tactics." He allowed his frustration to come forward. "I have to know how they plan to proceed. I haven't come this far to sit back and wait for events to transpire. I've devoted my life to this."

"Have you tried asking them?"

What an insulting question—and she asked it with a smirk playing at the corners of her lips. Not an outright smile, but a hint of all the disdain she felt deep in her gut.

"To put it mildly, my relationship with the Grigori has… devolved." The discomfort of his wounds flared as though to emphasize this point. "But there is one to whom we could turn for answers."

"Ira would know what to do," Elisabeth said quietly. She turned away, her eyes downcast.

"Ira was a fool," Lagati said.

"Was?"

Lagati hesitated. Should he reveal the truth, that Ira had vanished from the mountainside in the midst of a conflagration that had claimed at least six others? That he didn't know what had become of the rabbi?

"He's dead." Lagati modulated his tone to deliver it softly, sympathetically. Persuasively. From her reaction, she believed the lie. She grew pale, on the verge of tears. This surprised him; he hadn't expected these two had shared a connection. "I didn't realize you were close."

"We were the opposite of close," Elisabeth said. "I despised him, almost. He tried to stop us from coming here. He warned us. We should have listened, and if he were here now he would know what to do."

"You give him too much credit. He wasn't infallible."

"No, but he was often right."

Lagati didn't want to pursue this line of thought. "Regardless, I wasn't talking about Ira. The person I mean to ask is close by."

"On the base?"

"In a manner of speaking."

Elisabeth wasn't stupid, but she put it together faster than he had anticipated. "I won't go back through the barrier, if that's what you mean."

There would be risks, Lagati knew, but Elisabeth had risen to the occasion once before. With the right incentive, he hoped she would do it again. Entering Shamballa wasn't for the faint-hearted, though the prospect might not be so intimidating now that Barakel was its only resident. The real risk was whether it would be possible to leave again. The old lock had been picked—he said a silent thank-you to Brighton, wherever he might be—but Semyaza and the others would have altered the security system to keep Barakel contained. Lagati wouldn't gamble his future on it. Not unless he was certain.

Using Elisabeth had one other big advantage. Whereas the Grigori were keeping tabs on him, they barely seemed aware Elisabeth existed at all.

"His name is Barakel, and he's one of the Grigori," Lagati said.

"I thought the Grigori were all free."

Lagati nodded. "They were, briefly. They put Barakel back inside, as a punishment for betraying them to Jehovah six thousand years ago. Understandably, they haven't gotten over it."

"Why are you working against them now? You just finished saying that you've devoted your life to their cause. What's changed in the last few days?"

A fair question, and one he hadn't managed to reconcile. He hadn't switched sides, as much as it might look that way from his recent behavior. He begrudged how the Grigori had treated him, yes, but he still believed in what they were doing. Humanity had been oppressed and manipulated for years by Jehovah and his zealous followers in all their varied religious guises. The Grigori could change things for the better. They couldn't be worse than the alternative.

But that's not what Elisabeth needed to hear. She needed to think they shared a goal.

"You wouldn't ask that if you'd seen the abuse I've taken," Lagati said, cooking up a potent mix of truth and falsity.

This had the intended effect.

"And you want me to pass through the barrier and see what this Barakel has to say," she said.

"That's right. In exchange, I'll see what I can do about getting you out of this cage. Do we have a deal?"

Elisabeth took her time answering.

SEVENTEEN

Yellowknife, Canada
JULY 31

Local time was eleven o'clock and the sun had gone down, yet dark cerulean twilight filled the skies as Brighton watched the airport terminal grow larger through the window. The building was plainer than porridge with its white aluminum siding and baby blue trim. The sign outside read YELLOWKNIFE, its letters gleaming under the plane's forward running lights. Brighton's heart leapt at the realization that they had arrived in an honest-to-God port of civilization, not some abandoned airstrip in the middle of the tundra.

We're in Canada, Brighton thought, feeling a measure of relief. He knew next to nothing about Yellowknife except its existence on the fringes of the Arctic frontier. Semyaza had said they were heading somewhere in North America, far to the north, and this certainly fit the bill.

The plane stopped and the pilot came out to lower the steps.

Brighton stepped onto the pavement, hesitating at the bottom as he took in this foreign locale. He'd been to Canada before, a number of times, but hundreds of miles farther south. In some ways, what he saw was nonetheless familiar. Spruce trees sprouted up from a patchwork of rocky hills, though these trees were a bit stunted. This likely had something to do with the high latitude. They couldn't be far from the tree line, the point at which the soil and climate became too inhospitable for full-grown trees to survive.

Yet it wasn't cold. In fact, Brighton felt quite warm under the stiff summer breeze, a welcome change after their Kamchatka pit stop.

"Warmer than I expected," Brighton called to the pilot, still aboard the plane.

The pilot stuck his head out. "Twenty degrees, according to the temperature gauge."

Brighton knew he meant Celsius degrees. "Is that usual for this time of year?"

"Beats me."

Just then, Brighton spotted a woman approaching. Her long, dark-haired braid hung over the shoulder of her uniform. Security? Brighton instinctively backed up, wary, but she didn't seem to be armed.

"Good evening," Brighton began—and got no further.

The pilot clomped down the stairs, pressing forward to shake the woman's hand. "You must be Nicole. We radioed in."

Radioed in? Brighton wondered to Abranel. *Given our covert mission, I'm surprised Semyaza would allow us to land at a municipal airport, with all the red tape and bureaucracy—*

"There was no way around it," Abranel assured him.

"Documentation," Nicole said, grim-faced.

The pilot disappeared into the plane and reemerged a few moments later with a thin folder, bits of paper poking out around the edges.

Nicole took the folder and opened it with one hand, aiming her flashlight with the other. Once satisfied, she clicked off the light and handed it all back.

"Everything checks out," she said. "I hope you find what you're looking for."

As she walked back toward the terminal, Brighton reran the brief exchange in his head. Was that it? Would there be no further security hassles? Were they truly free to go?

The pilot pointed toward a gate next to the terminal building. "Let's go. No reason to invite further questioning."

"What does she think we're looking for?" Brighton asked.

"You ask a lot of questions."

Brighton shrugged. Asking questions had long been his tendency. "Is it such a horrible thing to want to know what's going on?"

"I suppose not. She thinks we're with the RCMP."

"RCMP?"

"The national police force. Our cover is that we're hunting a Japanese fugitive who entered the country illegally, under a forged tourist visa. If anyone asks, we've just come from Japan."

Brighton narrowed his eyes. "That sounds unnecessarily complex."

"Their radar has been tracking us since international airspace, over the Pacific. We needed a story to explain our origin and invite as little scrutiny as possible. The folks back at Khunjerab worked out the cover and provided us with the necessary paperwork." He scowled at Brighton's skepticism. "You know what they say about looking gift horses in the mouth, sir?"

Brighton wondered at this as they passed through the gate into a parking lot riven by thick concrete dividers to demarcate the roadway. He couldn't believe how quickly they'd gotten through.

"Our masters were clever," Abranel postulated.

He bristled at the suggestion that the Grigori were his masters. This was nonetheless a reality he would have to accept. In time. But not today.

A lone taxi occupied the center of the parking lot. Its driver must have spotted them because the taxi's engine roared to life and it rolled toward them over cracked pavement.

"You need a ride," the taxi driver said in a thick accent. Brighton pegged him as having come from an African country, though he couldn't guess which one. He marveled at the untold story that traced this man's path from the overheated wastes of Africa to a small, isolated city in the far-flung borderlands of the Canadian Arctic.

Brighton exchanged a look with the pilot. "Where are we going?"

"Into town, I guess. It's up to you."

"Yes then," Brighton said. "Could you take us to a hotel?"

A few moments later, the taxi turned onto a two-lane highway. Were it not for the airport, Brighton might not have believed they had reached civilization after all. He saw no buildings, and barely any signs for the next mile. As they crested a hill, however, the city came into focus. This was no sprawling metropolis, certainly not by the definition of the great cities Brighton had visited, but neither was it a backwater. A cluster of tall buildings towered over the countryside, their lights overpowering the expanse of weak stars only now making their appearance in the twilight.

"Which hotel?" the driver asked as they coasted down an incline.

"Anywhere. Doesn't have to be fancy." Brighton looked over just as the pilot reached into his pocket and withdrew a credit card. "Would you take credit when we get there?"

"Cash only."

"In that case, we'll need to find an ATM."

They rode in silence. The unique architecture spoke to the many months of bitter cold these buildings were subjected to in winter. The barebones structures were draped in the same warehouse siding as the airport, a reminder that they were built for survival, not luxury. Each building's grid of small windows offered its occupants a few coveted peeks into the outside world.

The taxi stopped next to a bank. Brighton looked out the window and saw the ATM built into the exterior wall.

The pilot unbuckled his seatbelt and reached for the door handle.

"I want you to get the money," Abranel told Brighton.

Why?

"I'll explain later. Just do it."

Brighton awkwardly reached out his hand, palm up. "Could I have the card, please?"

The pilot froze, a look of surprise on his face. Brighton couldn't believe he was asking the man to turn over his card, but Abranel could not be bargained with.

"It's not his card."

That, at least, made Brighton feel less intrusive. The pilot turned it over, though he did so begrudgingly.

Only after Brighton inserted the card into the slot did Abranel reveal the four-digit PIN. He proceeded to take out a few hundred dollars, enough to pay for the cab, the motel, and any unforeseen expenses the next day. As for himself, Brighton needed some fresh clothes, soap, a toothbrush… just the necessities to ensure people didn't treat him like a street person.

Brighton swung himself back into the taxi, but this time they only drove around the block. The seedy motel they'd come to offered no amenities beyond four walls and a door for privacy. The walls were painted a somber grey, though off-white patches showed up where the paint had peeled, either by extreme weather or occupants with nothing better to do. Steel bars obstructed the windows, making it look more like a cell block than a place to voluntarily spend the night.

"It's perfect," Abranel said with a hint of excitement. Perhaps he was hoping they'd be mugged in their sleep, robbed at gunpoint and relieved of… well, they carried no luggage, so at least that worked in

their favor.

"It's the last place anyone would look for us," the pilot murmured.

"It'll do." It wasn't the worst place Brighton had spent a night.

They paid for the taxi and watched as it disappeared back in the direction of the airport.

"Now, go in alone. Pay for one room."

Brighton left the pilot outside and pulled open the door to the office, finding it surprisingly heavy. He really had to heave the metal door to get it open.

Inside, the office was as dingy as the exterior suggested. The overhead light had burnt out, so the only illumination was a desk lamp in the center of a round table. An aboriginal woman in her mid-fifties sat next to the table, a well-worn paperback in one hand and a cigarette in the other. When she saw him, she emptied nearly an inch of ash into the tray next to her.

"What you want?"

"A room for the night," Brighton said.

"Just you?"

"Tell her you're alone."

Brighton didn't let his confusion show. "Yup. Just me."

The woman pulled out a notebook. "Name?"

Brighton decided to wait for Abranel to provide it. Abranel didn't say a word.

What name should I give? Brighton asked.

"Use the one on the card."

"Name," the woman repeated.

With her staring straight at him, there was no way to avoid the inelegance of digging his hand into his pocket and checking the name on his own credit card. "Raj Peters."

She grunted, then cocked her head at him. Brighton tried not to blush, but the heat rushed straight to his cheeks and neck.

Damn it. Could I look any less like a Raj? He thought he sensed Abranel laughing at him.

Fortunately, she didn't ask questions. She pulled a pen out of her pocket, uncapped it, and scribbled the name. Her writing was illegible.

"It's forty bucks."

Well, at least they would get what they paid for. Brighton dug out a couple of twenties and placed them on the table. The woman stuffed the bills in her own pocket. Next, she reached up to a row of hooks and extracted a key attached to a comically large keychain, its only marking the giant "15" scrawled in felt marker on the white plastic slat.

Brighton accepted the key and left the office.

"We should have gotten two rooms," the pilot remarked as they made their way to the door of their motel room.

How to explain that the spirit inside my head told me not to? Brighton inserted the key in the lock and pushed open the heavy door. The carpet had been worn thin, the paint was peeling where any remained at all, and he heard water dripping from the tap.

Brighton walked to the edge of the bed and prepared to lower himself onto the floral-patterned bedspread, its color faded from several thousand runs through the washing machine. Before he could bend his knees, he felt a point of pressure deep in his head, and then he straightened again. Brighton's heart raced. Abranel hadn't taken over like this in nearly two days.

"It's very important that nobody knows where we are," Abranel said as the pilot went to the sink and washed his hands.

The pilot dried his hands on a towel and turned to face him. "It's late, and I'm tired."

Abranel, on the other hand, seemed well-rested. "You're an excellent pilot. I want to thank you for the ride."

"Excuse me?"

Abranel approached him. "I said thank you."

The pilot rubbed his tired eyes. "Okay then."

"I don't think you ever told me your name. What can I call you?"

The pilot didn't answer.

No, Brighton pleaded, suddenly realizing where all this was headed—and had been headed the whole time. *Don't do it, Abranel. He's one of us.*

"He's not one of us," Abranel said aloud. "A hired gun. No more."

"Who are you talking to?" the pilot asked.

Brighton felt his lips pull back in a thin smile. Not his smile. He wanted to scream, to tell the pilot to run, to get the hell out. Abranel seemed to laugh at these ineffective attempts.

"You're really no different than the taxi driver," Abranel said, directing himself to the pilot again. "Except the taxi driver doesn't know who we are, or where we came from, or what we're doing here. None of his business. You? Different story."

The pilot had frozen in place. Brighton recognized it as a fear response.

"One man is hard enough to control. Two is ungainly." Abranel took three measured steps toward the pilot. "I'm afraid one will have to go."

The pilot made a run for it, bounding around Brighton and launching himself over the bed. His right foot trailed behind him, then failed to clear the bed. He tripped, crashing into the wall—and then the floor.

The look of abject terror on the man's face struck Brighton like a hammer to the stomach. Brighton had been nothing but kind to him, and now? He thought Brighton was going to kill him. He had no reason to believe otherwise, and Brighton had no way to explain what was really going on.

Stop it! Brighton shouted in desperation. *Stop this! Stop it now!*

The pilot hoisted himself up again and almost—*almost*—made it to the door. Brighton's hand lashed out and swatted the man away just as he grazed the metallic doorknob, the only taste of freedom he was likely to feel in the short moments remaining to him.

You don't have—

"Shut up," Abranel said in an even tone as he squeezed the pilot's wrist. The pilot let out a cry of shock as Abranel snapped the wrist back, separating the hand from the bones of the lower arm. The sharp corner of one of those bones broke the surface, puncturing the skin and spraying blood over the carpet.

Brighton wept internally at the horror, but he couldn't stop it, couldn't close his eyes, couldn't shut down his sensory input. He had no choice but to experience it, every moment, every gruesome second of the assault. He tried to retreat into his subconscious, but Abranel refused to let him off the hook.

Abranel pulled the pilot to his knees, holding him by the throat in a firm grip. The pilot wheezed quick breaths through Abranel's tightening fingers, each growing more labored than the last.

"Please," the man gasped.

As Brighton sobbed, his fingers began to squeeze the life from the man, feeling the throb of his pulse, the slick of sweat on his skin, the feeble grasping of his hand as he struggled to free himself, to no avail.

"Do you understand why I'm doing this?" Abranel demanded.

The pilot looked up at him with a mixture of confusion and fear, with the certain knowledge of his death. Of course he didn't understand, but Brighton knew well that the question hadn't been trained on him. The question was meant for Brighton.

No, Brighton insisted between his undemonstrated but deeply felt sobs. *This isn't necessary. You don't need to do this!*

"It is necessary," Abranel said, enjoying the pilot's bewilderment.

You don't know if he would have betrayed us.

"That's not why I did it. Though I suppose there was some risk of betrayal."

Then why?

"You needed a further demonstration of your place in this relationship. I make the decisions. You are not in control, even if I allow you some momentary perception of free will." Abranel paused, waiting for a response which didn't come. "Do you understand?"

Yes, yes—

"Do you think he's ready?"

End this, please.

"Yes, I think so."

With that, Brighton felt his fist close ever tighter around the man's throat, crushing the windpipe yet not letting up. He gripped harder, harder, harder until his thumb and forefingers touched on the other side of the pilot's lifeless neck.

"Yes," Abranel repeated, somewhat casually. "Yes, that does it."

Abranel's control subsided.

Brighton fell forward as his body went limp. Just in time, he saw that he was going to land atop the pilot's body, but it was too late to do anything about it. He bounced off the dead man's chest and rolled onto the floor. In revulsion, he reared back, hitting the back of his head against the wall.

Now that an opportunity for real tears presented itself, they coursed down his cheeks in a torrent. He didn't try to brush them away as he dropped onto the carpet, mingling with the glossy puddle of blood that had formed there. He stared unblinking at the body, wracked with guilt, even though it made no sense to feel guilty. He'd had nothing to do with it!

But that was a lie. He hadn't been in control, but he'd allowed himself to be put in this position. He'd given himself away. He couldn't claim ignorance, merely haste. He hadn't thought it through, just like he hadn't thought through a hundred little decisions in the past weeks. He'd been a walking, talking ball of rage—and this pilot had unjustly paid the price.

Ira, if you could only see me now.

"Abranel, are you there?"

A stupid question. Of course Abranel was there, but it suited him to remain silent, to force Brighton to confront the loneliness which struck him full-force.

Brighton used the wall to help himself to his feet. He turned away from the pilot, even knowing that he couldn't ignore what had happened. He had to deal with the corpse, dispose of it and clean the blood out of the carpet.

I can't do this, he thought.

But he had to do it. Abranel would force him, one way or another.

EIGHTEEN

Mount Khunjerab, Pakistan
AUGUST 1

Lagati thought his limp was a bit less pronounced now that he'd taken a second dose of medication. Not only had the pain receded, but he felt strong. Normal. It helped to mask his subterfuge when he returned to Elisabeth's cell with a pair of folded blue coveralls.

She approached him from the kitchen, rubbing the coarse fabric between her thumb and forefinger.

"I saw the others wearing these," she said, almost to herself. "The ones in the hangar, around that ship."

"Most of the workers wear them. They won't draw attention." Lagati turned his back to her. "Put it on, quick."

"Right now?"

"We should get going. Strike while the iron's hot and all that."

He closed his eyes, savoring the sounds of Elisabeth undressing; it was more a reflection of how badly he had come to miss Antoinette than latent attraction to Elisabeth. He had committed any number of wrongs, many of them objectively terrible, but he couldn't even entertain the prospect of cheating on Antoinette. He had a responsibility to her, and her to him.

"How do I look?" she asked.

Lagati turned and beheld her. She fit into the coverall very well, if not a bit snugly around the hips, but to his eyes she still looked like a masquerading prisoner.

"Tired," he replied. "You look like you haven't slept."

"So do you."

"Point taken. Still, perhaps if you washed up a bit."

Her expression radiated irritation, but she walked to the kitchen sink and splashed water on her face, rubbing her cheeks and the bags under her eyes. She ran her fingers through her curly brown hair to work out a few tangles.

"Better?" she asked.

Lagati nodded. "The Shamballa barrier is a five-minute walk through well-trafficked corridors. Fortunately, the base will be quiet this evening."

"Will your people recognize me?"

"Some, certainly. You must not be seen."

Elisabeth smoothed the front of her new outfit. "Sounds risky."

"I won't lie—" He registered her slight smile at the aborted remark. "Let me put it this way: what we're doing is dangerous. If we're caught, we may not survive the night."

"Better than spending another minute in here," she said.

He strode into the anteroom and triggered the outer door. It slid open and they stepped out. Lagati braced himself, half-expecting Elisabeth to make a run for it, but instead she waited patiently for him to set their course.

Just as they approached a junction, Amir came around the corner and stopped right in the center of their path.

Elisabeth tensed, but Lagati put a hand on her shoulder.

"He's with us," Lagati assured her. He turned to Amir. "How many people are in the corridor?"

"Very few." Amir spared a nervous glance at Elisabeth. "Are you sure you want to go through with this?"

Lagati sighed. "Very sure. Now go on, and warn us if you see anyone coming."

Amir inclined his head, a gesture of obeisance, and trotted down the corridor. Lagati waited until Amir was out of sight around the curve, then started to walk a safe distance behind him.

"You trust that man?" Elisabeth whispered.

"Only barely."

Elisabeth let it drop, falling into silence as they moved as quickly as they dared without appearing suspicious to surveillance cameras or wandering eyes.

"Hey, Suzanne!" Amir called out.

Lagati rolled his eyes at the volume of Amir's voice. Did his warning have to be so obvious?

"Act natural," Lagati said under his breath.

Sure enough, just ahead Amir stood alongside two women clad in their own blue coveralls. He had engaged them in conversation. A distraction.

Lagati passed nonchalantly, his eyes trained forward. Just this once, he cursed his bad luck for having such a prominent role; one woman's eyes met his and locked on. Any other time, he might have appreciated the small act of deference, but not tonight. Tonight it was extremely inconvenient. Amir chattered away, doing his level best to draw her attention back, but it did no good.

"Hi," Elisabeth said to the staring woman.

Lagati wanted to strangle her, but instead he offered his own nod of greeting as they continued on their way.

"What were you thinking?" he hissed when they were out of view.

"Acting natural, like you said. She didn't seem to recognize me."

"You shouldn't have said anything."

"Wouldn't it have been weirder if I'd stared at the floor?"

Maybe she was right. In any event, they'd gotten through un-scathed. But now Amir's usefulness had been spent. They were truly on their own.

His head jerked up at the sound of further voices. Another pair was approaching, and by the increasing volume of their conversation they were very close.

Lagati thrust himself against a door to the right and thumbed its square pad, praying that his access would work. The door slid open. Lagati pushed Elisabeth through, then went in after her.

He pressed his ear against the closed door and listened.

"But where will we go?" a high-pitched voice asked. It took Lagati a moment to place it. A Grigori. Batraal, maybe?

"Semyaza has not said." Someone unrecognizable.

"Perhaps it has something to do with Singapore."

"Singapore!"

"A few of our children are there now…"

Lagati desperately wanted to hear the rest of that conversation, but there was nothing for it.

"Who's going to Singapore?" Elisabeth asked as they left their hiding spot and resumed their surreptitious march.

"I don't have a clue."

Less than a minute later, Elisabeth slowed. "We're close. I recog-nize the way. We take a right up ahead, onto a corridor that descends deep underground."

"That's right, but keep up the pace. We're still vulnerable."

The corridor walls gradually grew rockier, rougher, and in moments they were hurrying down the aluminum steps which led toward the barrier chamber.

Lagati came up short when a pair of guards stepped out of the shadows and blocked the way. Each wore the same blue jumpsuits as everyone else, but the getup took on a more threatening character when coupled with rifles—locked, loaded, and pointed straight at them.

"Stop there," one of the guards warned. A woman. She glanced once at her male companion, then fixed Lagati with her piercing eyes. "This is a secure area."

Lagati didn't recognize her, but he vaguely remembered having hired the man. Or at least being consulted. The Pakistani man had come from a local village. Lagati had been reluctant to take on people with no training or experience, but dozens of unskilled laborers had been needed.

"Surely you must know who I am," Lagati said, out of breath.

The woman lowered her rifle a bit. Now instead of hitting him in the forehead, she would put a bullet in his groin.

"Our orders are to let no one through, sir," the woman said.

"Who gave those orders? Surely they didn't mean me."

The guards shared another glance.

"Azazel didn't mention any exceptions," the woman replied. "How about you, Lu?"

Lu? Lagati thought. *That can't be his real name.*

"I've never been prevented from coming down here before," Lagati said.

"We will check," the man said in stilted English. "Wait here."

Lagati waved this off. "No, no. Don't go to the trouble."

"Who's the girl?" the woman asked. "I've never seen her before."

"Sure you have," Elisabeth piped up. "I've seen you. Lots of times."

The woman shrugged as though to acknowledge that her memory might be at fault.

"Listen, there haven't been guards here before," Lagati said.

"What's changed?"

"Don't know the details," the woman said. "Someone's been eavesdropping on the Grigori. That's the rumor anyway." Her rifle came all the way up again.

"Watch where you point that thing." Lagati reached forward and gently aimed the rifle away from him. She tensed, but didn't turn its muzzle toward him again. At least Lagati still carried enough authority to save himself from these capricious underlings.

Damn, Lagati silently cursed. If it hadn't been for his own foolish snooping, this would all be so much simpler. *But then I wouldn't have found out about Brighton—and wouldn't have sent Antoinette away.*

He cursed again. She would still be here now, sorting out the situation alongside him. Instead he had to rely on virtual strangers. All he wanted was Antoinette back.

I should be so lucky.

Lucky.

His eyes shot up, hardly able to believe his good fortune.

"Lutfi," Lagati blurted to the Pakistani man. "I hired you personally two years ago. Remember?"

Lutfi nodded stiffly. "Yes. I remember."

"You've been a fine addition to the team." Damn it, his motives were so transparent. It would never work. He had to change tacks. "Azazel is very busy. In fact, I don't even think he's currently on base. He's gone to Singapore for a day or two."

"What's he doing in Singapore?" the woman asked.

Lagati shrugged. "I can't actually tell you."

The woman lowered the weapon entirely this time. "How long will you be down there?"

"Not long. Semyaza sent us to check on…" He'd been about to name Barakel, but he didn't know whether these guards knew anything about that. Probably not. "Well, I can't tell you that either."

It had the ring of authenticity. More importantly, it was enough. The woman stepped aside, creating a path down the steps into the darkness lit only by the occasional glow rock.

As they came into view of the enormous, shimmering barrier, its sleek cylindrical walls piercing straight through the rock above and below, Lagati couldn't help but reflect on the hundreds of times he'd come down here. The most memorable day of his life had been the day he'd discovered it. October 5. It had taken a week of exploring the abandoned base before he finally got to the barrier. He'd picked through steep caverns for two long days to find it! The memory of all the work, the pain of the scratches he'd suffered because of it, had vanished upon his first sight of the barrier. And the voices! Those voices had called to him, a verbal caress, the ultimate reward for such a difficult journey. He remembered it like it was yesterday. Meticulously he'd cleared a spot on the ground and sat in a meditative posture, just as he'd been taught, and reached out with his mind. To make contact. To commune with the Grigori, for the first time in person, or as near to in person as he could achieve without bodily entering the barrier. Entering Shamballa. The shock of discovering heaven and earth—a real, experiential place. At the beginning, the Grigori had soothed him with haughty words and revelatory lessons. He'd soaked it up, absorbing every principle in which they could instruct him. The power, the belief, the history… it had been an overwhelming experience. To meet living gods!

He realized he'd closed his eyes and rapturously placed his bare hands against the cool surface of the barrier. When he opened his eyes to the dim but magnificent cavern, his soul filled with a deep, unshakeable melancholy.

I am so alone.

"You are not alone," a voice whispered. Shockingly intimate.

Who had spoken that? He turned, expecting Elisabeth to be leaning into his ear, but she was nowhere nearby. She stood at least twenty feet behind him.

"What are you doing back there?" he asked.

She took halting steps toward him. In the same way that the barrier filled him with the rapture he'd felt on previous visits, she seemed to feel only fear and loathing.

"Maybe I'm not ready for this." Even speaking in her lowest tone, her voice carried through the chamber.

Lagati frowned. "That's not an option, Elisabeth. If you don't go in, I'll make sure you stay locked up forever. Do you think I won't do it?"

Let her chew on that, he thought while studying the slack, brooding expression on her face.

"You are not alone."

Lagati straightened, double-checking to ensure Elisabeth hadn't spoken it. Indeed, she stood silent, exactly where she'd planted herself. "Did you hear that?"

"Hear what?" Elisabeth asked.

"A voice."

Lagati faced the barrier with fresh realization. It was so clear to him, so obvious that he was embarrassed for only catching it now.

"Barakel, it's you," he whispered. "You can sense me, can't you?"

"Yes." A pause. "And another."

Elisabeth stepped up beside him. "Now I hear," she said.

Somehow Barakel had the ability to direct his thoughts to particular minds. A marvelous way to effect covert communication, Lagati thought. What he wouldn't do to obtain such a skill.

It may not be out of reach, Lagati thought. *If Ira Binyamin can do what he did on that mountainside, nothing's impossible anymore.*

"Why have you come?" Barakel asked.

The question caught Lagati flat-footed. To his mind, his purpose should have been self-evident, but perhaps he would need to connect the dots. "To speak with you."

A beat, then Barakel continued. "You want to know what the Grigori are planning."

Perhaps I won't have to connect the dots after all. "Yes, that's right."

"Who is the woman?"

"Her name is Elisabeth."

"Ah. Yes, I remember now. Semyaza drew her here. She accompanied the man named..." Barakel trailed off into recollection. "Brighton, I believe. Yes. That is his name."

"Right," Elisabeth spoke up. "Sherwood Brighton was my friend."

Was? Lagati asked himself. Did she know something he didn't?

"The others would be most upset if they learned you came here," Barakel said.

Lagati nodded to himself. "That's an understatement. Our need—or at least, our curiosity—outweighs the risk."

"And are you prepared to enter?"

Lagati found himself hesitating. He had never entered the barrier bodily. Before Brighton's arrival, Lagati had worried that entering the barrier was a one-way trip. Even now, the possibility concerned him. Obviously the Grigori had reinstated some kind of locking mechanism to keep Barakel from escaping.

"I am," Elisabeth said.

Lagati stood in awe of her. So bold, so confident suddenly. And that confidence seemed to stem from some inner earnestness; it wasn't solely a factor of his threat. True, she had little to lose at this point, but he suspected she yearned to know the truth of things as much as he did.

"Then I await you," Barakel said, sounding patient.

It struck Lagati that Barakel's voice was different than the other Grigori's, in pointed ways. Barakel didn't seem so quick to anger— ironic, since Barakel had the greatest reason of all to be angry. His voice also didn't contain the false sincerity that characterized the others' manipulative tactics. He was quieter, more resigned. Lagati felt himself ready to trust Barakel, but he knew this was a mistake, and perhaps a costly one. Barakel might only be a more skilled manipulator.

Elisabeth stood right up against the barrier while Lagati hung back.

"You must both enter," Barakel said. "It's easier to show you the answers than merely tell them."

"Can you guarantee we will be able to leave?" Lagati asked.

"Yes, of course."

But the Grigori were famously accomplished liars.

He watched in astonishment as Elisabeth fearlessly closed her eyes and stepped through the barrier without leaving so much as a ripple in her wake.

Illogically, he felt some panic about being left behind. Alone. He turned and peered up the dim passageway. Perhaps it was only a matter of time before they were discovered down here. He couldn't afford to stand around indefinitely.

Lagati summoned all his nerve and counted to three. Gritting his teeth, he stepped forward, half-expecting to smash his nose against the cool barrier.

He slipped through unscathed.

At first, he didn't know where he was. The air was so dry that it leached moisture from his face. Dust floated in the air; he couldn't see the motes, but he felt them brushing against his skin as he walked.

The darkness was near absolute, except for the crackling of a campfire nestled amidst a henge of strangely misshapen rocks. Billions of stars glistened overhead, each pinprick shining so brightly that Lagati couldn't believe such a place existed. Not even in the most unpolluted, unpopulated frontiers of the planet could such a pure wilderness exist. He sensed intrinsically that wherever they were hadn't been embraced by the cold, destructive encroach of civilization.

Elisabeth stood silhouetted by the light of the campfire, and next to her an unusually tall man. Barakel's eyes shifted to regard Lagati, his eyes so dark that all Lagati could make out were ominous black cavities.

"Where are we?" Lagati asked, walking toward the fire.

"Physically, we are still under the mountains. Inside the barrier, I have the ability to manipulate my surroundings at will."

Lagati put out his hands. The fire certainly felt warm enough, simulated flames or otherwise.

Elisabeth cleared her throat. "Yes, but where *are* we?"

Once his eyes adjusted to the darkness, Lagati could make out greater detail. Beyond the rocks extended a line of stony hills and mountains devoid of vegetation. Their camp was situated on the slope of a shallow valley.

And then he knew exactly where they were. Not *right* here, by the fire, but up in those distant mountains. He'd visited dozens of times. Azazel had always shown a great fondness for this setting.

"Mount Hermon," Lagati said before Barakel could answer.

Barakel pointed toward the tallest of the peaks, flattened at the top where Lagati knew an almost perfectly circular crater resided.

"Azazel directed me there in my meditations. It's where I often met with the other Grigori." Lagati surveyed Barakel. "But never with you. They didn't trust you."

"True," Barakel said. "I sought peace, but the rest of my comrades had no room in their hearts for anything but war. They blamed me for their captivity."

Lagati remembered well the day Semyaza had taken him to see Barakel, when he'd sentenced Barakel to further confinement. Semyaza had intended it as an object lesson, a reminder for Lagati to do what he'd been told.

I guess I didn't take the lesson to heart. I always was stubborn.

A flash of light in the sky caught Lagati's attention. He looked up as a shooting star burned through the cosmos, leaving a faint contrail in its wake. Its hooked arc took it straight to the peak of Mount Hermon. Surely not a coincidence.

The three of them stood in silence as more streaks of light passed overhead, each converging at the same point.

"I come here often." Barakel poked the fire with a jagged stick. Lagati wondered where he'd gotten the wood for the fire, as there weren't any trees or bushes nearby. Then again, Barakel had the power here to create anything he wanted, so why not a campfire? "This is where it all began, you see. Where the future may have taken a different course."

Lagati didn't know what he was talking about, and by the puzzled look on Elisabeth's face, neither did she.

"What's so special about that mountain?" Elisabeth asked.

"It was the site of the Grigori's first council. Azazel invited two hundred of us to join him there and discuss the fallout of our schism with Jehovah. I suspect Semyaza pushed him to do it, but Azazel, always the passionate one, leapt at the opportunity to take action. His rage ran unchecked. Semyaza could have manipulated him to do anything." He paused, perhaps realizing he'd gotten off on a tangent. "You'll have to excuse me. I rarely think along straight lines. The centuries go by, and I have no way to pass the time except to think. And regret. Indeed, the regret is constant, and especially potent when combined with hopelessness. Take care to learn from my example, if you can."

"I try to live my life without regrets," Lagati said.

Barakel grunted. "No one lives ten thousand years without regret."

"You've lived ten thousand years?" Elisabeth asked.

"At least." Barakel gazed at Mount Hermon with palpable disgust. "Azazel is convincing them as we speak. Not just them. Us. I was among them. He persuaded me as much as anyone, caused me to believe in his plan." He spat at the ground. "I committed terrible acts in the name of that plan."

This was not the story they'd told Lagati. Similarities abounded, but the history of the Grigori had sounded much nobler through Semyaza's florid descriptions.

"Tell me," Lagati said guardedly. "What was this plan?"

Barakel laughed. A mirthless laugh. "You are doubting the story they gave you. As you should. Azazel rallied us to mate with human women, to disrupt Jehovah's genetic designs on humanity. We chose our women with great determination, chose quickly and often."

The desert rocks vanished, replaced with a courtyard surrounded by tall, orange wattle-and-daub walls. Wind rustled through nearby palm trees whose long, deep green fronds peeked over the tops of the courtyard on two sides. The other two walls contained doors and windows, indicating a home. The air was humid; Lagati thought he heard waves crashing in the distance.

Barakel stood with his back to a table upon which rested an oil lamp. Except for the stars, it provided the only light.

"I've always loved the stars," Barakel said with a hint of blissful distraction. "During the day, it's easy to lose perspective of our place in the universe. At night, the stars make it impossible to forget."

A woman's scream wrenched the air. Lagati whipped around toward one of the doors into the home's dark interior. He listened closely in the silence that followed, but all he heard was his own ragged breath. Just as he was about to ask Barakel about it, the woman screamed again, louder this time, and the commotion preceded a crash.

Elisabeth made several strides toward the door, but Barakel clamped a hand on her shoulder.

"That woman's in trouble," Elisabeth said.

Barakel removed his hand and cast his gaze to the ground, covered by an even layer of gravel. It crunched underfoot as he made a circle around the table. "Nothing can be done about it. All this happened six thousand years ago."

"Why have you brought us here?" Lagati asked.

"Because I must never forget," Barakel said, making eye contact with him. His eyes were dry but tinged with shame.

Lagati heard another crash as a woman stumbled out into the courtyard. No, a girl. She couldn't have been older than thirteen or fourteen. Her simple grey dress was torn down the middle, exposing small breasts, and a thick red cut oozed blood down her too-thin stomach. She ran to the corner of the courtyard, clutching the tatters of her dress and scrabbling against the walls. There was no escape to be had.

Elisabeth turned away, unable to watch. Lagati, for his part, couldn't take his eyes off the scene. The girl turned her mud-streaked face toward the door she'd come from, but the way was blocked by a tall man barely lit by the oil lamp's long, flickering shadows.

That's not just any man. Indeed, it was Barakel himself. This younger version of Barakel stalked toward the girl with lascivious intent, a zealous gleam in his eyes.

Lagati's stomach turned. Now he, too, wished Barakel would change the channel, as it were. He didn't want to see this, yet he couldn't turn away as Elisabeth had. Some ghastly, evil impulse deep inside him kept his gaze fixed on the terrified girl. He hated himself for it, but his heart raced with a combination of disgust and excitement.

The younger Barakel grabbed the girl by the waist and forced her down, pressing her supple skin into the gravel. He tore away the rest of her clothes in three efficient flourishes, then loomed over her. His hand settled over her mouth, muffling her screams. He let out an ugly laugh as he penetrated her.

Then, blessedly, Lagati did summon the courage to look away.

"She bore my first child," Barakel said, stepping away from the ongoing rape. "The child was monstrous from the start. None of us could have predicted the genetic effects of mingling our seed with human DNA. In the years that followed, the world was overrun with our creations. Giant, hulking creatures that gave us pleasure at mankind's expense." He looked behind him, regarding the poor girl with downcast eyes. "Their mothers never survived childbirth."

Lagati shook his head from side to side, unable to believe what he was hearing. This was not the way the story went. The Nephilim had not been such monsters. They'd been leaders and men of renown.

At long last, the rape complete, the courtyard vanished, leaving nothing but darkness all around. Lagati's arms pinwheeled at the discovery that his feet were no longer anchored to the ground, but then he realized he was perfectly stable, neither sinking nor floating. They stood in a void, absent of form.

"Some of the children assimilated better than others," Barakel said. "I myself had over a hundred, and a handful weren't particularly evil. I hesitate to call any of them *good*." He faltered. "Except perhaps for one."

He didn't follow up on this cryptic statement, no matter how long Lagati and Elisabeth waited.

"There could be no peace with Jehovah, despite my best efforts," Barakel continued at last. "The Nephilim died—bound to the earth for all eternity, just as Enoch promised. No hope for them. No hope for us."

"Not all of them died," Elisabeth pointed out.

Barakel came to stand in front of her. "I assure you, they did."

"It can't be," she insisted. "At least one survived, preserved beneath the surface of the ocean. He carried the Book of Creation."

Lagati spun on her. "You mean this Mahaway story you mentioned? You didn't say anything about the Book of Creation!"

It made a kind of bizarre sense. Lagati had always been certain Brighton, Wörtlich, and Binyamin had found the Book, but despite a lengthy search there remained no trace of it. If Brighton had encountered a giant named Mahaway—as improbable as that sounded—it followed that Mahaway had also been the source of the Book. He should have seen it earlier.

Barakel was beset by an equal amount of shock. "But we saw it in Brighton's memory, in the King's Chamber. Mahaway was not…"

Lagati could hardly believe his ears, but Barakel was choking back tears. Tears!

"He wasn't there," Barakel stumbled. "I didn't see him. No one told me."

"Who's Mahaway?" Lagati demanded. Whoever Mahaway was, he had obviously been important to Barakel. Important enough to extract tears from a Grigori.

Barakel let out a long, shuddering breath. "My son."

"The one who was closest to good," Elisabeth finished, completing the puzzle.

Barakel nodded. "Such a long time to wait. And for nothing. Jehovah would never change his mind. Jehovah the implacable. Jehovah the immovable. Jehovah the intractable."

Lagati smiled internally. Despite Barakel's ancient betrayal, he now exposed his true allegiance. He was no defender of Jehovah. So the Grigori had been honest about that much. Jehovah was not the pious, righteous deity he revealed to the world.

"You still haven't answered my original question," Lagati said. "What are the Grigori planning?"

Barakel overcame his emotion, lowering his gaze to Lagati. His eyes burned like coals, his grief having turned to anger. Rage. "They will do what is necessary."

"What is necessary?" Elisabeth repeated. "What does that mean?"

"It means Jehovah will regret what he's done to us. My compatriots are freed, and Jehovah has lost his advantage. It's two hundred against one now." Barakel approached Lagati, treading slowly through the infinite blackness. "But the plan is not the real reason you have come to me."

Lagati looked up at him, startled. "It is. I swear it."

"Your oaths mean nothing."

"But I insist—"

Barakel brought a single finger to his lips. "What you really want is to be in the thick of it. You want a part to play."

He sees right through me, Lagati recognized. "Is that so much to ask? I orchestrated the Grigori's release, but they've cast me aside. Would you believe that they have me archiving the crates that have been shipped down from the moon?"

"The moon!" Elisabeth exclaimed.

Lagati ignored her. "I could be put to better use. Though the things I've discovered in those crates are enough to curdle one's blood."

Barakel laughed. "I'm not surprised you haven't the stomach for it. I presume you've found the bodies of a number of the Nephilim, preserved as well as our advanced technology allows."

Lagati acknowledged the truth of this with a shrug.

"Those bodies can be brought back to life," Barakel said, almost lazily. "Our children's spirits can inhabit the willing… or the dead. Their original bodies would make fearsome hosts, I think you'd agree. They won't last long now, but they'll make excellent short-term weapons against Jehovah's faithful. Against the world at large." He laughed. Not quite the rancorous sound his younger self had made while raping the girl, but close. "What I wouldn't give to witness it."

This seemed to give Barakel an idea. He placed both his enormous hands on Lagati's shoulders. Even worse, the Grigori leaned forward until his face was nose-to-nose with Lagati's.

"How would you feel about an exchange?" Barakel asked.

"What kind of exchange?"

To Lagati's left, a strange-looking device flashed into existence. Lagati had never before seen its like. Only after staring at it for several seconds did he realize he was looking at a very large bulb of some kind, attached via a series of interconnected blocks and tubes to a monolithic base. The base looked like a solid block of gold, reflecting the pale light of the bulb's long, sinuous filament.

"It broadcasts an unlimited supply of energy, allowing all this," Barakel indicated their darkened surroundings, "to function. The device also serves as a locking mechanism, requiring a complex key. The text of this… I think you called it the Book of Creation, but I know it only as Jehovah's creation science… anyway, the text provided the key, which we culled from Brighton's memory. Alas, the key has been changed to keep me inside." Barakel paused. "If you discover the latest key, I have a reward for you."

Lagati's ears perked. "I'm listening."

"You and Azazel have never seen eye to eye, is that right?"

"None of the Grigori have treated me with any affection."

Barakel let go of his shoulders. "Indeed, it is not in their nature. But there is something you could do about it."

"Which is?"

"I could restore your place of importance." Barakel stepped closer to the machine, grazing its smooth surfaces with his long, lean fingers.

Lagati waited for Barakel to finish, but he seemed in no hurry to do so. "Yes?" he prompted.

"I know a trick that would allow you to control your Grigori masters, just as our children's spirits control their human hosts. Are you interested?"

Lagati thought this was a rather stupid question.

NINETEEN

Srinagar, India
AUGUST 2

Gayle left her hotel under grey skies, just six hours after arriving in picturesque Srinagar, and arranged for a taxi. The city, nestled in the claustrophobic Kashmir Valley and surrounded by Himalayan daggers, was truly a paradise. A languid river flowed through the seemingly endless wetlands and sprawling suburbs of the perpetually conflict-ridden Kashmiri capital. In many ways, this was Venice's spiritual cousin. Forks of the river cut everywhere amidst a bevy of locals in low-riding wooden boats, many en route to market loaded with vegetables and fish. And the mountains! The Rockies east of Provo were rugged and snow-capped in their own right, but these were different. Taller. Sharper. Alien.

The taxi moved swiftly through streets packed with women in long, flowing abayat and men in t-shirts and blue jeans. Gayle resented the incongruity, but who was she to judge?

Today she had only one task on her mind.

Her ramshackle cab stopped on the edge of a busy plaza. A quick look out the window revealed the reason: the main street was adorned with tables displaying various wares—fruits and vegetables, fresh fish, bushels of grain, and clothing. The driver didn't speak English, but from the way he was gesturing it was clear he wanted her to get out. She wondered if he'd taken her to the right address or had simply gotten "close enough." She couldn't see any street signs or numbers on buildings, most of which were plastered in colorful posters and signage. Nevertheless, she got out and watched as the cab pulled around in a wide circle and drove back up the road.

Gayle walked through the tables, averting her eyes from the aggressive salesmen shouting at her in Urdu. She stopped occasionally to inspect the items on display. One rack held a selection of lovely front-buttoned caftans in colors other than the ominous black so prevalent on the city streets. She briefly fingered one before getting chased off by the dark-eyed gaze of the saleswoman. Maybe she just didn't like dealing with foreigners.

She headed for the sidewalk—well, what passed for a sidewalk, though it was actually finely trampled sand and mud—and looked for those accursed numbers. Nothing. The only markings were signs for local vendors.

Loud barking stole her attention. A woman screamed as a pack of dogs—three or four creatures with matted brown fur—hurtled through the tables, knocking the legs out from one and causing its contents to slide into the mud. The man minding the display cursed and kicked one of the mangy animals as it fled.

Faisal, where on earth are you?

She'd known Faisal for several years, though they'd never met in person. He was a member of her network of fellow sensitives and had been the first to report the influx of energy in the region. She had reached out to him before booking her flight to Srinigar, but he hadn't gotten back to her until this morning.

She felt a hand graze her right shoulder and she spun around.

"Peace, peace!" her assailant said as forcefully as he could through clenched teeth. Gayle readied herself to spring out of danger when he grabbed her hand. "It's me. Faisal."

Amazing how quickly terror could transform into relief! "How did you recognize me?"

"It was not hard." He cracked a smile. "Have you seen yourself?"

She took a few deep breaths, calming herself. She supposed she looked more than a little conspicuous. Western tourists probably crawled all over Srinagar, but not in this neighborhood.

"I have been watching for you," Faisal said. "Come with me."

"Where are we going?"

"I have a place."

He kept his hand clamped around her wrist, grasping a little too tightly, but she didn't complain.

Rain began to fall as Faisal led her to the end of the market, then crossed the street into a narrow alley bounded by low brick walls. Rainwater puddled in troughs in the gutted pavement, as wide and frequent as moon craters and almost impossible to avoid. Four houses down, Faisal reached into his pocket for a hefty skeleton key; the sweat on his forehead spoke to the exertion required to turn it in the lock and swing open the heavy metal gate.

"This way, this way," he beckoned, hurrying up to the door. He used the same key to open it.

Once inside, the door's own weight caused it to slam shut again.

Gayle's eyes adjusted to the low lighting. Faisal took off his shoes, his bare feet gliding over the concrete floor. Light poured in from a room at the back of the house, which is where they seemed to be headed. They reached a parlor with wooden chairs pulled tight in a circle around a Persian rug. Rain splashed against three tall windows.

"You came just in time," Gayle said. "I was starting to worry."

"I still can hardly believe you are here."

Gayle had to strain to make out Faisal's mumbled speech. His accent and low intonation made the words run together.

"Your email said you are looking for someone." Faisal picked up a lighter from a table just outside the circle and used it to ignite the wick of a bowl-shaped earthen oil lamp. The flame flickered to life as Faisal sat down and faced her. "Tell me why you are here."

Gayle slumped down. "My friend Elisabeth is missing. She came here, I believe, or somewhere nearby. She was investigating last week's burst of energy, so she may have been looking for the node."

"I see." Faisal appeared deep in thought, looking at the floor and rubbing his stubbled chin. "Then finding her could be a problem."

"Well, yes, I didn't think it would easy."

"You do not understand. If she was investigating the node, she may not have come to Srinagar."

"Why is that important?"

Faisal glanced up, making eye contact. "The politics in Kashmir are very complicated. You understand?"

"Yes." She wasn't sure she really did understand.

"That is good. I have determined that the node is not in the Indian-controlled region. Maybe somewhere near Gilgit. North."

"Near the Chinese border," Gayle said. "I already know this, Faisal. Near the Pakistan-Chinese border."

"Yes. You see the problem. Not in India. Pakistan."

Gayle hesitated, realizing her mistake. And what a colossal mistake. "Damn it. I thought it was in Kashmir, near Pakistan. Not *in* Pakistan."

"Kashmir is split, Gayle."

"So we need a way to get into Pakistan then. Is it difficult?"

"In Kashmir, everything is difficult. You must cross the Line of Control." Faisal returned a short time later with a piece of paper. He drew a crude line dividing the center of the page and turned it to her. He pointed to the left division. "This is Pakistan. Only one road goes there from Srinagar, a high mountain pass. Private cars are not allowed, only commercial traffic and a bus."

"Then I'll take the bus."

"For that, you will need an entry permit for Pakistan. Bus goes from Srinagar to Muzaffarabad. You can make application at the Regional Passport Office."

Her heart dropped. She didn't want to scuttle through this country's bureaucratic maze. "How long will that take?"

Faisal answered with a shrug. "I have never tried this. Never been to Pakistan."

In fact, Gayle got the impression he had never been out of India. Perhaps never out of the province. "Will you go with me?"

"Bring your papers and we can go now. I do not know if they will see you today, but we can try." He extinguished the oil lamp with his fingers. A trail of smoke sizzled up from the blackened wick. "Did you bring papers? Documents?"

"If you mean my passport, then yes."

"Good. Very good. We will take a taxi."

They left the house, hurrying down the alley in the opposite direction from the market. A ten-minute walk took them to the banks of a river, where a sea of those flat wooden boats bobbed in the water.

Faisal left Gayle on the road as he went down the muddy banks toward a group of boatmen. She felt a small thrill at the prospect of touring the city by water instead of the bumpy, barely navigable concrete trails that passed for roads.

Faisal's haggling only took a few moments, and then he was waving her down the embankment. Gayle watched her step to avoid the indignity of splashing head-first into the river.

"Come now," Faisal said as they climbed aboard. He indicated the boat. "Shikara. Fastest way. You will see."

The rear section of the boat had been covered by a brown tarpaulin to keep the rain out. Gayle sat on a low bench and breathed deeply. The boat's driver got down into the front, a lower position, and began to row them away from shore. Gayle dropped her hand over the side of the boat—the shikara, she corrected herself—and trailed her fingers through the cool water. Some small part of her anxiety evaporated.

The driver piloted the shikara with remarkable swiftness, cutting a sometimes jagged path through the crowded waterway. Gayle was astonished by the armada of similar boats; dozens crossed every which way. It seemed a miracle there weren't constant collisions, but these drivers knew what they were doing.

Precipitously tall brick and wooden structures leapt up along the banks, sometimes hugging vertical hills, interspersed against the accent of broad-leafed chinar trees. Men and women stood on balconies watching the chaotic traffic, some even from the steeply angled rooftops. The buildings were beautifully, if haphazardly, constructed.

Gayle held on to the edge of the boat as the driver suddenly took them on an abrupt turn, heading for the entrance to one of the river's tributaries. Their progress slowed somewhat as they fought their way upstream.

She looked up at the sound of the driver and Faisal speaking. When they were done, Faisal called back to her, "We are almost there. Just five minutes more."

She smiled and nodded, the wind blowing through her hair. In truth she wasn't in the smallest hurry for the ride to end. She hadn't been this stress-free in a long time. She savored every moment, knowing the bliss was momentary.

To her surprise, the river took a sharp bend, then widened until she could no longer keep the opposing banks in view at the same time.

"Dal Lake," Faisal informed her as they sped over the water, its traffic only barely less crowded than the maze of canals in the city proper. The sky had cleared somewhat, allowing a few columns of sun to bear down on the lake's myriad inhabitants. "A famous place. Very beautiful."

He was certainly on-point about the lake's beauty. Tiny islands teemed with trees, their long branches drooping into the water. Most of the islands were home to stilted houses only accessible by boat.

The shikara's driver angled toward shore and a busy highway. Her anxiety returned in full force when she beheld the enormous concrete cube awaiting them. A long horizontal sign stretched from one side of the building to the other, the length required to fit all its text, transcribed in several languages. The only English word Gayle spotted was the one she needed to know they'd come to the right place: PASSPORT.

When they stopped, Faisal paid the driver and they disembarked.

They waited on the side of the road for the traffic to either clear or stop long enough for them to scurry across. Neither eventuality seemed likely. The minutes crept by without a break in traffic, and Gayle grew increasingly impatient.

At last, Faisal grew tired of waiting, grabbed her by the arm, and made a break for it. Gayle let slip an involuntary scream. On two occasions, she was sure they would be hit, but the car always slowed or swerved in time, without so much as a honk of the horn.

When in Srinagar, she thought as they reached safety.

Faisal stopped outside the doors to the passport office. "I will wait."

"Outside? No, Faisal, I need you to come with me."

"You go alone. I will be here."

"But what if they don't speak English?"

"It is government. Someone will speak English, I am very sure."

Faisal seemed to have grown roots. For whatever reason, his body language said he absolutely did not want to go inside the passport office. Gayle didn't understand it, and to be honest she felt a little bit offended that he would take her all this way and not go in with her. Then again, she barely knew the man. He had already gone miles out of his way, so perhaps it wasn't reasonable to presume too much.

She missed Henry most of all in moments like these. He had given her the confidence to undertake the sorts of profoundly uncomfortable tasks now required of her with little or no support.

"All right," she said in resignation. "Don't go anywhere. I'll be back."

"Even if you take an hour—or two hours—I will stay."

And if it takes three or four? she wondered, haunted by the sorts of endless DMV queues back home. She didn't ask the question. Faisal wouldn't come in, but he also wouldn't abandon her. She knew honor when she saw it.

As soon as she stepped inside, she knew she needn't have worried about queues. The only furniture in the front room were two desks, just one of them occupied, and five empty chairs whose metallic legs stabbed into the well-scratched laminate floor.

A bearded man behind the desk stared at her through sad eyes and said something in Urdu, slowly, emphasizing the language's long vowels. He may as well have been speaking Korean. Didn't matter how slowly he said it.

"I'm sorry," Gayle said. "I don't speak Urdu. Only English."

The man stared uncomprehendingly, scratched the long greying hairs in his thick beard, then repeated himself. Afterward he stared at her through suspicious beady eyes. Stalemate.

"English?" She tried to sound as apologetic as possible.

He frowned, his lips forming an impressive upside-down U, then stood gruffly and exited through a squeaky door whose hinges hadn't been oiled in some time. Gayle sat in one of the metal chairs and waited.

And waited and waited. At least ten minutes passed before she looked up at the sound of the door's atonal whine. Two men came out—the first was the bearded man, and the second was younger, with unkempt jet-black hair and profuse eyebrows. He couldn't have been more than twenty.

"You, English?" the younger man asked, moving to the unoccupied desk.

Gayle got up and took a chair on that side of the room. "Yes, thank you. I would like to apply for an entry permit for Pakistan."

The man's forehead stitched up in a look of perfect confusion. "You are Kashmiri citizen?"

"No. American."

He lowered his palm flat against the desktop. "No permit for American. Just Kashmiri. You see?"

No, I don't see, she didn't say. "Let me explain," she said instead, trying to use simple vocabulary he would be more likely to understand. "I have to go to Pakistan. Take the bus."

"You want Srinagar-Muzaffarabad line, yes?"

"That's right." She recognized the name of the Pakistani city, the one Faisal had mentioned. "As soon as possible."

"No, no," he said, shaking his head with great vigor. "Bus for Kashmiri only. No tourist."

Gayle sat in shocked silence. Could it be true? She didn't have time to cross anywhere else.

"I say sorry, but no ride for American."

She made eye contact with the bearded man at the other desk, hoping for a respite against these nonsensical rules. All she got from him was a dark glare which didn't need translation.

She didn't say anything as she stood up and hurried outside.

"You get the permit?" Faisal asked, coming alongside her.

"Apparently the bus can only carry Kashmiri citizens."

"So you are staying in Srinagar."

"No, Faisal." She put an arm on his shoulder. "So we will find another way."

TWENTY

Yellowknife, Canada
AUGUST 2

The tundra looked nothing like Brighton had imagined. He'd pictured grey, squishy swampland as far as the eye could see. Perhaps if the float plane were to land, he'd find the ground as marshy and smelly as an old sponge, but the aerial view made it out to be a vast, flat garden sprouting flowers of innumerable vibrant colors. The ground rolled from one low rise to the next, interspersed with occasional outcroppings of rock. A strong wind made the scrubland dance. He had spotted a handful of abandoned mines so far, marked by towers of rotting wood, steel scaffolding, and open pits. The pilot of the float plane, Regan, explained that most of these were gold mines, the former lifeblood of the northern economy.

While the plane was in the air, Abranel forced Brighton to stare out the craft's small window, forced him to stare so long and hard that his eyes watered. Abranel wouldn't even let him blink, keeping his eyes open for so long that he thought his eyes would dry up, shrivel, and fall out of their sockets. But when compared to being compelled to kill another human being in cold blood, it didn't seem so bad. At least the pain was only inflicted on himself. He could endure it.

"I find you to be a curiosity, Sherwood," Abranel spoke quietly.

How so?

"You are quite selfless. You didn't even know that man's name."

I didn't need to know him. I certainly didn't want him to die.

"In all things, sacrifices must be made." Abranel allowed him to blink. Profound physical relief washed over Brighton. "I think I like you."

You have a funny way of showing it.

"Whatever my level of affection for you, I have been given an important assignment. I must attend to my duties. My grandfather would be displeased if I failed to teach you such valuable lessons, and when my grandfather is displeased…" He pursed his lips. "Well, you must have an inkling of how he expresses his displeasure. It pales in comparison to mine."

Abranel was a psychopath.

"That's an unkind characterization, especially between friends."

We are not friends.

"We will be, in time. Once you come to appreciate what I bring to this relationship, and I am allowed to make it more reciprocal in nature."

Brighton felt his lips turn up in an inappropriate smile.

"Yes, we will be great friends, and accomplish great things together."

Brighton did his best to silence his thoughts as the plane turned in a wide arc and began its return run to Yellowknife. It wasn't possible to stop thinking altogether, but mindlessness was the only thing that kept Abranel quiet. Abranel used Brighton's own thoughts to bait him again and again. Brighton strived to give him as few opportunities as possible.

How do you know we're searching in the right area?

"We received telemetry as the ship was going down. We're at least in the neighborhood."

Nearly an hour later, they swung out over the choppy waters of Great Slave Lake. Brighton had grown accustomed to this view. The plane only had enough fuel to stay in the air five or six hours, so they returned at least once a day to take advantage of the long daylight.

As they banked, Abranel reached down and unclicked the seatbelt just before the plane veered into Yellowknife Bay. Brighton tumbled headfirst out of the seat and smacked his forehead against the bulkhead in front of him.

"You okay?" Regan called back.

"Yeah," Abranel said as he slid back into the chair, that same inappropriate smile plastered to his face. "Forgot the seatbelt."

"Careful there. That's a good way to get yourself seriously hurt."

Damn you.

Abranel said nothing except turn and look out the window. A steady trickle of blood dripped down his forehead and onto his nose. Abranel refused to wipe it away.

The city rose on a rocky promontory to the west. Houses and apartment blocks crowded the lakefront, with the more prominent downtown rising atop the hills behind. The city was small enough that it all more or less fit into one panoramic view.

Brighton felt only a slight bump as the twin pontoons hit the water. After the initial splash, the plane taxied through the bay, its nose pointing up over the horizon. Regan cut their speed of approach and angled toward the narrow opening between the mainland and a forested island fronted by a few dozen mousy houseboats with sailboats and dinghies tethered to them.

Beyond the city's marina stood a long series of warehouses and historical buildings reflecting the rugged character of the region's gold rush nearly a century before. These were long rectangular structures, often constructed from thin logs and cedar siding. Most were outfitted with steep-pitched tin roofs, probably to prevent snow buildup during the harsh winter months. Their destination, one such warehouse with red-and-white siding, housed a small private airport that served the prospecting companies who set up shop here.

"Same time tomorrow," Abranel said as he jumped out the door and landed with both feet on a wooden dock. The cool wind whistled off the water, and he shivered.

"You wanna tell me what you're looking for?" Regan joined him on the dock and slammed the door behind him. "That'll make it three days. Getting mighty expensive."

"I'll make another deposit in the morning. Whatever it costs, I'll pay. I can't afford an interruption."

"Let's talk details tomorrow," Regan said. "I can promise at least one more day. After that, I've got other commitments."

Brighton knew that if Abranel needed the plane for a fourth day, he'd get it.

Abranel trotted toward the street snaking through the warehouse district. He then generously turned over control for the fifteen-minute walk uphill to the hotel. Not so generous, really.

*   *   *

When Brighton opened his eyes, fresh off the climax of a harrowing nightmare whose fuzzy details grew all the fuzzier as he tried to recollect them, he found himself alone. Really alone—the first time he'd felt that way since Pakistan. He flexed his fingers as a test. Obligingly, they slid over the sheets. He could hardly believe his good fortune. Every other time he'd awoken, Abranel had been right there, ready and determined to pluck every precious moment of his freedom away. That damned Abra—

Don't even think the name, he thought, trying and failing in the attempt. Thinking the name was like calling him.

Brighton approached the window and drew back the heavy blinds, heavy enough to keep the room in darkness even during the most persistent summer daylight. Just now, however, the sky was good and dark save for a smudge of faint purple over the lake.

Suddenly, Brighton didn't know what to do with himself.

Abranel—hard to avoid thinking it when Brighton's whole life revolved around him—had been exercising almost constant control since arriving in Yellowknife. Was it possible he'd reached his limits? Was Abranel exhausted?

Brighton decided to find out by staying up. Besides, it would be a waste of free time to go back to bed, no matter his physical exhaustion.

He rode the elevator to the main floor and crossed the lobby to the bar. He was disappointed to find it closed, despite the fact that it was only a little past midnight. Inconvenient as hell.

He turned and headed for the front door. There were other establishments nearby, and he didn't mind taking a walk.

The view outside the hotel's front door caught him off-guard. The building was perched on one of the highest points in the city, so the view was particularly lovely.

But the terrestrial view was nothing compared to the celestial ballet overhead. Constantly shifting prisms of multihued green and white performed an unearthly dance, swirling in concentric rings like a miniature spiral galaxy, expanding and intensifying.

The aurora, he realized, spellbound. The shock of it made his mouth fall open, and no natural force could force him to clamp it shut again. He hadn't expected such a sight in these waning days of high summer.

He'd seen images of the aurora borealis, and even a few poorly rendered videos on social media, but none had prepared him for the awesome experience of seeing its unrestrained majesty in real-time. For a moment, he felt as though he stood just below a glass bowl as milk was poured into it from above, splashing and cascading through the heavens over a transparent barrier that prevented the light from falling to earth and drowning them all in its cosmic radiance.

In the presence of such spectacle, Brighton felt something he hadn't felt in ages—joy. The joy coursed through him in waves, bringing a sting of tears to his eyes. The lights moved to their own silent rhythm, a strangely literal manifestation of the freedom he'd been robbed of, and the hope that one day his freedom might be restored to him, if only he persevered against the almost overwhelming temptation to give up.

The doors to the hotel opened and Brighton turned to regard a dark, human-shaped outline.

"Have you seen the lights?" Brighton asked the stranger.

The stranger cautiously came out from under the shadow of the building and Brighton saw she was a woman. The aurora lights played off her face as she looked up.

"No, not until today," she said with a hint of French inflexion to belie her staunch Japanese features. "It is beautiful."

Brighton nodded. That was a transcendent understatement, but words could only go so far.

"What brings you to Yellowknife?" he asked.

"I'm a tourist."

Indeed, Brighton had seen a number of Japanese tourists wandering the streets, though Regan had told them the tourist population exploded during the winter months, high season for the Japanese despite the bone-chilling cold. He'd said there was a saying in their culture asserting that conceiving under the northern lights brought good fortune. Or a higher proportion of sons versus daughters. Or gifted youngsters in general. Brighton was unclear on the specifics.

"Did you bring someone to conceive with?" Brighton asked, allowing himself a smile.

She stared back at him with confusion and a sizable helping of well-earned indignation. "Excuse me?"

"Sorry, I didn't mean…" He blushed, feeling mortified. "That really was a stupid thing to say. Someone told me a story about… well, it doesn't matter."

The woman turned her attention back to the sky. It was impossible to look away for more than a few moments.

"You have a name?" Brighton asked.

She didn't answer for the longest time. At first, Brighton interpreted her silence as mere distraction. The lights *were* distracting. But as the moment stretched on, Brighton began to wonder if there was something deeper at work. Reluctance. He was certain he'd never met this woman before, so what reason did she have to play coy?

"Annie," she said at last, though she didn't make eye contact.

"It's good to meet you, Annie."

Without warning, she retreated toward the hotel. "Me too," she tossed over her shoulder as she went back inside.

He didn't need a degree in psychology to know she didn't mean it. He also didn't have much time to dwell on his odd encounter, for a moment later Abranel woke up.

TWENTY-ONE

Singapore

AUGUST 3

The bustling port of Singapore stretched south of the main island like a hundred stubby fingers curling possessively around the tiny city-state's bays and inlets. Islands crowded the strait, many with shorelines too angular to be natural. Land reclaimed from the sea, Dario presumed. In Singapore, where the scarcity of land dictated its high value, the incredible cost of raising these precious square feet could be easily justified.

All around, towers of glass and steel reflected the humbling blues, oranges, and pinks of the setting sun. Each of these innumerable highrises was marked by row upon row of stacked windows, their horizontal fluorescent hues imposing a sense of order against the chaotic backdrop of the financial district.

Dario sucked back a breath, overwhelmed. He brought up his half-empty glass of red wine and drained it in a single gulp—not the way his nona had taught him. He put the glass down on a passing server's tray and smoothed the front of his suit. More of a tuxedo, really. He felt uncomfortable despite the impeccably tailored folds clinging to him like he'd been born to wear them. He would have preferred the khaki work garb he'd thrown on every day of his tenure at Herculaneum, but it would have drawn inordinate attention at a swanky dinner party like this one. He did his best to walk with confidence, comporting himself as though he often ran in such urbane circles.

From the legion of humorless waiters sprang a young man with an expression one could charitably describe as "slackened." Dario thought Singaporeans must have a social stigma against overt emotionalism, for most of the people he'd met so far were friendly but as bland as his great-aunt's homemade pasta. Perhaps this waiter, having been instructed to ensure no guest's wine ran empty, had seen him deposit his empty glass on the tray; Dario soon held a fresh supply in his right hand and some sort of flaky pastry in the other, balanced carefully in the center of a white cloth napkin with blue hand-stitched embroidery.

He brought the wine glass to his lips and sipped at its contents. He had to control his nerves; there'd be no upside to drinking too much, and plenty of downsides.

He looked clear across the crowded reception room packed to the gills with guests moving around with expressions of muted excitement. It worked to his advantage that few of these guests knew each other as close, personal friends and therefore might not notice Dario's discomfiture. It was a trade conference, attended by the overly formal government officials of fifty or more countries, not a backyard family wedding.

It's not wise to stand so long in one place, he told himself. *People might start to notice your lack of engagement.*

Dario chose a random spot on the other end of the room and began to walk slowly toward it, nodding and smiling at the occasional person who dared make eye contact. As he did so, he made quick note of a few very particular details Ira had instructed him about—their height, the set of their jaws, their posture, and the symmetry of their facial features. In other words, how closely did they resemble Trevor?

"The Watchers will almost certainly be there, expecting to go undetected," Ira had told him upon their arrival in Singapore. "This is the perfect event to infiltrate, with representatives from most major governments present."

Dario felt vaguely promiscuous as he found himself evaluating every man's physique. Despite his best efforts at discretion, many of these men noticed the undue attention. There was no way around it. Most men ignored him, but a few looked back. In one mortifying case, a man looked back *invitingly*. Dario wanted to crawl under a rock—or a table, at least, seeing as there were no rocks handy.

"Can I help you?" a dark-haired Asian man asked.

Dario realized he'd been caught staring again. He swallowed his embarrassment while dutifully noting the man was too short by far. "No. No, I don't think so."

He hurried off, picking up speed as he felt the man's eyes drilling into his back.

Dario stepped through an opening in the crowd and discovered himself standing adjacent to the string quartet whose music he'd so far barely registered. The violinists were trilling their way through one of Vivaldi's Four Seasons—Spring, he thought. Twin spotlights aimed down at them from the high ceilings. Lines of sweat on the cellist's forehead betrayed just how hotly those lights shone. Just a few feet away, an open door led onto the terrace. Clutching his wine glass, Dario slipped out.

The night air offered little respite. Even with the sun having set an hour or two before, the heat and humidity felt oppressive.

The terrace formed a long isosceles triangle, its far point a lengthy walk from the reception room entrance, though the walk seemed appealing enough. Tall emperor palms guided the path on either side, and for a short while Dario was able to forget that he was on the one hundredth floor of a high-rise. When he reached the end of the path, however, he found himself perched at the farthest extent of the terrace, shaped like the prow of a mighty ship. The view of the city might have been breathtaking had he not felt like throwing up from the vertigo. How easy it would be to clamber up the railing and fling himself into a lethal freefall.

Dario turned back toward the building, noticing for the first time that the ground to either side of the path was covered in lush grass. This was more of a garden than a terrace. A stunning architectural achievement, not that he needed to look far to find other examples in Singapore.

Far off, he heard the quartet's harmonies trail into silence, and a moment later the season turned. Winter, with its distinctive pizzicato highlights, a small part of him annoyed that they were performing the concertos out of order.

"You are one of the European delegates?" someone to his right asked. "Which country?"

Dario turned to find a man and a woman approaching, the woman in an arresting blue gown that shimmered under the park lamps. He braced himself for… well, he didn't know what he braced himself for, but he didn't know these people. Why were they drawing him out?

It could be they're just friendly, he told himself, though he scoffed at the improbability. He'd grown accustomed to harboring suspicions of anyone who showed kindness when polite indifference would do.

"Italy," Dario said guardedly. That was what his fake credentials said. It had the added benefit of being his actual homeland.

"Oh, Italy is wonderful," the woman said. "I spent a month in Rome last year. There's nothing like it."

Dario forced a smile. When people found out where he was from, they almost universally regaled him with details of their trips to Rome.

He said nothing, hoping his silence would encourage them to move on.

The man put out of his hand, and Dario shook it with reluctance.

"Stewart Dougherty, from the Australian delegation," he said.

Dario wished he had an equivalent story of some misbegotten college adventure in Melbourne, so much so that he almost made one up. Not worth the risk, even if he hadn't been on a clandestine mission.

"Isn't Singapore lovely? Is this your first time?" The woman smiled at him. A sweet smile. Potentially insincere.

"Yes, it is," Dario said in answer to either question. Didn't matter which. "I'll see you inside."

He knew it would be interpreted rudely, but he spun toward the reception room and walked at a steady clip. The couple hadn't met the physical characteristics of the Watchers, so likely their interest was innocent. Still, he didn't want to spend his time in idle conversation.

As he passed, he noticed a young woman staring at him. She leaned against a park bench, bathed by yellow lamplight. She had close-cropped blond hair, but that was about the only observation he had time to make as he hurried past. He could feel her eyes on him even with his back turned, but he dared not stop and do a prominent double-take.

How paranoid of him! In the last hour, no one he'd seen had fit Ira's description. Ira was probably wrong, and the trip a waste of time. These party guests were human, human, incontrovertibly human.

Dario aimed himself for the door, once again on the lookout for Watcher lookalikes. Before he could get inside, a security guard blocked his path.

"Excuse me, sir, could I see your identification?"

Dario hesitated, wondering at how tight the security was that they wouldn't let people back into the party even after they'd already been cleared downstairs. He reached into his pocket and retrieved his credentials. The guard shone a flashlight onto it, then snatched it away from him.

"A moment, sir."

The security guard pulled a stapled booklet of paper from the inside of his jacket and scanned its contents. A guest list, Dario realized. If it was the same as the list downstairs, he'd be okay.

The guard flipped through the pages, then lowered them to get a better view in the low light. The viewing angle was now flat enough for Dario to see some of the names, one of which happened to be Stewart Dougherty from Australia.

But then Dario caught the name just under it—a name so surprising, so conspicuous that he couldn't believe he'd read it until he looked again and confirmed that it was there, in black and white. There could be no mistake.

It's not possible, he told himself.

The name stared back at him long after the guard had flipped to another page of his makeshift book. Rhea Dunford.

Rhea Dunford!

The odds implied this was a simple coincidence. Coincidences did happen, with some frequency, in everyday life. But he couldn't accept that, not tonight, and not under these circumstances.

"Very good, I see it now." The guard handed Dario his credentials. "Sorry to disturb you. Go on inside."

Dario continued on, but he did so with hackles raised. At least one other person at this event wasn't who she appeared to be.

*   *   *

Ira looked up at the sound of knocking. Before he could get up, Janene rushed to the door and looked through the peephole.

"Who is it?" Ira asked.

Janene turned to him. "Three men in suits."

"Well, that could be anybody. As long as it's not hotel security."

They heard more knocks, and this time a voice called from the hall. "Mr. Binyamin? I'm here with the ambassador."

Ira stood and snapped his fingers at Janene. She glared at him as she pried the door open. Two security men pushed into the suite, performing a routine inspection. One of them entered the bathroom, then came back in.

"All clear," the slighter of the two guards called toward the door.

A moment later, a man with chubby cheeks and a pasty-white complexion entered at a saunter. His jacket was open, one hand in his pocket, his other hand loosening his necktie.

"You Ira Binyamin?" he asked in a Texas drawl.

Ira nodded. "And you must be Ambassador Kirkland."

"That's me." Kirkland gestured to his two security agents. "Sorry, but I had to take the precaution. They've tightened security around here before the trade pact's signing. Some threats, if I hear correctly."

"It's perfectly understandable, Your Excellency," Ira said.

"You know it's serious business when they call you 'Your Excellency,' don't you think?"

"I believe that's the official protocol for addressing a sitting ambassador, sir."

Kirkland nodded once. "But I can't stand it."

"Very well. Ambassador then."

"Yes, that's fine." Kirkland pointed to one of the seats clustered around the window. "Mind if I sit?"

"Please do."

"My office informs me you requested a meeting three times. If you don't mind me saying so, that makes your business sound a mite urgent. Either that or you're a waste of my time."

"It is urgent," Ira said. He spared a moment to check on Janene, perched on the side of the bed. "Hopefully you'll agree with that assessment."

"We checked into you. You're not a member of any of the participating nations' diplomatic staffs. That leaves me wondering what you're doing here, and whether you're a security threat."

"There *is* a security threat, I'm afraid, but it's not me."

"Those are ominous words, Mr. Binyamin."

"I don't deny it. But there's a faction out to infiltrate this conference and interfere with the signing. Count on it."

Kirkland drew a long breath, obviously troubled. "Go on then."

*   *   *

Dario maintained his calm all the way to the elevator, and then during the long wait between pressing the button and the door opening. He had to share the elevator ride with several strangers, so he still couldn't afford to lose his cool.

Rhea Dunford is dead, he repeated over and over, picturing her face, hearing her voice. *Rhea Dunford is dead. Rhea Dunford is dead.*

He got off on the sixtieth floor and held himself from running through the hall, even though there were no eyes to observe him. No human eyes, anyway; the place must be swarming with security cameras.

He stopped at Ira's suite and knocked, perhaps harder than he'd intended. No one answered for a moment.

"Ira, it's Dario. Let me in."

The door opened. Janene's face showed annoyance. "Dario, he's in the middle of a meeting with the ambassador."

"Sorry, but I think I found what we're looking for."

Janene raised an eyebrow and closed the door behind Dario.

A middle-aged man with receding hair sat in one of the chairs by the window. America's ambassador to Singapore, the Honorable Jonathan Kirkland. And two security agents who crowded around Dario upon his entrance.

"He's with me," Ira told them. The men backed off. "What did you see, Dario?"

"Do you want me to say it here, Ira?"

A befuddled expression crossed the poor ambassador's face. He clearly had no idea what to make of all this excitement.

"Yes, right here," Ira said. "I was just telling the ambassador to expect trouble at the conference. May I presume you have found some trouble?"

"One of the attendees is using an alias." Dario left out the part about his own credentials being forged. There were some things the ambassador didn't need explained just now.

"The Grigori then."

"Actually, I'm not so sure. I looked for people bearing the physical characteristics you mentioned but didn't see any obvious examples."

Ira joined Janene at the foot of the bed. "Then how do you know someone's using—"

"Because I saw a name on the security list that belongs to a dead woman."

Kirkland stood up. "Son, how do you know she's dead?"

"She died right in front me, sir. About a week ago, in Bolivia."

"What's her name?" Kirkland asked.

"Rhea Dunford."

"You do realize there's bound to be more than one person with that name."

"The ambassador's right, Dario," Ira said. "There must be dozens of Rhea Dunfords."

Intellectually, Dario knew this was true. "There's a connection. I know it."

"Has this person used the alias in the past?" Kirkland asked.

"No." It sounded feeble in Dario's own ears. Still, there was no room for doubt. "It's not like that. I believe the person," and he used the term loosely, "who killed Rhea is now impersonating her. Or at least using her name."

Kirkland weighed this. "All right, son. We'll look into it." He nodded once at his security team. One of them sprang to life, pressing a button on the comm looped over his ear. He immediately began speaking to someone in another part of the building.

"I think we should investigate this ourselves," Ira said, already on his way toward the door.

The second security guard intervened and put his hand against the closed door.

"I wouldn't advise that," Kirkland said. "In fact, I forbid it. Mr. Binyamin, you've already acknowledged that you don't have security clearance. I'm going to have you escorted from the premises." He turned to Dario. "You, too. We'll take it from here."

The guard at the door clamped down a hand on Ira's shoulder. The rabbi winced in pain, but then closed his eyes and seemed to accept it. That was unlike Ira, but at least they'd done their part by alerting security to the threat.

Except we didn't come here to stop the threat to the conference, Dario reminded himself. *We came to find the Grigori, and we haven't found them yet.*

The guard emitted a howl of surprise, then yanked his hand back from Ira's shoulder. Ira's hand glowed warmly as he reached up to remove the guard's grip.

"Ira, don't do it," Janene said, raising her voice.

"Don't worry, Janene. I can control it this time. You'll see."

"What are you talking about?" Kirkland asked.

Dario watched, helpless, as Ira placed his red-hot hand against the guard's chest. The guard slumped. Kirkland called out for help, and the other guard was on them a second later.

Ira raised his palm against the other guard, and this was enough for the man to think twice. He stopped in midstride.

"Ambassador, back away," the second guard said.

The warning was unnecessary, for Kirkland had already escaped to the far side of the room, the bed and several other pieces of furniture between him and Ira.

"Mr. Binyamin, I believed you when you said you weren't a threat," Kirkland said. "I see that I shouldn't have."

"I have no time to explain," Ira said. "You'll be safer if you stay put."

"Safe from what?"

Ira declined to answer. "Dario, we need to find this imposter. Now."

Dario wasted no time. He reached down and pulled the first guard just far enough away from the door for Dario to squeeze into the hall. The corridor was empty all the way to the elevators three doors down.

"Are you coming?" Dario asked, throwing a glance over his shoulder. Behind them, Janene stayed put. That was probably for the best.

Ira stood halfway in the doorway. "In a minute. Go on ahead."

*   *   *

Ira held his palms up to his face, staring at the familiar creases in the skin. They were the same hands as always, the same human hands, endowed with Jehovah's power, the same potential he believed was available to every man and woman, though rarely fanned into flame.

"What the hell did you do?" Kirkland tried to keep his voice flat, but Ira detected a quaver of fear.

"Don't be afraid of me."

"Why did you ask for this meeting?"

Ira walked closer to the bed; in response, Kirkland backed up against the wall. Meanwhile, Janene sank into one of the chairs by the window. She watched the scene transpire, silent and speechless.

"I told you there's a faction out to interfere with the conference," Ira said. "I didn't get a chance to explain that it's not a *human* faction."

Kirkland scoffed.

Ira raised the palm he'd just used on the guard now sprawled on the floor. He didn't mean it as a threat; nonetheless, Kirkland shied away.

"Don't scoff." Ira poured all his effort into delivering the statement as nonthreateningly as possible. "The power I've just demonstrated has…" How could he say this without coming across as a religious nut job? "What you saw was a demonstration of extraterrestrial power."

Misleading, yes, but *extraterrestrial* was certainly accurate in the strictest sense.

"Are you saying you're an alien?" Kirkland asked.

"Of course not." Ira sighed, realizing he'd inadvertently led the ambassador to exactly that conclusion. "Rather, I learned how to do this through an extraterrestrial."

"And they're trying to stop the conference?"

"I didn't say that. In fact, I believe they want the trade pact signed. They're here to infiltrate, not obliterate."

The obliteration will come later, he thought grimly.

Explaining the Grigori threat would be next to impossible without resorting to religious intimations—and there was no better way to get someone's back up than to go on about religion.

A further demonstration would do the talking for him.

TWENTY-TWO

Singapore

AUGUST 3

When Dario returned to the reception room, the quartet had swapped Vivaldi for Mozart. Well-heeled men and women slipped past each other in tight, constantly shifting configurations like a school of fish avoiding a predator—though the identity of the predator thwarted Dario as he stared into the mass of blank expressions and politic smiles. He could think of only one person who might want to use Rhea's name, and that was the one who had killed her—Ohia. And Ohia could have taken any host, anyone at all.

He has shown a preference for women, he reminded himself. First Yasmine, then Rhea, followed by that unknown redhead who'd led the attack on the Khunjerab slope. All of them dead now, but together they formed a pattern. Not that it helped. At least a third of the delegates were women. He could look right at Ohia and be none the wiser.

Providence chose that moment to shine down on him. Amidst the crowd, Dario's searching gaze lingered on a woman he had seen before. The young woman who had stared at him out on the terrace earlier, the blond by the park bench, under the lamp.

Could it be so simple? It was unreasonable to suspect her based on a brief moment of shared eye contact.

Dario turned away and walked in the opposite direction, planning to circle around the room, behind the quartet, and catch her unawares.

And then what?

He had no friggin' clue.

Dario deployed as quickly as he dared without drawing attention to himself, declining three offers of dessert wine. He kept close to the outside walls and avoided looking back except for the occasional glance to ensure his target hadn't moved out of position.

As he crossed behind the quartet, he got his first unobstructed look at the woman. She wore a green gown with a slit halfway up her right thigh, revealing milky flesh. She was deep in conversation with a man of average build. His hair was swept to the left, pressed so tightly to his scalp that it revealed a straight white crease along the part. The man laughed at something she said, then turned his face just enough for Dario to get a good look—

Dario took a step backward.

It couldn't be him. Not here. It made no sense.

He dared a closer inspection of the man's face, holding it just long enough to confirm that this was truly Doctor Wallis Christophe. His ID badge even bore the flag of Bolivia, even though Dario knew Christophe wasn't originally from there.

His mind whirled at the implications. Christophe's presence certainly supported Dario's hunch that this woman might be Ohia. The site coordinator at Tiahuanaco had been enraptured with Ohia from the start, had summoned government officials to the city to meet her.

Dario changed his mind. It made perfect sense. Christophe and his contacts in the Bolivian government would have been the ideal way for Ohia to infiltrate the signing.

Indecision paralyzed him. *Ira, I need you.*

*   *   *

Ira swept out of the elevator and stopped in front of the security checkpoint. Beyond the line of Singaporeans in uniform, he saw the party in full swing. Mournful strings poured out of the reception hall just loud enough to obscure the many private conversations all around him.

He had to get into the reception hall, and he didn't have a badge. He also didn't have much time. Kirkland and his guards were safe in the hotel suite, out cold, with Janene watching over them; they wouldn't stay that way forever.

Let's get in and out, he thought to himself.

Ira closed his eyes and envisioned a minimally invasive way into the room. A wave of dizziness hit him as he waded into the river's shallow banks, feeling the sand squish between his toes. He fell backward against the wall next to the elevator, steadying himself. So odd to perceive himself in two places at once…

"Are you okay, sir?" someone asked.

Ira opened his eyes to find one of the checkpoint guards watching him closely. With concern? With suspicion? The man's features didn't give away his emotional state.

"Yes, I'm fine." Ira closed his eyes again, shutting out the real world and focusing on the river which he'd spent so much time in these past few days. The water embraced him up to his hips.

He imagined perfect stillness, and all the sounds of the enclosing forest stopped—no chirping of birds or buzzing of insects, no splashing of fish or whistling of wind. Only the steady downward pull of water.

When Ira opened his senses to the hotel again, the first thing he heard was the music. The party went on unabated, but the men at the checkpoint had frozen like flies trapped in amber. He wished he had the skill to affect the entire party, but he had to be satisfied with a ten-foot radius. Next to him, people had stopped in midstride, mid-sentence. They weren't truly frozen, he knew, just moving at a pace so sluggish as to be imperceptible.

Ira walked into the midst of the checkpoint, stepping around the guard who had enquired after him. How long before everyone no-ticed? He hadn't tried this before. He couldn't even guess how it would work on the human mind.

A chorus of screams answered that question. People were begin-ning to take notice. He had to move fast or risk losing his advantage.

*   *   *

Dario's head shot up when he heard screaming. He jumped onto the quartet's raised dais for a better view and saw that people were push-ing at each other in a rush to get away from the room's main entrance. People streamed out onto the terrace. Right next to him, the violinist threw his chair back and made a run for it. Conversely, the people closest to the entrance weren't moving at all. In fact, they seemed more or less frozen.

What the hell was going on?

But not everyone at the doors was immobile. A solitary figure swept into the reception room, the eye of an extraordinarily still hurri-cane, a bubble-like tableau spreading around him in a circular perime-ter. Dario didn't need to look closely to know it was Ira. As people tried to get away, many became entrapped in Ira's wake. The effect was that everyone could *see* him, but no one could get close enough to stop him. A few security types gathered at the boundary, trying to formulate a plan while continually gauging its edges so as not to get entangled. Dario smiled at the futility of their efforts. Ira was savvier and more powerful than they could ever hope to be.

"Ira!" Dario shouted over the din. "Ira, over here!"

Ira didn't seem to hear him, but Ohia certainly did. The woman in the green dress looked up at him right away, then reacted by pulling Christophe with her toward the terrace doors.

"Ira!" he tried again.

Dario had to act fast. Another few seconds and Ohia and Christophe might get outside, and from there he would lose them. He hurled himself after Ohia, leaping off the dais and hitting the woman in the back. He knocked her over. It felt strange tackling a woman, never mind such a beautiful one, but Dario felt no regret. She fought him, trying to buck him off, but Dario grabbed her arms and pinned them behind her back.

"Ira, I've got her!" Dario suddenly remembered Christophe, and looked up just in time to catch the man disappearing into the herd of panicking delegates.

Ohia's frenzied struggle slackened, but only to the degree that Dario noticed his own movements had slowed considerably. Was it his imagination? No. He attempted to crane his neck to check Ira's position, but he didn't need to; Ira had to be close. Very close. Nearly on top of them, he'd wager.

Dario felt his mental capacities grow frustratingly lethargic, thick, weighty, every thought and movement requiring an interminably long time to process.

And then he had no thoughts at all.

*   *   *

Panic faded into the background of Ira's awareness as he knelt next to the strange scene: Dario perched atop a short-haired blond woman in a green dress, his knee jammed into the small of her back while he kept her arms pinned tight. She obviously wasn't a Grigori; it was a Nephilim spirit possessing a hapless woman's body. That made her extraordinarily dangerous.

And knowledgeable, he added. A source of information was exactly what they needed, and here it was, delivered as though from on high.

As strenuous as his efforts had been so far, what came next would be much harder. He stooped down next to the pair locked in a fighting stance, then placed one palm on each body, warm despite their death-like appearance. Both of their hearts beat, ever so faintly, their metabolic activities reduced to the lowest levels needed to sustain life.

"I may need some help with this," Ira whispered. If Jehovah was listening and aware of what was happening here, he gave no indication.

Ira had so much power to balance—the stasis effect, with so many bodies caught in its intricate web, was incredibly draining—and now he needed to add a fresh set of calculations. The complexities needed to achieve translation were near impossible in the best of circumstances; this was among one of the worst. He closed his eyes, the skin on his forehead stitching into deep trenches. Numbers large and small, variables, coefficients, polynomials, and quadratic formulas floated in his intellectual ether, resisting the pull to cohere. The current raged as he fought for control. Profuse sweat broke out all over his face, on his arms and legs, crawling over his skin like a colony of stinging red ants.

I can't do it, he realized. It was that simple.

No! another, more persistent part of him shouted back, his mind breaking, fragmenting. *Focus! Focus on the result, the perception, the desire.*

It's too hard!

When he'd struggled in the past, he had been dispassionate. He needed emotion, the deep-seated rage in his gut that propelled him in his worst moments. When his friends had abandoned him. When Trevor had walked away. When Sherwood had refused to do what he was told. Ira embraced the cold anger and tasted its bitter piquancy.

He formed an image of Fair Haven, the farmhouse, the orchard, the plush carpet of grass undulating over gentle hills.

It's not enough, it's not enough.

By sheer resolve, he bent the mathematics to his will, his mind assembling data in a way no human brain ever had, transcending its design to accomplish something new, something extraordinary, something impossible.

"Ira!"

Where was that voice coming from?

"Ira! What's happening?"

Had the stasis failed? No, no, it couldn't. It couldn't have—

"Ira!" And then: "Quick, call for help!"

He lifted his closed fist and realized with a start that it was full of freshly pulled grass, its wiry brown roots tugged from the soft earth.

He opened his eyes and for a moment disbelieved what he saw: Fair Haven, in all its country glory. In all its safety, far from distant Singapore and Grigori threats.

A young man was running toward them. David the younger.

Thank you, he prayed, gushing gratitude. *Thank you thank you thank—*

His thought was interrupted by the sound of a hard fist hitting bone. Ira came fully into the present as he saw Dario retract his fist; beside them, the woman groaned and rolled onto her side, clutching herself.

"It's Ohia," Dario said, coming to his feet.

Ira raised an eyebrow. Ohia? The same creature who had attacked them outside the Khunjerab base. Dario had been right about the Rhea connection.

"Ira!" Junior shouted, dropping to his knees next to the rabbi.

"I'm all right, David," Ira said, marveling again at just how much

Aaron's grandson resembled his younger self. "Calm down and help me get this woman into the house."

"Who is she?"

"Her name is Ohia, and she's very dangerous."

Junior took Ohia by the hands and forced her to her feet, prodding her toward the farmhouse in a forced march. Dario joined them, flanking Ohia on her left side.

Ira followed slowly, massaging his temples. He was so tired. He could barely feel his own body.

Suddenly, Ira's legs went out from under him and he collapsed, his head narrowly missing the first step up to the veranda.

A moment later, Junior was at his side.

"I'll live," Ira rasped. "I just need to rest."

Junior helped him up. "The guest room is ready. You can sleep all day as far as I'm concerned."

"I'm afraid we don't have that kind of time." Ira made it up the steps and shuffled, with the young man's assistance, to the door of the house.

"Where's Janene?" Junior asked as they climbed to the second floor.

"What?"

"Janene was with you when you left."

Ira stopped short of the top stair and sat gingerly on sore muscles. He clutched his head, willing its steady throb to level out. "Janene…"

Oh Lord, what have I done?

TWENTY-THREE

Srinagar, India
AUGUST 3

G ayle awoke before dawn on the most stressful day of her life and slapped the alarm clock on the nightstand, missing the snooze button. She tried three more times, all the while enduring its sadistic siren, before finally managing to hit the target. While smothering herself with a fluffy white hotel pillow, wanting to cry and feeling like she hadn't gotten any sleep at all, she came within a hair's breadth of lapsing back into unconsciousness. Instead a surge of determination kicked in and forced her out of bed. Faisal would be here in a half-hour, and she had to pack and get ready.

She showered and changed into the most conservative outfit she'd brought—a long-sleeved grey blouse and black pants. She tied her hair into a ponytail, tucked it into the back of her blouse, then covered her hair with a ball cap.

When Faisal arrived and she let him in, he laughed at her choice of clothing. "You cannot wear that. It is," he searched for the correct word, "ridiculous."

She fought the urge to feel offended.

He unslung a pack from his shoulders and placed it on the un-made bed. "I brought something."

"What is it?"

From the deep recesses of the pack he unfolded a long black aba-ya. Faisal handed it to her as he dug out a matching scarf. Perhaps it was selfish and impractical, but all she could think about was how hot and ill at ease she would feel concealed in this sartorial fortress. None-theless, she knew it was the only way.

Gayle took the scarf from him and conveyed the change of clothes into the bathroom. She stripped off her comfortable Western attire, except for a simple white t-shirt. She wriggled her arms through the cavernous sleeves of the abaya and eventually popped her head out through the opening on top. The fabric enfolded her head on all sides, like the hood of a winter parka.

She didn't look Faisal in the eye as she exited the bathroom, un-zipped her suitcase, and put away her original outfit.

He grazed his chin and watched her appraisingly. "Too big. Do you have a belt?"

She dug through her suitcase. Near the bottom was a thin black belt which she only ever wore with jeans.

"Yes, yes." He pointed to his own upper waist. "Right here. Wear it high. And tight."

Gayle clasped the belt and tightened it until it was roughly in the position he had indicated. When she glanced at herself in the mirror, she had to admit it didn't look half-bad. She could see how the robes could be fashionable when worn correctly.

"Perfect. You look very good."

"Thank you," she said, feeling a bit better about the situation.

"But now we go. We have little time."

There were no shikara taxis plying the waterways this early, but Faisal had brought a small car. Gayle loaded her suitcase into the trunk, then settled into the passenger seat, saying nothing as Faisal drove away from the hotel.

"I should have checked out," Gayle murmured as the sun rose, its light hitting her in the eyes.

"Better you did not. Now they will not know you are missing."

At least not for two days, Gayle considered. That was how long she had extended her reservation.

"I went back to the Regional Passport Office last night. They will grant my application, both for me," Faisal paused, throwing her a meaningful look, "and my wife."

"That was very quick!"

"Yes, very. I explained it as a family emergency. My father, who lives in Gilgit, is ill." He paused. "My father is not really dying, Gayle."

"I understand. It's a cover." She nodded. "I can't thank you enough for what you're doing, Faisal. You are helping to save a woman's life."

"I know. This Elisabeth is important to you."

The passport office opened at six o'clock, but they arrived a few minutes early.

"Stay here," Faisal instructed as he got out of the car. "I need to pick up our permits."

"Will they check my identification?"

"If you were travelling alone, yes. Because you are travelling with your husband, there may not be a need." He reached through the open window, adjusting her scarf so that it truly covered everything but her eyes. "From a distance, they may not see you are not Kashmiri. It is still dark out. Okay. Wait here."

Faisal waited outside the doors for several minutes before someone came to open it. Gayle recognized the bearded man from the day before. He didn't give her a second glance as he let Faisal inside.

As dawn turned to full morning, she heard the distinctive sounds of the city coming awake. Traffic increased, with the frequent blasts of horns drowning out the quiet lapping of Dal Lake. Shikara drivers congregated just across the highway, conversing loudly with each other—so loudly, in fact, that Gayle suspected they were engaged in an argument.

A knock on the car window got her attention. Faisal leaned in, practically nose to nose with her, and whispered, "I will now say something in Urdu. When I do, get out, and face the man in the doorway."

Without waiting for her to acknowledge him, he pulled open the door and allowed her enough to space to exit the vehicle. But first he began to speak—whatever it was, she imagined it had something to do with presenting herself to the bearded man.

She slowly got out of the car and looked straight at the bearded man in the doorway. He stood far enough away that she couldn't be sure if he would remember her. No light of recognition flashed in his eyes.

Faisal whispered again. "Now you are to go to him and claim your permit. Do not be afraid."

Fear clutched her heart at the prospect of getting so close. She took deliberate steps, also careful not to walk too slowly. Nothing to make him leery. She walked up to him and reached out to grasp the piece of paper. Once it was in her hands, she turned and walked away, not daring to breathe until she was back in the safety of the car.

Faisal waved at the man and said goodbye, and then they were off.

"I can't believe he didn't want to see my ID," she said.

"My word as your husband is enough. Not unusual in India."

Normally such a display of gender inequality would have turned her stomach, but all she could feel today was gratitude.

She raised her hand to loosen the scarf pulling tightly across the front of her neck.

"Leave it," Faisal said. "We will soon be at the bus. You must remain covered."

"Thank you again, Faisal."

"Do not thank me. Not yet. The real test will be when we reach the Line of Control. Pakistani officials might ask questions."

"But I won't be able to answer them. At least not in Urdu."

"That is my fear. We must pray they let me speak for you."

The bus depot turned out to be a small, rundown building with broken plaster and cracked concrete. The depot's two windows were so opaquely filthy that Gayle couldn't see anything through them except a funhouse-mirror reflection of her own scarf-covered visage.

"What will happen if we're caught?" she said to Faisal as they approached the depot.

"I do not wish to frighten you."

"But I'm already frightened."

"Illegal aliens are severely punished. Put in jail for long periods. Or worse."

Faisal had brought a small suitcase of his own. He carried both his and Gayle's luggage out of the car and placed it in front of the idling bus next to the depot. This was nothing like the luxurious buses she had seen back home, long and sleek vehicles with beautifully upholstered seats, mounted televisions, and onboard washrooms. It was short and in poor condition, its muffler coughing up acrid clouds of black smoke. In the midst of those clouds, a young boy with dark, shadowed eyes stared at them; he sat propped up against one of the back wheels. He wore shorts that emphasized several bloody gashes on his shins and calves. Gayle hoped those injuries had no more sinister a cause than childish horseplay.

"Should we go inside?" Gayle asked.

"Yes. Come with me."

He led the way through the dingy entrance. Two overhead lights, one of them a bulb attached to the ceiling through a frayed wire, lit the room in swinging pools of light. Faisal exchanged words with the official behind a wooden desk. Faisal pulled Gayle behind him, then took the permit from her outstretched hand and displayed it. The official stamped both permits with a red-inked word in cursive Urdu. Gayle didn't need to understand the language to know it read the English equivalent of "Approved."

Gayle drew a deep breath of the heavy, humid air when they ventured outside again. The air in the depot had smelled of urine and cigarette smoke.

"When does the bus leave?" Gayle asked, keeping her voice low. It wouldn't do for the other passengers to notice she only spoke English.

"We must be patient. Maybe hours."

His warning proved prophetic. The sun climbed to its midday height and began its gradual swing downward before Gayle noticed any hint of further activity. A glut of new passengers arrived, milling around the bus.

At last, Gayle climbed aboard with Faisal, ascending a couple of steep stairs and walking past the empty driver's seat. Only two other passengers had beaten them aboard, and both sat near the front. Faisal led Gayle to the back, where she hoped the ride would be relatively peaceful.

She clutched the scarf in place as the bus filled. Among the passengers she recognized the boy with the scuffed knees, dragged behind a woman dressed similarly to Gayle. The boy's eyes met hers, despite sitting nearly a full bus length away. He stared and stared.

"That boy is staring at me," Gayle whispered to Faisal.

Faisal looked up, but already the boy had averted his gaze. "What boy?"

"Two rows behind the driver. The boy with his mother."

"You are showing paranoia."

God knew she had a lot to be paranoid about.

Half an hour later, the bus lurched over the pitted parking lot. Gayle pressed her closed fist into the seat's cracked leather to prevent herself from pitching over into Faisal's lap.

The bus made its way through the streets of Srinagar, the buildings getting smaller and the traffic sparser. Gayle said goodbye to the place, knowing she was unlikely to return regardless of what happened at the border.

"Are you all right?" Faisal asked once they were in the country, climbing a steep road into the towering mountains.

"No. How could I be?"

"It is out of your control now. Be at peace, my friend."

Be at peace. Excellent advice, assuming there was any reserve of peace left intact within her. She touched her forehead to the glass and gaped unblinkingly at the snowy peaks. *And today I must cross through them.*

*   *   *

The valley opened wide to receive them into its hungry gullet. The bus stopped three times in remote mountain villages to take on additional passengers, each delay longer than the last. Faisal showed no nervousness, however, and his strength buttressed Gayle. He was risking just as much as she by helping her, and he had so little to gain. In a way, she couldn't understand what motivated him. His strength and loyalty flew in the face of what she knew of human nature. If she succeeded in finding Elisabeth and bringing her home, it would only be because Faisal had put himself on the line. How could she repay such a debt?

The last Indian town was known as Salambad, along a portion of the highway where the valley walls rose like cliffs. Dozens of white-roofed houses ornamented the slopes, nestled onto narrow strips of terraced farmland. They gleamed under the fading sun.

"You see that hill ahead?" Faisal pointed out the window at the front of the bus.

The hill was hard to miss. It bulged out from the north wall of the valley like a cancerous growth, cutting across their path and forcing the highway to dogleg sharply to the south.

"Yes, I see it."

"I recognize it from a map. It marks the border. We will come to a checkpoint soon." He put a hand on her knee. "Are you ready?"

She shook her head.

"There is nothing to prepare for," Faisal told her. She wasn't sure if it was a statement of encouragement or resignation. "Now we wait and see."

These last two miles rushed by. As they approached the hill and the unknown possibilities it represented, she felt helpless. She clutched her hands together, her knuckles turning white. Even Faisal looked nervous, despite his best efforts to control his emotions.

The highway wrapped around the base of that rocky hill, then crossed a dry, scree-filled streambed by way of a concrete bridge that more resembled a ramp. A line of commercial trucks had stopped along the bridge, and the bus pulled in behind them. All Gayle could see was the bright orange paint of the truck in front of them, and a blue sign that stretched across the roadway, supported by twin poles. English featured prominently among the multiple languages on the sign. Despite her stress, Gayle smiled at the disingenuous message: "Welcome to Pakistan Land of Peace Love and Friendship." Ironic, Gayle thought, considering Pakistan's poor human rights record. It certainly wasn't known for its peace, love, and friendship.

Nor for its grasp of punctuation, she added.

Her short-lived humor dissipated upon catching sight of an armed guard patrolling the shoulder of the highway, holding a machine gun. Nothing said peace, love, and friendship quite like a machine gun.

"Standard procedure, I am sure," Faisal reassured her. "This is a turbulent region."

The traffic inched forward, revealing the corner of a white wall cozied up to the side of the hill. Trees sprouted all around its base so that only the top of the wall remained visible. Atop it flew the flag of Pakistan, its trademark crescent and star superimposed over a field of dark green.

The bus rocked to a sudden stop, followed a moment later by sharp knocking against the door. The driver didn't hesitate to open it, allowing a pair of soldiers to climb inside. They stood at the front of the aisle in their imposing green-and-brown army fatigues.

One of the soldiers shouted something, and in response all the passengers began to reach into their bags—including Faisal, who withdrew the two entry permits they had gotten from the passport office.

"Hold it up," Faisal whispered to her. "And do not speak."

Before the soldiers reached the back of the bus, shouts from outside stole their attention. Both of them tramped back out onto the road, brandishing their weapons.

"What's going on?" Gayle asked.

Faisal leaned forward, straining to listen. Frightened chatter had erupted among the other passengers, making it even more difficult to tell what was going on.

Gayle opened her mouth to repeat the question when the air broke into an explosion of gunfire. She instinctively threw herself down—and just in time, too, as a bullet collided with the window next to her. Shards of glass rained down. She squeezed her eyes closed, feeling a fragment of glass slice into her cheek. Blood dripped from the fresh wound onto the dark folds of her abaya.

"What should we do?" Gayle cried out as she crouched low to the floor.

"Stay here. I do not think they are attacking the bus," Faisal said.

"Who's they? The Pakistani soldiers?"

"I do not think so."

A fireball flared to life just outside the window, transforming the clear blue sky into a flash of white. The bus rocked sideways. Gayle grabbed the top of the seat as the bus tilted onto two wheels. It tottered for the longest second of Gayle's life, then lost its war with gravity and hit the edge of the road, sliding into the narrow shoulder between pavement and rocky hillside. Gayle's head bounced off the floor—no, the ceiling, she realized, feeling disoriented. She got to her feet, the former ceiling's metal warping underfoot.

"Faisal," she said, looking around for her friend. He had been thrown into the aisle, crumpled against one the seats several rows in front of them. Other passengers lay scattered about like discarded ragdolls. Those who were conscious wailed as they attended to their loved ones.

Don't be dead. You deserve so much better. I shouldn't have gotten you into this.

Gayle got down next to him and cradled his head in her arms. "Faisal! Say something!"

For a few scary moments, he said nothing, but then he let out a cough, releasing a stream of phlegm and blood.

"I am well," he croaked. "Perhaps I was wrong about staying on the bus."

"I'd say so. Can you walk?"

He shifted his legs, uncurling them and using a seat, suspended from above, to help him up. "I will try. Come, now."

"What about the others?" Gayle asked.

"Those who can come will join us."

Already three others had congregated around them. Somehow they had recognized a leadership quality in Faisal; no matter where they came from, people had an uncanny ability to pick out exactly who to follow in a crisis. A powerful survival trait.

Gayle listened as Faisal consulted with a couple of their fellow survivors, their strange-sounding words interspersed by further explosions and bursts of gunfire. Each eruption of violence reminded her to move quickly.

Before leaving the bus, she bent low to help a young boy stand. It was the same boy who'd been watching her so intently earlier; though previously suspicious, all she felt now was compassion. His mother was gone, probably dead, so she inserted her hand under his arm. He limped next to her, not saying a word during their escape.

In all, seven of them emerged from the wreck. Faisal pointed toward the relative safety of the hillside. Everything was happening too quickly. They didn't have time to get their bearings, never mind figure out who was attacking them, why, or from where.

They ran up the hill, fumbling for purchase on stones, brambles, and dry roots breaking the surface. Eventually the hill's slope proved impassable, so Faisal leveled their ascent. A series of boulders ten feet up would make for excellent cover, if they could climb that high.

Faisal went first, kicking into the dusty ground to make handholds and footholds. Gayle had only attempted rock-climbing once in her life, and she'd chickened out less than a third of the way up the wall—all in the safety of a gym. Today she found the motivation the conditioning class had failed to instill in her; she'd have had no trouble getting up that wall if her instructor had tried lobbing grenades.

Gayle became the third person to reach the boulders and the little sanctuary Faisal had found behind them. All seven refugees fit when they hugged tight, but it was a near thing. Gayle had to practically sit in Faisal's lap. Such intimacy would have made her nervous the day before, but today she thought nothing of it. Bigger fish to fry.

Faisal looked out from behind the largest boulder, and his face slackened, his mocha-colored skin turning slate grey.

While climbing the rocks, Gayle had been too busy to risk a peek over her shoulder, but now she inched up to steal a look. Whatever had scared the daylights out of Faisal—

Her thoughts ran into a dead-end as an impossible scene played out before her eyes. The valley had descended into a maelstrom of chaos. Fire tore through the queue of vehicles stopped on the road, including the burning husk that had been their bus.

Such violence was enough to strike her dumb, but it paled when she registered those carrying out the attacks. These were not soldiers or terrorists or civilians. They weren't even *human*. They were giants! The ground shook from the lumbering creatures' strides. Gayle saw three of them, as tall or taller than the fire-consumed commercial trucks, and they walked amid the warzone unfazed by the smoke and flames. Their skin looked dry and cracked, desiccated, covered in lesions. Death walking. They carried torches, setting ablaze everything in their path—cars, trucks, trees... even people. Shocked screams ripped through the air, undiminished in speed and intensity as they travelled all the way up to Gayle's hiding place.

She looked away, but too late. She would never excise this madness from her head.

"What's happening?" she whispered through tears.

Faisal, too, had been weeping. "It cannot be real."

Gayle cringed as yet another death shriek washed over her. "We have to get out of here."

"Back down the road," Faisal agreed. He pointed east, the way they had come. The path was easiest in that direction.

"No." Gayle shook her head, stunned by the forcefulness of her own conviction. "I've come too far. I must go west. Elisabeth is counting on me."

TWENTY-FOUR

Canadian Arctic
AUGUST 3

There! Do you see it?"

Abranel squinted out the window at a bright spot interrupting the tundra a few miles to the east of the plane. Brighton thought it seemed vaguely triangular, like the ship they were looking for, and the brightness might be sunlight reflecting off its surface.

Instead it turned out to be nothing but a pointed boulder sticking out of a thick patch of dwarf birch trees. Brighton didn't feel much disappointment, but Abranel's frustration grew more potent by the hour.

Is there a deadline I'm not aware of? Brighton asked.

"Do not distract me. I must remain focused at all times."

Not at all times. Last night, you disappeared without a trace. You were asleep.

"Sleep is a physical limitation."

I have a theory.

"Charming."

I think you were too tired to exercise full control.

"Why do you insist on deluding yourself?"

You were out for nearly an hour. That was no delusion.

An hour later, hundreds of miles from the nearest port of civilization—if mines could be considered ports of civilization—they found it. The wreck was unmistakable. The ship had come in fast, blazingly fast, its nose plowing an enormous black trench almost a mile long. At the end of this track, now brimming with the inflow from a nearby stream, the ship stuck out of the ground, its triangular body waving to them like a pennant.

Abranel lurched out of his seat and hovered behind the pilot.

"I see it," Regan said, banking the plane. "Just have to find somewhere to land."

"There are lakes everywhere," Abranel said.

Regan nodded. "But not all are long enough to facilitate a landing."

A brief search identified a narrow lake, but Regan was reluctant to land on it.

"If we keep going, it'll take too long to walk back to the crash site," Abranel protested. "Make the landing."

"The lake is narrow and can't be longer than three thousand feet, end to end."

"Can you do it?"

Regan hesitated. "It's right at the limit. And I can't tell if there are obstructions in the water."

"We have to get to that crash site," Abranel insisted. "I'm not giving you a choice."

"You don't give me orders," Regan grunted back, the first sign in three days of anything but a cheerful disposition. "Not when it comes to safety, leastways."

Brighton was concerned for Regan. Abranel had already killed one pilot this week, and he supposed it wouldn't much bother Abranel to kill a second. Of course, Regan was safe as long as the plane remained in the air. At the moment, Abranel wasn't in a position to bargain. He was subject to Regan's assessment of the situation, and it infuriated him.

"Well, it looks deep enough," Regan mused.

"Then we'll land."

"We'll *attempt* to land. Get back in your seat—and brace yourself, just in case."

Subservience didn't come naturally to Abranel, but he returned to the chair and tightened the belt around Brighton's waist.

This landing was far bumpier than the ones in Yellowknife Bay. As the plane screamed toward the edge of the lake, Brighton wondered if Regan had made the right decision. They only barely cleared the lake's rock-strewn southern shore before the pontoons hit the water. His throat constricted as they raced along the surface of the lake.

Regan knew what he was doing, however, and they came to a stop with plenty of room to spare. Brighton thought he might have overstated the difficulty of the landing.

Abranel unstrapped his belt and walked toward the door. He played with the handle.

"Not yet!" Regan shouted.

Abranel struck him with a look of open contempt. "What is it now?"

"Look outside. You see that smudge in the air?" Sure enough, hazy spots of black hovered over the terrain. "That's a mosquito swarm. In such numbers, they're more than pests. I've got some strong repellent to discourage them, but you'll still get bitten. You can't discourage them all."

The repellent was so strong that Brighton almost choked on it.

"Breathe through your nose," Regan advised. Next, he showed them a handheld GPS. "By my reckoning, that crash site is north-

northwesterly, three hundred forty degrees. If we head straight for two miles, we won't miss it."

"I'm going alone."

Regan shook his head. "No chance. I get the feeling you've never hiked tundra before, so you'll need a guide. You could get into trouble on your own, and the terrain could suck you under if you step in the wrong place. It's gonna be real boggy."

"I can handle it."

"No offence, but why take the risk?"

Abranel drew himself up. "You don't understand. The crash site is highly classified. If you see it, I'll have to—"

Kill you, Brighton finished when Abranel stopped short of confirming the dirty truth. Instead he allowed the pilot to fill in the blank with whatever seemed most reasonable. He probably had no idea of the danger he was in.

"I can't be held responsible for what might happen to you."

Abranel met the man's glare head-on. "Back down. This has nothing to do with flight safety."

Abranel put a hand on both of Regan's shoulders and squeezed—not so hard as to hurt the man, but enough to emphasize the threat.

"Okay," Regan finally said, stepping out of the way. "I'll wait three hours. If you're not back by then, I'm coming after you."

"Agreed. But make it four."

"Four hours is too long a—"

"I'll probably be back much sooner, but let's say four to be safe." Abranel pointed out the window. "Daylight won't be an issue, and neither will fuel."

Reluctantly, Regan agreed.

The pilot furnished them with a few extra provisions before sending them on their way, principally an adjustable hiking pole to help navigate the bumpy ground. Abranel loaded up his backpack with two bottles of water, a thick waterproof blanket, and a lighter. He stuck the GPS in his pocket. Regan also wanted him to wear heavy boots that climbed all the way up to his knees; he resisted at first, then relented when Regan described what it was like to get sucked into the mire of a tundra bog. The pilot warned them that it would be soft as a sponge in places, so they had to stick to exposed rock wherever possible, especially when hiking up even the easiest-looking grades.

Errant mosquitoes swam into the plane the moment the door opened, though most were rebuffed by the still-strong scent of repellent in the air.

"Hurry, you have to jump," Regan said.

Abranel stepped to the edge and looked down. The plane had drifted up to within a couple feet of the shore, where the solid blue water of the lake splashed against moss-covered stones. They looked slippery.

"What are you waiting for?" Regan came to stand beside him. "Jump!"

Abranel played the coward and handed off control to Brighton.

I'm not going to do it, Brighton thought. He had so few opportunities for genuine passive resistance. It made him feel empowered.

Finally Abranel accepted it and pushed off. He landed just beyond the wet rocks in a patch of syrupy mud. He sank into it, then struggled to stand. The brown sludge coated the right side of his jacket and pant leg.

Regan laughed. "Four hours, and I'm coming after you."

"I'll be fine!" Abranel insisted gruffly as Regan pulled shut the door with a strident crunch. He then pulled out the GPS and stared at it, waiting for the readings to appear. The moment they did, he began to march.

The mosquitoes flocked to him like schoolchildren to Halloween candy. The bugs were relentless. Ferocious. Most stopped short of his oily, DEET-covered skin, but a few intrepid warriors touched down and drew blood. Those that evaded Abranel's furious slaps scarcely escaped with their lives, though Brighton wistfully imagined them dropping dead a few minutes later from the toxins they'd picked up.

Aside from the constant swarm, Brighton was surprised at the sound. He'd expected the tundra to be quiet, without any signs of human settlement anywhere to be found; instead those kamikaze mosquitoes kept diving at his eyeballs, giving rise to a constant cacophony. Combined with the wind whistling through shrubbery, the burbling of frequent streams, and a flock of geese overhead this wasn't really any quieter than a city street.

Abranel stopped next to a stubby blueberry bush and wiped sweat from his forehead. He consulted the GPS again.

Strange that we can't see it from here, Brighton thought. *It didn't seem that far.*

"Distances can be deceiving from the air."

They soon arrived in a low-lying marsh, revealing a trough that snaked down from the northwest carrying a creek. Abranel aimed slightly west, clomping those black knee-high boots over the lichen-covered stones on the creek bed. The boots weighed a ton, but at least they kept out the mosquitoes.

They couldn't avoid the trough forever, as it lay directly in their path. Now more than ever, Brighton was grateful for the boots. Even through the thick rubber, he could feel how cold the water was. He wouldn't have wanted to trudge through it in his usual sneakers.

Once safely across, Abranel mounted a low rise. Ahead lay a bank of ten-foot willows too dense to cross and pockmarked with water-holes. The only quick alternative would be to scramble up an escarpment of exposed rock, so Abranel decided to take a longer detour around the willows.

Thirty minutes later, Brighton got his first view of the crashed ship. Somehow this was more profound than the brief sighting he'd had at the Khunjerab base. Out in the open, the ship looked bizarre, anachronistic, like it had no place in the midst of nature. None of this shock had a physiological effect. His pulse didn't quicken, his pupils didn't dilate. Abranel radiated calm expectancy as they approached.

As they'd seen from above, the ship had skidded along the ground for almost a mile before coming to rest with its front cone planted in the earth like a misshapen tree. The silver body of the craft glistened in the sun except where dirt had flown up, coating it in patches of black grit. The triangular body had ended up almost perpendicular to the ground; the only force keeping it from falling over was the mossy boulder against which its underside rested. All around that point of impact were long, jagged scratches in the metal. Water lapped against the edges of the trench created by the crash, probably water from the very stream they had crossed earlier.

The ship's not as big as I remember, Brighton thought.

He mounted the boulder, then scaled the ship's sheer edge onto the ventral plating. It shook a little under the added weight, and for a moment Brighton thought they were going to fall off.

And hit my head on a boulder and meet my end. An ignominious death.

Abranel ignored him as he balanced carefully. From here, Brighton had a better appreciation of the ship's scale. As Abranel applied pressure to a certain point on the hull, he heard a hiss. A recessed compartment revealed itself, the seams in the metal becoming obvious at last. The compartment seemed like the ideal place for a pilot to enter, but it was much too large for a human. Thirty feet, at least.

"Not too large for the pilot it was designed for," Abranel said as he pushed the compartment open wide.

Brighton detected a quick burst of movement, then a splash, and this time even Abranel reacted. He recoiled and lost his balance, sliding down the ship and tumbling onto his stomach as he hit the ground.

Told you so, Brighton thought.

"Shut up. You're fine." Abranel got back to his feet without pause and looked toward the water. A body floated in the ship's shadow, face down and creating ripples.

Finally, someone for the mosquitoes to feast on in peace.

Abranel climbed back up to the pilot's compartment and looked around for a while, doing nothing. Perhaps he didn't know what to do.

"It's been a few thousand years, but we used to fly ships very much like this one."

Who do you mean by "we"?

"My brothers."

The ship was remarkably low-tech, its main compartment surrounded on three sides by some kind of soft, ergonomic material Brighton didn't recognize; it would have snuggled in close to the pilot's unique body shape. A great way of preventing injury during a crash—if only it had worked out in this case. Brighton glanced toward the dead body in the water.

"In my original form, I would have survived. Any of us would have."

Abranel seemed to find what he was looking for. He hit a pressure point on the wall of the compartment, and the ship shuddered. At first Brighton thought it was powering up, and he even entertained the possibility that it might fly again.

"I doubt it," Abranel said. "Not without major repairs."

Brighton heard a grinding noise from somewhere deep in the bowels of the craft's machinery, and then he felt another shudder, stronger than before.

What was that?

"The cargo hold."

And what is the cargo?

"You'll see."

Abranel swung himself out of the pilot's compartment and went around to the underside of the craft, which had cracked open but failed to extend all the way out. Brighton wasn't too surprised by the failure, seeing as the ship was perched on its nose.

Abranel didn't say a word as he pried at the edges of the cargo hold opening. Eventually, he was able to force the door to deploy. He had to step out of the way to avoid getting hit.

Brighton couldn't see a thing once they entered the interior. The cargo hold had been constructed to be just large enough to carry a payload of six coffin-like crates. The first one Abranel felt was cool and smooth. Some kind of metal.

How do we open them?

"We don't," Abranel said. "Our job is only to secure the cargo. Besides, the crates are locked and I don't have the key."

You can't be serious. I didn't come all this way not to get answers. Brighton fought down his rage. *You know, don't you?*

"What do I know?"

Don't be obtuse. You know what's in the cargo. You've known the whole time.

"Of course I have."

Then tell me, damn it.

"There's no advantage in telling you. Why would I do that?"

Because we're supposed to have a reciprocal relationship. Remember?

Abranel chuckled as he held onto the side of the first crate and began to drag it toward the cargo hold's door. Whatever was inside the crate was extremely heavy. Too heavy to lift, but Brighton was strong enough that they could drag it. Even so, it took nearly five minutes to work it toward the door. With a final shove, Abranel pushed it out. It fell like an anvil, sinking into the permafrost.

Brighton felt disappointed. If only there'd been a giant boulder there, the impact might have been enough to crack it open.

There wasn't time to lament that which hadn't happened, however, for Abranel was already climbing back for the next crate. This would be a long afternoon if they had to extract each and every one of them.

What's the endgame here? he asked as they heaved the second crate over the edge. It smashed into the top of the first crate, but Abranel seemed blissfully unconcerned about the possibility of damage. *How are we going to get the cargo back to the plane?*

"We're not," Abranel grunted from exertion. "I've already activated the ship's emergency transponder. Another ship will be here soon. We just have to wait."

And what about Regan? He's not going to leave without us.

"Sadly, you're probably right. We already have a tried and true solution, though."

Brighton recoiled. *I won't go through that again.*

"You won't have a choice," Abranel said as the third crate hit the ground and rolled end over end before coming to a stop. "Regan is yet another loose end we can't afford. You don't have to kill him yourself. Just watch."

In some ways, watching was worse.

Abranel heard a loud creak and pivoted toward the cargo hold's door. He crept back to the opening and looked out.

Maybe the wind is picking up, Brighton suggested. *Occam's razor in action, which means—*

"I know what Occam's razor is. I may be a few thousand years old, but I get around." He climbed down from the ship, even with three crates left to free from the hold.

You thought it might be Regan.

Abranel turned in a slow circle, surveying the horizon in all directions. "The thought occurred to me. It would save us some trouble. I'm not eager to hike across the tundra again."

They heard the same sound, this time accompanied by movement. One of the crates they'd tossed out of the ship—the one that had rolled end over end—now lay on a bed of smooth stones washed up by the water in the newly formed lake.

The wind? No, the wind wasn't nearly strong enough to move it.

Abranel, what's in these crates? Brighton asked again.

That crate rocked from side to side, gently at first and then hard enough to roll itself over. Abranel backed away, then climbed into the cargo hold again. He moved slowly. Cautiously.

There's something alive in there.

"Not sure 'alive' is the right word."

Under different circumstances, Brighton might have found that more shocking. And if he'd been in control of his body, he would have run as fast as he could back toward the plane.

Are you planning on locking us inside here? How is that going to end?

Abranel's uncertainty chilled him to the bone.

TWENTY-FIVE

Fair Haven, Vermont
AUGUST 3

I have to go back!" Ira bolted upright, clutching the sheets of the double bed. The morning sun cascaded through the second-story window. He was too frantic to register its beauty.

A frumpy woman appeared in the doorway, hands on her hips.

Celeste, he remembered, the events of the last few hours coming back to him like water being poured into a jar. He was at Aaron's house in Fair Haven.

Ira leaned over the side of the bed and reached for his pants, which had been neatly folded on the wooden stool that doubled as a nightstand.

Celeste snatched the stool away. "You're exhausted."

"I have to get Janene," Ira said, sitting up. "She's in trouble, and it's my fault."

Celeste returned to stand in the doorframe. "Can't argue with you there, but you're too tired to do anything about it. One way or another, you gotta sleep."

"I can't sleep. It would be irresponsible."

"Okay, try getting past me."

"I need to put my clothes on first. Otherwise I'll end up in that Singapore hotel wearing nothing but…" Ira peeked under the covers. "Absolutely nothing, apparently. It's a black-tie affair, you understand?"

"Sure do. David said to keep you in bed until at least noon, and to make sure you spend that time resting. That's two hours from now."

"David doesn't know what he's talking about."

Hands on hips again. "And I happen to agree with him!"

"I guess we know how I feel about you then." Ira regretted the words instantly. "Sorry, that was harsh."

"I understand the urgency," Celeste assured him. "I do. But you didn't see yourself when you got here. You can't let yourself deteriorate like that again. I've spent years watching Trevor, and he's never once lost control the way you did."

"Trevor is a coward." Now that he didn't regret. "And I won't apologize for that one."

Celeste sighed. Ira could tell she was just as disappointed in Trevor as he was.

"I won't lie here a minute longer." Ira swung his legs out of bed.

"Fine." Celeste walked up to the dresser and picked up a glass of water that had been sitting there. "You'll need to recover your strength, though. Feeling thirsty? Taking care of a man's thirst is my specialty."

Ira accepted the glass and took two long gulps. The water felt cool as it rushed down his throat. "Thank you. Now get my pants."

Celeste obliged by returning the stool to its original position, within arm's reach.

"And I'd prefer some privacy, if you don't mind." Ira waited for a few seconds, raising his eyebrow at her.

Finally she turned and walked out into the hallway.

"Tell David I'm going to need some food before I leave," Ira said as he struggled into the pair of black dress pants, still more or less wrinkle-free despite their adventures. He only got them up to his knees before a wave of dizziness overcame him. He fell back onto the bed.

"Celeste, something's wrong." Panic crept into Ira's voice.

"Nothing wrong, Rabbi. Like I said, you gotta sleep." She paused. "One way or another."

Ira glanced at the half-empty glass of water. It must have been laced with something.

"It's quick acting. Keep you out for another few hours." Celeste had come back into the room to adjust the blankets. He felt rage that she was seeing him in such a vulnerable state. The way she flipped the blankets over him without giving him a second look told Ira just how little she cared. "You'll thank us later."

I seriously doubt that, he thought before kicking and screaming his way into unconsciousness.

*   *   *

Dario's internal clock was all screwed up. He remembered feeling some jetlag after the initial jump from Pakistan. But now? Three jumps and how many days later? That initial disorientation seemed quaint in comparison.

"I'm tired," he admitted. *But not as tired as Ira.*

The elder David sat on the porch swing next to him. The chair did what it was designed to do—swing a few degrees to the side, then swing back, rinse and repeat. It made Dario a bit lightheaded, a symptom of all this jumping around he hadn't yet gotten used to. He didn't say anything as David pushed the swing, talking all the while.

David had so many questions about Singapore, and Dario did his best to answer them. They seemed to have all moved past secrets now—a huge relief in itself. The secrets had been stifling; Dario wasn't sure humans had been built to endure such systematic dishonesty.

For half an hour, the two men discussed the trade conference. But really all David wanted to know were the particulars of Ohia's capture.

"You hear anything about this in the news?" Dario suddenly asked, only now realizing the likelihood that their activities were being reported in the media. Maybe they'd even been caught on camera.

David shook his head. "My son has been monitoring the internet all morning. Nothing so far, but it's still early."

Dario worried that his anonymity might soon be a luxury of the past. He couldn't control that, though. Best to focus on the things he *could* control. "Have you checked on Ohia?"

"She's secure."

"It's not a she," Dario pointed out. "Not even a he, I don't think. Just a narcissistic monster."

"Perhaps it's time you spoke to… it."

Dario planted his feet on the wooden slats of the veranda, hard enough to make the swing stop in mid-motion. "Let's go then."

David led him through the house to the rickety stairs descending into the cellar. The dank concrete walls pressed in from all sides, but Dario no longer suffered the anxiety elicited by tight spaces. Especially underground ones. His experiences in Tiahuanaco had seen to that.

The cellar floor was composed of concrete so festooned with tiny cracks that it was impossible to take a step without covering one. His shoes scuffed over grey pebbles and thin, fragile chips of concrete broken off over the years.

He needed a few moments for his eyes to adjust. Two bulbs lit the path toward an old deepfreeze, though it had been unplugged and pulled away from the wall.

Dario knew what awaited them behind the freezer, but the incongruity still caught him off-guard. A tall, leggy blond in a green dress lay on the ground, fresh cuts on her exposed thigh evidence of her rough handling upon arrival. Her arms were tied behind her back, the skin of her wrists chaffed by a coarse rope David had retrieved from a shed out by the orchard.

"I'll be right here," David said, his hand on the back of a chair they'd dragged down from the kitchen earlier that morning.

Dario kicked the woman in the shin, putting aside his rule against hitting women.

This isn't even a person, he had to remind himself. *It doesn't deserve my pity or remorse.*

Though it was hard to excise his feelings of pity and remorse. The woman was a goddess. Ohia had chosen well. What had she been like before the possession? Had she been a willing host, or had Ohia violated her as roughly as he had Rhea? Was her human consciousness still in there somewhere, hanging on to life in the distant recesses of her mind? Could she still feel pain?

He hoped not, because it would complicate what he had to do next.

"Your name is Ohia," Dario said, giving the creature another kick when it failed to respond. "Come on, I want to talk to you."

Makeup was smeared all over its face, traces of garish red lipstick running down its chin, murky pools of mascara flooding its cheeks. It didn't say a word, but the dark sneer on its face did all the talking.

"Aren't you going to say something?" Dario asked. "You have a lot to answer for."

Not a word.

"Don't you want to deny it? Claim you don't know what I'm talking about?"

"No."

Dario's eyebrows raised in surprise. He hadn't expected it to answer. "No?"

It let out an exasperated sigh. "No. I will not deny it."

"What won't you deny?"

"That my name is Ohia, and that I killed your friend. Of course I remember you. You are an idiot if you think I care about your threats." Its singsong voice might once have been sweet, but now it was as biting as a gust of Andean wind.

"We can hurt you."

Dario expected it to laugh at him, or toy with him some other way, like it had the last time. Instead it stared at him with a vacant expression that spoke to how badly it wanted to shred that rope, wrap its fingers around Dario's soft throat, and squeeze until his head popped free like a grape from a vine.

"You cannot hurt me," it said, its tone even and sinister. "You can hurt this body, but I am not confined here. I can leave at any time."

"Then why don't you?"

"Because a willing host is hard to find. And this one is lovely, don't you agree?"

Was that a lie? Could this woman truly have given herself over to the creature? There must have been some deception involved.

"My fathers and sons are moving," it said. "Nothing can stop them. You're too late."

Dario took several backward steps, reluctant to show his back to the creature. He returned to David, got down, and whispered in the man's ear.

"Do you have any questions?" Dario asked him.

"Ira will want to go after Janene," David said. "But we need to find the Grigori. They're massing somewhere."

"It won't tell us." Regardless, they needed answers. Dario turned back to Ohia. "What were you doing in Singapore?"

"Building alliances, making friends, recruiting," it answered boldly. "You're surprised that I answer your question so openly, but you already surmised my purpose in Singapore. I only confirm what you know."

"Then what don't I know?"

"There are too many items to mention. But I suspect you wish to learn my fathers' location." Ohia tilted its head, looking almost thoughtful. "It is no great secret. You will learn the answer soon enough. They won't remain hidden much longer."

"They'll make their presence known? Why would they do that?"

"You are an idiot," it repeated. "Both of you. It serves our purposes to make our presence known."

Dario heard footsteps on the stairs. He turned his head just as Junior stepped into the dim light.

The elder David stood up and went to his son. "What is it?"

"There's something in the news you should see."

Dario herded them as far from Ohia as possible so it wouldn't overhear. "Tell us," Dario said. "Is it about Singapore?"

"No, it's something else." Junior ran a hand through his short hair. "Something far worse."

*   *   *

Ira heard their voices before he had enough strength to open his eyes. His eyelids felt heavy.

"Ira, you have to wake up."

It was David's voice. The older David. Aaron's son. Ira tried to reply, but his mouth didn't respond.

Damn it, what did that infernal barkeep do to me?

At last his eyelids were open, though not by his own effort. David's face filled his vision. Ira felt the man's touch against his clammy skin, holding his eyes open with two fingers.

"Ira. Wake. Up."

I'm trying, I'm trying, I'm trying—!" Ira stopped himself, grasping that he'd somehow gone from thought to speech without even thinking about it.

David removed his fingers, and Ira's eyes stayed open of their own accord.

"He's awake," David called, turning his head to look toward the bedroom door.

A woman appeared next to him. Celeste, damn her.

"I'm sorry, Rabbi." She sounded truly apologetic. "I was following instructions."

"My instructions," David added. "You can't blame her. Besides, you needed the rest."

Ira jammed his elbows back, drawing his torso up off the mattress. "If I needed rest so badly, why are you interrupting it?"

"There's been a development," David said.

"Janene," Ira breathed. "Is she still alive?"

David hesitated. "I don't know, Ira. This isn't about Janene. There's been an attack."

Ira wasn't sure he'd heard correctly. "What kind of attack?"

"A very public one, near the Indo-Pakistan border. It's all over television, Ira. My god, they're real-life giants! Just like my father said."

"The giants are out in the open?" Ira asked. It didn't make sense. Aside from Mahaway, the giants had long been dead. "Let me see."

They helped Ira sit up, and a moment later Junior hurried into the room and thrust a laptop into his hands. Ira squinted at the images playing out on the screen. A long line of burning commercial trucks lay tossed along the side of a narrow highway, billowing huge stacks of black smoke. Screams tore through the computer's tiny speakers.

"I don't see giants," he murmured.

But then he did see them, two of them, walking side by side through the underbrush. One minute they were in view and the next they had walked through the frame. It had happened so quickly that Ira wasn't sure they'd really been there.

As though sensing his thoughts, Junior rewound the video and let it play from the beginning. He paused it just as the pair of giants came into view.

"In Pakistan, you said," Ira said.

"That's right."

"We have to go." Ira stopped himself from standing up, remembering that he wasn't wearing any clothes. "Get out of here and let me dress."

Everyone herded out into the hallway.

"Where's Dario?" Ira asked just as David was about to shut the door.

"He's outside." David paused. "Ira, are you ready? What are you going to do?"

Ira admitted to himself that he didn't know. But whatever he did, he'd do it quickly.

TWENTY-SIX

Chakothi, Pakistan
AUGUST 3

The first mile almost killed her, but Gayle bit back the litany of complaints about to burst forth. Her feet ached; how long would it be before she couldn't put weight on them? Her eyes stung from the choking black smoke. Her damned clothes were causing her to overheat, and she kept tripping over the suffocating abaya's low hemline. She wanted to rip it off and wear nothing but her underwear, but her fellow refugees still didn't have reason to suspect she was anyone other than Faisal's demure wife.

There was no path west, just a steep climb through mountain brush, and they had to keep their distance from the road to remain unseen. Gayle only hoped that if the marauding giants looked in their direction, they would be indistinguishable from animals.

She heard a strangled cry as the young boy in their group fell, clutching his leg in pain. One of the men tried pulling him up, but he couldn't stand. The boy leaned against the man, his injured leg bent at the knee.

"What's wrong with him?" Gayle whispered to Faisal, unable to understand the chatter between the other passengers.

"Twisted his ankle, I think."

Gayle watched as the boy struggled to climb up onto the man's back, but her attention was pulled to the valley. Every vehicle on the road had gone up in a ball of fire, leaving behind a cemetery of twisted metal frames. Several bodies had been reduced to skeletal remains, billowing ash in every direction.

She gagged, realizing only too late that she wouldn't be able to hold down her stomach contents. She got down on her knees and heaved the unrecognizable vestiges of breakfast, closing her eyes as she heard it splash onto a layer of smooth stones. Groaning, she wiped her mouth and looked away from the group so she'd have time to re-adjust her scarf.

"We will soon be away from it," Faisal said. "Come now. We must keep moving."

"What are they?" She didn't expect him to have an answer, but asking the question somehow made her feel better.

Except he did have an answer. "The Starseed people. Who else?"

The words stunned her. They also made perfect sense, given the burst of nodal energy they were chasing.

"Faisal, I was never sure if I really believed."

"There can be no doubting now."

Gayle strained to stay next to Faisal at the front of the pack. Her lower legs didn't much care for all this exercise.

"Do you know where we're going?" Gayle asked him.

"Over the hill. One of the men says there is a town there called Chakothi. It is very close."

"And probably it is very destroyed."

Faisal didn't reply. He probably didn't see the point—and once she gave it serious thought, neither did she.

*   *   *

The blue sky brightened steadily until Dario couldn't keep his eyes open. Much more suddenly, the light went away, replaced by darkness.

No, not darkness, he realized. *Dusk.*

The sun was cut in half by a towering ridge of mountains, casting the valley in shadow. The encroaching nightfall barely registered against the tangy scent of blood and fire. Smoke swelled over burned-out commercial trucks, their steel bones enclosing piles of ash and cinder—the remains of whatever cargo they'd once carried.

Dario took a tentative step and felt his shoe crunch over… something. He looked down and saw that it was a smoldering piece of bone. He stepped back, and almost bumped into Ira.

"Do you see that?" Dario asked, but the rabbi was too busy focusing on the two dozen other specimens of charred flesh littering the road. "What happened here?"

The ground shook, subtly at first and then more rhythmic and pronounced. Like approaching footsteps.

"Holy hell, Ira!" Dario spun in time to see a trio of enormous creatures coming toward them from the east. One held a flame-thrower that looked like a toothpick in its colossal hand.

Ira raised both his hands in front of him, fixing the giants with a glassy stare.

"Run. Now," Ira said, his voice calm. Mostly calm. Dario thought he could detect a touch of anxiety on the last syllable.

Dario took off, his arms and legs pumping wildly. At first he didn't have a destination in mind, but the burnt, peeling skin of a big rig, its cab detached from its trailer, offered the best shelter. He hurtled around the side of it and crouched, his head between his knees. He waited for several achingly long seconds, his quickened pulse making his whole body throb. He listened carefully for a sound, any sound to indicate what was going on, but all he heard was the wind. Even the grinding thud of footsteps had stopped.

"You, little man," a voice boomed, carrying easily to Dario's ears, and likely from one end of the valley to the other, the slopes forming a natural amplifier. "What's this now? Ah, we did not expect Jehovah's ilk."

Dario risked a peek around the side of the rig. He half-expected Ira to be crushed against the pavement like a swatted fly, but instead the rabbi's hands were held aloft, raging with fire. The heat distorted the air all around him in a conflagration as deadly as the one Dario had seen him make at Khunjerab.

Ira, I hope you know what you're doing.

As one of the giants lumbered toward the rabbi, Dario saw how deformed they were. They looked like walking corpses, as though their appendages had been assembled by a ten-year-old with no appreciation for anatomical correctness. Their withered, parched skin had separated into splotchy white patches, leaving deep, bloodless troughs between them.

Ira seemed unfazed by this madness. He calmly knelt and touched his hands to the ground. The earth began to shift, moisture rising to the surface and then breaking into a boil. A moment later, the dirt erupted into tar-black gouts of fire.

The giants fell back as the black inferno consumed the ground outward from Ira, growing in a circular pattern a few inches per second. When Ira stood up, the black fire fizzled and died, leaving a swatch of charred grass in a wide ring.

The giants growled, then one of them hurled itself back toward Ira at frightening speed, its unshod feet crackling through the charred grass and stone.

"Ira!" Dario screamed, though Ira clearly saw the beast coming.

The giant's feet churned ever closer, and Dario realized they were driving more and more sluggishly. Whereas Dario had thought it would reach Ira in seconds, it now seemed the creature was at least a minute away. He was doing what he had done in Singapore, managing to slow time in a wide radius around him. The creature plodded perilously close to Ira, and Dario knew it would never reach him, not as long as the spell held.

Was spell the right word? Dario didn't have an adequate vocabulary to describe it. Whatever it was, he prayed Ira had the strength to keep it up.

A second giant broke into a run, and then the third. Within moments, all three were converging on the besieged rabbi. Even from this distance, Dario could see Ira struggling to contain them. His shoulders twitched. Sweat poured down the back of his neck, soaking his shirt.

He wouldn't be able to keep this up much longer. If he failed, he'd be dead.

Dario made an impulsive decision. He stepped out from behind the rig. If those creatures did care about him, perhaps he could take some of the pressure off Ira, even for a moment. Maybe long enough for Ira to change strategies.

Dario screamed at the creatures, trying to draw their attention, and slowly—for everything they did now was very slow—they reacted. Their inertia was such that his sudden appearance didn't take an immediate effect, but then, just as Dario's heart fell, one of the three creatures shifted its trajectory. Ever so slightly. Toward Dario.

And it picked up speed as it moved out of Ira's influence.

It was exactly what he'd wanted, and exactly what he feared. Dario broke into a sprint. He knew he didn't have a prayer of actually outrunning the giant, but it was the only way to buy Ira time. Hopefully it would be enough.

He ran until he was out of breath. Once, he dared look behind him. The giant remained a good distance away, Dario having enjoyed a head start while the giant was still enmeshed in Ira's dampening field. Now the giant was gaining—fast.

Dario heard a roar in the distance, tempting him to chance another look, but he worried even the act of turning his head would slow him down. Fighting for breath, he plunged ahead. The vibrating earth betrayed the giant's approach. He didn't have long now.

Ira, you bastard.

On cue, the air sizzled ten feet in front of Dario, and Ira exploded into view. Dario reeled to avoid him, steering out of the way just as a gigantic leg zipped through the space he'd just occupied. The giant let out a grating snarl as Ira, too, dodged it. The creature overshot them by a wide margin, but immediately turned back.

"Ira, where did you come from?"

Instead of answering, Ira grabbed him tight by the wrist and closed his eyes, his lips trembling as though reciting some frantic, silent petition. As the giant bore down on them, Dario considered wriggling free and making another run for it, even though he knew intellectually that it would be useless.

"Stop him!" Dario shouted.

"I can only do one thing at a time." Ira clenched his eyes even tighter. "Just… once more…"

Dario felt like he might have a heart attack from the terror, but just in time—as it so often happened these days—he heard a crackling sound in his ears and knew the impending safety and relief it portended.

*   *   *

Chakothi proved lifeless, as did the village after that. They came across several dozen shell-shocked refugees in the surrounding hills and assimilated them into their pack. As their numbers swelled, Gayle felt all the more alien. It was only a matter of time before someone noticed she wasn't who she appeared to be.

As night fell, there was some conversation of stopping and making camp. Gayle didn't want to stop, but she also recognized the near-impossibility of making headway in the dark through unfamiliar territory. Faisal proved an excellent guide, but even he had no direct knowledge of the terrain. He also no longer served as the group's de facto leader, as several local men took charge. From their gestures, it seemed as though they wanted the group to press on until they came across a village untouched by the violence.

Gayle had other plans.

"They will go south in the morning, toward more remote territory," Faisal told her as they settled down for the night next to a thick-trunked silver fir.

"We can't stay," Gayle said. "We're better off traveling alone."

"But where to?"

"West."

"Safer to go south, hmm?"

Gayle looked in the direction she thought was northwest. "I told you about Elisabeth. She went missing somewhere far north of here. We need to get to a town and look for transportation. A car, preferably."

"That might be hard to find."

"We have to try. And we shouldn't wait until morning. We'll leave before the sun comes up. The others won't even notice we're gone."

She slept fitfully, startling awake every half-hour, in large part due to the stress of not wanting to sleep too late and get caught up with the refugees again. After opening her eyes for the fifth or sixth time, she awkwardly emptied her bladder in the forest.

"Are you sure this is the right decision?" Faisal asked after she woke him. "We have no food or water."

"We'll get some in the next town."

Under the light of the stars, they resumed their long march.

TWENTY-SEVEN

Canadian Arctic

AUGUST 3

Abranel breathed slowly but evenly. He didn't seem afraid, only wary. Something had moved inside the crate, and Abranel hadn't expected it.

It's one of the Nephilim, isn't it? Brighton asked. It was the only possibility that made sense. The crates held dead bodies, Brighton was sure of it, and this one had been possessed. The spirits usually required living, willing hosts, but he had witnessed firsthand the way they could also inhabit the dead. How easily he could recall the face of that dead girl in Tiahuanaco, the one who had fallen victim to Ohia's machinations.

"Yes," Abranel admitted.

Aren't these the brothers you mentioned? Are you frightened of your own brother?

"I'm not frightened." Abranel hesitated, and Brighton wondered what he was thinking. "But I'm the only one my grandfather sent."

Who else would have sent someone?

"Semyaza controls all the Grigori, and there is only one group of Grigori."

In other words, you don't know.

Abranel peered toward the crate in question. It hadn't moved in a minute, but that didn't mean it would stay that way. As though to drive home the point, it leapt into the air and landed on its end. The crate teetered for several seconds before falling over again.

In the expectant silence that followed, Abranel barely breathed.

The crate exploded—or near enough to it that Brighton couldn't tell the difference. The lid lifted from the release of enormous force and flew through the air before diving into the water. It sank straight to the bottom.

Brighton expected a body to rise out of the crate, but nothing emerged—and Abranel refused to investigate.

It knows we're here, Brighton pointed out. *We're not fooling it by hiding.*

"You don't know that."

You may as well find out who it is. Then you can find out what's going on.

"Shut up!"

Brighton was pleased to have pissed him off enough to elicit such an emotional reaction, and he decided to press his advantage. *You are a coward. You exude confidence and charm when you enjoy total control, but the moment there's any uncertainty your instinct is to run and hide. It's pathetic.*

Abranel growled quietly. "You can't bait me. I've been doing this for millennia."

But I have baited you. You're not as strong as you think.

"Your opinion means nothing. I'll never release my grip on you. I'm never going to leave. Do you understand how hopeless your situation is? It's like you don't even exist."

Brighton felt he had goaded him into revealing the naked truth. Despite the occasional kind word and moment of hope, Abranel had laid it bare.

You're a monster.

Abranel laughed. "A monster? Is that the best you can do? I've been called a monster my whole life. It's what the humans thought of us—and they paid for it with their lives."

You failed to destroy them. We're still here, and you and your brothers are gone.

"We're still here, too."

Yes, you exist. And that's all that can be said of you and your wretched kind. Forced to wander the earth for all eternity, with no bodies of your own. Unable to die, unable to live. Where does that leave you? Relegated to the dregs of humanity. And corpses.

"I suppose that makes you the dregs of humanity."

Well, Abranel had him there. *I've made my bed. I'll sleep in it.*

Abranel might have responded, but instead he was distracted by a voice on the wind: "I can hear you. Can you hear me?"

The voice was deep and raspy, as though issuing from a throat that hadn't spoken a word in a very long time. The voice of the dead.

Brighton had noticed Abranel's tendency to get very quiet when faced with something he didn't want to talk about, and here he was at it again. The wind whistled and wailed. Water lapped over rocks. Abranel remained mute.

"I want to speak with Sherwood Brighton," the voice called.

Brighton couldn't believe his ears. Surely he hadn't heard right. But he had.

"I want to talk to you!" it said.

Coward, Brighton thought. *Coward. Coward. Coward!*

Brighton couldn't be sure whether he'd persuaded Abranel to take action or Abranel had made the decision on his own, but he stepped into the cargo hold doorway, making himself visible.

"What do you want with him?" Abranel called.

"I've been following him for several days."

"And what is your name?"

A long pause. "I'm called Nariman."

Abranel's eyes widened. Whoever Nariman was, Abranel knew of him. But as Brighton rolled that name over in his thoughts, he realized the name was familiar to him, too. He'd heard it before. Somewhere dark. Somewhere wet. A fireplace. An enormous chair. Giants. Ancient kings.

Gilgamesh, Mahaway, Nariman. He repeated the names over and over. *Gilgamesh. Mahaway. Nariman. Gilgamesh. Mahaway. Nariman. Gilgamesh…*

"I know who they are," Abranel whispered. "You don't have to—"

The three men from the vision I had over a year ago. Ira walked us through it, a vision from Barakel's memory. They were giants, and one was Barakel's own son. Mahaway. He had just seen something in a dream.

As Brighton reviewed this memory, it came back clear as day. Sickly yellow flames blazed in a hearth, casting long shadows. Three giants sat in enormous wooden chairs, cloaked in darkness, but their gruff voices reverberated off the cold stone walls.

"A vision came to me," Mahaway had said. "It concerned a stone tablet, and upon that tablet were names. Perhaps every name, of every man who lives, and every woman, and every child. And the tablet was drenched in water."

Brighton gasped at the memory. Was this how it was supposed to work? Was this the kind of perfect recall Ira had tried so unsuccessfully to teach him?

"They were our names," Abranel said.

Whose names?

"The names on the tablet Mahaway saw. My name, my brothers, and all our descendants. Jehovah sent a cataclysmic flood to wipe us out. We were murdered."

For the first time, Brighton found himself able to sense Abranel. His emotions were too strong to ignore. They drove through him like a nail through drywall, the sadness so profound that Brighton, despite himself, couldn't help but empathize with the pain of losing everyone he'd ever known. Except it had been a fate worse than death, for they hadn't died. Their spirits had lingered. Stayed behind in this pitiable form, reduced to leeches, able to get by…

…*on the dregs of humanity,* Brighton finished, overwhelmed by the blunt force of connecting the dots.

"This penalty is too severe!" Nariman had cried out to Mahaway. Brighton found that he could call on the memory at will. "It is not for us! We have done nothing. It was Azazel! We are but the children, the byproducts, neglected and forgotten."

I'm sorry, Brighton thought.

Abranel let loose his rage. "I don't care about your pity!"

It was enough for Brighton to remember that despite everything that had happened to Abranel, he truly *was* a monster, guilty of thousands of atrocities. How many men and women had he killed? How many of his own brothers? How could it be justified? An abused child who grew up to be a killer was still a killer.

"You can't have him," Abranel called out, this time to the crate. "You'll have to talk to me."

"Why don't you come out where I can see you?"

Abranel clearly didn't want to show himself. Did Nariman represent some kind of threat that Brighton didn't understand? Perhaps they'd been on different sides of a conflict. Even still, Abranel himself couldn't be injured in the event Nariman attacked him, so why the reluctance?

For that matter, why didn't Nariman come to them? He couldn't be too determined to speak to them if he didn't leave his crate.

Abranel, let me speak with him.

"I will decide to whom you speak," Abranel said.

It was amazing how quickly Brighton's empathy transformed to hatred. Abranel was dead-set on making his life as miserable as possible.

I can't live this way.

"Isn't that the point?" Abranel growled under his breath.

I don't understand why you're doing this. It's unnecessary!

"Fine," Nariman called over the intervening space. "If you won't come to me, I will come to you."

Brighton again expected a ghoulish body to rise out of the crate, but nothing happened. Nariman no longer spoke at all.

And neither did Abranel.

The reason took about five seconds to register, and those were amongst the most pivotal five seconds of Brighton's life. First he felt a flare of almost unbearable heat around his shoulders, pressing down with crushing force. He would have screamed were he able; he smelled rather than felt the singed flesh. His jacket tore open, its frayed threads catching fire. Abranel thrust the jacket off him before it worsened the burn, though Brighton knew his skin was already as red as a lobster. As it turned out, he lacked the capacity to even think about the pain or where it came from, because the heat then entered his chest, throbbing to the rhythm of his heart—and his heart raced. It made sense that his heart would beat so quickly, except this wasn't a symptom of his own fear, but Abranel's. Abranel wasn't just afraid; he was on the edge of panic. Brighton's whole body burned with a shifting fever that raged one second in his abdomen, and the next in the base of his neck. It settled in his head, shoving his consciousness aside in a violent demonstration of strength. Brighton had grown accustomed to the familiar pattern of Abranel's presence, and he knew this was something different. *Someone* different.

As these whirlwind five seconds came to a close, the crowning realization struck that a war of titans was being waged inside him, between Abranel and Nariman. The war only lasted a fleeting moment, and when it ended only one presence remained.

And it wasn't Abranel.

Hello? Brighton thought.

He then heard his own voice, but its cadence and structure were foreign. "At last we can speak in peace."

Are you Nariman?

"Yes. The other one is gone. He's no longer welcome here."

Neither are you. Brighton pushed his consciousness forward into… he didn't know how to think of it except to conclude it was the center of his being, the part of his mind he resided at when he was in control. Abranel had surrounded it like an impenetrable barrier. No amount of force had been able to affect Abranel's iron hold, but Nariman was a different story. He was soft, malleable clay to Abranel's steel. With hardly any mental effort, Brighton pushed Nariman *out.*

At first Brighton felt only confusion. His body ached from the strain it had been put through, and he could barely move. He looked down and realized he was sitting half in the shallow water at the base of the ship. The cargo hold loomed above him; Brighton had no recollection of falling. Or had he climbed down? Had Abranel done it?

Abranel…

His own thought reflected back at him. He blinked in shock as he remembered that this was the way it was supposed to be, the way it had always been before Abranel's residency. Brighton blinked repeatedly, unable to grasp what had happened—and *how* it had happened—and between those blinks, tears rained down, splattering his cheeks.

I'm free.

And he whispered it.

"I'm free."

And he shouted it at the top of his lungs.

"I'm free!"

The words soared through the air, swept up by the wind before returning to earth and being absorbed into the tundra. What a glorious luxury to think and to speak and to act! He would never again take for granted such simple pleasures.

"You let go," Brighton said. "You could have held on."

"I could not." Nariman's voice came from the crate once more, deeper and more gravelly than ever. "I entered, but only to free you. We can inhabit only the willing or the dead. You were neither."

Brighton tried to stand and felt the sharp sting of blisters marring his mosquito-bitten skin. He stood, the pain fading. Perhaps he only needed another minute to adjust. After all the torment he'd endured, a little bit of physical pain barely registered.

"What happened to Abranel?" he asked.

"He has been... expelled. I trust I wasn't out of line."

Brighton almost wept from the exultation of knowing he was his own person again. "But why did you help me? Why did you come?"

"By helping you, I help myself," Nariman said. "Now, come closer. I want you to see me."

Suddenly, Brighton didn't want to approach. He was afraid of what he would find in that crate. But how could he deny such a simple request, after all Nariman had done for him?

Brighton crept closer, moving slowly on account of his injuries. Nariman didn't rush him.

When he looked down into the box, it was fully as repulsive as he had feared. A gnarled, disfigured face leered up at him, covered in flesh shredded by extreme age.

"It's important to see us for who we really are," Nariman said.

Brighton jumped back at the startlement of seeing the dead face animate. "This is your body?"

"Not my original body, no. As far as I know, it has long returned to the earth. What you see is the preserved remains of my fellow Nephilim. Before the flood, during the war with Jehovah, the Twenty preserved a number of our bodies."

The Twenty, Brighton thought, turning his thoughts back to his meeting with Semyaza.

"Semyaza said he was the first of the Twenty," Brighton said.

Nariman pursed his mutilated lips. "Semyaza lies about much, but in this he told the truth."

"That's why the crates were so important to him. He wanted them as part of his war efforts." Unafraid, Brighton stepped closer—and saw to his surprise that the crate only contained the top half of Nariman's body. He peered at the other crates strewn across the grass. Perhaps one of those contained the bottom half.

No wonder Nariman wasn't able to walk to us earlier. He doesn't have any legs!

"Did you know the one whose body you now occupy?"

"Yes, I knew him," Nariman said. "He was one of the most important of all the Nephilim, a general in the Grigori's forces. He was very dear to Semyaza. His favorite son."

"What was his name?"

"It's unimportant." But then Nariman seemed to change his mind. "He was known by many names, but the one you might be familiar with is Nimrod."

"Never heard of him."

Aside from the schoolyard pejorative, he remarked silently.

"Whatever Semyaza is trying to accomplish, and I don't claim special knowledge, Nimrod will have been central to it. That's always been the way of things. That's why I targeted this ship, took it down by interfering with the pilot. I wanted to draw their attention." The creature's cadaverous eyes blinked. "We can put an end to all this."

"How?"

"We must destroy these bodies. It won't stop the Grigori, but it will be a step in the right direction." The creature smiled, a hideous sight. "And it will enrage Semyaza."

"All the better," Brighton agreed. "But why are you turning against them?"

Nariman didn't say anything for a few long moments, and Brighton realized this was a complex question. More complex than he'd intended.

"The Grigori created us to wage war against Jehovah, and for no other reason," Nariman said. "They didn't care for the women they raped, and they didn't respect the children they sired. We were monsters, plain and simple, tasked with carrying out atrocities."

"You didn't want to carry them out? You're saying you were forced?"

"No. I wish that were true. Most of my brothers all too willingly maimed and murdered. They were bred to enjoy it." His face turned hard. "But there were exceptions—and some of us came to embrace our peaceful natures. When the threat of the flood first reached us, we began to meet in secret."

"You mean with Gilgamesh and Mahaway," Brighton said.

Nariman's raised his eyebrows. "You know of them?"

"It's a long story." When Brighton saw that a longer explanation was called for, he added, "Barakel told me."

It wasn't quite true, but at least it resembled the truth. In a way, Barakel *had* told him.

"I'm pleased at least some know the truth," Nariman finished in a voice heavy with sorrow. "I myself am filled with regret."

Brighton could tell Nariman hadn't told the whole story. This version of the tale was an oversimplification, but in the face of such a long history it had to suffice. Brighton didn't sense any dishonesty in him.

Nariman instructed him to gather wood for a fire. For ten minutes, Brighton wandered the tundra looking for sticks amidst the brambles. It wasn't easy, and soon he resorted to collecting the driest-looking grasses as well. He returned to the crash site with just enough for kindling, but it would be an anemic fire.

"I need you to open the rest of the crates," Nariman said as Brighton made a pile of the kindling.

"But they're locked."

"In the cockpit, there's a specialized device for opening them."

Brighton gazed at the ship. "Why didn't Abranel know about it?"

"I imagine he did," Nariman said.

"He said he didn't."

"Then he lied. Are you surprised?" When Brighton said nothing, Nariman continued. "The walls of the cockpit are pressure-sensitive. Feel the area behind where the pilot's head would rest. You'll find a storage compartment. The item you're after looks like a wand, about ten inches long."

Brighton walked back to the ship and stared up along its smooth, nearly vertical edifice. An imposing climb, though one Abranel had handled with ease.

He started off by clambering overtop the cargo hold door, then moved slowly upward, using the rubber soles of his boots to maintain traction. He tried to stay focused on the ship, looking into his distorted reflection in the vessel's hull; the height was especially daunting now that he controlled his own fate again.

He slid into the safety of the cockpit after a minute of climbing and probed the wall of the compartment. The material felt soft yet firm, like a cross between steel and a sponge. The combination seemed so implausible, but his hands told him otherwise.

Just as Nariman had said, a small opening revealed itself. A jumble of items had been placed inside. He picked up each one and inspected it, acting more out of curiosity than need since only one item resembled the wand in question. A handful of black cubes were scattered around the small space, and Brighton noticed that they clamped together magnetically. He couldn't even guess at their purpose, but they might have value. Another item, elliptical in shape, had an antenna-like protrusion from one end. Perhaps this was the emergency transponder Abranel had referred to.

He pocketed the wand, as well as the black cubes, and carefully picked his way back to the ground.

"I found it," Brighton said, a little out of breath. He settled down on the ground next to one of the unopened crates.

"Place it lengthwise along the thin seam marking the lid. Then press down on either end of the device, doesn't matter which, and the lid should pop free."

"How does it work?"

"Don't worry about that. Just get the crates open and remove the bodies. They must not be recovered by the Grigori. We only have an hour or two."

Less than that, Brighton knew, if he was going to beat Regan. He was cutting it close.

The two crates already free of the ship popped open easily. Both contained heads and torsos. Brighton struggled to lift the giant bodies out of the crates, but fortunately Nariman was able to assist. The spirit occupied each body as Brighton lugged it out onto the ground. Nariman was only able to move them in a limited fashion, but he could use the arms to hoist the bodies up. Without that help, Brighton would have had to work twice as hard.

Unfortunately, there were three other crates still in the cargo hold, and Brighton strongly suspected all three would contain cadavers from the waist down. Nariman wouldn't be much help with those.

His concerns proved unjustified, as the legs were much lighter and easier to maneuver. It took half an hour, but he had soon assembled the bodies in a stubby tower. The tiny amount of kindling he'd collected looked ridiculous now. Burning these bodies would require an inferno.

"There's another option," Nariman suggested from the only torso not yet thrown onto the pile. "Use the ship's unused fuel."

Nariman had to instruct him in how to retrieve the fuel. The fuel itself was volatile and might ignite the oxygen in the air. Therefore, Brighton could only extract it in very small amounts, and it had to remain contained.

The best container option was the metallic lighter Brighton carried in his backpack. Brighton fumbled with it for a minute before figuring out how to remove the lighter insert and access the fuel reservoir. He pried open the latch on the bottom and emptied the lighter fuel already inside. The opening was only large enough to accommodate a drip or two at a time, so he worried their plan wouldn't work.

Nariman explained where to find the fuel hatch on the exterior of the ship. One had to know exactly where to push against the hull to reveal it, and Brighton only located the round hole after several tries. There was no gas cap like on modern cars, but instead an intake valve designed to keep the fuel from coming into contact with the air. It took a minor adjustment to reverse the tiny pump's flow. Nariman assured him it would only come out a few drops at a time, seeing as the ship required such a small amount. He thought Brighton should be able to capture the fuel without difficulty.

As though sensing Brighton's tension and striving to make it worse, a mosquito landed on his forehead. He swatted it away, then another. He would just have to ignore them and let them have their feast, at least for the moment. He had to keep his hands steady. He hadn't just gotten his life back to blow himself up, had he? When he expressed this fear, Nariman didn't provide the total reassurance Brighton had hoped for.

"It's a possibility," Nariman said. "But it must be done."

Brighton clutched the fuel reservoir and placed one finger on its small opening; his other hand rested on the ship's fuel valve. He pressed the two as closely together as their shapes allowed, but they didn't quite touch.

"We must hurry," Nariman reminded him.

Now or never. Brighton sunk his teeth into his lower lip and opened the valve. One two three four drops came out, slowly and methodically. Not wanting to press his luck, Brighton closed the valve and snapped the reservoir's seal back into place.

He hadn't been killed yet, but the ordeal wasn't over.

"Place it at the base of the bodies, alongside the kindling," Nariman said. Brighton did as he was told, grateful to put the lighter on the ground and back away from it. "Now, how good a shot are you?"

"Excuse me?"

"With a rock. Keep your distance, just in case, but do you think you could hit the lighter with a rock from twenty feet away?"

Brighton backed up to the suggested distance and appraised the situation. He might need a few tries, but it was doable. He searched the ground for a medium-sized rock, and found several perfect specimens near the edge of the water. He picked one up, tossed it into the air, and caught it.

He was about to toss it at the pile when he stopped, realizing the gravity of what he was about to do.

"Nariman, are you sure you want me to do this?"

The body Nariman inhabited lifted its grotesque head. "We have to say goodbye to what we were. It's the only way."

Brighton still hesitated. "We won't be able to speak again. Is there anything else you want to say?"

"I'll stay close in the difficult time to come, an invisible ally should you need me," Nariman said. "Now do it. They'll be here soon. You need to get away."

"Where do I go?"

"Just do it!"

Brighton released the rock. It flew through the air, missing the lighter and hitting Nariman in the face.

"Try again."

The second rock hit the ground, short of the pile.

The third hit the mark.

Brighton rocked backward in the resulting explosion. The fireball billowed high, releasing a huge cloud of smoke. Brighton knew it would be visible for miles in every direction. Regan would have seen it for sure, and so might the approaching Grigori.

He turned and ran, only slowing when he nearly fell on his face trying to climb around a copse of willows. He adjusted to a jog as he navigated the ups and downs of the soft ground, only turning occasionally to stare at the column of smoke behind him.

When he came to the top of a hill, he saw the creek they had been forced to cross earlier. Before venturing through the cold water, he looked back and admired the fire. A second and much larger explosion erupted—somehow the fire had grown to encompass the ship. That was a lucky outcome, as he didn't want the Grigori—or anyone else—getting their hands on it.

As he continued on his way, the float plane came into view. Regan stood in front of it, waving his hands frantically.

"What have you done?" Regan demanded. "Did you start that fire?"

Brighton passed the pilot, waded through the shallow water, and climbed onto the pontoon. He swung open the door and got inside.

"Let's go," Brighton said, scratching a row of bug bites on the back of his neck.

Within minutes, Regan turned the plane around and took off, heading south toward Yellowknife.

"What's our ETA?" Brighton asked over the noise of the engine.

"An hour and a half."

Plenty of time to think about what I've done.

*   *   *

Once back in Yellowknife, Brighton headed straight to the hotel, intent on holing himself up in his room as long as it took to figure out what to do next. He hurriedly packed, even though he had no idea where to go once he left the city. He just knew he had to leave.

I'll go back for Elisabeth. The last thing he wanted was to get thrown back into the Grigori conflict, but he didn't have much choice. He owed her, simple as that.

He would make a plan, but first he needed rest.

When he awoke, the sky had gone dark. He checked the time and confirmed that it was the middle of the night. 1:45. It would be too late to slake his thirst at the bar, so tap water would have to do.

Brighton grabbed the empty ice bucket on the hutch next to the television and went in search of the ice machine. He heard its distinctive rattle somewhere off to his left.

As he approached the corner at the end of the hall, a woman swerved around it and narrowly avoided a collision with him.

"Sorry," she mumbled.

"Annie!" Brighton said. "Looks like you're as much of a night owl as I am."

The Japanese woman's eyes shifted and Brighton realized she was actually looking over his shoulder. He turned just far enough to see that someone else was converging on them. Someone he recognized.

Brighton dropped the empty ice bucket in surprise.

"Like I said, I'm sorry," Annie said.

Wendell, the new arrival, grabbed him by the wrist and pulled hard, refusing to let go.

TWENTY-EIGHT

Chilas, Pakistan
AUGUST 4

The valley was covered in scars—trees ripped from the ground, buildings and homes cleaved from their foundations, crops leveled. Gayle got out of their stolen car and took in the devastation. "What happened here?" she asked as Faisal joined her outside.

"The river."

Gayle's eyes fixed on the river, flowing strong but hardly out of control. It didn't seem wider than normal given the single bridge spanning it. Nonetheless, a watery cataclysm had no doubt struck here. Chunks of pavement had been pried out of the highway and carried off.

"Perhaps a dam broke open?" Gayle suggested, looking upriver.

Faisal shrugged. He didn't have the answer.

"Continuing will be difficult." Faisal pointed to the broken pavement. "The highway is not passable."

"But the node is north of here. More than a hundred miles."

They had to abandon the car and walk to the river on foot. Great sinkholes of mud blocked their way, and navigating around them took precious time.

"Hundreds must have died," Gayle murmured as they walked.

"And it is a very long valley," Faisal added.

He was drowned out by the sound of an approaching motor. Gayle shielded her eyes and spotted a motorboat. Two men occupied it—one standing, the other sitting. The sitting man was the driver, and the standing man served as lookout, pointing out debris in the waterway so the driver could steer around it.

Gayle hurried closer to the water, waving her arms. "Hey!"

Faisal caught up to her. "Let me speak."

The lookout spotted him and stared with suspicion, but nonetheless instructed the driver to come closer.

Faisal spoke to the men for a few minutes, and Gayle did her best to follow along. The lookout raised his voice as he spoke, growing more animated. At one point, he mimed a huge wave washing down upon them from somewhere upstream.

"There was a lake two hundred kilometers from here, blocked by an earthen dam," Faisal whispered to her. "They say giants broke through the dam and released the flood. They will ferry survivors to Gilgit. They will take us."

"That's perfect," Gayle said.

The lookout heard her. "You speak English?"

Surprised, Gayle turned to him. She cleared her throat and lowered her scarf, exposing her face.

"I am…" She had been about to say American, but then changed her mind. Who knew what opinion these people held toward Americans? "…Canadian."

This didn't seem to be much better, because the man still threw her a look of disgust. "There are others. Lots of visitors this month."

Intrigued, she allowed the lookout to help her onto the boat. She sat next to Faisal, acting as demurely as she could tolerate. They raced farther downstream, searching for other survivors but finding none. Before long, they turned around and headed to Gilgit.

The city was just as decimated as the rest of the valley, with only small pockets of buildings on the more highly elevated fringes still standing. Their destination was a handful of warehouse-like structures.

Inside, a crowd milled in confusion. The chorus of strident voices made it difficult for Gayle to make sense of what was going on. Faisal explained that in one part of the building survivors were working on a registration to keep track of everyone, making it easier for survivors to find friends and family. In another corner, people were dispensing food; she felt hungry, but not enough to brave the crush of humanity converging there.

"They will not have enough food," Faisal remarked sadly.

Gayle felt a wave of lightheadedness. She put a hand to her forehead and breathed deeply. She needed some fresh air. An open door beckoned.

"I'm going to go out," Gayle said, pulling on Faisal's arm.

He resisted. "I must find a way to help."

"Good man, Faisal. I'll come back and find you."

She breathed more easily outside, and she saw she hadn't been the only one to feel claustrophobic. A number of others sat on rocks, staring in dejected silence at their ruined home.

Gayle's spirit lifted when she saw a group who looked like Western tourists. As she neared, she heard that they were conversing in English.

"Can I join you?" she asked.

A man turned and Gayle saw that he had tears in his eyes. He stood aside to make room for her. Gayle didn't dare say a word as she struggled to catch up with the situation. The conversation revolved around some fellow travelers who had gone missing. When they discovered Gayle had been all the way downriver to Chilas, they broke into a litany of questions.

"We came from far to the east," Gayle clarified.

"Did you see the giants?" someone asked.

Gayle nodded, reliving the terror of escaping the overturned bus. "In fact, we barely escaped them."

The crying man put a hand on her shoulder. "When you were in the mountains, did you run into a South African couple? Carter and Marilyn de Vries?"

"I'm afraid not," Gayle said. "Did you lose them in the flood?"

"They've been gone a couple of days. We don't know what happened." The man pointed his chin to encompass the group. "You'll think it strange, but we're not here to admire the scenery. We're... well, I guess you could say we're alien chasers."

Gayle didn't quite know how to respond to that, but she certainly didn't think it strange. "Have you ever heard of the Starseed people?" she asked.

"Not by that name," a young woman said. "But the aliens we're looking for go by many names. Their ships are often spotted in the skies over these mountains."

Evening descended before anyone could decide what to do next. Gayle went back inside to look for Faisal. It took almost half an hour to track him down in the crowded warehouse, which had only gotten more crowded as additional refugees poured in.

Faisal sat against a wall, sweat covering his forehead. Going by his blank, almost despondent expression, he'd been worn to a nub.

"You look like you could use a rest," Gayle said.

"Yes."

She helped him up, and together they found a cool spot in which to rest.

"Why has no help has arrived?" Gayle wondered aloud.

"The damage is very widespread. These giants... there may be many, keeping the government occupied."

Gayle couldn't recall falling asleep, but she must have for she awoke, startled, when someone touched her on the shoulder. The young woman from the alien chasers hunched down next to her.

"What is it?" Gayle asked, peering toward a window and seeing that the sun had started to rise.

"We've decided to hike south. You should join us."

Gayle looked over at Faisal, still asleep. He would probably approve of fleeing to the safety of a larger city, but Gayle had come too far to give up.

"I can't," Gayle said. "I have a missing friend of my own, and I won't abandon her."

The woman lowered her moistened eyes, and Gayle regretted her choice of words.

"Thank you for thinking of me," Gayle called, but the woman had already left.

Faisal raised himself up, blinking the sleep from his eyes. "Who was that?"

"No one." She sat up straight. "We should keep moving. Do you think we could rent a boat, or commission someone to take us upriver?"

"Will be hard. Everyone is afraid."

"That may be. But we'll have to find a way."

*   *   *

By eleven o'clock, after hours of asking around, Faisal found a boat owner willing to take them as far as a place called Shishkat, but no farther. Faisal agreed to pay the boater for his trouble, and within an hour of reaching an agreement they were motoring north.

Gayle's heart broke as they passed village after village washed away by the flood. The most troubling sights were the bodies in the water. Gayle spotted three, including a girl who couldn't have been more than five or six. The driver was disinclined to fish corpses out of the river, but Gayle stared behind them until the little girl was no longer visible.

Amidst the heartbreak, she began to feel something else. Gayle remembered the overwhelming influx of energy she'd first felt three weeks ago. It had intensified for several days before fellow sensitives began contacting her about it. Great bursts of energy were bombarding the earth. Henry had died trying to channel that energy.

All that energy accumulated here, she told herself. *Whether it's the Starseed people or something else, the answers are close.*

Faisal interrupted her thoughts by pointing to the remains of an enormous earthen dyke on either side of the river.

"The flood started here," he said. "Giants breached the dam and released the lake's water."

Anybody could see the truth of it, for the portion of the valley they now entered showed many signs of having been submerged. A highway had once twined through the narrow gulley, but all that remained were crumbling ledges covered in thick mud. Not a tree grew, not even a blade of grass.

Just as small patches of green returned to the landscape, they arrived at Shishkat. Several docks extended out from the center of town, a strange sight since there was no lake to receive them.

The driver stopped the boat and handed Faisal the end of a thick rope. Faisal hopped out onto one of those docks and tied the rope around its pier. Gayle got out behind him, hands on her hips. The street at the end of the dock seemed practically deserted, though a few eyes peeked out through windows. Gayle made a point of pretending she didn't see them.

"Are you sure we can't convince him to take us farther?" Gayle asked as she and Faisal walked into town.

He shook his head. "He was insistent. We can look for another car."

Several abandoned trucks were parked in the streets, but neither Gayle nor Faisal could find keys to go with them.

"Do you still sense energy?" Faisal asked an hour into the search. They approached a vintage Toyota with faded red paint.

"I can, but it is growing weaker. We have to hurry."

None of the Toyota's four doors would open, but on a whim Gayle decided to check the trunk. To her surprise, the latch opened easily. She peered in and saw that she would be able to push down the back seat and crawl inside.

"I don't suppose you see the keys?" Gayle asked.

Faisal leaned his head to one of the side windows and scanned the interior. "There!"

After double-checking to confirm the presence of a ring of keys stuffed almost out of view in the center console, Gayle crawled into the trunk. The bottom hem of her abaya tore when it snagged a sharp corner of the folding back seat.

Soon they were on the move again, cruising north along the pitted highway, dodging potholes and boulders placed at such regular intervals that Gayle presumed they'd been put there to stymie travel.

But they were moving.

*   *   *

The energy continued to burn in the distance. A faint beacon, and growing fainter by the hour, but a beacon nonetheless.

"It's up there," Gayle said, pointing to a glacier. "Not too far, I think. A mile or two at most, but it'll be a steep climb."

"Map calls it Khunjerab." Faisal looked up at the sun falling quickly from its noonday peek. "If we go now, we may get there before dark."

Gayle liked this plan. She didn't want to spend another night camping under the stars.

They began the long walk, pushing forward despite their mounting fatigue. By the time they reached the side of the glacier, Gayle didn't know if she would be able to make it to the top. The only thing keeping her going was the occasional burst of energy. They had to locate its source before it died completely.

"Do you see that?" Faisal asked.

Gayle glanced up, only to realize they were considerably farther up the slope than the last time she'd checked. The tedium of climbing this barren path had caused her to fall into a sort of trance.

"See what?"

Faisal pointed toward a flat patch of ground cleared of stone. In the center, a pile of sticks had been burned to ash, leaving scorch marks on the grey rock.

"A campfire," Gayle murmured.

"A recent one. Only a few days old."

Gayle's urgency increased as they climbed. She guessed they still had a half-hour of climbing ahead when the last vestiges of energy fizzled out, disappearing entirely from her perception.

She stopped and touched Faisal's arm. "Faisal, did you feel that?"

He nodded solemnly. "It's gone."

"We may be too late."

But once they reached the top of the saddle between the mountains on either side, Gayle gazed into the hidden valley beyond and smiled. Their destination was even closer than she had reckoned. A vaguely oval-shaped hole tunneled down into blackness. Whatever this place was, it had been built by someone highly intelligent. The energy couldn't have come from anywhere else.

Hang on, Elisabeth. I'm close.

*   *   *

"This is a very strange place," Faisal said.

Under the dim light of mounted fluorescents, they saw that the hole had a metallic floor which looked suspiciously like the opening to a hangar underneath. Gayle felt certain this is where the ships came from—the ones the alien chasers had mentioned.

They walked a few hundred feet around the circumference of the opening to reach a set of modern-looking stairs. Gayle didn't hesitate to begin descending them, though Faisal stopped on the top landing.

"Is this a good idea?"

"No," Gayle called back, "but it's the only idea I have. We didn't come all this way to stand around."

"We also didn't come to get killed."

Didn't we? If Gayle was honest with herself, getting killed had always been a possible outcome.

She continued down without looking back to check if Faisal would follow.

"I see something," Faisal said when he finally joined her at the bottom. He pointed into the near darkness. "Over there."

Gayle squinted, then saw what he was referring to—two lumpy mounds of a substance so dark that the low light nearly blanketed it from view. She stopped directly over the mounds and studied them with a critical eye.

"Human remains," she decided, stepping away. "Two people. Incinerated, by the looks of it."

"We might be next."

A bright light beckoned from across the vast metallic floor, and she saw that it emanated from a doorway. She hurried toward it, wondering how deep underground this mysterious facility would burrow.

Ahead of them stretched a curved corridor with rough rock walls and doors built into them at even intervals. Gayle marveled at the base's construction. To her surprise, nobody stopped her. It was as though nobody here cared that she and Faisal had invaded their sanctuary.

"Where is everyone?" she asked, more to herself than to Faisal.

They turned into another corridor, this one wider and appearing to run in a circle around the hangar door they had entered from. She looked down the corridor in both directions, waiting for something. Anything. If anyone was home to take notice, they didn't come out of hiding. The base appeared to be abandoned.

"No one here," Faisal offered.

"Then why were the lights on?" Gayle began to explore again. Each door they passed had an accompanying pad, perhaps coded to recognize the fingerprints of authorized personnel. She tried to enter several doors, but none opened for her. "It doesn't make sense…"

"Perhaps the giants left no one behind."

Gayle considered that. "Perhaps."

Upon reflection, though, she didn't believe it. She got the impression that the giants weren't the Starseed people themselves. More like proxies. Lackeys.

Her heart leapt with excitement when they came upon the entrance to an immense chamber. Gayle deduced right away that this was, indeed, a hangar. She looked up and saw the same diagonal lines across the ceiling that she'd noticed on the metallic floor above.

Gayle's footsteps echoed as she entered. "This was a hangar deck."

"I agree." Faisal gestured to the empty space. "But no ships."

"Perhaps the Starseed people used them to abandon the base."

Their attention was stolen by the sound of a clearing throat. Gayle turned quickly, preparing to either defend herself or run—whichever reaction proved appropriate—but instead froze when she saw only a single figure blocking the way back into the corridor.

"Starseed?" the male figure said in a deep voice. "I have never heard such a term."

The newcomer strode toward them with slow and steady paces,

as though stalking them. Gayle wanted to run, but she had nowhere to go. Her only alternative was to stand firm and appear confident. The man stood nearly seven feet tall, slim but also muscular. His cold, appraising eyes dissected her.

"Who are you?" Gayle demanded, forcing iron into her voice.

"My name is Barakel," he said. "I am one of these… Starseed people? Is that what you called us? A clumsy term, but it is generally accurate. We come from the stars."

"And the seed part?" Gayle asked. "Did you create us?"

"No. You were here before we arrived. But we… helped you grow."

Gayle didn't know what to say. She had not expected such a literal confirmation of the beliefs she'd carried around most of her adult life.

Faisal spoke up. "You are responsible for the burst of energy we felt?"

"The burst of energy?" Barakel turned to him as though seeing him for the first time. "Ah, you mean the energy from the machine." He anticipated their next question and answered it. "A locking mechanism. You see, my people were imprisoned here for many years. The energy you felt was caused by their release."

"The energy came from many other places," Gayle said slowly. "For weeks, it poured down from the skies."

"My people have many facilities. Not all are… local."

"Where did the people go?" Gayle asked, referring to the empty base.

"They did everything they could here," Barakel said. "They need privacy for what comes next."

Well, that sounded ominous. "And why did they leave you behind?"

Barakel refused to answer this question. He stood impassively, acting as though the question hadn't even been asked.

"Ask about your friend," Faisal said to her quietly.

Gayle nodded to him, then turned back to Barakel. "We are looking for someone who was here recently. Her name is Elisabeth Macfarlane. Do you know what happened to her?"

"I know this woman, yes," Barakel said.

Relief flushed through her as she waited for more. Barakel offered no further details. "Well, what happened to her?"

"I could take you to her," Barakel said, drawing out the words. "Would you like that?"

Gayle wasn't sure whether Barakel could be trusted. The obvious answer was no, but she feared she might not find another way to reach Elisabeth. Of all the risks she'd taken so far, this would be the greatest—but also the most necessary.

"Yes," she said.

Faisal looked shocked by this. "Gayle, this is not smart. I will not go."

"Then stay." Gayle didn't speak with irritation or impatience. She took him by the hand, squeezing his palm. "Faisal, you could do so much good if you stayed. Return to Gilgit and assist the refugees. Or go back to Srinagar. I fear your hometown may be the giants' next target."

Faisal took a long time to respond. "I cannot leave you."

"Of course you can. I have to do this. You don't."

"Too dangerous, Gayle."

Gayle smiled at him. "I appreciate the concern, but I can take care of myself. I release you from your obligation to me."

Faisal nodded, but only with great reluctance.

"Very good," Barakel said. "I warn you, my people will not be happy to see you." His mouth spread open into a peculiar smile. "They will not be happy to see me, either."

TWENTY-NINE

Linthal, Switzerland

AUGUST 4

The spider skittered away. Lagati adjusted the tiny device in his hand, wondering if it even worked, then closed his fist around it. The cube was half the size of a game die and barely identifiable as a device at all. It had no buttons or lights or human interface of any kind. It had no discernible moving parts, and it emitted no sound, though Lagati had pressed it to his ear and strained to pick up even the faintest mechanic whir. To the most vigorous examination, the shiny device offered no hints as to its purpose or function. Lagati had nothing to go on, save Barakel's solemn word that it would work as advertised—that it would allow Lagati to control his Grigori masters, or at least one at a time.

One in particular, Lagati thought, conjuring an image of Azazel leering at him as he delivered a swift kick. He would make Azazel pay dearly for those beatings.

Lagati clenched his jaw in irritation. If Barakel had told the truth about this device, then the spider should not have been able to move.

I must not be using it right. Barakel did say it would require practice.

He secured the cube in his pocket, then stretched out his leg and stomped the spider before it could escape. Even if the device hadn't worked, there was no good reason to let the spider have its run of Lagati's own home.

The upper floor of the house was eerily quiet now that the Grigori had purged their human workforce. They didn't require so much labor here as they had at Khunjerab. Lagati's Swiss estate was large by any standard, but nothing compared to the sprawling base they had left behind.

Lagati stared sadly at the thick door Turel had moved here from the vault. One didn't just turn the knob and push it open; one tapped in the correct code, then heaved against it with all one's might, a much greater challenge now that the door was no longer connected to the computer system that had once facilitated its automatic opening and closing.

He was about to enter the code when he reconsidered. The last time he'd walked in on Elisabeth, she'd made him pay dearly. Instead he knocked, hoping the sound would penetrate the thick door.

"Elisabeth, it's me." Lagati waited for some kind of signal that she'd heard, but nothing came. "I'm coming in. Don't attack me. Do you understand?"

He punched in the code and grasped the steel door handle. It took several tries to open the door wide enough for him to slip inside. To his surprise, Elisabeth didn't try squeezing through the narrow opening and making a dash for freedom. He was glad she hadn't made the attempt; she wouldn't have gotten far.

She sat cross-legged in the middle of the room, her head down. All the furniture had been broken or pushed to the corners.

"Thank you for not hitting me in the head with a bedpost," Lagati said with a wry smile. There certainly had been enough ammunition in this room, and Lagati knew just how determined she could be.

Elisabeth slowly got to her feet. "You promised you'd get me out of my cage if I helped you. You lied—again. All you've done is substitute one cage for another."

"I didn't even know you were here. Nobody bothered to tell me," Lagati said. "Frankly, they were under no obligation to keep you alive at all. The only reason you're with us is because I argued on your behalf."

In truth, he really had intended to keep his word, but after they had exited the barrier and started climbing back up to the base, several security guards had surrounded them. There had been no opportunity to help Elisabeth get away, so they had taken her back into custody.

For the next two days, Semyaza had kept the ships busy transporting personnel and equipment from Pakistan to Switzerland, all without raising alarm from the many nations in between. Not an easy task. Of course, the chaos being sown along the Indo-Pakistan border had helped cover their exit. Such a perfect crisis!

"Don't be ungrateful," Lagati said. "I'm here now."

"So you really are going to let me go?"

"Of course. I'm going to smuggle you out." Lagati took her by the arm and pulled her toward the door. "Unless you have any objections."

The scowl on Elisabeth's face lightened, but she resisted him.

"I assure you, this is no trick," Lagati told her. "And as always, time is limited. But if you don't trust me, you can remain here. It's up to you."

Elisabeth nodded, then followed him through the narrow opening and waited as he shoved the door closed behind them.

"Don't think you've earned my trust," she said as they walked along the corridor.

"And you needn't think I care about your trust one way or the other."

This kept her quiet. He stepped lightly around the stairs, tracing the wooden banister with his fingers. They came away with a hint of dust, and he grimaced, aggravated by the fact that the Grigori had dispensed with most of his household staff.

He lingered just long enough to notice movement several levels below—on the mezzanine, he thought. He stepped backward to keep out of sight.

On the other side of the mansion were a number of rooms he rarely used, except for one which was furnished like an office. Lagati didn't come here for business, but for transportation.

Elisabeth stood just inside the door, confusion writ large in her wide eyes. "What are we doing?"

He raised a single finger, and this was enough to shut her up. He opened the door to a closet only to face yet another door, this one paneled in dark cedar, with no handle. Standing directly in front of it caused a pinprick of red light to appear on the wood panel.

"What is this?" Elisabeth asked.

The door slid open to reveal an elevator. Lagati pulled her inside.

Elisabeth leaned against one of the obsidian walls. "Who lives in a house with a secret elevator?"

Lagati pressed one of the three unmarked buttons, and immediately the elevator began to lift. "Indeed, it's a small club."

"Where is it taking us?"

"You ask a lot of questions."

"That's because you're not giving me anything to work with."

Lagati smiled, not because he felt amused but because he was on the verge of losing his patience and the smile helped cover it. "It's not in my interest to tell you exactly what's going on. Shouldn't you be satisfied that you're about to be free again?"

"Yes, I suppose I should." She didn't sound like she meant it.

The elevator had been one of the most expensive installations during the long decade spent excavating the mountain and reinforcing the home such that it wouldn't be crushed in some random yet deadly and inevitable geologic event. The shaft through which the elevator ascended would take them to a helipad two thousand feet up the mountain.

When the elevator stopped, they exited into a long tunnel which ended in the bright light of day. Lagati crossed the distance quickly, paying little attention to Elisabeth's open-mouthed display of amazement.

A gleaming yellow helicopter sat in the center of the crosshairs painted on a cement floor.

"Who's going to fly me out of here?" Elisabeth asked as they entered the circular chamber at the end of the tunnel.

"I am."

Lagati stepped to the right side of the helicopter and unlatched the cowl door. He scanned a bank of switches and confirmed they were set to the on position. The master switch, the oil pressure, the alternator, everything good to go. His hand moved by instinct down to a panel of buttons, and he pushed each in turn to ensure the warning lights were operating normally. He then swung himself up into the cockpit and confirmed that the lights glowed green. They did.

"You know how to fly?" Elisabeth asked.

"I wouldn't be risking my life for you if I didn't."

He got out and closed the cowl door after confirming there were no obvious leaks in the fuel lines. In perfect conditions, he would give himself twenty minutes to look at everything from the control rods to the air ducts. Today he couldn't count on more than five minutes for a preflight check, just long enough to make sure they wouldn't be killed by blatant negligence. Still, he felt uneasy as he returned to the cockpit. Any one of a thousand things could go wrong during a flight, even a short one.

"Get in," he ordered as the blades began their slow rotation. Elisabeth grasped one of the struts and climbed a short ladder into the rear compartment. She settled into the cushioned chair.

"Let's go then."

Lagati nodded as he focused on a few final tasks. He fastened his seatbelt, stowed the loose items scattered on the dash, and ensured the instruments were all powered up.

The helicopter lifted off the ground and hovered in place as he rolled the nose to face the opening to the cavern. He felt the tail and its rotor swing in an obedient arc—and then the clear blue-tinged panorama came into view through the wraparound front window. He throttled forward and curved out into open sky.

He steered west, which necessitated a longer flight path to the airfield south of Linthal, but if he took the shorter route around the eastern flank of the mountain he would be visible from the front of the estate. Too great a risk. Someone would see him.

Within ten minutes, Lagati set down the helicopter on the edge of the airfield. The only other craft in sight was a small private jet on the far side of the runway. He didn't have time to linger on it, but he wondered if it was one of his fleet. It certainly looked familiar. He'd caught wind that the Grigori planned to use them to ferry political dignitaries in advance of the coming campaign.

"Get out," he shouted to Elisabeth over the roar of the engine.

Elisabeth unhooked her seatbelt. "Why don't you come with me?"

A part of him wanted to do just that. Antoinette was out there, free and clear, and he could find her. They could be free and clear together.

He shook his head. "I have to finish what I started."

"What does that mean?"

"Elisabeth, get out or come back with me. I don't have time for this."

Without another word, Elisabeth hopped down onto the pavement and looked toward the town of Linthal, its tiny cluster of buildings occupying the lowest and flattest real estate of the rolling valley.

Lagati immediately lifted the helicopter back into the air and soared overtop her. In his final glimpse of Elisabeth, she was nothing but a tiny pixel streaking across a vast canvas.

He didn't remember much of the return flight. When he set the helicopter back down in the center of the painted crosshairs, he realized he'd drifted into autopilot. He withdrew his hands from the control, reached into his pocket, and pulled out the shiny cube Barakel had given him. Such a strange little object.

"You must practice," Barakel had told him. "It will not come easily."

And it certainly hadn't. Lagati had always prided himself on his mental discipline, but this required a level of concentration he couldn't fathom. He stared at the cube, stroking its edges with his thumb.

As much as Lagati wanted to, he couldn't truly make himself believe that Barakel had lied to him about this device. Barakel had an axe to grind with the rest of the Grigori; it felt right, somehow, that he would recruit Lagati to add his own brand of chaos to the mix.

I just have to keep trying, Lagati thought as he exited the helicopter.

Lagati returned to the elevator and descended. He heard noises in the hallway, so he remained in the office for several minutes. Once he deemed it safe, he stepped out into the hall.

The loft was deserted, just like he'd left it.

Well, not quite. He stopped near the stairs and looked toward the heavy door that had recently barricaded Elisabeth. Lagati had made sure to close it when they left, but it now hung wide open. Someone had been here recently and discovered that Elisabeth was missing.

Lagati padded down the stairs as quickly and quietly as he could. A few people scurried about the second and third floors, but he managed to slip through them without drawing attention to himself. They all looked terrified, and the fear wasn't unjustified. Only a fraction of the team Lagati had assembled in Pakistan still drew breath.

He found his way to the library on the mezzanine level. He hesitated only a moment to admire his collection of old books before proceeding to the glass door that led to a small terrace.

Lagati turned the handle and stepped into the fresh mountain air. The strong breeze whipped his hair into a frenzy. This had always been a favorite haunt, the place he most often came to meditate. He loved this view, and the sheer drop down the face of the mountain. This wild, untouched vista exhilarated him like it always had.

He gripped the railing and breathed deeply. It felt good to be home, even though it didn't feel as homey as it once had. The Grigori had assailed Lagati's house as thoroughly as they had the rest of his life.

He shucked off his shoes, sat on the floor, and assumed the lotus position. He closed his eyes and lowered his palms against the hardened skin of his upturned feet. He struggled for several minutes to fall into his usual meditative state—slow his breathing, set the rhythm of his heartbeat, relax his thoughts, seek insight. His body relaxed, but not his mind.

After some time, he gave up. For years, he had meditated as a means of contacting the Grigori. Now he could just walk downstairs and talk to Semyaza or Azazel in person if he wanted—

A knock on the door made him turn. Amir Balasubramian stood behind the glass, eclipsing Lagati's view of the library.

Lagati slipped his shoes back on and opened the terrace door. "What do you want?"

"There's some commotion downstairs. See for yourself."

The two men descended to the first floor in silence. When they reached the main hall, Lagati saw that several of the Grigori were shouting at each other. The argument had seemingly broken out in the dining room and extended into the hall.

"What do you know about this?" Lagati asked Amir. He wondered if it had something to do with Elisabeth.

No, he decided. *They don't care about her enough to warrant an argument like this.*

"Listen to me!" a shrill voice cried, cutting through the raised voices. It belonged to the one named Batraal. "We do not require permission!"

"Not from him," added another Grigori whose face Lagati didn't recognize. He spoke in a low voice, hard as granite, which belied his smooth, almost effeminate features.

The hall fell silent, and Lagati was able to count six Grigori in the main cluster, and another large group watched from inside the dining room. Notable among them was Azazel, standing with his back against the edge of the stairs, a self-satisfied grin on his face.

"That is enough," said Semyaza in a commanding tone. He stepped out of the dining room, grabbing each dissenting Grigori by the shoulder and pushing them back into the makeshift council chamber. As the leader herded his quarrelsome subjects, Lagati noted that the long wooden table had been removed, and in its place rested a circle of high-backed chairs. As the Grigori took their seats and resumed whatever discussion had so enraged them, Azazel closed the door.

"Well, that was certainly interesting," Amir remarked. "What do you suppose it means?"

"It means very little." Which was blatantly false, of course, and Lagati knew Amir wouldn't be fooled by it. "All it shows is that the Grigori have differences of opinion."

"But to let it boil over that way!"

Lagati shrugged. "We all lose control from time to time."

"We all…?" Amir broke off, looking at him in astonishment.

Lagati couldn't blame him. What they'd just witnessed *had* been extraordinary, no matter how much Lagati attempted to downplay it.

"There's something else," Amir said in a low voice.

Lagati feigned disinterest. "Oh?"

"Elisabeth Macfarlane is gone."

"What do you mean, she's gone?" Lagati felt some relief that Amir had made the discovery and not someone else. Amir was far easier to manage and control.

"I checked on her. She was not inside."

Lagati kept his eyes on Amir, but his focus lingered on the closed dining room door and the deliberations going on just behind it.

"The Grigori must have done something with her," Lagati said, pretending to have put some thought into it.

But Amir wasn't buying it. "The Grigori have been in conference most of the morning. I doubt they—"

"Do you have a better idea?" Lagati turned and began climbing the stairs again. "In truth, Ms. Macfarlane is not important."

"I agree."

"You do?"

"Of course I do. All that's important is what we found in those crates." Amir put a hand on Lagati's shoulder. Lagati bristled, very briefly. He didn't think it had showed. "Have you seen the reports from Pakistan? They brought those creatures to life!"

"I don't see how it's possible."

"Neither do I, but I saw the pictures for myself. Giants, wreaking havoc in the countryside, setting fire to entire towns. It'll start a war!"

Indeed it will, Lagati mused. *I'm sure that's the plan.*

"Lagati!"

It hadn't been a shout, per se, but spoken with enough spiritual force that Lagati felt his spine stiffen. He looked over the banister.

The dining room door was open and Semyaza stood in front of it, beckoning with his right hand. "We request your presence."

Lagati didn't know how to react. Well, he did know—he couldn't refuse a Grigori, and he thrilled at the possibility of quenching his curiosity about what went on in their private sessions. Being summoned into the Grigori lair might have terrified him half to death at one time. It still rattled him now, but as he descended the stairs he dropped his hand into his pocket and fingered the little cube Barakel had given him.

"I'm coming," Lagati called out, nursing his secret. It infused him with confidence.

THIRTY

Singapore

AUGUST 4

Dario felt no surprise or excitement at all when Ira popped out of existence. It had become such an ordinary occurrence, with the rabbi having become a sort of supernatural taxi ferrying him from place to place. Dario studied the buildings shooting up all around him; they made him feel like an ant lost amidst a tangle of weeds.

After confirming that their arrival had gone unobserved, he walked toward the alley opening. Cars buzzed through all four lanes— including, Dario noted, a handful of taxis. He raised a hand to flag one down, and soon he found himself in the backseat of a bright blue cab.

"Police headquarters," Dario instructed.

The taxi joined the free flow of traffic out of the financial district and over a bridge into a more sparsely populated canton. Sparse seemed the wrong word considering the island city's density; these buildings rose only thirty stories instead of fifty or more. Practically rural by Singaporean standards.

Ten minutes later, they stopped in front of two twenty-story octagonal structures surrounded by concrete surface lots and well-treed parks.

"This is it?" Dario asked.

The driver pointed to a squat building beyond the twin octagons. "Police headquarters."

Dario reached into his pocket for a handful of Singapore dollar bills. "Thanks."

The long shadows of the octagonal towers cloaked the path leading to the precinct. Dario stepped quickly, passing knots of uniformed officers along the way. He didn't look them in the eyes, which might have been interpreted as suspicious in other nations, but not this one.

Dario felt a stab of bitterness that Ira had left him to do his dirty work while he took care of "more important" matters. Dario wanted to think that if it had been one of his own close friends, he would have been more interested in effecting the rescue personally.

Then again, Ira seemed to believe the fate of the world rested in his hands. Perhaps that excused his recent behavior.

Once inside, Dario followed a handful of signs to a square reception room with a desk on one side and a row of chairs on the other. It resembled a classroom.

"What do you want?" the officer behind the desk asked. Dario had to remind himself that Singaporean directness should not always be interpreted as discourtesy.

"I'm looking for someone you have in custody."

"Name."

"Janene Kaplan."

The man tapped a few keys on his computer, narrowing his eyes at whatever results appeared on the screen just outside Dario's vision.

"One minute." He pushed his chair back and called in Malay to a couple of fellow officers who had been walking down a hall behind him. They exchanged a few words before the man returned to the desk. "She's not here."

"What do you mean, she's not here? I read a report that said you brought her in this morning."

"She was given over to the custody of the American embassy."

Dario paused. Ira had gotten Junior to check the records only a few hours ago, and they hadn't said anything about a transfer of custody.

"Thank you," Dario said as he turned to go.

"The ambassador came himself."

The officer peered at him with a strange sense of urgency. Dario almost replied, but then the officer went back to whatever he'd been doing before Dario's arrival.

He left the building and returned to the street, craning his neck in both directions, hoping to see another taxi. He was about to go back inside to ask the officer to call the cab company when a green cab flew down the street. Speeding, Dario thought. A risky behavior right outside police headquarters. The driver saw Dario, angled toward the curb, and screeched to a halt.

"U.S. embassy, please," Dario requested.

One of the nice things about Singapore was that traffic flowed lightly for a city of its population—and everything was compressed into such a small area that no trip took longer than a few minutes. The ride to the embassy proved no exception.

The white-walled building was a concrete fortress surrounded by a sloping lawn and a black wrought-iron fence that towered well over Dario's head. He got out of the cab and walked toward the gatehouse.

A pair of soldiers emerged to greet him.

"Stop there," one of them said.

Dario did as instructed. "I've come to speak with the ambassador."

"Do you have an appointment?" the same soldier asked. The other stood mutely at his side, content to let his compatriot do all the talking.

"No, but he will want to see me. My name is Dario Katsulas."

"Do you know the ambassador? Can I see your passport?"

Dario hesitated. Not having an American passport could be a deal-breaker. "Just mention that I'm an associate of Ira Binyamin's."

"There's nothing we can do if you don't have an appointment or a passport, sir."

"I promise the ambassador will want to see me," Dario insisted. "I'm on urgent business."

"What does it concern?"

"There's a woman in your custody. Janene Kaplan. She was picked up this morning from the police. I understand that the ambassador has taken a personal interest in her case." He fell silent. He had to give them a more compelling reason to let him inside. "I'm her lawyer."

The men consulted each other, whispering. After a couple of moments, however, a call came through on the spokesman's radio. He unclipped it from his belt and brought it to his lips.

"What is it?" he asked.

Dario strained to make out the response, but it was too quiet and he didn't dare step any closer. The men carried sidearms and he didn't want them to view him as a threat.

The spokesman lowered the radio and called to him. "Not today, sir. We're on lockdown."

"Lockdown? She has the right to an attorney!"

Neither man answered as they hastened back to the gatehouse.

No one followed as Dario made his way back to the street, cold comfort though it was. He looked back at the embassy's high fence and impregnable walls. Without Ira here to jump from A to B, there was no way to get inside.

He entered a grove of trees and leaned against the rough bark, swearing to himself. Sweat matted his forehead as the tropical humidity hit him. Even with the sun going down, the temperature soared.

Ira would be back in that downtown alley in an hour. Should he wait for the rabbi to find him and admit that he couldn't do this on his own?

It was Ira's own damned fault they were in this position. He should have saved some of his energy to go back for Janene before she'd gotten swept up in the post-conference chaos. The simple truth was that he'd forgotten about her. For all the good Ira had done lately, he seemed equally capable of thoughtlessness and self-absorption. Dario's mind went back to the many unflattering things Brighton had said about Ira during their journey to Khunjerab. At the time, Dario had taken those descriptions with a grain of salt. Not anymore.

The bushes rustled behind him and he turned to see a maintenance worker in brown civvies. The man walked along the fence line for a while before taking note of Dario. His first thought was that this worker was patrolling the embassy's perimeter, for some reason associated with the lockdown, but that didn't quite make sense; that job would have fallen to soldiers, and this was no soldier.

Then another thought struck him: perhaps this worker was the *cause* of the lockdown.

Dario averted his gaze, his heart beating faster.

"Wait," the maintenance worker called.

Dario stopped in his tracks and realized it wasn't a maintenance worker. It wasn't even a man.

"Janene!"

"Keep it down," Janene said, adjusting her cap to make sure it contained her mop of brown hair. "What in heaven's name are you doing here?"

Dario steered her into the shadow of the trees. "I'm here to rescue you. Why else?"

She yanked herself free. "Well, you needn't have bothered. As you can see, I'm just fine. How were you planning on getting me out?"

"I was formulating a plan."

"You were waiting for Ira, that's what you were doing."

Dario pursed his lips. "Fine. I didn't have a plan."

"Good thing I did then. Let's get out of here."

"We should still wait for Ira. He'll be able to get us—"

She spun on him, her eyes angry. Dario recoiled, surprised to see her this way. He hadn't known her for more than a couple of days, and she'd only ever been a loyal sidekick at Ira's side.

"I'm not some damsel in distress," she snapped. "I had the wherewithal to rescue myself, as you can see. You could use some help, though. You look as lost as a stray cat."

Dario said nothing.

"Let's get going." She pulled him by the arm. "They'll be out in force soon, and we'll want to be as far away as possible."

*   *   *

Ira tugged at the door handle, but it wouldn't budge. He leaned in close to the pub's window, peering into the dank interior.

"Pub's closed," a passerby called from across the street.

Ira glanced at the burly local, his face hidden by a scruffy brown beard. He wore grimy work clothes as though he'd just climbed off an oil rig. Considering the nearby shipyards, that assessment may not have been far off. "I know."

"Why ya pounding on the door then?"

"My friend lives upstairs. I thought he might be home."

The man grunted and moved on. But he was right. If Trevor was here, he would have heard all the racket and come down. Unless Trevor didn't want to speak with him.

"Trevor!" Ira called toward the second floor window. He didn't care if he made a scene. "Trevor, I need to talk to you!"

He placed his hand against the brick exterior with grim resolve.

Could Trevor really be ignoring him? Ira returned to the door and grazed it with the back of his hand. If he mustered enough force, could he break it down?

No, Ira concluded. *There's another way. A better way.*

He massaged each shoulder in turn, trying to relax himself—not an easy task. He blew a stream of air through his gritted teeth, then remembered to ease the tension in his jaw. When he tried to form the image of the river, a wave of nausea rolled in. He secured himself against the current.

He popped into Trevor's parlor. The shades had been pulled down over the windows and the overhead light was dark. Ira blinked as a mote of dust lodged in his eye. He wiped it away and turned in a circle, getting his bearings. Gradually, shapes formed out of the darkness—furniture, doors, the kitchen counter, a bookshelf—

"I'm disappointed," a low voice said.

A lamp burst to life and Ira averted his eyes. Once he was used to the glow, he saw a man sitting on the couch. His clothes were as shabby as the thin, worn upholstery.

It was the man from outside on the street.

"What are you—" Ira frowned. "I don't under—"

"I said I'm disappointed."

Ira's heart leapt when he realized this man was no stranger. The face, the eyes, the beard…

"Enoch, it's you!" He stepped closer. "Thank Jehovah. Where's Trevor?"

Enoch patted the empty space next to him on the couch. "Sit, Ira. Rest for a while."

"Trevor and the others, they're launching a counterstrike, aren't they?" Ira let out a long breath, relief overwhelming him. "Then Jehovah hasn't abandoned us."

"Of course he hasn't, but that—"

"Enoch, listen to me. The Grigori are expanding outward. There have been attacks throughout the mountains. Pakistan and India are overrun, and they've been in contact with several prominent governments..." He broke off. "Why are you disappointed?"

"Trevor wasn't here, and you knew it," Enoch said. "Yet you summoned your newfound capabilities to translate inside. It was a waste."

"I needed to find help."

"Help has never been withheld from you. All you needed to do was *ask*."

Ira sat down next to him. "Okay, so I'm asking. Help me. As for Semyaza and Azazel and all the rest, where can I find them? I sense that they've gone away."

"The help you've come for is not the help I'm here to give. Do you understand me?"

"I understand that we're going to lose this war!" Ira stood again and walked across the room. He laid his palms flat against the kitchen counter and breathed deeply, once again trying to relax—not only his exhausted body, but his mind. "You want me to do nothing. To sit on my hands! Who will stop the Grigori if not me?"

"Perhaps no one."

There had been a time in his life when he would have paid any price for just such an audience with Enoch, a flesh and blood human who had managed to get closer to the Creator of the universe than anyone else in history. Not only had he done it once now, but twice. Nonetheless, Ira wanted to reach his hands around the man's long, slender neck and squeeze it dry. Harsh as this sounded, Enoch's words filled him with rage transcending all reason. The man wanted him to be rendered helpless in the face of the greatest threat humankind had ever faced.

There's something wrong here, he realized. Enoch professed to speak for Jehovah, but he had denied Ira the opportunity to see him with his own eyes. Enoch wanted him to trust, yet it occurred to Ira that he had no proof of Enoch's supernatural claims. In fact, he had no proof at all that Enoch was who he said he was. *Yes, there's something very wrong here.*

"Ira, what are you thinking?"

Ira narrowed his eyes. Was there a hint of uncertainty in Enoch's features? It came as a shock to him that Enoch had no idea what was going to happen next. If Enoch was an agent of Jehovah—the real Jehovah, the one Ira had spent a lifetime worshipping—then he should feel little to no uncertainty. There had to be a plan.

"You're not who I thought you were," Ira said slowly, still coming to terms with it.

Enoch said nothing more as he reached for the lamp and clicked off the light.

Ira waited a moment, his breath the only other sound in the room. Enoch hadn't just fallen silent, though; as Ira flicked the light back to the on position, he saw that the spot where Enoch had been sitting was empty.

He was afraid, Ira thought. *He was afraid of what I might do, what I might discover.*

"I've wasted too much time counting on these so-called allies," he murmured as he got to his feet.

Fortunately, he had a few allies of his own. Allies he could trust.

THIRTY-ONE

Over Greenland
AUGUST 4

Wendell and Annie huddled near the back of the plane for most of the trip across the Canadian Arctic. They spoke in low voices, casting furtive glances in Brighton's direction. Brighton could do nothing but stew in frustration, straining to pick up snatches of conversation between the conspirators.

"We'll be setting down in Portugal to refuel," Wendell told him after several hours. Near as Brighton could tell, they were cruising somewhere over Greenland. The ice sheet gleamed pearly white from horizon to horizon.

"Let me off there," Brighton said, even and collected. "I've spent most of the week on one plane or another, and almost all of it imprisoned in my own mind. It's the least you can do."

Wendell sat in the seat next to him. "Don't you want to know where we're going?"

"Honestly, I'm past caring." He looked Wendell deep in the eyes, recalling the first time the two had met, at an outdoor café in D.C. Even then, he had thought Wendell sported a strange countenance, both striking and plain at the same time. "Anyway, you won't tell me."

"I will, actually. Mr. Lagati needs our help in Switzerland."

"I'm not interested in helping him. I have someone else to rescue, and she isn't anywhere near Switzerland."

"Don't be so sure. I have it under good authority that Elisabeth isn't in Pakistan anymore."

"How did you…" Brighton let the question drift off. "Never mind. Stupid question. I take it we're all headed to the same place?"

"That's right. We'll go after Lagati, you can go after Ms. Macfarlane. You can even go free afterward. We won't try to stop you."

It sounded too good to be true. "Why?"

"Because even Raff Lagati isn't a free man anymore," Annie said, approaching. She took a seat and swiveled to face them. "The Grigori have him in their grip, Mr. Brighton, and this may be my only chance to get him out alive."

"Who are you?" Brighton asked.

"I'm Raff's… friend."

"Didn't know he had any of those."

"He selects his friends very carefully," Annie said.

Wendell nodded. Did he consider himself Lagati's friend as well? If so, he was in a different friendship category than Annie, who seemed to be on a first-name basis with the megalomaniacal Frenchman.

"If you don't want a part in this, we'll understand," Wendell said. "You can go your own way in Portugal. We won't come after you."

"How can I believe that?"

"I don't know. You just do it." Wendell let out a long breath. "You're not that important anymore. The Grigori got what they needed from you, and they've moved on to bigger things. I doubt they even remember who you are."

Brighton desperately wanted to believe this was true. "You could have left me behind in Yellowknife. Why didn't you?"

"Because Raff sent me to track you down, to find out more about your mission." Annie set her jaw in a look of determination.

"Then you must want to know what I was doing in Yellowknife."

"We already have a good idea," Wendell said. "You were meant to retrieve a crashed spacecraft, isn't that right? There were rumors in the city about a crash. A family of Inuit hunters claimed to witness it."

Brighton didn't reply.

Wendell sighed. "I'll take that as confirmation. It might seem difficult, but you can trust us. All three of us are on the same side now."

It went against all his experiences of the last year. "What is the Grigori's plan then, if it doesn't involve me?"

Wendell lifted his index finger. "Just wait. I have something to show you."

He got up and ventured toward the cockpit.

"Why did the Grigori take Lagati captive?" Brighton asked Annie once they were alone.

"Raff had a very specific role to play, and once he played it the Grigori no longer needed him. Wasn't the same true of you? Once you released them, they trundled you off halfway around the world."

"Halfway around the world, sure, but on an important mission."

Annie smiled. "They didn't send you, I suspect. They sent the spirit inhabiting you. Who no doubt you are happily rid of."

"Was Lagati—"

"No. He would never allow himself to be taken over." She spoke it with a fierce dose of condescension. Clearly, she thought poorly of Brighton and his choices. In the end, he didn't care what she thought of him. "Raff facilitated their return, but he has little to contribute now."

"I would think he has invaluable connections."

"He certainly counted on that." She rubbed her tired eyes. "Turns out they had other schemes in mind."

Wendell rejoined them, holding out a tablet. On it Brighton saw headlines running the full length of the glowing screen.

"What's all this?" Brighton asked.

"The news from Pakistan," Wendell said. "Take a few minutes to read it over. We have time."

A rising sense of unease filled Brighton as he scrolled from one news item to the next, scanning the content of each story. Attacks in the tinderbox border regions of Pakistan, India, and China had led to a state of near-war. The various news agencies disagreed on the nature of the attacks, but the growing consensus was that the perpetrators weren't quite… human. Brighton gazed down at a gallery of images featuring giant, rotting behemoths scorching the countryside. Entire villages burned, thousands dead—and the violence spilling over into neighboring countries.

"They're destabilizing the region," Brighton murmured. He held his tongue, withholding the parts of the story Nariman had filled in.

"That's right," Wendell said. "The Grigori will use the situation to their own advantage. I'm sure their emissaries have already reached out to key governments. Events will move very quickly."

"Which is why we must act now," Annie said.

They don't know the plan, Brighton realized. It didn't matter. The world would soon learn the truth, and Brighton suspected the resulting conflict would tear the world apart.

*   *   *

When Brighton stepped off the plane onto Linthal's tiny airfield, he saw that the town could barely be thought of as a town at all. A few streets crisscrossed each other, lined by houses and buildings so characteristic of Swiss chalets that he briefly considered the possibility that he'd wandered into a painting. But the ground beneath him felt real enough.

Somewhere in the heart of the village, he heard a train screeching into its berth. Elsewhere a mountain creek churned over slippery rocks. As he craned his neck, he spotted a cow in a nearby field, chewing a wad of grass just beyond the squat wooden fence that enclosed it.

"I'll say one thing for my recent travels," he mused to Annie and Wendell, who came down the flight of steps behind him. "They've brought me to some rather tranquil locales."

"The Grigori like to stay out of the limelight," Wendell said.

With an air of self-assurance that came from long familiarity with a place, Annie hurried toward the road leading to town. Chief amongst the copse of steep roofs pierced the tower of the local church. As Brighton stared at the structure, its bell began to toll the time. He counted the strokes. Five o'clock.

"You said you would let me go," Brighton shouted.

Annie turned her head. "Then go."

To the north loomed the rounded bulge of an intimidatingly large mountain. If Brighton remembered right, Lagati's estate was situated along its eastern flank, accessible only by a private drive. Annie and Wendell wouldn't approach that way. They had to have another plan, another way in. Brighton sure didn't plan on walking right back into the hands of the enemy, so he'd have to take the same route.

"I should have tagged along a while longer," Brighton mumbled as he marched into town. Maybe it wasn't too late to do just that.

As he crossed a vaulted bridge, he heard the distinctive sound of a helicopter overhead. He shielded his eyes and searched the sky for the approaching aircraft. Just then, a yellow helicopter banked low over the valley.

Something told him this locale was about to get a lot less tranquil.

THIRTY-TWO

Linthal, Switzerland
AUGUST 4

emyaza circled him, eyeing him like a predator might regard a soon-to-be-devoured meal. Lagati forced himself to look into the leader's eyes every time he circled around, though it pained him to do so. All the while, Lagati held onto the tiny cube in his pocket and considered Barakel's promise.

"Do we need him?" Turel asked from his seat in the dining room. "Perhaps Ramuel is right."

Turel pointed across the room at a Grigori with moderately feminine features. That must have been Ramuel. Lagati recognized him from the argument that had spilled over into the hall. Long black hair fell nearly to Ramuel's waist, each strand straight and untangled.

As they continued their enigmatic dispute, Lagati counted the Grigori present. He was not surprised to discover there were exactly twenty, though he only knew the names of a handful—Semyaza, Azazel, Turel, Batraal… and now this Ramuel.

"He has a part to play," Semyaza spoke with authority, loud enough to silence the others. He stepped away from Lagati and placed his hand on the only empty chair, caressing the wood with his long fingers.

The dining room fell into an uneasy silence. No one said a word, but Lagati felt each pair of rapacious eyes raking over him.

Semyaza gestured for Lagati to come closer. "Join us, please."

Lagati took a series of slow, careful steps toward the circle. "Do you need me for something?"

"Need is a strong word," Azazel remarked.

Semyaza shot him a hard look, then pulled out the empty chair. "Sit."

It took Lagati a few awkward moments to realize the command had been directed at him. Sit? Among the Twenty? He hadn't heard right.

"You heard correctly," Azazel said in a perfect echo. "You are our guest this evening."

Lagati stepped between the empty chair and the one occupied by Batraal, who literally looked down his long nose at the human. Lagati settled down, took a deep breath, and forced himself to face them.

You've shown enough weakness, Lagati said, encouraging himself. *It's time to show them your strength.*

Azazel in particular would get a front-row seat.

"Very good," Semyaza said, beginning to pace around the outside of the circle. "I cede the floor to Ramuel, who I believe has a thought to contribute."

Ramuel angled his lean upper body in a graceful, gravity-defying transfer of weight. "I say again that we do not need this man's, or any other's, permission to—"

Semyaza cut him off with a glance. "We have moved on, Ramuel. I believe you have something else on your mind."

"Something else?" Ramuel seethed. "Yes, I have a question about the status of my sons' activities. What can you tell me?"

"Your sons? Well, Talmai has been in contact with us," Azazel said, rubbing his knuckles in a bid to appear uninterested. "He and his comrades met with success in Lahore and await a fresh deployment."

Ramuel leaned even further forward. "And Seshai, his brother?"

Azazel made a point of looking Ramuel in the eyes, failing to disguise a thin smile. "Seshai is dead, I'm sorry to say."

The ensuing uproar saw several Grigori leap to their feet, but no one made a move on Azazel. Semyaza managed to silence them with the subtle lift of his index finger. Lagati marveled that everyone observed and responded to the almost imperceptible gesture.

"You're not sorry," Ramuel spat.

Azazel shrugged. "Not in the least."

Looks like I'm not the only one who has it in for Azazel, Lagati pondered as he took stock of Ramuel.

"We aren't making a good impression on our guest," Semyaza said as he reached the far side of the circle from Lagati. "I suggest we stay on point. We have pressing business."

"And we're on a timetable," Turel said in his characteristically low voice. "Jehovah will not wait for us to act."

Batraal nodded. "True. We have received indications that Jehovah has a network of agents observing the giants. As you predicted, Semyaza, they have proved the perfect distraction."

"Then we will erect the barrier on schedule?" Semyaza asked.

A long pause followed.

"Assuming this one cooperates," Batraal inclined his head toward Lagati, "the schedule will hold."

*   *   *

Brighton stalked the streets for thirty minutes, frustrated at having lost track of Annie and Wendell, but the frustration melted away when he reached the main square in time to see his targets enter a tavern. He came closer, his nostrils filling with the familiar aroma of beer, a gentle yet sour concoction of wheat and wistfulness. No two beers smelled—or tasted—alike, and he felt a strong compunction to give this brew the courtesy of a fair shake.

He paused too long and almost didn't step out of the way in time to avoid a woman hurrying out the front door. She wore an overlarge dark sweater whose long sleeves slipped halfway down her palms, and her wild mane of brown curls had been pulled back into a barely restrained ponytail.

"Sorry," Brighton mumbled as he pivoted. He returned his attention to the tavern, considering what he might say to Annie and Wendell to get them to cooperate.

"Sherwood?"

Brighton turned. The woman had come to a stop in the middle of the street, a look of shock on her face.

"Can it be?" she said as she closed the distance between them.

Brighton's throat restricted, strangling off his vocal cords as he recognized Elisabeth Macfarlane, looking a bit worse for wear but in otherwise good health.

"Elisabeth," he blurted, recovering his voice. "I can't believe you're—that you're here. Right here." He stammered, opening and closing his mouth like a hooked trout. "I was coming to... to look for... Elisabeth, is it really you?"

"Of course it's me, you idiot." She planted herself a few feet from him, her posture stiff and guarded. "The question is, are you *you*?"

At first, he didn't know what she meant. His brain caught up a moment later as the translation slammed home.

"Yes, yes, it's me," he said in a rush. "I'm myself again."

She came even closer, searching his eyes. "It is you, isn't it?" she said quietly, more to herself than to Brighton.

A flood of relief overtook him as tears sprang to his eyes. He blinked them away, embarrassed and confused at the strength of his delight. He couldn't have predicted the suddenness of the reunion, and it took an emotional toll.

He didn't move as Elisabeth wrapped her arms around his shoulders and hugged him tight. His delayed reaction was to hug back and release these pent-up emotions he hadn't expected to burst out of him. Elisabeth served as a poignant reminder of his adventure's humble beginning—a connection to Emery Wörtlich, his passion, his friendship, his determination. And his death, of course.

She pulled away after the long embrace and he wiped tears from his eyes. The salty moisture clung to his cheeks.

"Are you crying?" she asked with a smile.

He blinked rapidly. "I'm as surprised as you are."

"When you said goodbye, I didn't think I would see you again. Not with Abranel inside your head, and you heading north on some errand." Her keen eyes snapped back to the tavern. "We have to go."

"Of course," he said. "Now that I know you're safe, there's nothing left for me here."

"There's a more specific reason. I saw a man come into the tavern a minute ago, a man I've seen before."

"You mean Wendell," Brighton said.

"That's right. He works for Lagati, and he might try to stop us if he knows we're here."

"You don't have to worry about him. Or Lagati. Elisabeth, we're free of all that."

They had reached the main thoroughfare. Elisabeth took him around the corner of a storefront, just far enough that they were out of sight of the tavern.

"Did Lagati tell you that?" she asked. "You can't trust that man, or anyone who works for him."

He took her by the arm. "Lagati is as much a prisoner of the

Grigori now as you were. The Grigori don't care about any of us any-more. This is our chance to get out for good." He began to walk again. "To be honest, I thought I'd be running forever."

"You're wrong about Lagati. He's not a prisoner."

Brighton was about to press her for details, but his response got cut off by a cacophonous explosion somewhere off in the distance. He stopped and stared up at the mountain and its bulbous prominence.

"What was that?" Elisabeth wondered aloud.

"If we get out now, we may never know." He made eye contact with her. "I'm good with that if you are."

She nodded. Vigorously.

*   *   *

Ira transported Dario and a pissed-off Janene back to Fair Haven. Al-ready tired from the effort, he forced himself to jump again, after only thirty minutes of downtime. His first destination was a spot just out-side Cairo, within view of the Giza pyramids. He reached out with his mind, trying to detect any unusual supernatural activity in the area. He didn't find anything, though it had been a long shot. He left quick-ly, making a succession of jumps from one hotspot to another, search-ing for clues as to where the Grigori had gone to ground.

Enoch could have saved him the exhaustion. The thought left Ira intensely bitter. He had no doubt Enoch knew more than he had said. Why did he and Trevor insist on being so unhelpful?

Nothing in Tiahuanaco, and then nothing in Tubuai. Ira nearly collapsed from the effort of translating to the Norwegian base in Ant-arctica, now abandoned; he stayed less than a minute, long enough to determine the Grigori hadn't been there.

He finally did collapse on a stone-floored terrace beneath the verdant seaside cliffs of Malta, ivy clinging to every surface. He remained on the floor, unable to raise himself to his feet.

So it's come to this, he thought.

"Who are you?" a voice asked in accented English. "And where did you come from?"

Ira looked up to see a dark-skinned Maltese man in a white shirt and pants. Ira opened his mouth to speak, but his throat was too dry. He closed it again and worked in some moisture.

"My name is Ira," he finally managed, ignoring the man's second and more problematic question.

The man said nothing, but Ira assumed he was one of Lagati's servants. A steward or a cook. This getaway, the restoration of an original Greek boathouse, had been one of Lagati's favorite spots. Ira could almost reimagine that long-ago day when he and Wörtlich and Sherwood had gathered here late into the night, leaning against the railing and discussing the mysteries of the universe.

"Is your master at home?" Ira asked.

"Not for many weeks."

Ira lowered his head, having already confirmed that the Grigori hadn't come here, either. This madcap search was getting him nowhere.

"Do you know where he's gone?"

The man's blank stare confirmed that he didn't.

If Lagati wasn't here, and he wasn't in Pakistan, it stood to reason he might very well have returned to his estate in Switzerland. Could it be that he'd brought the Grigori home with him? Or perhaps it had gone the other way around.

The possibility brought him renewed vigor, and this time when he waded into the river's current, he had no difficulty planting his feet and imagining his destination.

A moment later, he stood along a narrow road wrapped around the side of a mountain. Its width was so tight, the drop so sheer, that it caused him a moment's panic. He flattened himself against the cliff to make sure he didn't tumble off it.

Once he'd reached relative safety, he looked off into the distance and took in the sight of Lagati's mansion. It was a fortress entombed in the mountainside, surrounded by solid, impenetrable rock. Only the front of the three-story edifice saw the light of day, and it was impossible to tell from the outside just how deep the house delved.

More importantly, a black car idled in the carport, perhaps waiting for a passenger. Which implied there was some activity going on here.

He heard an engine's thrum and the rhythmic thwacking of a helicopter. He scanned the skies for the helicopter he knew was there—somewhere—but he couldn't see it. Perhaps it was on the other side of the ridge.

Still, he smiled. That was the evidence he was looking for. He could only think of one reason a helicopter would fly at these elevations.

Lagati had come home at last.

*   *   *

Dario straightened as he heard pounding footsteps on the stairs. He put down the glass of water he'd poured for Janene and turned, nearly colliding with Junior. They joined his father at the bottom of the stairs and rushed onto the veranda.

Ira had returned to the same spot on the lawn he always did. He was hunched over in pain, which also fit the pattern of his travels.

"Bring him inside," Dario said, holding the door open. The Davids each took a shoulder as they led Ira into the house. Ira waved them aside and sank onto the bottom step.

"You can't keep doing this, Ira," the elder David said.

The rabbi coughed into his hand. "I know. The power is taking its toll on me."

Dario rushed into the kitchen and plucked the glass of water off the countertop where he'd left it. He pushed it into Ira's hands, and the old man drank deeply.

"Teach me what you do," Junior said earnestly. "I can help. We can work together."

"I'm afraid it's too late for that. You would need years to master it." Ira finished the water. "Besides, it's all coming to a head."

They looked up as Janene and Celeste appeared at the top of the stairs. The women descended to the landing, with Janene choosing to sit cross-legged while Celeste leaned against the banister.

"He found the Grigori," Junior said, surmising the reason for Ira's quick return.

"They're in Switzerland," Ira rasped.

Dario knelt in front of Ira. "Why there?"

"It's where Lagati lived, in the Central Alps. Very remote." Ira wiped the back of his hand across his forehead, but it did nothing to remove the sheen of sweat. "I've been there before. I should have thought to check sooner."

"So what do we do?" Janene asked. "I don't plan to sit here while the world needs saving."

Ira's eyes brightened. "You couldn't have said it better, my dear. What comes next will require all our participation. No more little missions. This time, we go en masse."

Ira grunted, then pushed his weight forward onto his knees.

Dario realized he might very well topple over, so he thrust his arms out to catch him. Ira pushed him away, straightening his stiff back. Dario thought he heard a cracking sound.

The elder David took him by the hand as Ira walked outside, the rest of the group only a step behind.

"Ira, are you sure you can do this?" David asked. "I saw how quickly my father deteriorated at the end. You may not have it in you."

"He's right," Dario agreed. "Just getting us there will require an enormous amount of energy."

It could be a one-way trip, he added silently.

"Trust me," Ira said. "I can do it."

"But do we have to do it right now?" Celeste looked back toward the house. "And what about Ohia?"

"Leave it in chains," Dario growled. He would prefer to kill Ohia, but it seemed pointless. Ohia couldn't truly be killed, only the woman whose body the creature occupied, and Dario wasn't sure he could bring himself to dispatch her.

Ira walked ever so gingerly to the usual spot on the lawn. The grass all around it had been trampled as though by a team of horses. "We go now," he said in a firm voice. "Everyone put their hands on me."

"All at once?" Junior sounded skeptical.

"Yes, David. Do as I say."

They crowded together, six pairs of arms and legs packed into an uncomfortable human tangle. Dario barely breathed as he tried to come to terms with the urgency of the situation. He looked down at his clothes, still smelling from the two hours he'd spent in Singapore.

"Do you have a plan?" Dario asked as they waited for Ira to work his magic.

"Oh yes." Ira smiled widely without opening his eyes. "Rest assured, I know exactly what I have to do."

THIRTY-THREE

Linthal, Switzerland

AUGUST 4

A gust of wind shook loose a branch. Gayle heard it fall, hitting the middle of the mountain path. She'd left Linthal that morning with instructions from Barakel to climb until she intersected with a dirt trail just short of the tree line. She stepped around the fallen branch and kept going. Once this would have been a challenging climb, but the hike up and down the Khunjerab glacier had been good training. She barely felt winded.

At first she had worried Barakel was sending her to her doom, but the GPS she had rented in town confirmed the route. A couple of paths visible only on the satellite imagery suggested she could cross over to the mansion without having to take the main road. She'd need to approach with stealth if she had any prayer of finding Elisabeth and getting her out, but Lagati had situated his home to make stealth nearly impossible.

She heard the helicopter only a moment before she saw it. The aircraft rose almost directly in front of her, veering around the side of the mountain and continuing its ascent. She ducked into the under-brush, praying she hadn't been spotted by the pilot. It had flown too close to have been going anywhere except Lagati's mansion. What other destination could there be at these heights, on this particular mountain?

Ten minutes later, the path forked almost imperceptibly. One route descended around a swollen glut of grey rock jutting out from the ridge. The other offered a more punishing climb well past the tree line.

She knew she should take the safer path. If the goal was to get over the mountain, the lower track would take her there. But the more vertical course led exactly in the direction the helicopter had gone.

Following her hunch, she headed *up*.

*   *   *

Dario faced the otherworldly mansion across the wide gorge. Ira had chosen to land them on a flat shelf of rock where they'd be unlikely to be spotted from the road. Dario agreed this was a perfect staging ground.

Behind him, Ira huddled with Celeste and Janene, dispensing in-structions. Ira had already deployed the Davids and translated them away from here. As Dario watched, Ira vanished with the women, leav-ing him alone. He didn't know what Ira had planned, and in a sense he didn't want to know. He achieved a certain clarity by being able to focus on a particular task instead of the big picture.

"Beautiful, don't you think?" Ira's voice carried over the gorge.

Dario hadn't heard the rabbi return. "I suppose it is. A tremen-dous feat of engineering."

The mansion hewed to an inspired design, but Dario found it cold and impersonal. He'd never want to spend any length of time in this mountain fortress. Indeed, the design spoke volumes about Raff Lagati.

Over the last week, Dario had heard many stories about the infamous Frenchman, and when he combined them with the few bits of near-legend he'd absorbed from Lagati's very public persona, it made for a perplexing character profile. Raff Lagati: unconscionably wealthy, but philanthropic. Hands in many endeavors. Seen only on rare occasions. But what of his personality? His drives and ambitions? Lagati maintained an intensely guarded image. A difficult puzzle to assemble from the scattered pieces.

The wealthy often seemed out-of-touch with the world. The effect was almost pathogenic. As one rose to such stratospheric heights, it could be easy to lose one's sense of place. One's sense of humanity. Regardless of how a man like Lagati might view himself, he was such a different creature from the average low-wage laborer that he may as well have evolved into a new species. And what made such people appear not only alien to the common man, but in some way inherently evil? Surely these perceptions weren't based in flesh-and-blood reality. It didn't seem fair to classify Lagati as an evil man. Yet what other conclusion could Dario draw from the stories? Ira didn't need convincing. To the rabbi, Lagati was the epitome of the worst humanity could produce.

Ira didn't cut a perfect figure himself. He had unmistakably changed in the short time Dario had known him. At the beginning, Dario had listened to Brighton's tirades and chalked up the enmity to something personal. Certainly Ira didn't resemble the monster Brighton had made him out to be. As the days passed, as Ira became more deeply invested in rooting out the Grigori, Dario found himself recognizing attributes of the monster. Dwindling patience. Mounting obstinacy. More obsession than measured and thoughtful resolve.

It wasn't any one thing, but the fusion of all these factors painted an unflattering portrait. Dario couldn't deny that Ira had grown to become a dangerous man in his own right, employing questionable tactics on a regular basis.

But Ira had saved Dario's life more than once. Therefore, Dario wouldn't judge him. He didn't think anyone could. At the end of the day, Ira was only answerable to Ira himself.

"A feat of engineering," Ira repeated. "Yes, I think that sums it up. If not beautiful then at least remarkable." He stared at the distant mansion with hard, uncompromising eyes. "We don't have time to admire it. Lagati is a remarkable man, but what he has unleashed… Dario, we've come to the end. I haven't known you long, but I've come to rely on you."

In Ira's mouth, the words sounded almost like a compliment. Was he saying it to grease the wheel, to flatter him? Ira hadn't much relied on anyone but himself.

"Are we going to kill them?" Dario asked.

"We have to try."

"Perhaps they can't be killed. These giants, I mean. Their spirits are capable of moving from one host to the next, and they've been doing it for thousands of years. How does one kill a spirit?"

Perhaps the spirits couldn't be killed, only corralled. The metallic barrier in Tiahuanaco had trapped Ohia for a very long time.

"The spirits are mere nuisances," Ira said.

"One of those 'mere nuisances' killed a close friend of mine."

Ira hesitated before speaking, and Dario was glad. Dario felt certain the rabbi had been about to say something spectacularly offensive—that Rhea's death, while regrettable, did not count for much in the larger scheme.

"You're right," Ira finally said. It didn't bring Dario any closure to know Ira seemed to agree with him. Besides, Ira might be attempting to placate him. Who could say what the rabbi really believed on this subject? "Anyway, the spirits are already dead. The same cannot be said about the Grigori themselves. And if I'm not mistaken, Jehovah has reserved a fiery place for them."

Dario had seen enough to believe wholeheartedly in the existence of beings with superior power and insight, but this sort of religious mumbo-jumbo troubled him. Dario was inclined to believe the Grigori had extraterrestrial origins, not supernatural ones. Jehovah was real, but not necessarily God. If Ira was truly God's representative, he was doing a poor job.

"You said you had a plan," Dario prompted. He thought Ira had gained a bit of color in his cheeks. Was he recharging his proverbial battery? How much time would he need to get back to full strength?

"I do." Ira nodded, more to himself than to Dario. "And you're the lynchpin."

*   *   *

The road north of Linthal unspooled in a straight line, following the constantly burbling creek, and it offered extravagant views. Brighton didn't mind the fatigue he felt after the first two miles, given that his exertion had been spent as a free man. The journey was aided by long conversation and a constant pageant of chalet-dotted towns and villages, and the short and scenic tunnels along the highway that connected them. First Rüti, then Betschwanden, and then, as the valley widened somewhat, Luchsingen. What an improvement this was over the far-flung Karakorams, where one could drive mile after desolate mile without encountering any sign of habitation. Brighton drew energy from being surrounded by people again.

None of this erased the deep-seated sense that he was making a mistake.

From time to time, he looked to Elisabeth to see if she shared his reservations. She had passed the time telling him of her experiences with Lagati—notably their meeting with Barakel in Shamballa, and then the helicopter rescue. Throughout the stories, her principal emotion was elation. She would not want to go back, making it difficult for Brighton to suggest it.

How many times did you wonder whether you could go on living with Abranel? his conscience seemed to ask as they went along. Indeed, he had wondered this many times. *How long do you think you'll be able to live with the knowledge that human lives hung in the balance and you just walked away? Is that the future you looked forward to, that you fought for?*

"Do you see that?" Elisabeth asked, pointing up the road.

A procession of black town cars slithered out of the next town like a snake. There had to be two dozen of them. They took up the whole road, driving straight down the middle of the highway's dividing line.

"What do you think it is? A wedding? A funeral?" She didn't sound like she believed these suggestions. Like Brighton, she had to suspect it was related to that explosion they'd heard. Which meant it must have something to do with whatever was going on at Lagati's home.

Brighton stopped completely to watch as the first of the vehicles passed. It drove slowly enough that Brighton tried peering through the tinted windows. Anyone could be in there, but only one type of person: a VIP. These people were rich and important—and they weren't here for a wedding or funeral. Not in these numbers.

"Dignitaries," he said after another half-dozen cars had gone by.

"Dignitaries for what?"

Brighton weighed his opinion before answering. "Governments probably. Or they could be corporate CEOs."

Elisabeth didn't need to ask the next question: *What is their business here?* The elation had slipped off her face, replaced with caution and doubt. And indecision.

"Whatever's going on, you know they're headed for Lagati's estate," she said quietly. "It can't be chance."

"It would be hard to believe."

She blew out a stream of air. "We have to go back, don't we." It was a bland, emotionless statement.

Brighton wanted to make the opposing argument.

But he didn't have it in him.

*   *   *

"Before I brought everyone here, I heard a helicopter." Ira pointed to the north face of the mountain. "I think it came from that direction."

"You think the helicopter belonged to Lagati?" Dario asked.

"I'm sure of it," Ira said. "It seems obvious that Lagati would have a helipad attached to his main residence, and it's just as obvious that there isn't one out front. It must be hidden somewhere up the slope."

Dario frowned at him. "You're making a lot of leaps of logic, Ira."

"Am I?" Ira widened his eyes, sincerely surprised. "One assumption follows another. I can see the fallacy in following a series of assumptions, mistaking them for certainties, but in this case…?"

Dario opened his mouth to reply, but Ira cut him off.

"No doubt you're going to advise me not to be governed by my feelings. Don't bother." Ira could hear the sharpness in his voice, but he couldn't control it. Besides, he had thought this through. This wasn't a democratic process. "It sounds harsh, but you have to understand that I know what's required of us now." Ira didn't wait for Dario to agree. "If there's a helipad, then there's another way into the mansion. You need to find it."

"But why can't you deposit me inside the mountain itself?"

Ira closed his eyes, and in deference to Dario he tried for the second time to make a jump into the house's cavernous main hall. No matter how hard he tried, how hard he concentrated, every effort was rebuffed.

"There's some kind of barrier in place," he said, opening his eyes again. "They know I'm coming, and they've taken steps to keep me out."

"What kind of steps?"

Ira felt annoyed at this barrage of questions. "I don't know, Dario. If I knew, don't you think I'd *tell* you?"

"No," Dario said plainly. "There's a lot you don't tell me."

This was true, of course, but Ira's irritation only grew at having the truth served to him on such a blunt platter. "The Grigori are on the cusp of taking a critical step. Once you're inside, your assignment is to disrupt it—or at least delay it."

"What are you going to be doing?"

"Distracting them as best I can." Ira reached out his hand and waited for Dario to take it. They had to make physical contact to attempt the jump. "We have to hurry. I'll deposit you on that northern slope."

Dario stood up and joined him, looking resigned to his situation. Ira felt a twinge of empathy for the reluctant warrior, but he didn't want to dwell on it. There would be plenty of time for empathy when the danger had passed.

"I need you to promise you'll do as I say," Ira said. "It will be tempting to turn aside, to favor your own life over the lives of others. We're built for self-preservation, after all. But you must understand by now that the evil beings in that house," he gestured across the gorge, "have come to destroy the world. Maybe not all at once, but they will take it bit by bit, corrupting and distorting it until nothing good remains. They will remake the earth according to their own selfish desires. They aren't here to lead the people but to rule, and their rule will be devastating."

He stopped, stepping forward and taking Dario by the hand.

"Everything hinges on you, my friend. We have fought them, but now we must find a way to finish them. I regret asking this of you. In fact, I regret many things. I regret that I was chosen for this fight, and that so many innocents have been caught up in it. I regret that we cannot switch roles, but I cannot go inside there. The barrier prevents me. You must be the hero. Indeed, you are small enough that they may not see you coming. I believe you have a chance."

Dario didn't say anything.

"Did you hear me, Dario? I need you to promise."

Dario's words came with great reluctance. "I promise."

"Oh, and Dario, one more thing," Ira added, his voice losing its compassionate edge. "Stopping them may not be enough. If you get a chance to kill any of the Grigori, take it."

*   *   *

If I kill a Grigori, it will likely be the last thing I ever do, Dario thought grimly once Ira abandoned him on the side of the mountain. One wrong step and he'd plummet a thousand feet, at least, and a stiff north wind seemed determined to make it so. At this rate, he might never even get a chance to *see* a Grigori, never mind kill one.

He shielded his eyes from the sun and looked in the direction Ira had indicated. The rabbi had deposited him on a high ledge, at about the same elevation at which the helicopter would have landed. But it had been only a rough estimate. Dario worried he'd never find this imaginary helipad.

Killing a Grigori...

Dario imagined how the scene might play out, then he imagined it again. He replayed different scenarios, and not a single one ended well. He hoped Ira would be content with a mere disruption, because even that could not be guaranteed.

He picked his way over rocks, moving on all fours most of the time to keep his center of gravity as low as possible. This offset the risk of a gust of wind wiping him clean off the mountain, though it did a number on his knees. After twenty minutes of clambering around, his arms and legs were badly battered.

He asked himself one question over and over: *Is it worth it?*

If Ira was right that the human race depended on their actions to-day, it clearly was worth it. Despite all the evidence—and the sum of it was damning—Dario remained unconvinced. Saving the world was an intangible goal. Even if the stakes really were that high, the real question he contended with was more portentous: *Am I willing to sacrifice myself to save others?* Ira's impassioned speech aside, Dario had doubts.

Yes, he was willing, if Ira could be trusted. Given that he wasn't certain of that, he wondered what he was doing here. If he were perfectly altruistic, the prospect of the death of millions—millions of strangers—should be motivation enough. Perhaps it made him a monster, but Dario had to acknowledge that he could claim no such altruism.

He wanted to get his hands around the throats of whoever was responsible for senselessly killing Rhea, then pissing on her memory by occupying her corpse. Ohia had animated Rhea's broken body like a damned puppet. Even now, weeks later, Dario didn't know if she'd been properly laid to rest. Perhaps that would provide enough rage to fuel him. Ohia could not be killed, but Ohia was a small fish in this festering pond Dario had been forced to splash around in—and he wanted to make someone pay. Killing a Grigori would be… gratifying.

It wasn't altruism; in his estimation, it was better.

*   *   *

Ira returned to the staging ground and reveled in the silence. Being alone helped him think clearly. He hadn't rested nearly long enough, and the last few hours had required a near-constant outpouring of energy. Unfortunately, there was no end in sight, with his greatest challenge still to come.

Once in the flow of the river, he began to devise a new formula. The effect would be nothing like Aaron ever imagined in those halcyon training days on the quiet streets of Queens. Aaron had been a tremendous asset, but his failing had been his inability to foresee the lengths one might have to go in service to the mission. Now, Ira needed a creative approach. A distracting approach. A *devastating* approach.

He sunk deep into the water as equations he didn't understand unspooled across his vision. He didn't need to understand them; he was confident they would do his bidding, like they always had.

His hands glowed, and then came the accompanying heat. He substituted a few figures, moved numbers as he felt led, and from his palms burst a conflagration terrifying enough to put even the most belligerent Moses in his place. Ira was proud of the way he was able to direct the energy; he no longer felt at the edge of control while wielding it. More substitutions allowed him to concentrate the heat into a very tight beam, ever-narrowing. This would be no burning bush; he would wipe Lagati's mansion off the face of the earth.

Ira lifted his hands into the air and stretched them out toward the mansion. Triumphantly, he loosed all the fire he could muster. The deadly beam surged across the gorge, sizzling the air. An instant later, fire erupted upon Lagati's doorstep with a deafening explosion, and Ira exulted in his achievement.

*   *   *

Lagati cleared his throat. "I have a question."

The Twenty turned as though they had forgotten he was there.

"Who gave him permission to speak?" Azazel asked.

Semyaza gave his rival a hard swat across the back of the head. The sound reverberated through the dining room. "He sits in the circle, and thus he may speak." He gestured for Lagati to continue.

"You, Ramuel." Lagati looked across the circle to the Grigori he'd just met. "Azazel said your son died, but surely that can't be possible.

Your children… they are bound to the earth as immortal spirits, are they not? My understanding is that only their hosts can die."

"The rules have changed." Ramuel made eye contact with Semyaza. "Why are we wasting time with this man? Why must we explain the patently obvious?"

"Because we are fostering good will, remember?" Semyaza's voice sounded from almost directly behind Lagati's chair. Lagati's back stiffened. He waited for Semyaza to pass, but then he realized Semyaza had stopped. Out of the corner of his eye, he saw Semyaza's long fingers curled around the sides of the chair Lagati sat in. "We want Mr. Lagati to feel welcome in our company."

The expression on Azazel's face showed disagreement—and Azazel wasn't the only one who felt this way, though none made threatening moves.

"Nothing about this is patently obvious to me," Lagati said, asserting his place.

Ramuel grunted at him, but answered anyway. "To protect our new headquarters," and by this he seemed to mean Lagati's own house, "we've erected a barrier to keep out any agents of Jehovah who might seek to disrupt our activities."

Lagati nodded. "You mean Ira Binyamin."

"He is one such man, yes," Ramuel said.

"And what does this have to do with your dead son?"

Ramuel bristled and sat back in his chair.

Semyaza picked up the story and resumed his path around the circle. "Our barrier requires a great deal of reinforcement, because the weight of the physical plane exerts constant pressure. The Earth's gravity well makes it difficult to maintain the barrier, and many of our sons are involved in buttressing it. While they're engaged in this task, they are vulnerable to our enemy's attacks. If one is killed, he is not necessarily able to escape the host body in time."

"So their spirits aren't eternal?" Lagati asked.

"That's not exactly it," Semyaza said. "Their spirits go on when they leave our plane. It's just that they exist… somewhere else. Just think of them as gone."

Ramuel appeared unsatisfied. "We could have minimized that risk!"

"At too great a cost to our endeavor, fool." Semyaza grasped the back of Ramuel's chair, then flung it backward in a sudden motion that caught Lagati off-guard. Ramuel let out a startled cry as he landed in an undignified heap on the hard floor. He remained there for several moments before lifting his head and brushing aside his long straight hair. He seethed with rage.

"You do not speak for us!" Ramuel said.

Semyaza turned his back on Ramuel. "We speak in one voice, as we always have. I provide that voice." His cold eyes found Lagati. "Mr. Lagati, you are probably wondering about this endeavor I mentioned. Indeed, it is the main reason you have been invited to join us today."

Lagati worked strength into his vocal cords. "Yes. I would like to know more about it."

"That is sensible. We request," and Lagati thought the Grigori leader had chosen that word very carefully, "to join your people in common cause, to form an agreement. A coalition, you might say, against our mutual enemy." Semyaza cast a glance at the fallen Ramuel, who was just now returning to his feet. "It is not Lagati's permission we seek, but his partnership."

THIRTY-FOUR

Linthal, Switzerland
AUGUST 4

Everyone stared as Ramuel turned his chair right-side up and slid it back into place. He settled into it, his eyes swollen red from anger. Was this all it took for Semyaza to assert authority over the Twenty? Pulling back a chair and dumping one Grigori on his ass?

"Would you like to hear our proposal?" Semyaza asked.

"Yes, of course." Lagati had been angling for this, but he didn't betray his enthusiasm.

Semyaza displayed an off-putting smile. "Good. Jehovah must be stopped, and we have little time before he launches an attack against us—assuming one isn't already underway. For thousands of years, Jehovah held us captive. What humanity doesn't realize is that he has kept your entire race captive for just as long. He pretends to be your creator, your God, when the truth is that the Grigori had an equal hand in lifting mankind out of the primordial sludge. And now we must work together to ensure Jehovah is not allowed to commit further atrocities.

"I trust you will forgive my brazenness, but in your name, Mr. Lagati, we've invited dozens of world leaders to join us for a global peace summit. They are on their way now to negotiate treaties with us. When they arrive, I will tell them exactly what I'm telling you. In the same way that we have erected a barrier around this site to keep Jehovah and his agents out of our business, we intend to create another barrier, this one on a much larger scale—a planetary scale, in fact—that will keep Jehovah out of our affairs. Permanently."

Lagati put a hand on his forehead to steady himself.

"You look overwhelmed, Mr. Lagati," Semyaza said. "Do you understand what I'm saying?"

"To be honest, I'm not sure."

"It may take time to—"

"Actually, I have another question," Lagati interrupted, an audacious move he felt he could get away with now that Semyaza had taken to behaving so magnanimously. "You said reinforcing your barrier is a strenuous job. A planetary barrier would be—"

"Far easier." Semyaza had that same menacing smile on his face, as though to say, *Don't interrupt me again.* "I know, it seems counterintuitive. Erecting the planetary barrier will be difficult to put in place, but once it has formed a complete seal in orbit, it should hold with little maintenance. And just like that, Jehovah will never bother us again." He paused. "We insist on working with mankind. It's your planet, and therefore your decision. Our role is to support you against Jehovah."

Lagati allowed his gaze to trail over the Twenty one by one. Azazel had averted his gaze, and Turel seemed almost disinterested in the proceedings. Ramuel whispered with an unnamed Grigori next to him, quietly enough that Semyaza either didn't notice or chose not to comment.

"These world leaders," Lagati began, "when will they arrive?"

"Any time. They've been gathering in Zurich."

"Who's bringing them in?"

"One of your valets. Fitz, his name is." Semyaza spoke the name with an air of distaste.

Lagati meant to ask the names of these leaders, but before he could get the words out the entire room shuddered. Semyaza's head jerked up as an explosion ripped across the front window, shattering the glass.

*   *   *

Gayle's arduous climb came to a halt when she arrived at a cliff slightly too high to scale and with no observable handholds. She spared a glance back the way she'd come and realized she couldn't see the valley anymore. Even the last of the knobby, oxygen-starved trees were a few hundred feet downslope. Cuts traversed her hands and shins. Her fingers throbbed from the pressure she'd placed on them in scrambling up and over one outcropping after another. The path had long since disappeared, leaving her to navigate by memory: she was certain the helicopter had come this way—and that it had landed.

Not for the first time on this hike, she thought back to Henry. They had been avid hikers and spent many days in the Rockies. Henry had always felt close to nature, which is why he had suggested getting married in that alpine meadow—

An explosion sounded in the distance and the ground shook. Gayle nearly lost her balance. Only at the last second did she snag the edge of a rock with her left hand. She let out a cry of pain as her fingers curled over its blade-like contours. She hung on for dear life as the rock sliced through the tender flesh of her palm.

Once the shaking subsided, Gayle pulled herself onto her knees and cradled her hand, bloodied from the deep cut. She clenched her fist, hoping to stem the bleeding, but the pain only got worse.

She gritted her teeth and let out a howl of agony.

Once the keening of the wind reasserted itself, she looked down at her tightened fist and tried flexing it. She sucked back another scream and slammed her eyes shut. She counted to three, then continued to ten before opening them again.

A man's face was peering over the top of the unscalable cliff, staring right at her.

Gayle struggled to her feet. "Who are you?" she shouted, her hands clutched in an effort to stymie the pain. It seemed to help. The more pressure she applied, the better.

"My name is Dario. I heard you screaming."

"I hurt myself on the rocks… and here I was trying to be covert."

"I'd say your technique could use some work."

Was that supposed to be funny? "I'm new to this."

"I told you my name. What's yours?"

She clammed up, in a state of disbelief over the speed at which she'd given away her purpose. She could have said she was on a hike and had gotten lost—anything except carrying out a covert mission.

Still, this man had offered his own name without hesitation. Either he was just as terrible at espionage, or they were on the same side. More likely he wasn't on any side at all.

She didn't really believe that. No way was he on this mountain, on this day, by coincidence.

"Were you on that helicopter?" she asked.

"Helicopter?" Dario paused, thinking this over. "You saw it, too?"

"If you weren't aboard, how did you get up there? The cliff isn't passable. Not without specialized equipment."

"I came from the other direction. You need a hand up?"

She glanced down at her injury and grimaced. Had that, too, been intended as a joke?

Laughter bubbled up inside her and came out in a burst. She

brought her good hand to her mouth in an effort to stifle it, then gave in as it blossomed into a full-blown belly laugh.

Dario's head withdrew behind the cliff and Gayle wondered if she'd said something wrong.

"You still there?" She missed the stranger now that he was gone.

"Just a minute. I'll be right back!"

A few moments later, he reappeared farther west along the cliff, at the point where the drop was shortest. She walked carefully along the smooth slope until she was right beneath his outstretched hand.

"I can pull you up," he said.

"Or you could come down."

"Then neither of us will get where we're going, and I have a feeling we're going to the same place."

Gayle held up her wounded hand, still dripping blood though the worst of it had dried into dark red flakes. Maybe it wasn't as bad as she first thought. "Don't you think I'll need both hands to hold on?"

"We can try. It might be very painful."

"I can't!" she insisted.

Unexpectedly, he raised his voice at her. "Then go back down!"

That's another thing I can't do, she thought.

Stuck between two impossible options, she settled on the more courageous one.

*   *   *

Linthal's central square soon filled with locals looking up at the mountains, theorizing about the sounds they'd heard. Brighton latched onto a bit of conversation here and there; the people were unconcerned, more curious than frightened, though a handful of instigators—tourists, by all appearances—were trying to whip the people into a frenzy.

"Do you think the people are safe in the town?" Elisabeth asked, as though lifting the thought straight from Brighton's mind.

"Not really."

The ground shook, pushing them into action. They hurried south, but stopped before reaching the road that would take them to Lagati's estate. The parade of black town cars had halted, parking in single file along the side of the motorway. A collection of men and women in uniforms stood shoulder to shoulder, packed so tightly that from this distance they seemed to form a single dark mass of humanity.

"Security personnel," Brighton said. "They don't know what to do."

"If you're right that the people in those cars are dignitaries, their security won't be keen to take them into harm's way."

"I don't want to head into harm's way, either, but I think we have to." Brighton turned his attention back to town. "With the townspeople distracted, we should be able to find a car unattended, don't you think?"

They were in luck: some careless owner had left his or her silver Volkswagen unlocked. Brighton opened the door confidently, hoping that if they were being watched it would look as though they were the car's rightful owners. He crinkled his nose when the smell hit him: fish, of all things.

"Must be some kind of fisherman," Elisabeth said, dropping into the seat next to him as he started up the engine.

Sure enough, a tackle box occupied the middle of the backseat, and on the floor rested a blue cooler which he suspected contained the displaced denizens of nearby lakes and streams.

"It's full of fish," Elisabeth confirmed when she opened the lid.

"Leave it on the side of the road." But the smell lingered even as he performed a U-turn and accelerated through the back alley.

Their Volkswagen passed the idling town cars moments later, laboring to climb out of the valley. At each switchback they were afforded a view of picturesque Linthal. Brighton checked each time to see if those town cars had moved; they never did.

"There's not much gas," he mused when he remembered to check the gauges.

Elisabeth shrugged. "Won't matter. It's not far."

Brighton remembered very little of the directions. On his first and only previous trip here, he'd relaxed in the backseat and left all navigation to the thickly accented chauffeur, a swarthy little man who hadn't been much for conversation.

"I don't suppose there's a map in the glove box," Brighton said.

"Lagati's place isn't going to be marked on a map, Sherwood."

"No, but seeing one might jog my memory."

Elisabeth conceded this and opened the glove box. Brighton kept his eyes on the road, but couldn't help looking out of the corner of his eye as Elisabeth removed a bulky leather sleeve. Its drawstring was pulled tight.

"What have you got there?" Brighton asked.

Elisabeth loosened the drawstring and reached inside. She smiled as she withdrew a fileting knife by its hard plastic handle. A bit on the dull side, but dangerous nonetheless.

"My, my," Elisabeth said.

Brighton glanced away as they came to a series of private drives. He searched his memory, trying to remember which of these—if any—would take them to Lagati's estate.

A bank of clouds ahead obscured the area in fog. If they drove much further, it would be very difficult to see where they were going, never mind get a sense for—

The ground shook again, stronger this time.

"We must be close," Elisabeth said.

Brighton practically screeched to a stop as he spotted a gravel track. The car came to a rest right in front of the road's mouth, though Brighton still couldn't see where it led.

Elisabeth rolled down her window to get a better view. "Is this it?"

"I remember a sharp turn when we left the main road." He scowled, wishing he had paid more attention two years earlier. He backed up a couple of car lengths, then shifted into first gear and moved slowly onto the little road. "We'll find out soon enough."

*   *   *

"You can call me Gayle," the woman finally revealed once Dario had helped her over the ledge. She spoke while wincing, obviously in a great deal of pain.

"Let me take a look at that." He knelt next to her and took her closed fist in both hands. "Could you loosen your grip?"

"If I keep the pressure up, it doesn't hurt so bad."

"You've been holding it that way for almost ten minutes," Dario said. "The bleeding may have slowed."

Gayle didn't appear convinced, but she loosened her grip enough for Dario to pry back her stiff fingers. As he'd thought, the bleeding had mostly stopped, the cut not as deep as it had appeared. Her palm was encrusted by flecks of the darkest red he had ever seen, almost black.

Could Ira heal this? He felt the mountain rumble beneath him and remembered that Ira had other things on his mind just now.

"Looks worse than it probably feels," he said. "Still, we should wrap it just in case. Wouldn't want it to get infected."

He tore a strip off his own shirt sleeve and proceeded to wrap it around Gayle's wrist. He looped the cloth between her thumb and forefinger a couple of times to keep it from slipping out of place. Not the most ideal solution, but a reasonable stopgap.

"Come on, we should keep moving," he prodded. "Which way did you say that helicopter went?"

She stumbled after him with a pained expression. "Just over the ledge. It must have landed nearby. It might lead to—" She clammed up.

"What were you going to say?"

She frowned at him. "I don't know if I can trust you."

"Fair enough, but it looks like I was right."

"Right about what?"

"About us going to the same place," Dario said. "I'm trying to find a way into Lagati's estate, too."

So he knew. "And what are you going to do when you get there?"

"I don't know what you've been told, but there's a group of"—well, they weren't *people*, but what could he call them them?—"I guess you could call them aliens. Sort of. Sounds crazy, I know."

"You mean the Grigori," Gayle said, almost offhandedly. "They go by a lot of names, some even crazier. I used to call them the Starseed people, a race of aliens who came to Earth thousands of years ago to help life flourish here."

Dario slowed down, shocked. "Do you really believe that?"

"I don't know what to believe anymore. What do you believe?"

The question made him want to laugh. He was tempted to repeat all the things *Ira* believed. His own beliefs were so much more complicated. "Wish I could tell you. All I know is that I'm supposed to get inside, find out what they're up to, and stop them. Somehow."

They continued in silence, each chewing on what the other had said. On this shoulder of the mountain, the angle of ascent wasn't nearly so steep as where Ira had left him, allowing them to move more quickly.

"My friend's name is Elisabeth, by the way."

Dario smiled. "I guess you've decided you can trust me then?"

"Seems we're probably on the same side. Either that or you're a very good liar."

He braced himself against a gust of wind, slowing down to compensate. "Elisabeth, you say. Is her last name Macfarlane?"

"You know her?"

"I did. I mean, I do." Dario picked up the pace again. "But not well. We travelled together for a while."

Gayle shook her head. Not in disagreement, Dario thought, but rather to shake out the cobwebs. "There were four of you. Yourself and Elisabeth, a man named Brighton and a rabbi. Is that right?"

"How on earth could you know that?"

"Because I'm the one who directed you to Pakistan."

Dario snapped his head around. "Excuse me?"

"Elisabeth was in Peru when I got a call from her, asking for help finding a place called Shamballa. You must have heard of it. A mystical place, home to an interdimensional portal? Never mind. Turns out I was wrong about most everything, except for one thing: its location. I told Elisabeth where to look—and she found it. I mean, you all found it."

"Well, it didn't exactly go as planned," Dario said, finishing off the story. He said nothing as they approached another steep ascent. "You're sure the helicopter came this way."

"In truth, I'm beginning to doubt myself."

No sooner had the words left her mouth than Dario saw what he thought might be the opening to a cavern. At first the low angle of the sun made it seem like a giant shadow, only without an accompanying protrusion of rock to cast it.

He pointed toward it. "Is that what I think it is?"

"A wide cavern," she said, coming to the same conclusion. "Perhaps even wide enough to accommodate a helicopter."

Dario tried to assess the climb. He was sure he could get up there, but the steepest section would give Gayle trouble.

"What are we waiting for?" she asked.

"I'm worried about your hand. Maybe I should go first." She didn't look happy with his suggestion. "I promise I won't leave you here."

*   *   *

Ira stumbled as the beam of power leapt from his outstretched hands, threatening to tumble him backward in one of the worst recoil effects imaginable. He managed to hold his ground, though he didn't know how. He *lived* in the power, in the ecstasy it elicited as he channeled it outward in wave after wave of devastating fire. The front edifice of Lagati's mansion had been consumed in a wall of leaping flames and towering smoke.

But it wasn't enough to damage the house; he had to destroy it, to bring the mountain down upon it. There couldn't be any survivors.

If I fail, at least Dario will have a fighting chance. His thoughts then meandered in a darker direction. *If I succeed, Dario will die at my hands.*

Fighting nausea, he turned up the temperature by collecting oxygen from the air, compressing it, and feeding it into the stream. The fire responded immediately, softening from bright red to yellow to green and then to deadly blue. Even the blue soon faded, the fire growing hotter as it paled into near-invisibility.

Under this fresh onslaught, the rock face shook and smoldered as though the subject of a never-ending earthquake. Ira knew that the house wasn't just on fire; the rock itself was beginning to boil.

*   *   *

Blowback from the fire forced the Twenty's meeting deeper into the house. Its explosions were so strong that Lagati couldn't understand why they hadn't all been burned to a crisp—until he asked the question aloud to whoever was near enough to answer, and Turel explained that the barrier around the house provided sufficient shelter. For the time being, anyway.

That didn't reassure Lagati in the slightest.

He fell in with the press of bodies as they were led toward the back of the house, first through the drawing room and then through a vestibule into an enclosed space far enough from the fire that there seemed little immediate risk. The walls were thick with titanium supports.

When they finally stopped to catch their breath, Lagati saw that only a handful of fellow humans had been carried along—including Amir, he was pleased to note.

Azazel approached, shoving Lagati out of the way. "This isn't an ideal place to perform the ritual."

"I have come to the same conclusion," Semyaza said. "But we cannot delay any longer. If anything, we need to quicken our schedule."

"Agreed." Azazel turned just far enough to glare at Lagati. "We will take the humans and go somewhere safe."

Lagati reached into his pocket and gripped the cube tightly. It made him feel secure.

Turel came closer, having overheard the discussion. "The barrier will hold if we move quickly. We have to act. Now."

"What about those world leaders you mentioned?" Lagati broke in. "They'll need to be brought in somehow."

The nearby Grigori fell silent as they pondered this problem.

Lagati smiled, realizing that he had the perfect solution. Unfortunately, it would require him to postpone his plans for Azazel. It couldn't be helped.

THIRTY-FIVE

Linthal, Switzerland
AUGUST 4

righton drove with exceeding care, struggling to make out the road through the fog. He feared the possibility of having come this far only to plummet off a cliff and be killed in a fiery blaze. An ignoble way to go.

Elisabeth stuck her head out the window to get a better view. "You smell that? This isn't fog."

She was right. Smoke billowed all around them.

"We must be close."

At last, the air cleared enough for them to see that they were skirting the edge of a deep gorge—and Lagati's mansion lay directly ahead. Or at least it had. What Brighton remembered as an architectural wonder—the modern-day reimagining of ancient Petra—had fallen in on itself. Dust and smoke rose in titanic blooms, wafting high into the atmosphere. The wind had temporarily shifted the smoke away from the road and out over the gorge. Not that being able to see the remains of Lagati's fortress would get them any closer to it; the road ahead was blocked where rocks had crashed into the pavement.

Brighton got out of the car. "What happened here?"

Elisabeth joined him, bringing the knife. With it, she indicated an almost invisible shelter in the rocks opposite the road. The only reason either of them noticed it was the spasms of flame spouting up into the air. Each spasm was less brilliant than the one before, diminishing until the only evidence of activity was a smoky tendril.

A figure tumbled forward from the spot. To Brighton, it looked like an old man. And he knew right away who it was.

"Take the car and get help," Brighton said in a rush. "Leave the knife, though."

"Can't you see that the house has collapsed? There can't have been any survivors."

"Not for the people in the house, damn it." He pointed toward the figure of the old man. "For him!"

Elisabeth narrowed her eyes. "Are you sure it's a man?"

"I'm sure. As sure as I know his name is Ira Binyamin."

*   *   *

Straining against gravity, Dario pulled himself over the lip of the cavern. He rubbed some of the grime off his face as he got his bearings. He sat on the edge of a smooth concrete floor that stretched deeper into the mountainside than he would have thought possible. Near the back, resting upon painted crosshairs, sat a yellow helicopter. It shone like a beacon, and Dario realized it was because a pair of recessed lights in the ceiling had been aimed onto its gleaming surface.

"We were right!" Dario called behind him, heaving to catch his breath. "The helicopter is here. I'm looking right at it."

When he peered over the edge, he saw Gayle a hundred feet below, cradling her closed fist. "Can you get me up?"

He marched toward the helicopter, an idea forming in his mind. He needed something like a rope, something she could use as a support. On the far side of the helicopter he encountered a line of metal cabinets, six in a row. He tried the first five, all locked, but the sixth came open when he gave it a tug.

Inside, he found little canisters containing God only knew what and a pile of oil-soaked rags. Not much help there. He closed the door and immediately noticed a thick orange cable snaking from the rear of the helicopter to an elaborate socket in the wall. A fuel pump? An electrical cord? It didn't matter. He unhooked both ends and dragged it to the brink of the cavern.

"Hold onto this." He lowered the bulky cable over the side. Its metallic end pinged against stone until it came to a rest at Gayle's feet. He braced himself against the cavern wall and held on as tightly as he could as she began to climb.

She used her good hand to find purchase on the mountainside and her bad hand to grasp the cable. It took her twice as long to reach the top as it had taken him. Sweat poured down her face from the effort.

She came to her feet and took her first look around, seeming undaunted. "This must lead into the house."

The cavern was long, but aside from the helicopter and those cabinets, there wasn't much to see.

"Looks an elevator," Gayle said, having wandered to the opposite side of the cavern. When he joined her, he saw a sliding door with a single button installed on its steel frame. She stabbed at the button. "Going down?"

"Maybe we should give this more thought. Make a specific plan."

She brushed aside a clump of tangled hair. "We don't know what we'll find down there. Hard to make a specific plan for that."

*   *   *

Lagati's heart raced as he climbed the stairs, hoping the route to the loft's tiny office remained clear. The attack seemed to have finally stopped—or at least the constant shaking had—but he suspected entire portions of the house had collapsed. He had to sidestep some alarmingly huge boulders that had smashed their way through the ceiling.

He stood in front of the wood-paneled elevator door, waiting for the sensor to recognize him. Nothing happened for twenty seconds, and he assumed the circuitry had been damaged. He slapped the manual button to the left of the door, holding his breath and hoping against hope that it would work. He thought he might be able to climb the elevator shaft by hand, but he certainly didn't want to find out for himself.

The door slid open and he jumped into the waiting car. He tried to settle himself down by looking into the small compartment's dark, non-reflective walls. That only seemed to make his anxiety worse.

I could get out of here and let the mountain collapse on them, Lagati thought, knowing he could never go through with it. He feared what would happen to him if the Grigori weren't all killed—and he equally feared what would happen to the rest of the world if they were. Their warnings about Jehovah had struck a chord. He believed them. It was obvious that Jehovah's various, world-spanning religions had done nothing but choke the life out of human progress. Such ancient and misguided beliefs were incompatible with modern civilization, and they would continue to be a millstone around humanity's neck until a way was found to discard them. The Grigori had provided a way.

"Get a grip," he whispered to himself. "You can do this. Down to the village, get the dignitaries, bring them back."

It wouldn't be easy, but saving the world wasn't the sort of thing that ever came easy.

*   *   *

The doors slid apart, revealing a dark-haired man with blue eyes and a slightly slumped demeanor—and he looked as surprised to see them as they were to see him. Dario instinctively sidled up between the stranger and Gayle.

"Who are you?" Gayle asked, and then a moment later, "Never mind. Stupid question."

Dario threw her a sidelong glance. "Stupid?"

"Can't you see who it is? Raff Lagati. He has a rather famous face."

Startled, Dario gave the man in the elevator a longer inspection. His face was a bit gaunt, his cheekbones sharper than the magazine covers had suggested, the eyes deeper set and balanced atop globular eye bags that must have taken months—years?—to accumulate.

"What are you doing in my house?" Lagati demanded.

Dario didn't know what came over Gayle, but she shoved past him and got in the famous billionaire's face. "You kidnapped my friend!"

"Gayle, maybe that isn't the best way to—"

She silenced Dario with a look. "He has to answer for his crimes."

"I haven't kidnapped anyone," Lagati said, smiling. An anxious smile, though. "You're the trespasser here. You don't have the right to speak to me this way."

"What do rights have to do with it?" Gayle said.

Dario grabbed her by her good hand and pulled her backward. "Gayle, there are better ways to handle this." He turned to Lagati. "Elisabeth Macfarlane went into that base in Pakistan and didn't come out again. Do you know what happened to her?"

"Elisabeth is your friend?" Lagati asked derisively, eyeing Gayle.

Gayle nodded. "Yes. And I know you still have her."

"She was here, I admit, but I didn't kidnap her—not personally—and in fact I let her go." Lagati pointed to the helicopter behind them.

"I flew her down into the valley myself."

Gayle was silent for a moment. "When did this happen?"

"A couple of hours ago."

He was probably telling the truth. That would have been around the same time Ira and Gayle had seen the helicopter fly by. But even if he had flown the helicopter, he might have been lying about freeing Elisabeth.

"I have no reason to lie about that," Lagati said, reading his mind. "Elisabeth has never mattered to me. If she had been important, I would have kept her. Rest assured of that."

"We know what's going on down in your house." Dario met the man's gaze. "We know the Grigori are there, and we felt the explosion."

"It was Ira, wasn't it?" Lagati asked.

Dario's instinct was to keep the truth to himself, but Lagati would find out one way or another. "Yes, that's right."

"I expected nothing less. That so-called man of God has been a thorn in my side for longer than I care to say." Lagati stepped out of the elevator, and Dario and Gayle stood aside to make room. "In other circumstances, I would escort you off the property, or call the police. But as you have already supposed, we're past all that. What are you going to do, surprise the Grigori? By yourselves? You make for pitiful resistance." He smiled again, more confidently this time. "So I don't need to stop you, or kill you, or do anything at all. They'll do it for me."

Lagati spoke smoothly, like an orator predisposed toward grandiloquent speeches. Even when his words revealed him for a monster, he had the ability to persuade and entice.

In fact, that's his most monstrous trait, Dario thought.

"Fortunately for you, I'm feeling magnanimous," Lagati continued. "Despite the way you've treated me, I'll take you to Linthal. If Elisabeth is all you're after, you might find her there. It will be your best chance."

Gayle looked satisfied, and Dario thought she might take him up on the offer. He, on the other hand, didn't have the luxury. Ira was depending on him to carry out his mission.

I made him a promise. Plus, Rhea would want me to do it.

But would Rhea really want that? As fond of her as he'd been, he hadn't gotten the opportunity to know her very well. A few lousy weeks. For all he knew, she would want him to run as far away as he could and make a life for himself.

"There's no reason for you to throw your lives away," Lagati said. "You can choose to stay—and die. Or come with me—and live. There it is: life or death. The choice is yours. I recommend life."

Gayle turned to Dario with pleading eyes. "Dario, come with us. He's right. There's no reason for us to die. Not today."

"That's right, Dario." Lagati used his name as though they had been friends for years. "I suggest you listen to her."

I would like nothing better, Dario thought, *but I made a promise.*

*   *   *

"Ira, can you hear me? Ira!"

Brighton screamed until his voice was hoarse, but the crumpled figure didn't move. At this distance, Brighton couldn't tell if Ira was alive or dead. No matter his level of personal anger at the old man, he still cared. More than he had expected.

"Ira, it's me, Sherwood!"

The figure winked out of the air—there one minute, gone the next. This only made Brighton's panic rise faster.

"Ira!"

"You don't need to shout," a weak voice rasped behind him.

Brighton spun on his heel, shocked to see Ira in the middle of the road right where the Volkswagen had been parked. The rabbi was on his side, curled into a fetal position. Brighton rushed to him and propped up his head. His lips were dry and caked with dust. In one week, Ira had aged at least ten years.

"My God, what's happened to you?"

Ira coughed out a thick spurt of blood and mucus. "It's too long..." he fought for breath "...a story to get into..."

"Elisabeth's gone to get help, so it's important that you hold on."

"Thank you, but there's nothing... to be done." Another cough. "You planning to stab me with that?"

Brighton looked down at the knife in his hand. He dropped it in the gravel. "Of course not."

"Let nature run its course," Ira said. "I've been locked in a mortal battle with nature for a week. About time it caught up with me."

"What are you talking about?"

A shadow seemed to fall over Ira's face. "As always, you listen but you don't really hear."

Brighton felt the old rage well up inside him. "Even now, you can't help yourself."

"Sorry," Ira said. "You've always been so much more than you appeared. I knew it in my gut, but I didn't trust it. Jehovah had big plans for you, but because of my failure..."

"Don't say that."

"Let me speak the truth. There's not much else I can do." He closed his eyes, then opened them again as though they weighed twenty pounds. "I'm the one who didn't listen. Oh yes, I have failed very badly."

Brighton took Ira by the hand. Seeing him this way, broken and left alone here on this mountain, filled him with pity. "I've made my choice now, Ira. I know which side I'm on, and what it means to be on that side. You were right all along."

"Quite the contrary," Ira rasped. "I've never felt more wrong.

Look at me. Look at what I've become."

"I think you did what was necessary."

"And it destroyed me." Ira sighed as Brighton checked his pulse. Very faint. Elisabeth would never make it back in time. "Just like Aaron predicted, all those years ago."

"Excuse me?"

"You remember Aaron."

Brighton smiled, a bid to distract Ira from his condition. "Aaron Roth. How could I forget?"

"And you remember the words he spoke to you. The prophecy."

Brighton needed no help recalling them. "'The black awakening is soon upon us. And you, a beacon of light in a dark place…'" He hadn't thought about those words for some time. "Except I'm no beacon, Ira. If you only knew what's happened to me, what I've *allowed* to happen. I've let you down."

"Hardly. It's the other way around. I should have mentored you."

Brighton smiled again. "Quite the pity party we're having, don't you think?"

"I suppose you're right."

Brighton looked toward the smoking ruins of Lagati's home. "Did you do that?"

Ira grunted, then spit up again. More blood. "Best I could do. Or rather, the worst I could do. I hope Dario was more successful."

"Dario was with you?"

"Went inside." Ira closed his eyes, and it took longer this time to open them again. "To stop them."

Brighton felt his stomach twist. "You sent him alone!?"

"I had no choice."

"What was the plan?" Brighton asked.

He leaned closer and listened as Ira for once told him everything.

THIRTY-SIX

Linthal, Switzerland

AUGUST 4

On approach, Lagati noticed a huge crowd in Linthal's central square. At most, the village had a population of about a thousand, but at least that many had poured in. He might have been concerned were it not for the temporary advantage it offered. The airfield was far from the central square, which meant almost no one was paying attention as he set the helicopter down.

"Get out," Lagati called over the *tic-tic-tic* of rotating blades.

"Where did you drop her off?" Gayle asked.

"Right here." He turned off the engine. "Best of luck."

Gayle hopped out and took off towards the town. His gaze followed her as he wondered whether he had done the right thing. He could have killed her and been done with it—just like he could have killed Elisabeth. It wasn't a matter of scruples; he hadn't seen any profit in it.

He switched on the radio. "Can you hear me, Fitz? It's Lagati."

Static burst from the speaker and Lagati turned down the volume.

He monitored the channel for a couple of minutes, checking in several times. No response came through. Lagati missed Wendell. His long-time valet had never kept him waiting.

"Come in, Fitz," he said on his fifth attempt. "Come in, damn it, come—"

"This is Fitz! That you, Jim?"

Who's Jim? Perhaps it was someone who worked for him. "Lagati here. What took you so long?"

"Left the car…" Infuriating static! "…south of town."

"Please repeat. Didn't catch that."

"Caravan's south of town. Big explosions up your way. You okay?"

"I'm in the bird," Lagati said. "How fast can you get to the airfield?"

"Lots of traffic. People everywhere. Estimate fifteen minutes, more or less."

"Make it less. I'm going to bring our guests up by air, but only four at a time."

"Roger that, boss. On our way."

Lagati swung himself out of the helicopter to get some fresh air while he waited. By now, Gayle would be hurrying through the swarm of humanity, checking every brown-haired woman in sight. A waste of time. Lagati was sure Elisabeth had left town at the first opportunity, and that had been hours ago.

He narrowed his eyes at two figures running toward him, waving their arms like madmen. His first thought was that they might try to prevent him from lifting off again. But then he recognized them.

Oh my god, it's Antoinette! His heart thudded in anticipation of seeing her again, and so unexpectedly, but his second reaction arrived almost as quickly: anger that she hadn't gotten away—and stayed away—when she had the chance.

"You shouldn't be here!" Lagati called to her as she reached the air-field. Wendell was right behind her. Lagati began walking toward them.

She sped up, and the two collided in a crush of passion. Despite his reservations over seeing her again, he didn't hold back. Their lips pressed together in a long kiss.

"Did you just say I shouldn't be here?" she asked when they pulled apart.

"It may not be the most romantic welcome, but it's what you need to hear. Linthal isn't safe."

"We gathered that," Wendell said. "We turned back toward town when the earthquakes started."

Lagati nodded slowly. "It's good you didn't try to get closer. Ira launched an attack, almost killed us all. In fact, the house may not hold up much longer."

"I can't believe that," Antoinette whispered. "That place is a fortress. It was built to withstand the weight of an entire mountain, let alone an old man with delusions—"

"Ira has no delusions, and he's more than an old man," Lagati said. "I don't know what's come over him, but he's grown powerful. Throwing lightning bolts, burning people alive… it's like that pile of torched corpses we found at Khunjerab, only worse."

"Jehovah is finally fighting back," Antoinette said.

"Looks that way." Lagati returned to the helicopter, but didn't get inside. "The Grigori have told me their plan, and it requires bringing up some dignitaries. I have an important part to play now." It felt good to say that last part aloud.

"We saw their cars stopped on the side of the road," Wendell said.

Lagati was grateful to have him back. "They're on their way here."

"There must be dozens of people in those cars." Antoinette touched her palm against the side of the helicopter. "We'll have to make several trips."

"Not we," Lagati corrected her. "I'm doing it alone. Wendell, take her as far from Linthal as possible. If I survive this, we'll meet up in

Zurich, at the usual spot. You remember?"

Wendell lowered his chin. "Of course."

"Don't send us away, Raff. We can help."

"No arguments, Antoinette. I won't fail in my responsibility." He kissed her again, not as passionately this time, and swung up into the cockpit. "Go, right now."

A lesser woman might have cried, but Antoinette just looked at him with fury in her eyes. "You *need* me, Raff."

"I love you, but I don't need you." He knew this would cut deep. That's partly why he said it. She needed a push. "Goodbye, Antoinette."

She would have argued forever, but Wendell took her by the arm and pulled her away.

Good man, Lagati thought. *He always comes through.*

He tuned out Antoinette's cries of frustration as he saw the first of the town cars approach. He smiled, glad to note they were well ahead of schedule. That certainly hadn't been fifteen minutes.

"Four passengers at a time," Lagati said to the driver. "And make it fast!"

*   *   *

At some point since landing, the sky had turned a violent shade of orange. Gayle shuddered, thinking it might be a bad omen for the night to come.

The crowd had swelled considerably beyond the confines of the central square, down side streets and even into some alleys. There might have been two thousand people riling each other up. It wouldn't take much to push the situation into a full-fledged riot.

"What is everyone doing here?" she asked a man at the edge of the crowd. "Don't you feel those quakes?"

He shrugged and gave her a blank look. Perhaps he didn't speak

English.

Gayle watched the crowd in frustration. She wouldn't get anywhere looking for Elisabeth here. Her friend would have done one of two things—get out of Dodge, in which case it would be almost impossible to track her down until she returned to the States, or head back up the mountain and get in on the fight, whatever form that might take. She had known Elisabeth long enough to suspect the second option might be closer to reality, but that didn't make it less foolish. Elisabeth tended to follow her heart when it made no sense to do so.

I'm not any different. Everyone's irrational in their own way.

She turned her attention to finding a way out of town. She considered stealing yet another car. It would be the third one on this long journey. She regretted treating strangers' private property like her own personal transit system, but what was a stolen vehicle when lives were at stake?

Out of the corner of her eye, she saw a parade of cars turning toward the airfield. Whatever they were up to, Lagati must be in the thick of it.

Gayle hurried into a nearby alley, then slowed as a pair of headlights shone right at her. Two blocks away, a car had turned into the alley. Gayle realized it was coming straight at her, and driving fast. She had just enough time to get out of the way.

The car shrieked to a halt, rocking on its tires from the sudden braking. The driver's door flew open and a woman with unkempt hair jumped out.

"Excuse me!" she yelled.

Gayle's instinct was to slink into the shadows. How had this woman known she was about to steal a car?

"I can see you there," the woman said, not as loudly. "For a moment, I thought maybe—"

Gayle stepped forward cautiously, avoiding the glare of the headlights. "What do you want?"

"Gayle?" The woman shook her head. "I must be going crazy. For a moment, you reminded me of someone … "

Gayle's breath caught. "Elisabeth!" she bounded into the light and embraced her friend.

Elisabeth hugged her back. "My lord, how many old friends am I going to run into today? Not that I'm complaining. How did you track me down?"

"Oh, it was nothing. Just four continents in a week."

"You're joking."

"Well, I really did hit four continents … " Gayle withdrew to arm's length. "It was worth it to know you're okay. You look exhausted!"

"So do you. What happened to your hand?"

Gayle had almost forgotten about that. She inspected her hand in the low light and realized it barely hurt anymore, as long as she didn't try to spread her fingers. Adrenaline!

They might have bantered all night, but Elisabeth's forehead suddenly stitched up in concern, as though she'd remembered something.

"I came to get help," Elisabeth said, getting back into the car. "Come with me."

"Help for whom? This is our chance to get out of here."

"A man will die if we don't—"

The babbling of the distant crowd rose in volume, turning into a symphony of screams.

Gayle's head shot up. "Sounds like there's trouble in the square."

No sooner had the words gotten out than a familiar site greeted her. Between a pair of three-story buildings at the mouth of the alley, an enormous figure lumbered into view, profiled against the blood-orange sky.

"I think a lot of people are about to die," Gayle said hollowly, her mind flashing back to that horrible night in Pakistan.

Elisabeth squinted through the windshield. "What's that?"

Gayle's heart fell. "A giant."

*   *   *

Dario stood at the back of the elevator as its doors opened into a darkened room. He waited for almost a minute, bracing himself for someone, anyone, to notice his arrival, but he appeared to be alone. He crept out of the elevator, his nerves spiking at the sound of the door sliding closed behind him.

As his eyes adjusted, Dario saw that this was a windowless office. Its lone door was open just a crack, allowing dim light to spill in from the hallway. He walked up to the door, slowed his breathing, and listened.

Almost immediately, he heard voices. He only picked up a few stray words.

"...generator's up... not sure how much longer... afraid..."

A different voice: "...doesn't want to go... the drawing room..."

And then a third voice, almost entirely unintelligible except for the only word that mattered: "Grigori."

Once he was sure they had moved on, Dario entered the hallway, the sound of his steps absorbed by the blessedly soft carpet. He stuck to the shadows, plentiful since most of the overhead lights had gone dark, most likely a consequence of the home running on generator power. Every once in a while, a light rumble shook the house, rattling the light fixtures.

The hallway ended at a stairwell. He stood with his hand on the banister and got a lay of the land.

An immensely tall figure strode into view at the bottom of the stairs and stopped, sensing Dario's presence. He looked up at Dario without any expression on his face, and Dario knew instantly this was one of the dreaded Grigori. Every muscle in his body tensed until the Grigori turned his gaze away and moved on.

His relief was short-lived.

"I don't know you," a voice said behind him.

Dario turned to see a young woman, no older than thirty, keeping a close eye on him from the hallway he had just navigated. Grey dust coated her hair and clothes.

Not a Grigori, this one. Just a regular human.

"You don't work here," she said.

He put a finger to his lips. "Please, don't—"

"This way." She took him by the hand and led him down a different corridor. "What's your name?"

Dario didn't answer.

They reached a closed wooden door and the woman gave it three solid raps. She didn't wait to turn the knob, instead opening the door just wide enough for them to slip through. She pulled him inside with her.

The space had once been a bedroom, though Dario didn't think it had seen recent use. The bed had been stripped and pushed lengthwise against the wall so it could function as a couch. Four downcast people sat on it, their legs dangling over the edge and not quite touching the floor.

"I've never seen him before," the young woman said to another woman, slightly older. "He was wandering by the stairs."

"You should be more careful, Sophie. You shouldn't have brought him." The older woman looked Dario up and down. She was clearly in charge. "Tell me who you are and how you got in here."

Dario hesitated.

"I'll make this easy. Tell us who you are, or we'll send you straight downstairs to meet the Grigori, and I'm sure you won't like what they do with you."

"I'm Dario," he said, deciding quickly to trust them, "and I came down from the helicopter cavern." From the looks on their faces, he determined that they had no idea what he was talking about. "Never mind that. Maybe you could tell me who *you* are."

"We work here, of course," the woman said. "Call me Edie."

"Okay, Edie, what's going on?"

"What's going on here is we're living on borrowed time. The Grigori have been taking us downstairs against our will, one by one. It doesn't take much imagination to figure out what they're doing."

"And what's that?"

Silence from the group. Dario realized that aside from thinking their compatriots were dead, they didn't know much more than he did. In fact, he likely had the advantage.

"Whatever it is, it's Lagati's doing," a man said from the bed-couch. "He's lost his mind."

"As far as I know, we're all that's left of the human staff," Edie said. She put an emphasis on the word *human*. "Have you come to help us?"

"I'll do what I can," Dario said, feeling a bit reluctant about it. But a plan had already started to form.

*　　*　　*

The giant made short work of an entire building, raining down stone and brick on the people in the square. Gayle watched, horrified, as the scene played out almost in slow-motion. Had there been anyone inside? If so, they were certainly dead by now.

"Get in!" Elisabeth shouted.

Gayle dove into the passenger seat as Elisabeth started the little Volkswagen's engine and kicked it into reverse. Too many people had crowded into the alley now, making a fast getaway impossible.

"Just get out and run," Gayle said, her door already open.

They abandoned the car and ran in the opposite direction from the giant, but they skidded to a stop when they reached the edge of town and saw three other giants lumbering toward Linthal, arms flailing at anything that moved.

Both women were caught speechless.

"*Get into your cars!*" a man bellowed behind them.

Gayle turned and saw a pickup truck headed their way. A portly middle-aged man had somehow squeezed his upper body through the passenger window. He cupped his hands to his mouth and hollered at anyone near enough to hear.

"*Use the cars as weapons! Ram their legs!*"

A stream of vehicles took off, most aiming at the single giant using the road. A pair of trucks, including the one with the shouting man, dared to bump its way through a rutted field to prevent the other two from reaching Linthal.

"If this was America, there'd be an army of gas-guzzlers ready to take these bastards," Gayle said. "Damn these small European cars."

"Gayle!" Elisabeth shouted. "Don't just stand there!"

Belatedly, she saw that the trucks had missed their mark and one of the giants had closed the distance to the town in only a few strides. He was headed straight for them. Gayle fled, knowing it was hopeless against the barreling creature. She felt a sudden swirl of wind to her left and correctly interpreted it as a giant swatting at her; she dove to the ground in time to avoid being caught up in the giant's fist, and she got a face full of gravel for her trouble. She watched helplessly as that same fist caught Elisabeth by the right ankle and hoisted her into the air.

Gayle lurched to her feet, ignoring the blood on her face and neck, and cried out for help until she spotted a car coming her way. It tottered to a stop next to her, but only long enough for Gayle to clamber inside.

"That one," Gayle said, pointing a shaky finger at the giant who still clutched Elisabeth.

The driver of the car nodded. "It's got your friend, yeah?" She had a thick British accent.

"Can't this bucket go any faster, Celeste?"

Only then did Gayle notice she wasn't alone in the back seat. Another woman, probably American and a couple of decades younger than the Brit, leaned over the center console.

"Fast as it goes," Celeste insisted.

As they sped toward the giant's feet, Gayle realized the collision would probably total their little car. Celeste gave the wheel a hard yank to avoid a group of lost and confused tourists. They careened forward with a previously unrealized burst of speed.

Gayle straightened her arms against the frame of the car and slammed her eyes shut in anticipation of the impact. Celeste and the other woman let loose a pair of discordant battle cries—

—which were strangled off as the car crunched into the back of the giant's leg. The windshield exploded inward, Gayle losing her sense of up and down as they went into a roll, glass raining all around.

They shuddered to a stop.

Gayle shook her head to clear it of the high-pitched squeal ringing in her ears.

"We did it!" the American woman crowed, unhurt except for a few cuts on her cheek and forehead. She was jiggling the handle of her door. It wouldn't open at first, but a couple of kicks did the trick and finally the door popped off its hinges. Gayle's door wouldn't budge, trapped against the hard ground.

A stab of pain flared outward from her shoulder. Just what she needed. A lacerated hand, gravel embedded in her cheeks, and now a dislocated shoulder. Boy, would she have a story to tell if she made it home alive.

The giant had stopped howling and was now using its hands to claw itself around. No blood gushed from its gaping wound. The creature's dry skin had sloughed off, revealing decomposed muscle and bone. Like the giants they'd seen in Pakistan, these too were walking cadavers. The hand that had clutched Elisabeth was now empty.

"Elisabeth!" Gayle shouted, turning in a circle, desperate to find her friend.

"Over here," Elisabeth called back.

With relief, Gayle saw that Elisabeth had fallen on her side only a short distance away. She knelt down to check her injuries.

"Can you feel your legs?" Gayle asked, jumping to the worst-case scenario.

Elisabeth looked down as she buckled her knee. "Yeah, I should be fine. Never been so scared in my life, though."

Suddenly, Gayle felt herself smile.

"What's so damned funny?" Elisabeth asked.

"Would you look at that... seems I managed to save you after all!"

*   *   *

Ira felt no panic, only acceptance as he slipped toward insentience. His mind gradually weakened, one errant thought after another tumbling out of his grasp. His overriding thought—so sticky that it might be the last to go—was that he somehow deserved this, that he had chosen it. Just behind that thought lived an insistence that he'd done something personally destructive but incredibly important, though his certainty diminished in concert with his mental control.

It had to be done.

It was a bit like drowning without water, and indeed this brought up a comparison to that metaphorical river he'd visited, a river whose waters were equal parts power and poison—and which now swept him under.

Distantly, Ira—his name?—was aware of that pleasant young

man shaking him in a maudlin display. All in vain, for there could be no coming back from this trip through the supernatural ether between worlds. Between dimensions?

What I did mattered.

But even as these words surfaced, he lost the ability to puzzle out their meaning.

And then a moment of surprise *hmm but I thought I would have more time*

THIRTY-SEVEN

Linthal, Switzerland

AUGUST 4

Brighton couldn't tear his gaze away from the body. Shooting fire from his palms hadn't turned out to be the most surprising of Ira's strange abilities. The man claimed to have traveled between dimensions… to have gone to heaven!

In his final minutes, Ira had told all, but Brighton couldn't recreate any of Ira's magnificent feats. This was perhaps the most damning of the rabbi's failings, that he hadn't found a way to pass on his knowledge to the next generation.

It should have been me, Brighton thought.

He returned his attention to the body, and nearly jumped out of his skin. Ira's eyes had snapped open! Brighton scrambled backward a few feet as Ira lifted his head in a mechanical motion.

Brighton quickly understood. "Nariman, is that you?"

Ira's dead eyes took in their surroundings. "It's me," the spirit said. "And I apologize for startling you. This was the easiest way to make contact."

"Did you…"

"No. He died of natural causes. In a manner of speaking."

Ira's body—it was impossible for Brighton to think of it any other way—began to move, and soon Nariman had gotten the corpse's arms and legs under control.

Nariman walked to the edge of the road, looking toward the rubble of Lagati's mansion. "There are survivors in the house."

"Hard to believe," Brighton said.

"My fellow Nephilim have erected a barrier. Near as I can tell, its primary function was to keep this man out." He gestured to himself. To Ira. "It also serves to reduce the load of the mountain, otherwise the structure would have collapsed by now."

"How many survivors?"

"All of the Grigori, and several humans. The Nephilim are taking losses, so new hosts will be needed."

"What do they need hosts for?" Brighton paused to rephrase that. "I mean, I understand that the Nephilim need hosts, but why the urgency?"

"The barrier I mentioned will soon fail, but the Grigori are planning to erect a much larger version. One that will encompass the entire planet, and require the use of many Nephilim."

"I don't understand. A barrier against what?"

"Jehovah. The Grigori will force him off this planet for good."

"Then I must deprive the Grigori of their supply of hosts. I'll rescue the survivors."

"An ally is already in place to do just that. Your task is more difficult."

"More difficult than rescuing a group of prisoners from alien madmen inside a collapsing mountain fortress?" Brighton laughed despite the gravity of the situation. "Okay, lay it on me."

Nariman contorted Ira's facial features into a grimace the rabbi never would have made. "You must kill my father."

*   *   *

Lagati helped a trio of ambassadors off the helicopter—Charmaine Olasiman from the Philippines, Alban Tansi from the Congo, and Mathieu Rouleau from France. A fourth passenger of vaguely South American descent hadn't revealed his name, and Lagati had been in too great a hurry to make a fuss over it.

"A diverse range of ethnicities. Semyaza will be pleased," Turel remarked upon seeing the group. "But less pleased that you kept this place secret from us."

"Why does Semyaza care about their ethnicities?" Lagati asked, ignoring the Grigori's closing comment.

"He wants the ritual to be as representative as possible of the human population."

"But these are only the first of many." He studied the ambassadors, who studied him back with justifiable confusion—and a touch of indignation.

Turel pulled him aside. "The barrier may not hold long, so we'll make do with these four." He gestured for the ambassadors to follow him toward the elevator. "Join us, please."

He looked physically pained to use the word *please*.

Turel wasn't wired for small talk and Lagati wasn't in the mood, so the ride into the house was quiet. The ambassadors appeared nervous, having been separated from their drivers and security personnel. The Congolese man was openly afraid.

"You are a very famous man among our people," Rouleau said to him in French once they exited into the loft office. "France's favorite son."

Lagati forced a smile. "It's good to meet you, sir."

"Perhaps you could explain what we're doing here. The invitation was not specific, but our government insisted on sending me." He lowered his voice. "There has been word of attacks."

Almost in reply, the mountain shook. A cloud of dust descended on them from a hole in the ceiling.

"In due time," Lagati said.

Turel took them straight to the drawing room.

* * *

Dario waited half a step behind Edie, looking over her shoulder through the sliver of the door as Raff Lagati and one of the Grigori led four people down the stairs.

"Who are they?" Dario asked.

"I don't know," Edie said, "but if we're going to make a move, now's the time. Before they come back."

Dario and Edie rounded up half of the occupants of the spare bedroom and instructed them to follow—quietly. It was a short walk to the office, but they had to pass in front of the open stairwell. Dario couldn't see any way around it.

Together, the group scooted past the stairs. As Dario crossed, he saw a Grigori standing at the bottom with his back turned. He hopped speedily out of view, realizing discovery had been a near thing.

"Where to?" Edie whispered as they entered the far hallway.

Dario directed them to the office, then pressed the button on the side of the elevator. "Ride it to the top, then wait. I'll join you shortly with the rest."

* * *

Brighton knew Nariman's father was one of the Grigori, and almost certainly one of the Twenty, but he didn't know any specifics. The Grigori's family connections were a confusing mess.

"Who is your father?" Brighton asked, fearing the answer.

With good reason, for the answer was the worst case: "Semyaza."

"It had to be Semyaza, didn't it!"

"I'm sorry I can't do it myself."

Brighton wondered if that was true. "Couldn't you, though?"

"The same barrier that kept your rabbi friend out will keep me out. I was banished from the rest of my family a long time ago, along with my coconspirators." He must have meant Barakel. And Mahaway and Gilgamesh, among others, though those were the only names Brighton knew. "So it has to be you."

"But what if I bring down the barrier?"

Nariman paused. "It's a difficult thing to kill one's own father. Even still, Semyaza might not suspect you are a danger—especially if he still thinks Abranel is inside you. He would recognize me right away, from any distance. I could never get close enough."

"How do you know he won't sense that Abranel's gone?"

"He might," Nariman admitted. "That's a risk. Abranel himself may have returned to them by now."

"You're not doing much to improve my confidence."

"Would you rather that I lie to you?"

Brighton smiled. "Actually, I might."

"I may be half-human, but your kind are difficult to understand."

It was strange to think of the Nephilim as half-human. They seemed to have inherited all the cruelty and alienness of their fathers, and only a tiny bit of biology from their mothers.

Brighton looked to the mountain again. The front entrance had all but been eradicated; if there were secondary entrances, Brighton expected they were closely guarded secrets. If only he had access to Ira-level powers.

"There has to be a way," Nariman said.

"That's it? You don't have any suggestions?"

"Let me think." Ira's face turned blank, almost as though Nariman had gone away. But not for long. "There was technology in the crashed ship that might have helped. I should have thought to salvage it."

Brighton couldn't believe his good fortune. He fished into his pocket and showed Nariman the handful of black cubes from the ship.

"What are these?" Brighton asked. "I found them in the same compartment as the crate-opener."

"What could have compelled you to take them?"

"See the way they clamp together, almost magnetically?" Brighton demonstrated by snapping a few of the cubes together. "I thought they might be valuable."

"Of course they're valuable. The whole ship was valuable. But these…" Nariman hesitated before continuing. "These are exactly what we need."

It seemed almost too good to be true, but Brighton had to admit he had forgotten about the cubes. He had only taken them on a whim.

"Give them to me," Nariman said.

Brighton placed the cubes in the spirit's outstretched hand. Nariman manipulated them slowly at first, as though he was having trouble controlling Ira's muscles. As the seconds passed and his work continued, he became more dexterous. He strung the cubes together into a shape vaguely resembling an oval with a line crossing through its heart.

"What are you doing?"

"The function varies according to shape. This is our version of a…" Nariman struggled to think of the English term. "A Swiss Army knife, I think you would call it. A device with many functions. Very versatile. Now, try touching it."

Brighton touched the cube closest to him and a red-tinged holographic display shot up from the center of the oval. It took Brighton a moment to understand what he was looking at: a topographic representation of the area for a couple of miles in every direction.

"The pilots use this for navigation. It scans one's surroundings and creates accurate maps of all landforms." Nariman looked Brighton in the eyes. "It will be able to map Lagati's mountain. If there are any back doors, so to speak, we will see them."

*   *   *

All four of the giants lay sprawled on the ground—two in the fields, and the other two having made it into the streets. Appalled silence had fallen over the town as the people took stock of what had transpired.

Gayle and Elisabeth limped past a wailing mother cradling a crushed child, the most tragic scene amidst a far larger tragedy. So many lost lives! Like Pakistan all over again, except far worse.

In the middle of the carnage, they came across the car that had come to their rescue. The American woman sat despondently next to a dead body which Gayle quickly recognized as the British driver, Celeste. Evidently she'd been thrown from the car in the impact.

Gayle wanted to comfort the woman, but she didn't have any comfort left in her.

"What's next for us?" Gayle said to Elisabeth.

Her friend sat on a curb. "I don't know. I tried to leave once already, but I came back. I thought there was something more I could do. Something to stop the people responsible for all this."

"What more is there?" Gayle sighed. "I think we've done all we can."

"Sherwood is still up there." Elisabeth inclined her head toward the mountain. "Whatever the Grigori are up to, it's not over yet."

A pickup truck stopped beside the American woman. Gayle recognized it as the truck that had rallied the rest of the townspeople, the one that had courageously headed straight for that first giant. Two men— the portly gentleman who'd pushed himself through the window, and a younger man who looked vaguely like him. Father and son, perhaps?

"Janene," the younger man said as he got out of the truck and came up behind the American woman. He began to massage her shoulders. "Is she gone?"

The American woman—Janene—nodded without saying a word.

"Do you know what's going on with Ira and Dario?" the portly man asked, looking at Janene.

Gayle perked up at the mention of Dario's name. She turned to Elisabeth. "Up on the mountain, I met someone named Dario, and he said he knew you. Does that mean you know those people?"

"I suppose we might have some mutual friends," Elisabeth said. "How did Dario get here?"

Instead of answering, Gayle got up and approached the small group, knowing Elisabeth was only a few steps behind her.

"Excuse me," Gayle said. "I couldn't help overhearing, but I think my friend and I have some information."

"Who are you?" the young man asked.

Janene brushed the man's hands off her shoulder as she got to her feet. "Are you hurt? And your friend?"

"We're fine," Elisabeth said. "I have some bad news, though. I saw Ira earlier, and he was badly hurt. Very badly."

"And Dario is inside Lagati's home," Gayle added. "I don't know his condition."

"How do you know them?" the portly man asked. "And you can call me David."

Elisabeth sighed. "It's a longer story than we have time for, David. I fear there's more trouble on the way, and these people have only started digging out. The townspeople need our help."

"Agreed," David said. "But what about Dario? I'll drive up—"

Elisabeth shook her head. "No point. I've already been up there, and the road's blocked."

Dario, I hardly knew you, Gayle thought. *Looks like you're on your own.*

*   *   *

The second group was ready to go by the time Dario returned to the spare bedroom. Sophie had supervised as they gathered a few possessions and wrapped them in the bed's discarded sheet.

He didn't say a word as he crept back into the hall, knowing they were pushing their luck by taking another large group. But whatever the Grigori were up to downstairs, it obviously monopolized their attention.

Halfway down the hall, they were caught. A dark-skinned East Indian man strode up the stairs and immediately spotted them. Dario tried to push the group back into the shadows, but it was too late.

"Come with me," the man said.

Dario stiffened. "Where are you going to take us?"

The man stared at him. "I don't recognize you—"

"You don't have to do this, Amir," Sophie said in a pleading voice. "Come along, and we can all get away."

"Sorry," Amir said. "They'll kill me if I don't follow instructions."

"What makes you think they won't kill you anyway?" Sophie asked.

"Because I've made a deal with them." Amir didn't sound confident. Maybe Dario could exploit that. "If you do as I say, they may make a deal with you as well."

Sophie grabbed the hand of the man beside her, and together they made a run for it. It was a desperate act, doomed to failure. Though Amir appeared torn, he eventually called down the stairs for reinforcements.

It arrived in the form of two hulking Grigori who were far too quick for Sophie and her friend. The Grigori each took one of the fleeing humans and forced their arms behind their backs. Dario lowered his eyes as he heard their necks snap.

"Please, do as they say," Amir implored them. "No one else needs to die."

They don't need to, Dario thought, *but they will.*

Dario fought to keep from staring as they descended the long, ornate stairwell to the mezzanine level. The space was cavernous,
though the ceiling had collapsed at the front of the house, covering at
least half the hall in impassable rubble. Dario looked up at the ceiling
more than once and wondered what was keeping it in place.

At the back of the mezzanine they came to a room surrounded by
marble pedestals of varying heights. Half of them had fallen over, spilling their contents on the hardwood floor. Most of the crowded room's
occupants were Grigori, though a handful of humans stood out.

One of them, Lagati, had spotted him.

"Oh, you again?" Lagati said, speaking over the din of voices.
"You should have followed my advice and stayed away."

Lagati seemed to want to say more, but they were interrupted
when a particularly fearsome Grigori emerged from a small vestibule.

"Is he the one in charge?" Dario asked.

Lagati smirked. "Azazel? Hardly."

"You!" Azazel pointed directly at Amir. "I only see half of the men
and women I sent you for. Where are the rest?"

"These were the only ones," Amir insisted.

"Check the helipad." Lagati jammed his finger into the side of Dario's arm. "I have reason to suspect this man may have shown them
the way out. We can still catch them."

Amir nodded before departing. The same two Grigori who had
accompanied him earlier followed after him.

Azazel clapped his hands together, loud enough to get everyone's
attention. "Okay, we've waited too long already. It's time for the ritual."

THIRTY-EIGHT

Linthal, Switzerland
AUGUST 4

Not everyone was allowed into the windowless room where the ritual was to take place. It wasn't large enough to accommodate everyone, even if Semyaza had wanted that, which he obviously didn't.

Lagati forced himself through the throng to the room's entrance, only to be yanked back by Azazel.

"Semyaza wants me in there," Lagati said.

Azazel relented, not only opening the way but shoving Lagati inside.

As usual, a circle of chairs had been brought in and the Twenty occupied them. Two empty seats remained—Azazel's and Semyaza's. Semyaza stood silently in the corner, watching as the human newcomers assembled, the four ambassadors prominent among them.

The leader of the Grigori sported that cold smile of his, made extra chilling by an amber emergency light fastened to the wall.

A third group stood near the door, wearing long white robes that draped to the floor, concealing even their feet. These were human, too, and Lagati recognized a couple of their faces. Sharon was among them, which suggested they were inhabited by Nephilim. Semyaza had said that several Nephilim were involved in maintaining the barrier; were these the ones he meant? They were in deep meditation, muttering as they went about their spiritual tasks.

Semyaza nodded to Batraal, who stood, stretched out his hands towards the humans, and spoke a long incantation. Lagati didn't understand the language. It had the ring of ancient Hebrew, each exacting syllable harsh and bitter. The abrasive language suited the Grigori perfectly.

"What is he saying?" Dario whispered into his ear.

Lagati shrugged. "I don't know the exact translation, but I suspect they're going to initiate you and the other humans."

"Initiate us?"

"They need more human hosts." Lagati watched the cold terror spread over the man's face. "You knew the risks. I gave you the chance to escape."

Semyaza swung his head toward them, and Dario turned pale under the scrutiny. "That's their leader, isn't it? Semyaza?"

"Not another word," Lagati whispered sharply.

When Batraal finished his incantation, all heads turned to acknowledge a bustle of activity behind them. As Lagati turned, he saw Amir arriving with a fresh batch of humans. Former household staff, all of them.

"Just in time," Semyaza said, brimming with anticipation.

*   *   *

The disappointment of seeing Edie and the others hit Dario hard. He wished he had done more to ensure they got away safely, but realistically he'd done all he could. It seemed unspeakably cruel that they'd come so close to freedom only to have it snatched away.

Turel stood up and instructed the soon-to-be hosts to form a queue. Not all the humans joined the line—Lagati was allowed to stand aside, as was the Indian man. Through a spot of bad luck, Dario found himself near the front of the line. To his left stood Edie—she wouldn't look him in the eyes—and to his right a man in a gray hoodie also averted his gaze.

Turel then herded four others—a Filipino, an African, a Chilean, and a man of indistinguishable European descent—to stand in the center of the Grigori's circle.

Dario watched warily as Semyaza spoke loudly enough for everyone to hear. "We're about to perform a ritual in which you are to play an important part. It has not been lost on me that you have no reason to trust us, and that you have recently tried to escape. When all is said and done, I think you will be glad it worked out this way, for we do not desire to hurt you. Quite the opposite! You are about to embark on a journey that will define your lives and imbue you with a greater sense of purpose than you've hitherto known." Semyaza smiled at them. "You look skeptical, and I don't blame you for that. Skepticism is to be expected, though I doubt it will last long."

"What are you going to do to us?" someone asked.

"We will do nothing *to* you. Rather, you will be invited to do something *with* us. What we propose is a magnificent partnership, the beginning of a long and vibrant relationship between our species and humanity."

Semyaza spoke for quite a long time, and the longer he went on the more Dario felt his compatriots' resolve breaking down. Dario could only squirm at the "partnership" one might share with the likes of Ohia or the giants who had attacked him and Ira in that remote valley in Pakistan. These were not wise and gentle creatures eager to bring wisdom and understanding.

But Dario had no illusions about what would happen if he spoke up. They would take him out and kill him. And if Dario persuaded any of the others to follow his lead, they would be killed as well. Would it be better to die or host one of these Nephilim?

"I won't do it," Dario decided aloud.

Semyaza barely glanced at him. "We will let everyone make their decisions individually."

So they weren't going to drag him out as a means of motivating the others. In hindsight, that made more strategic sense. It gave their prey the illusion of control.

Dario's stomach turned as the first person in the queue accepted the proposition. He felt certain the girl was only doing it because she didn't want to die. She would likely come to regret the choice.

Semyaza would reach him in the next minute or two, and it was the closest Dario was likely to get to one of the Grigori. Semyaza had to be much stronger than Dario, but if he *could* overpower the leader, would it spare the others? Would it create the kind of disruption Ira had hoped for? Or would it just make the Twenty angry enough to slaughter the lot of them?

Dario's heart raced, and there was nothing he could do to calm himself, as Semyaza stopped next to the man in the gray hoodie.

I'm about to die, Dario realized, and it filled him with grief.

The man in the hoodie moved closer to Semyaza, as though to whisper something. To Dario's surprise, Semyaza leaned in to meet him. Dario then heard the sound of something wet sliding over a smooth surface, like a dishrag over a countertop.

Semyaza emitted a strangled gasp as the man in the hoodie yanked himself back.

Dario couldn't believe that which his eyes laid bare. The man held a long, serrated knife, and it dripped with redder-than-red blood. Semyaza's blood. The normal reaction would have been to run, but Dario was too shocked for a normal reaction. He stared as the man lunged with the knife again. Semyaza tried to turn, but the knife caught him in the upper chest, only an inch below the neck. The blade sawed into the Grigori, cutting right to left. Blood spurted onto the human attacker's face.

Only then did it register: that face belonged to Sherwood Brighton.

*   *   *

The sight of Semyaza's blood took Brighton by surprise. He hadn't been sure the Grigori would bleed, or that he would die at all. It hadn't been a sure thing. He yanked the blade back, then shoved it into the soft flesh beneath Semyaza's neck. The blood sprayed at Brighton's eyes. He wiped it away dispassionately and turned to observe Dario staring at him with shock.

Semyaza sank to his knees, and for a few surprising moments nobody moved or uttered a word. Maybe they didn't know how to react. The leader's hands fluttered to the wound below his throat, pressing against it as though to plug the hole. He opened his mouth to speak, but no sound came out.

Azazel was the first to leap into action, but most of the other Grigori followed in his footsteps, coming at Brighton in a stream. Brighton turned and fled from the room, the general confusion allowing him to exit unscathed.

"Stop him!" Azazel shouted as he burst into the drawing room. "Round up the humans. Until they're joined, none should be trusted!"

Brighton was close enough to the edge of the mezzanine that he was able to build up a head start. The Grigori had much longer strides, however. It was only a matter of time before—

—he felt the breath knocked out of him. He tumbled forward, rolling over a pile of fallen debris. He put his arms up to protect his body from attack, only then realizing he no longer had the knife.

A pair of Grigori fists rained down, and he knew the end was near.

Ira, I may be joining you momentarily.

*   *   *

Lagati stood back as Ramuel and Batraal hurried to Semyaza, whose mouth continued to move soundlessly. They lifted him out of the pool of blood that had seeped into the fabric of his brown robe, his long arms falling to his side. His knuckles dragged along the floor.

"Is he dead?" Lagati asked, unable to believe what he'd just seen. His gaze fixed on the bloody spot on the floor. "How did Brighton get in here? Did he really kill Semyaza? Is it possible?"

He didn't normally allow himself to pose unanswerable questions, let alone a long string of them.

"I don't know," Amir said. Useless words for a useless man.

Lagati found it difficult to focus with all the chatter. In the background, he heard Azazel shouting incoherently from the drawing room.

A moment later, Azazel shoved himself back into the chamber.

"Did they get him?" Lagati asked, momentarily forgetting the enmity between them.

"I believe so." Azazel returned to the circle and tried to calm everyone down. "Let's have some quiet. The ritual must continue."

"Who will lead it?" Turel asked.

"I will. Do you have an objection?"

Indeed, Turel looked as though he might harbor several objections, but he didn't voice them.

Azazel looked to those few humans who remained. "Our first business is to facilitate the joining." He nodded to the Grigori around the circle, who collectively stood and moved to restrain the men and women. Lagati didn't react as they grabbed Amir and pushed him down onto his knees.

"Not me," Amir insisted. He shot Lagati a pleading look. "You can stop this!"

Lagati ignored him. In the grand scheme, this one man's fate meant nothing.

*   *   *

Dario ran into the drawing room, calling out Brighton's name; it was swallowed up by the crest of noise. Brighton then shifted into a whole other speed. No matter how fast he ran, he'd be caught.

Azazel stomped through the vestibule, directing the Grigori to round up the humans. The only thing Dario heard Azazel say was "They can't be trusted," or something to that effect, and he couldn't disagree with the logic.

"You will be joined," one of the Grigori said, herding Dario into a pack with several other men and women. Edie was the only one he knew.

"They can't make us," Dario said so the other humans could hear, hoping to encourage them. "It has to be our choice."

The Grigori kicked out his legs and Dario crumpled to the floor.

"That's not quite true," the Grigori corrected. "Our sons can inhabit the willing and the dead. If you're not willing, you can be dead. Either way, we'll get what we need."

Edie turned a terrified look to Dario, as though to ask, *What should we do?*

"I won't submit to you," Dario said through gritted teeth. "Kill me if you must."

"I'll do it," Edie said quickly.

The Grigori grasped her by the shoulder and hauled her to her knees. "That's more like it. In fact, one of our sons has specifically requested you."

"Me?" Edie asked. "What makes me so special?"

The Grigori jabbed a long, bony finger at Dario. "You are this man's friend, yes?"

Edie shook her head. "No. I barely know him."

The Grigori ignored her protestation. "The first thing you will notice is a warm sensation in your chest. You must not resist."

"Reconsider," Dario said to her. "Don't do this."

But Edie was more determined now to disassociate herself from him. Anything to save her life. "Okay, I'm ready."

The woman's eyes flared, and Dario knew the transfer had happened. No one could help her now.

"That's better," she said after several seconds had elapsed. Her voice had changed, going flat and taking on a monotonous quality. She craned her neck stiffly. "Travelling alone can be exhausting. A human host makes all the difference."

"Why did you request her?" Dario asked the newly inhabited woman. He could no longer think of her as Edie.

"Well, I have extracted a great deal of satisfaction from hurting your friends."

Dario didn't need to ask the creature its name to know it was Ohia.

*   *   *

A pair of strong arms reached into Brighton's view and restrained the Grigori pummeling the life out of him. Brighton scooched back, just enough to watch in amazement as his Grigori attacker was handled easily by one of those humans in the long white robes Brighton had seen inside the ritual chamber. The human beat the Grigori in the head with a craggy stone, blood oozing from the Grigori's forehead where the skull had begun to crater.

"Stop it," Brighton said when the human didn't stop; he continued mashing the rock into the Grigori's head until gray matter began to spray loose. The sight made Brighton sick. "I said, stop! Can't you see he's dead?"

At last the human ceased his pounding motion. He dropped the gray-splattered stone. It hit the floor and rolled away.

"Why did you save my life?" Brighton asked. "Tell me straight."

The human smoothed his robes, only now noticing that the white fabric had been blemished. "You and I, we go way back."

"Do we know each other?"

"Intimately." The human smiled, showing too many teeth. "Don't you recognize your old friend?"

Brighton squinted at him. He had no idea who this was.

"I did it so I would have the pleasure of ending your life," the robed man said. "I feel it's my right."

It clicked. "Abranel?"

"Who else?"

Brighton uncoiled in a fluid arc, tackling Abranel square in the chest. Abranel had been caught off-guard, and he went sprawling. Brighton reached for the same stone that had just been used to bash the Grigori's brains in; he smashed it as hard as he could into Abranel's shoulder.

Abranel lost his breath, then spun himself into a ball, squeezing out from beneath Brighton and rolling away. Brighton stood in time to meet a mix of kicks and punches. They winded him, but he didn't fall; he landed a hit or two of his own.

"You see? This is better," Abranel said, smiling despite his obvious pain. "After all we went through, it's proper that we should hash it out. A real fight to the death. The only kind of reconciliation we can have."

Brighton swiped a left hook, missing his target by an inch. "You're insane."

"Perhaps. If you'd gone all these years as a disembodied spirit, sustaining yourself on human corpses and animals, you'd go insane, too."

"Maybe if you weren't such a bad houseguest, you might have—"

Brighton doubled over as Abranel's fist sunk into his gut.

"Pay attention," Abranel spat. "Let's make this a good fight. One for the ages."

Brighton lost track of the bout; throwing punches and ducking others blended together until he couldn't discern one movement from another. He'd never moved with such grace and mobility, certainly not since he'd started drinking so heavily.

As he inched backward, Brighton sensed the broken banister behind him. It wouldn't be a long fall, but perhaps if he gave Abranel a solid push...

Slowly, he manipulated their arrangement until Abranel was the one with his back to the banister. Brighton seized his chance and dove for Abranel's legs. He caught Abranel in the knees and the creature fell backward, landing just short of the broken banister. A foot to the left and he would have sailed straight through and plummeted to the boulder-strewn floor below.

Abranel tried to leap back, but Brighton dragged him back down. He was closer to the edge now. Another inch and he'd—

"Please, don't!"

Brighton almost couldn't believe it, but Abranel's eyes widened in fear. It had to be a trick. Abranel knew him as well as anyone; he was appealing to Brighton's emotions. Trying to manipulate him, like always.

"Why?" Brighton asked. "You never showed me mercy."

But he felt drawn to those fear-filled eyes. Perhaps they didn't entirely belong to Abranel; there was a man underneath, a stranger Brighton didn't know. Was it still murder when a Nephilim was inside?

It was still murder when I was forced to kill that pilot...

But Abranel deserved to die. In fact, he deserved far worse.

*   *   *

Lagati watched impassively as Amir was inhabited right before his eyes. He felt no emotion over it.

Azazel lined up the four ambassadors and then pushed them to their knees, one by one. Mathieu Rouleau kept his eyes trained on Lagati, expressing his betrayal. Lagati took note, but once again felt no emotion. They were both Frenchmen, but their shared nationality imparted no special favors.

"I need your agreement," Azazel intoned while the Twenty looked on. "You must invite us."

"Invite you to do what?" Olasiman asked.

Azazel lifted an eyebrow. Was that a sign of amusement? "To end Jehovah's reign on this planet. The barrier we put in place will ensure mankind's continued freedom."

The Filipino woman unexpectedly rose to her feet. "You cannot be serious!"

"We are very serious," Azazel assured them.

"I won't agree to it," she said.

Azazel approached and lifted her casually into the air. She let out a scream as the Grigori flung her out of the circle. She hit the wall, hard, and slid to the ground. A single glance at her dead eyes told Lagati everything he needed to know.

I almost met the same fate at his hands, he thought. *And I would have, if I'd ever been so imprudent. Stupid woman.*

"Three invitations will have to be enough," Azazel said as he turned to the other ambassadors. They all nodded in hurried agreement. "Outstanding."

What happened next happened very quickly. The Grigori stood, leaving the ambassadors in their prone positions, and surrounded the white-robed Nephilim, including the new recruits, Amir among them.

Each of the Twenty pressed his hands to one of the Nephilim's foreheads and joined in their whispered incantations.

After some time—no more than ten, fifteen seconds—Azazel stepped away again.

"There," Azazel said with a self-satisfied grin. "It is done."

Lagati frowned. He hadn't felt a thing.

*   *   *

The sky flashed white, then faded back to purple twilight.

"Did you see that?" Gayle looked down at the injured woman she'd been attending to. All around her, the townspeople had deployed to gather the injured and the dead.

The woman looked confused. "No," she spoke in the local accent.

That was odd. The sky *had* changed color.

She helped the woman by placing a splint along the broken bone in her lower leg—this was the third one tonight—and then went in search of Elisabeth. She found her friend one block over, aiding a young boy who'd been rescued from a fallen building.

"Elisabeth," Gayle called. "I think something strange has happened."

Elisabeth wiped a combination of sweat and soot from her forehead. "Something stranger than being attacked by giants?"

"Yeah, stranger than that." Gayle felt a stab of pain and looked down at her clenched wound. She pushed it aside. "I saw a flash of light in the sky. Just for an instant. Did you see it?"

"Afraid not. This have something to do with that 'sensitive' stuff you're always talking about?"

"Maybe. I think there's been another burst of energy, like the one that killed Henry."

Elisabeth's face turned ashen. "Henry's dead? I'm so sorry, Gayle. I didn't know."

"It happened just after you left Provo. He got sick from trying to channel the energy." Such a clinical description!

"What do you think this burst means?" Elisabeth asked.

To Gayle's surprise, she didn't hear any doubt in her friend's voice. A lot had changed in the last couple of weeks. It felt good to be taken seriously.

Still, this new burst of energy didn't feel natural. Like poison being poured into a well.

"I'm not sure," Gayle said, "but I think it means we've lost."

THIRTY-NINE

Somewhere Else

The bulky gray clock ticked off the seconds so loudly that it was a wonder anyone could think, yet no one paid it any attention. A woman came through the door, pushing two children—a boy and girl—over to a wooden bench and making them sit. They quieted down as soon as their mother thrust brightly illustrated books into their grubby little hands.

The overhead fluorescent sang a shrill hymn, its fluctuating warble bouncing off the walls and ceiling before being absorbed by the faded blue carpet. The boy stared at the light, dropping the book into his lap, and covered his ears. What an unpleasant noise.

An older gentleman entered the waiting room next, making a quick stop at the receptionist's desk.

"I have a four-thirty," the man said, squinting overtop his glasses.

The receptionist passed him a magazine and pointed to the velour-covered chairs. "Take a seat, Mr. Cohen. The doctor is running behind."

"The doctor is always running behind."

But he took his seat anyway, and the receptionist went back to whatever it was she did with all those stacks of paper.

The boy glanced at his mother. "The light makes a strange sound."

"Just read your book," she said without looking up.

"It's very loud."

"I told you to read your book, Ira. Do what I say."

Hearing his own name made him sit up straight, though he wouldn't have been able to say why. After all, he had heard it before, a thousand times. Usually when his mother was angry with him.

The receptionist pushed her chair back. Ira watched as she swept around her desk in a graceful arc. She stopped directly in front of them, holding a clipboard over her chest.

"Ira Binyamin?"

Ira blinked up at her. Her voice sounded funny. The way she pronounced her words didn't sound anything like what he was used to. He almost laughed aloud, but his mother threw him one of those looks. It was so easy to get in trouble without meaning to.

"The nice woman is talking to you," his mother said. "Are you going to answer her question?"

Ira turned his attention back to the woman with the strange voice. "Yes. My name is Ira."

She bent down so they were on the same level. Now that Ira got a better look at her, he could see she was older than his mother. Small wrinkles had formed around her eyes.

"It's very good to see you, Ira."

"Do I know you?" Ira asked.

"Not very well. But we've met."

"I don't remember."

The woman took his hand. Ira was surprised his mother would let her get away with this, but she seemed entirely preoccupied with Ira's sister, helping her sound out the words in her book.

"Of course you don't remember," the receptionist said. "You have gone through a terrible trauma."

Trauma. Funny word. He didn't think he had heard it before.

"What's a trauma?"

"It's when something very terrible happens to you. I went through a trauma, too." She stood up, and suddenly Ira saw that the room was full of people. Where had they come from? "In fact, we've all been through a trauma."

"But nothing terrible has happened to me."

"You'll remember. Give it time."

Ira glanced from one face to another. He paused, fixating on a man with blond hair and high cheekbones.

"I know him," Ira said quietly. "Where do I know him from?"

"Maybe you should ask him. It could be important to find out."

Ira slid down off the chair, suddenly realizing that his legs weren't those of a child. In fact, he stood more than five and a half feet tall! He felt his chest with both palms, then brought one hand up to feel the scruffy hair on his chin.

I'm sixty-five years old, he remembered.

"Excuse me," Ira said, staring at the blond man.

The man glanced up and pressed his thin lips together. He didn't look too happy to see Ira. "What do you want?"

"I think I know you from somewhere. What's your name?"

"You *think* you know me?" The man blew air through his teeth impatiently. "You left me behind. I would hope you'd have some memory of that."

Ira frowned. "I'm sorry if I've done something to hurt you."

"What you did got me killed."

"That can't be. I would never kill anyone."

"You didn't do it with your own hands, but you may as well have."

The man stuck out his hand for Ira to shake, though the look on his face told Ira the gesture was intended to be sarcastic. "I'm Olaf Poulson. Does that jog your memory?"

It did. Ira had met this man somewhere very cold, covered in ice and snow. And then somewhere else—underground, hills covered with grass. And enormous bones. Olaf Poulson had stood just outside a broken stone tower, holding a notebook in his hands.

Ira couldn't believe what he had done. Poulson was right. Ira, Wörtlich, and Brighton had abandoned him in the ice dome without saying goodbye. They'd considered the Norwegian man a security risk.

"It was heartless," Ira said, feeling genuine sorrow. "I never imagined it might lead to your death. You have to believe that I would have acted differently if I had known."

"But you did know," Poulson said. "You were in a hurry. You thought what you were doing was so important."

Ira hesitated as he remembered the mission to retrieve the Book of Creation. If he hadn't gotten to it before Raff Lagati, the worst might have happened.

Except the worst did happen, Ira thought, as all the rest of his travels crashed in upon him, right up through his death in Brighton's arms. *Lagati did eventually get the Book, in a manner of speaking, and he used it to release the Watchers.*

"I'm sorry," Ira said, knowing the words were not enough. They were all he had. "Tell me what happened to you."

Poulson sighed. "It doesn't matter. I forgive you."

Ira surveyed the other faces in the waiting room and realized he knew them all. His mother and father, in their primes even though they had died at an advanced age. His sister, who remained fifteen, the age when they'd lost her.

"Where is this place?" Ira asked, his voice tentative.

The voice that answered sent a shock racing through him. Standing near the door to the waiting room was Emery Wörtlich. He still bore those hard German features, but they rested upon a younger face than Ira had ever borne witness to. This more vibrant version of Wörtlich was in his thirties.

"Welcome to the waiting room," Wörtlich said.

Ira walked toward the archaeologist. "Is it really you? I mean, are you a vision, or are you truly here?"

"It is hard to define the difference. It is not clear-cut, you must understand."

Ira wanted to laugh. That was precisely the kind of vague non-answer the people around Ira, Wörtlich included, had accused him of all his life.

"Ira, you have been damaged. Can you not feel it?" Wörtlich put a concerned hand on Ira's elbow, drawing the rabbi closer. It was a more affectionate display than the two men had ever shared in real life. "You have done terrible things to yourself, committed brutal acts."

Ira remembered each and every one of those acts—the very things Aaron had warned him against. In the end, Ira hadn't listened to his old mentor. Or anyone else. Even Trevor had tried to turn him back from his destructive course.

Ira slumped forward. "It still confuses me. Everything I did, I did it because it had to be done. The Watchers could not be allowed to succeed. Trevor would not help us. Even Enoch refused to step in. Why not?"

"I did not have spiritual answers in life," Wörtlich said. "Why would you think I have them now? You are asking the wrong person."

Wörtlich pushed him lightly toward the receptionist's desk.

The receptionist smiled up at him. "You remember now, Ira?"

"Yes, Celeste, I remember. Does this mean you died?"

"Don't be daft," Celeste said. "Everyone dies."

"Can you answer my questions?"

"No." She pointed to the door leading to the doctor's examination room. "But Trevor can. He's waiting for you."

Ira looked back at Wörtlich. "It was very good to see you again, my friend."

Wörtlich sat in one of the empty seats. "Same here, Ira."

"Will we see each other again?"

"Probably not."

Those two words filled Ira with incredible sadness. He lingered in the shadow of Trevor's door, wondering if he should delay. There were things he wanted to say to Wörtlich.

"Go," Wörtlich said. "You and I… we have different destinies."

If Ira stayed any longer, he realized he might never leave—and a waiting room was no place to spend eternity. He turned his back on everyone in the velour seats and knocked on the exam room door.

"Come in!"

Ira went inside.

Trevor had been facing a window, but he turned when Ira entered. Outside, horns blared and vintage Fords and Chevys clogged a busy New York street. The room had a low ceiling, emphasizing the Watcher's unusual height.

"Trevor, what am I doing here?"

"Didn't they tell you? It's the waiting room."

"But why does it look like my pediatrician's office from the fifties?"

"Your mind forms your reality here, and your mind was an appalling mess. I'm surprised any of this makes sense." He indicated the examination table. "Hop on up, young man, and let's see what's wrong with you."

Ira got up on the high table and settled on the white sheet that had been draped over it.

"Do you really think something's wrong with me?" Ira asked.

"Sure do, kiddo." Trevor's smile faded and he dropped the act.

"You followed your heart, and look where it brought you. Makes you wonder if there was something wrong with your heart, doesn't it? Something out of alignment."

Ira placed his hand to his chest and felt for a heartbeat. Was he even alive?

"Not that heart," Trevor said. "The other one. Don't pretend you don't know what I mean."

"When I came to you, I asked for help. You told me that you couldn't do anything, that it wasn't your decision."

"That's right. It's your world, and it's your own responsibility to shape it."

Ira bristled. "But the Grigori want to force you out of the world."

"If the world doesn't want Jehovah, he'll leave." Trevor's down-turned eyes radiated pain and frustration. "Don't you see? Maybe you can't. Maybe you never will. I don't know how else to explain it to you. The world is *yours*. Yours! You make decisions of your own free will."

Ira wanted to argue, but there was no point. Perhaps it was time to accept that Trevor was right, and he really didn't understand anything about Jehovah. A lifetime of study had been wasted trying to know a creator who seemed to act in ever more perplexing ways.

"You failed to stop them," Trevor said. "A few moments ago, insofar as time has any meaning here, the Grigori on earth succeeded in putting a barrier in place. All my brethren have been forced to leave. Seems it's the will of humanity—"

"But it's not *my* will," Ira insisted. "I was trying to stop it!"

"In all the wrong ways. Your demonstrations of supernatural strength changed no minds, affected no one's life in a positive way. You spread destruction. In the end, you were no different than those you fought against."

Ira jumped off the examination table and stormed to the window. Unexpected tears burst into his eyes as he comprehended the enormity of what had happened. "I can't accept that. Jehovah's plan, six thousand years in the making... comes to this? You're giving up?"

"None of us have given up," Trevor said. "Ira, it's so important for you to see how you've damaged yourself. When you tap into his reservoir of zohar, there are consequences. Call it the law of radiance, Ira. You were warned against its use."

"I only used it at the extreme end of need. The Grigori couldn't be defeated without it."

"But they succeeded despite your efforts." Trevor took him by the shoulder and led him back to the table. "Sit, Ira. There are things I wish to explain to you."

Ira sat, despondent. *What have I done to myself? How did I end up here, like this?*

"Jehovah himself has used the power only a handful of times," Trevor said. "Don't you think that's remarkable? All the power of creation at his disposal, and he restrains himself from applying it. That's because his own law prevents him from using it to interfere with the natural progression of the world. He cannot intercede against humanity's expressed will."

"But the Grigori have done just that, acting against humanity's expressed will."

Trevor shrugged. "Not exactly. They've gotten by the law on a technicality."

"You could have explained this to me days ago. Why didn't you?"

"It's not too late, Ira. It never is. Don't you understand that this creation is as timeless as Jehovah himself? The Grigori have no more dominion over the world than Jehovah himself does. Their actions are contingent on mankind's invitation to act. Jehovah has been waiting for the day when mankind will rise up against them."

"So they can still do something," Ira said, referring to Brighton and the others. "What about me?"

Trevor looked at him with a thoughtful expression. "You cannot proceed beyond this realm in your current state. The damage must be undone."

"What must I do?"

He took hold of Ira's elbow and turned him so that they faced each other. "You must lose yourself. Everything you know. Are you prepared for that?"

"How can I? I don't even know what it means."

"You will. Soon."

"And will I feel regret?"

Trevor shook his head sadly. "Ira, my friend, you will feel nothing at all."

FORTY

Linthal, Switzerland
AUGUST 4

"There," Azazel said with a self-satisfied grin. "It is done."

Lagati frowned. He hadn't felt a thing.

Azazel returned to the center of the circle, preening like a peacock. He lifted his hands into the air. "Do you feel that?" he asked the Twenty. "We have the place to ourselves! I can already feel Jehovah's power diminishing."

"What about Semyaza?" someone asked.

"What about him?" Azazel growled.

Another voice broke in. "This is not your victory, Azazel. The moment belongs to Semyaza. He fought longer and harder than anyone else."

Lagati backed away, worried that Azazel would tear the dissenter to shreds. Lagati inadvertently bumped into the Grigori who had spoken so boldly. He whipped around to stare into the eyes of none other than Barakel.

The exiled Grigori stepped forward, acting as though he owned the place. Lagati felt a small sense of annoyance at Barakel's proprietary attitude.

"Who let him in here?" Azazel asked, refusing to make eye contact with Barakel.

No one answered him.

"You were nothing but Semyaza's scapegoat," Barakel said. "The one to take the blame should anything go wrong."

Without Semyaza around to control his hair-trigger temper, Azazel lunged toward Barakel, picking up one of the tall-backed chairs and slamming it down over Barakel's head before Barakel could move out of the way.

As Barakel staggered under the blow, Lagati dug his hand into his pocket and gripped the shiny little cube hidden there. He stared hard at Barakel as the enormous man heaved himself back onto his feet.

He lifted the cube out of his pocket and held it between his left thumb and forefinger. Barakel had said it would respond to Lagati's will, were he strong enough to switch the device on from its inert state.

Do I lack the will? he asked himself, shutting out the clamor as the Twenty descended upon Barakel, abandoning the serenity they'd displayed under Semyaza and attacking Barakel en masse.

"Azazel," Lagati said slowly, drawing on all his loathing for the creature who had worked so hard to make his life miserable. Lagati felt every kick, every blow Azazel had ever inflicted—even the words that had struck like lashes. "Azazel, you coward." He raised his voice, gaining courage. "Azazel!"

Azazel's head shot up, somehow picking out Lagati's cry from the low-hanging cloud of ambient noise. He made a hateful smirk as his gaze stopped on Lagati. He separated himself from the beating and approached Lagati with long, purposeful strides.

"What did you call me?" Azazel demanded.

Lagati held the cube so tight that his fingers turned white. "I called you a coward. You live in the shadows, fueled by your emotions, ruled by anger. Tell me I'm wrong!"

"You didn't learn your lessons well." Azazel's face darkened in rage and Lagati knew he would snap Lagati's neck like it was nothing.

The moment had come. Either he'd bend the cube to his will, or he'd be too dead to care. Strangely, he felt at peace either way.

STOP.

A jolt of electricity ran through Lagati, beginning in his fingers and tingling its way up his arm. At first he thought he was being electrocuted, and he cursed Barakel for his treachery.

But then he noticed that Azazel had stopped in midstride, his arms stretched to within an inch of Lagati's own neck. He'd frozen, as though time had ceased to exist in a bubble all around him.

Lagati laughed out of sheer delight as he went to work.

*   *   *

Dario hated Ohia, and was glad he had only known Edie for twenty minutes. Knowing her longer, knowing her better, would have only made it more difficult to do what must be done.

"Are you going to try killing me?" Ohia asked. "It won't do you any good. You must know that I can't be killed."

"But I can rescue that poor woman you've desecrated."

"She gave me permission to enter. Who are you to say she didn't want this?"

Dario grunted. "If you're going to attempt to deceive me, at least put some effort into it."

"I cannot be bothered." The mountain shook, coating them with a thick layer of dust. "As you can see, time is short."

"Very well. I can move quickly." Dario rushed at Ohia, taking it by surprise. It slammed to the ground just as another stratum of dust fell, followed this time by a number of rocks the size of Dario's fist. One of them hit Dario in the back, knocking the air out of him. Fortunately, another had hit Ohia.

Ohia recovered a moment sooner, though, and lunged toward Dario on all fours. Dario scrambled backward, but he couldn't get out of the way. Ohia pressed Edie's delicate fingers into Dario's throat and squeezed with surprising strength.

"You've already lost," Ohia said. "The barrier is up. We have won."

Dario didn't believe it. He couldn't. He had to hope there was something further he could do, that all his pain and misery hadn't been for nothing. He slapped impotently at Ohia's stiff arms.

"I hoped from the first time we met that I would get the chance to kill you," Ohia said, the corner of its mouth dripping with a mucous-like mixture of dust and saliva.

Edie's hands were strong and uncompromising. As a last resort, Dario thrust his arms behind his head, feeling for anything he could use as a weapon. A rock would do the trick. Obligingly, several more bits of the ceiling crashed down—but they landed out of reach.

His vision blurred and he knew death was upon him. He thought he would feel sad, but instead he felt relieved. For weeks he had yearned for life to go back to normal; if death was the closest he could come to normal, he welcomed it.

But then he saw something... no, someone. Someone who shouldn't have been there. At first Dario thought he was hallucinating.

It was Junior, hovering just over Ohia's shoulder.

No, not Junior, he thought, thoroughly confused. And not the older David, either.

The reality was even more incongruous, for it was the groundskeeper from Fair Haven. The young stranger he'd conversed with in the orchard.

The stranger took hold of Ohia and pulled him loose, making it look effortless.

Ohia wasn't easily put off, and it just as quickly flung itself back at Dario. Dario twisted away, darting between a swarm of Grigori too busy running in the opposite direction to even register him. The house was finally coming down!

A force from behind took out his knees, and Dario once again sprawled, landing in a sea of sharp rocks. He twisted away as Ohia reached for his throat again.

Dario renewed his search for a weapon, and was shocked when his hands brushed aside a handful of pebbles to find the hilt of a slightly curved blade. The fileting knife Brighton had used to kill Semyaza!

Acting on instinct, he thrust the knife behind him and felt as it buried itself into something soft and yielding.

Dario pushed himself back as Ohia went limp. The light went out of Edie's eyes, the hilt of the embedded knife quivering in her upper chest as the room vibrated. He grieved for Edie. More than that, he was grateful she had escaped the lifetime of torment Ohia would have subjected her to.

He stood and dusted himself off, swaying as the floor quaked under his feet. The Grigori had all fled, and he was almost alone. Almost, because two figures were still visible in the dust-shrouded air. His heart leapt as he saw that one of them was Brighton, and the other was the groundskeeper.

*   *   *

Even with the house crumbling to dust around him, Lagati didn't leave Azazel's side. All the Grigori and Nephilim had fled the chamber in a blind panic.

Azazel stared with no expression as Lagati pushed him over. His frozen body crashed to the ground, still unable to move a single muscle. His eyes provided the only indication of life, and they shifted from side to side furiously.

"Perhaps you're regretting the way you treated me," Lagati said as he picked up a rock from the floor. He ran his finger along its ridge and found it sharp enough to draw a pinprick of blood. "Or perhaps not."

He lowered the sharp edge onto Azazel's forehead and pressed down as hard as he could, cutting a long, jagged scar into the skin. Lagati pulled away to admire his handiwork. Deciding he hadn't gone far enough, he ripped up the rest of the forehead, bit by bit. Blood oozed from the wounds and ran down his hands.

"Oh, would you like to say something?" Lagati pretended to consider it. "I think I prefer you silent. I want you to suffer just as you made me suffer." He wiped the blood away from Azazel's eyes to ensure the monster saw his fate coming. "If I go, there's a chance you'll regain control of your body in my absence. If I stay, we'll both die." He sighed heavily. "Quite a choice, isn't it? Am I willing to give my life to ensure you give yours?"

The sound of people in the drawing room made Lagati turn and peer through the vestibule. A group of humans had gathered there, abandoned by the departing Grigori.

Looking for a way out, Lagati thought. *They won't find one.*

He turned back to Azazel and felt an almost overwhelming surge of revulsion.

Do I hate you enough to give my life this way?

Suddenly, instead of settling in to die, those humans began to move toward the stairs. Where were they going?

No, Lagati decided, looking down at Azazel's ugly, bloody face. *I don't hate you that much.*

*   *   *

Brighton left Abranel behind, breathing heavily and already regretting having spared his tormentor's life. He wouldn't look back.

The last of the Grigori had departed, leaving behind two figures fighting in the middle of the drawing room. As he approached, he saw it was Dario and a young woman who pinned him down with surprising strength.

As though walking out of a mirage, a third figure appeared behind the main stairway. Brighton narrowed his eyes as the stranger came closer. He seemed familiar in some vague way.

Brighton watched as the stranger tried to intervene in Dario's fight by pulling the attacker away, but the possessed woman wrenched herself free like a wild animal and threw herself at Dario with renewed energy.

That's when it clicked. This was no stranger.

"Aaron Roth?" Brighton said. "That can't be you."

The stranger turned, his short dark hair matting his forehead. He was young, perhaps in his twenties, yet his face was unmistakable. This was the same person as the hundred-year-old man he'd met in a Syracuse hospital.

Aaron smiled at him, as though to confirm his identity. "Mr. Brighton, I'm surprised you recognize me. I look much different than the last time you saw me."

"You can say that again," Brighton said, amazement creeping into his voice. "What happened to you?"

"I died. Death does wonders for the complexion, don't you think?"

"You certainly have the same sense of humor."

Aaron shrugged. "Sometimes in a moment of crisis, humor is all you have."

"How did you get here?"

"The manner of my arrival isn't important. I've come to rescue you."

Brighton glanced up as the ceiling rumbled and an enormous chunk of rock sailed down, blasting a hole in the floor. "You have good timing!"

"Do you think we should stop the fight?"

No sooner had the words left his mouth than Dario plunged a knife into the young woman's heart. She fell immediately into a clump of gasping flesh.

Brighton fell into step behind Aaron as they approached Dario, who was trying to regain his breath as the entire house shook.

"Where did you come from?" Dario asked, blinking rapidly. His eyes fixed on Aaron's.

"He'll answer later," Brighton said. "For now, we have to run."

Aaron shook his head. "No need to run. I have a less exhausting means of escape—" He broke off as a half-dozen other men and women flew down the stairs and stopped just short of them, looking dazed. Aaron waved them over. "All of you, come this way."

"One day you'll have to tell me your part in this," Brighton said as they gathered.

"You'll see for yourself soon enough." Aaron clapped his hands once everyone had come together. "Everyone hug close. We're getting out."

"How?" someone asked.

Aaron's eyes glimmered with mischief. "In a flash."

As promised, the air brightened all around them, sweeping them out of harm's way.

FORTY-ONE

Linthal, Switzerland

AUGUST 4

Ira Binyamin felt young again. All his weariness had lifted as he was deposited in the middle of an eerily quiet town square, signs of battle all around. Buildings had been crushed to powder and the few visible townsfolk were occupied with pulling dead bodies out of the street.

He looked at the back of his smooth, wrinkle-free hands.

I don't deserve this second chance. Except of course it wasn't a second chance. Not precisely. *I'll make do with the time I've been given, however short.*

"We could use your help over here."

Ira identified Janene's voice right away. Light on his young adult feet, Ira walked toward his former assistant. She had turned out to be so much more to him, especially this week. She had almost paid the ultimate sacrifice.

"Janene, it's me," he said after realizing she didn't recognize him.

She squinted. "What do you mean, it's you?" Her mind caught up with her mouth a moment later, and she gasped. "I don't believe it."

"Believe it."

"You're like a new man." She approached slowly. "It's a cliché, but you really are a new man, aren't you? How did you get this way?"

Ira took her by the shoulders and pulled her into an embrace. "I died."

*   *   *

"Hey, I know this guy!" Elisabeth called.

Gayle glanced up when she heard her friend's voice. She and Elisabeth both stood in the middle of a street, helping to arrange the bodies in a grid. It was a grueling, fetid task.

"Who is it?" Gayle asked.

Elisabeth pointed to a corpse. "All I know is that he worked for Lagati."

Next to the man rested a woman with Asian features. Japanese maybe? Some kind soul had placed a jacket over the gaping wound covering her stomach. The poor woman had been eviscerated. Gayle didn't even want to guess how it had happened, or how long the woman had suffered. Hopefully death had come quick.

A commotion one street away soon stole Gayle's attention. She didn't need any prompting to investigate—anything to get away from the stench of blood and flesh.

Janene and Junior, both excited beyond what the situation called for, hurried toward them with a young man in tow.

"We're looking for my father," Junior said. "Have you seen him?"

Gayle shook her head.

They nearly passed by completely before Elisabeth's eyes widened. "Stop!"

Gayle looked at her friend with an unspoken question in her eyes. What had gotten into her?

"That man," Elisabeth said. She raised her voice again and called to the young stranger with Janene. "Do I know you?"

The man came closer. He stopped right in front of Elisabeth and looked deeply into her eyes.

"I don't know how it can be, but your name is Ira." Elisabeth stared at him even harder. Nothing would break her gaze. "Impossible!"

The man named Ira grinned. "It's been said that with Jehovah, all things are possible."

"Gayle, this is Ira," Elisabeth said. "I told you about him. He's the man Sherwood Brighton needed my help to rescue."

Gayle was puzzled, to put it mildly. "You said that man was in his sixties."

"He was." Elisabeth shrugged. "How old are you now, Ira?"

"I don't have a clue," Ira replied all too happily. "And I don't think it matters! But we could use your help. Your friend, too."

"Of course," Elisabeth said.

Gayle wanted to pull her aside and ask what had come over her. None of this made a lick of sense. "Where are we going?"

"To get my father," Junior spoke up.

"And after that?" Elisabeth prompted. "It's getting dark."

Ira didn't bat an eyelash. "True. I'd say it's time to turn on a light."

*   *   *

Like it had so many times before, the world shifted in a burst of light. When Dario dared open his eyes again, he found himself high up on a mountain. Night had fallen, bathing them in the light of more stars than anyone could count.

"That's quite the trick," Dario said, turning his attention to the groundskeeper. "You're not the first person to show it to me. Do you know a rabbi named Ira?"

"We're acquainted," the groundskeeper said. "You may as well use my name, though. I'm Aaron. And as it happens, Ira is just the man we're waiting for. He should be here any minute."

Aaron's sense of timing was impeccable, for the air in front of them lit up and resolved to reveal a half-dozen people. One of them was Elisabeth Macfarlane.

"Finally," Aaron said. "Everyone's in one place."

*   *   *

As soon as the light faded, Lagati struggled to orient himself. Fortunately, the alpine view was familiar. They had landed upon his mountain, probably very near the entrance to the helicopter bay—all that was left of his magnificent former home. It enraged him to think the Grigori had ruined the place. Of course, Azazel and Semyaza had paid no small price in the end. It was almost enough to even the score.

Now all he had to do was get down this accursed mountain and find Antoinette.

I couldn't have planned it better, he mused, still shaking from the unlikelihood of his rescue. He hung back. If he didn't say anything and averted his face, they might not realize who he was. He just needed an opportunity to sneak away.

A second flash of light lit the darkened slope, revealing Elisabeth Macfarlane and five others he couldn't place. Nor would he waste the time. As the group began to talk, embracing each other and shedding tears over long and dramatic reunions, Lagati hung back. The arrival provided the perfect distraction, and he was unlikely to get another.

Lagati identified two ridges of rock sufficiently tall for him to hide behind, though getting to either one might attract attention. He only allowed himself a moment of indecision before taking quick action; he stepped lightly away from the group, hoping the darkness covered his movements.

He didn't quite make it.

Someone hit him from behind and wrestled him to the ground. Lagati groaned as his abdomen slammed into the unyielding rock.

"I thought so," Elisabeth said, pinning him down. She had more strength than he would have guessed. She raised her voice and called for everyone's attention. "This is Raff Lagati. Personally, I don't think he deserves to leave this mountain with his life."

To Lagati's distress, he heard murmurs of agreement.

"What are you suggesting?" a male voice asked.

Lagati tried to sit up, but Elisabeth pushed him back down. "If it weren't for him, the Grigori wouldn't have come back. I wouldn't have been imprisoned." She looked pointedly at Brighton. "And you wouldn't have been put through hell, Sherwood."

The same male voice spoke up. "Are you saying we should kill him?"

Elisabeth held Lagati's gaze for several long moments. Her expression softened from righteous fury to pity, and then back again.

"Yes, I suppose that is what I'm saying." Elisabeth turned to Lagati. "What about you? Do you have anything to add?"

Lagati didn't know what to say—a problem that only rarely afflicted him. He got over it in a hurry. "You know, the two of us, we've been in this position before." He saw the flash of remembrance in her eyes. "Ah, you remember. Do you also see the irony? That I saved your life—twice—yet here you are, advocating for my death? I guess it's true what they say: there is no justice."

"You *saved* me?" Elisabeth countered. "Funny. I don't see how the man who singlehandedly conspired to release the Grigori on earth can claim to have saved anyone. Not when you weigh it in the balance of all those you are responsible for killing. You don't even know their names." She paused, correcting herself. "Well, I'm sure you know some of their names. The first, for instance."

Lagati didn't know what the hell she was talking about. "Excuse me?"

"The name of your first victim. Emery Wörtlich."

"I hired Wörtlich to perform a job. If he was killed in the process, that's his own failure. Nobody even told me he died. Certainly the whole affair is regrettable."

"Back off, Elisabeth," the male voice called again. "Let cooler heads prevail."

Lagati searched out the unknown man. His light-colored clothes shone under the starlight. He had a thick mop of dark hair and couldn't have been older than twenty-five or thirty.

"Yes, listen to your friend," Lagati urged.

"My friend?" Elisabeth laughed. "It would be truer to say that he's an old friend of yours. Don't you recognize him, Raff?"

Lagati chafed under the use of his first name, but he punted aside his annoyance to give the stranger a closer inspection. "I've never seen that man in my life," he concluded.

The man knelt down next to him. "You couldn't be more wrong. Don't you remember our first meeting? It was right here. You wanted to convince me to help you track down the Book of Creation."

"There were only three people that night…" Lagati choked back a breath. It couldn't be…

*   *   *

Brighton watched uneasily as the drama played out. He could understand Elisabeth's desire to see Lagati pay for his crimes. He had shared those sentiments for so long.

But he didn't share them anymore.

"Elisabeth, I think Ira's right," Brighton said. "There's been enough killing for one day."

"So we just forgive him?" Elisabeth asked, raising her voice. "He's a damned murderer!"

Brighton took a step forward. "And we're not."

These three words punched through the still night air. No one spoke for quite some time, not even Elisabeth, though her flushed cheeks suggested a torrent of words ready to fly out of her mouth at the slightest provocation.

"We should let him go," Brighton said.

"Let him go…" Elisabeth echoed.

"He's mostly harmless," Ira said softly. "What more can he do? The Grigori have abandoned him and his home has been destroyed. He's lost as much as we have. Maybe more. We can choose to be compassionate. We can choose to forgive."

Brighton smiled. Whoever that broken old man had been earlier tonight, the man who'd died in his arms, he'd been a stranger. This was the Ira he remembered, the kind and gentle soul who had mentored him through those grueling early days on the run, the grandfatherly rabbi who had kept his cool even in the furnace of the Egyptian desert. This was the Ira he had missed. The Ira he had needed.

Elisabeth kicked at a drift of scree in disgust. "Okay, let him go then. See if we don't come to regret it."

"You can get up," Ira said to Lagati. The young rabbi generously held out his hand.

As Brighton watched, the shaken Frenchman allowed himself to be helped up.

"I don't deserve this," Lagati said. "Elisabeth is right. You have every reason to kill me."

Ira chuckled. "It wouldn't be forgiveness if you'd done nothing wrong."

"Go," Brighton advised. "Before we change our minds."

Lagati didn't think twice before running off into the darkness. Brighton hoped he knew the way down, for the mountain was treacherous, especially at night. The stars didn't illuminate much.

"He'll find his way," Ira said as though reading his thoughts.

Nonetheless, Brighton worried that they were making a mistake.

*   *   *

Ira felt an outpouring of appreciation for Brighton. This was not the same man Ira had met a year and a half ago. Brighton had softened in a myriad of ways. Ironically, Ira's own journey had been the opposite. He had become as inflexible as steel. Trevor had been right; he'd inflicted so much damage on himself. He wasn't sure there was any way to atone for it.

This will be a start, he thought as he turned back to the others.

Both David and his son embraced Aaron, the progeny marveling at the youth and vitality of their patriarch. When Aaron and his grandson stood next to each other, Ira was struck by how alike they looked. The family reunion, though happy, filled Ira with regret that he had never had a family of his own. Sherwood Brighton was the closest he would ever have to a son.

Brighton patted him on the back. "Ira, I saw you die."

"Death isn't the final word, as you can see."

"It's good to see this side of you again," Brighton said. "You remind me of the man I first met all those months ago."

Tears tugged at the back of Ira's eyes, but this wasn't the time for tears. He'd been sent to do a job. He couldn't delay much longer. The Grigori barrier had only been in place an hour, but it was already an hour too long.

*   *   *

Gayle hung back as Ira took their hands and arranged them in a circle. What was this, a summer camp sing-along?

"You look skeptical," Elisabeth said to her quietly.

Gayle smirked. "I don't think you've ever called me that before. You're the skeptic in this relationship." She couldn't take her eyes off Ira. He looked radiant. "Do you know what this is about?"

"Can't say I do. But I'm willing to give him the benefit of the doubt."

Anyway, Brighton didn't seem to have any objections. He was actively corralling some of the survivors from among Lagati's household staff. The uncertainty on their faces mirrored Gayle's, but she took Elisabeth's hand on one side and Janene's on the other.

"I'm going to lead you through a series of meditations," Ira began. "The end goal is to align our intentions. The Grigori have erected a barrier to prevent Jehovah's creative power from reaching the world. They think they have succeeded, but if we act quickly there is still enough residual power for us to bring that barrier down." Once they had all joined hands and closed their eyes, he continued. "Form a mental picture of a river. This river is like the universe. Everything that exists is made up of streams of possibilities, and all those streams are caught in the current of the river. People get caught in the current, too—"

Gayle squeezed her eyes shut harder, feeling inundated by powerful energetic currents from all sides. She knew there was nothing physical to buffet her, but something had changed. It was the same feeling she'd had just before Henry started showing symptoms.

She swayed, and Elisabeth had to act quickly to catch her.

When Gayle's eyes opened, she saw that she no longer stood on the mountainside. The river Ira had described flowed by them, though it wasn't much of a river.

"Did you feel that?" Gayle asked her friend. "A wave of energy, strong enough to blow me over?"

Elisabeth nodded. "Yes. I can't call you crazy this time. Does it have something to do with Ira's meditation? With all this?"

"The river, I suppose. Such as it is. You see it too?"

"I think we all can."

Gayle saw the rest of the group along the riverbank—Ira, Bright-on, Elisabeth, Dario, and everyone else. The circle hadn't been bro-ken. In the real world, they stood on the mountainside. Now that she concentrated, she could feel the physical impression of Janene and Elisabeth holding her hands.

The river itself had clearly run a much wider course once. Its flow had been reduced to a lazy brown stream, and they'd have to hike through several meters of foot-sucking mud to reach it.

Ira looked around the scene with palpable dismay. "We're run-ning out of time," he murmured. "Without Jehovah, the river will die."

Gayle tried to shake the nauseous feeling out of her head, which only made it worse. "We're not alone here," she said in a whisper. "I can feel the weight of a great presence, oppressive energy..." She trailed off, not having the words to describe the sensation.

"Ira, it's like those memories we experienced," Brighton said. "Barakel's memories, when the Grigori were striking their bargain, when the giants were meeting in secret... but those only happened at hotspots. This isn't a hotspot."

"It is now, I think," Elisabeth said. "Ever since the Grigori brought the barrier up."

"But it feels like a person, a presence," Gayle insisted.

Brighton closed his eyes, trying to feel it for himself. "Is it Barakel again?"

As abruptly as if someone had changed the channel, the muddy river vanished, replaced by utter blackness. Gayle checked her com-panions' expressions to confirm they had all experienced the same shift. Obviously they had.

"Where are we?" Junior asked.

Nobody answered, not even Ira. Gayle found this profoundly unnerving.

A blinding flash ignited overhead. It immediately diffused, raining down pinpricks of light. They looked like stars, falling quickly all around them.

"I think Sherwood was right," Ira said quietly.

"Right about what?" Dario asked.

"We may be seeing Barakel's memories again. And if I'm not mistaken, it's one of his first."

FORTY-TWO

Somewhere Else

Brighton knew immediately what the stars signified. They were witnessing a pivotal event in the progression of life on earth: an occasion thousands of years ago—millions of years?—when the Grigori had first landed. Nothing had been the same since. It was difficult to accept that today's events, bringing down the barrier, would be the culmination of a story so long in the telling. Difficult to accept that he, a young and unexceptional man from rural Virginia, would come to play such a critical role. No one could ever have mistaken him for anyone important. That is, until he had encountered Ira and Wörtlich. From the very beginning, they had seen value in him no one else suspected. He'd had a career—a life—and he'd lost it all. But what had he gained?

Everything, he knew. *I gained everything that could possibly matter.*

"This is where it started," Brighton said softly to the rabbi—well, Brighton still thought of him as a rabbi even if the title no longer seemed to fit. "Are we seeing it as a dream, as shadows and symbols, or as it really happened?"

"Does it matter?" Ira asked.

"No, I don't suppose it does."

Their large assemblage had splintered into more intimate cliques, all of them admiring the view, their faces lit by the paroxysm of celestial light. The ambiance was both violent and romantic, even though such a pairing made little sense. Brighton watched Aaron fondly embrace his son and grandson, effecting an emotional reconciliation; Aaron had literally crossed time and space to be with them.

As Brighton and Ira stood in rapt attention, the scenes changed, replaying events Brighton was already intimately familiar with. The meeting on Mount Hermon, Barakel's choosing of a wife, the rape of that wife, and the council of the giants. Brighton spent an inordinate amount of time looking into Nariman's eyes and listening to the sound of his voice. Was this truly the same creature he had met? The little memory play culminated upon a blood-curdling scene beneath Giza. Brighton watched in despair as Enoch delivered Jehovah's declaration against the Grigori: "Your petition cannot be granted, for all the days of eternity. You shall not have peace. You shall not ascend. It has been decreed that you be bound to the earth. You shall witness the utter destruction of your beloved sons, and you shall not enjoy them." For the third time in Brighton's life, he winced upon hearing Azazel's cry of anguish.

In light of recent events, Brighton fully appreciated the gravity of Enoch's words. The Grigori had, indeed, witnessed the destruction of their sons. Over the centuries, their sons had wandered the earth as disembodied spirits, occupying the willing and the dead—even lowly animals who lacked the simple agency to cast out their interlopers. Some of these sons had even died in their vulnerable state in Lagati's mansion, thus bringing Enoch's prophecy to final fulfillment.

But not Abranel, Brighton thought. He wondered what had become of the tyrant spirit. Perhaps it had been foolish to spare him, but it had been the human thing to do. *I'm nothing if I deny my essential humanity.*

To Brighton's surprise, Barakel's memories continued to play out, well past the bits and pieces Brighton had witnessed before. Barakel stood with his son Mahaway in a darkened room. Heavy rain poured through the open window and thunder rumbled in the distance. Only the dimmest sliver of moonlight showed through the swift-moving clouds outside, just enough to light their faces. Mahaway had tears in his eyes as he reached his grotesquely huge hand to touch his father on the shoulder.

"You must go," Barakel insisted. "The flood waters are rising."

Barakel practically pushed Mahaway out the door onto a grassy hill. From here, Brighton saw that the building was a small tower. In every direction, he saw hills covered in thick grass, low trees, and lush shrubs. Enormous bones lay among them. He knew instinctively that Barakel and Mahaway had carefully laid those bones to point the way to Mahaway's hiding place.

Barakel pointed to a monstrous skull beside the hill. "Take the skull. It will serve as the final marker."

"Father, if the others discover what you have done—"

"That I have stolen the creation science?" Barakel gave a mirthless laugh. "The only way to save us is to preserve Jehovah's writings and return them. You must wait as long as you are able. Whether a hundred years or a thousand, Jehovah's servant will come for the writings. You must use them to negotiate a truce. Do you understand?"

Mahaway wiped his tears, an incongruous act given his intimidating size. "Yes, Father. I understand."

"Patience, my son. You must be patient."

A plan doomed to failure, Brighton thought. Jehovah's servant had, indeed, come for the Book of Creation, in the form of Ira Binyamin. And like Enoch before him, Ira hadn't been in a position to negotiate any truce. Mahaway had flown into a rage. Brighton couldn't fault him for reacting poorly when Ira delivered the bad news. The giant had endured in that underground pyramid for thousands of years on nothing but a slim hope.

"Not long after this, Barakel was entrapped with the other Grigori," Ira said in a steady voice. "For Barakel, it was a fate worse than death, for the Grigori certainly did learn of his treachery. He must have paid dearly for his betrayal."

"Barakel and Mahaway acted in good faith," Brighton said. "You shouldn't have rejected them."

"It was not my choice to make, but I share your sorrow. A very terrible tragedy."

The grassy hills transformed again, resolving into an eerily familiar scene. Brighton gasped as he registered the mountainside and the dozen people standing upon it. They were arranged in a circle, all of them holding hands.

"Ira, that's us!" Janene cried as she stepped away from the conversation she'd been having with Elisabeth and Gayle.

Ira looked puzzled. "I can see that."

"The meaning is clear." This came from Aaron, his arm draped over his son's shoulders. His lips straightened and pressed together in a grim expression. "We've moved out of Barakel's past, and into the present. He's with us, right now."

"What does he want?" Brighton asked.

Ira sighed. "I suppose we're about to find out."

*   *   *

Ira could almost feel Barakel's approach, but he refused to allow the renegade Grigori to disrupt the meditative circle. To his relief, the view of the mountainside disappeared and deposited the group back into Ira's original setting: the riverbank, diminished even further than it had been a few minutes before. Without Jehovah, the headwaters had been cut off. It wouldn't be long before the waters stopped flowing entirely—and then it would be too late.

Birds chirped as sunlight filtered through the rustling trees. Everyone stood, uneasy about the confrontation to come. No matter Barakel's past actions—and Ira admitted some of them had a redemptive element—his intentions remained as muddy as the riverbank.

Barakel emerged from the depths of the forest, a tall and hulking form concealed by shadow. He didn't come all the way onto the sunlit beach where Ira and the others waited, but far enough to reveal flesh wounds that might have been fatal to a human. The Grigori had been viciously beaten.

"I feel like I know you," Ira began, stepping forward and acting like the group's leader. Aaron joined him a moment later and the two stood shoulder to shoulder.

Barakel wiped blood from his chin. "Yet we've never met. You've only seen my memories."

"I've always wondered why we saw your memories, and no one else's," Brighton said. Ira heard the young man—well, who was the young man now?—come up behind him.

"You must have left them for us to find," Ira said.

"That's right," Barakel said. "It was important for my story to be told, and I knew the other Grigori would do whatever they could to silence me. Near the end, while the flood waters still rose, I seeded the memories where I hoped they would someday be found. Anyone sensitive enough would see and experience everything I did."

"What do you want, Grigori?" This, to Ira's surprise, from Aaron. Ira hadn't heard his mentor speak with such a hard edge in decades.

"What do I want? The same thing you do. To see the Grigori pay for their crimes."

"But that is not all you want," Ira said.

Barakel smiled. "True. I wish to see Jehovah pay for his part in this. You cannot deny that Jehovah created this mess."

"I do deny it, actually," Aaron said, much more casually. "You and the rest of your brethren have unleashed unmitigated terror."

"If Jehovah had listened to my petition, all that damage could have been rectified," Barakel pointed out. "I sacrificed everything, placing my own life—even my son's life—in Jehovah's hands. He ignored me. He still ignores me! Where is he now? He sends you to speak on his behalf. Does he ever speak for himself anymore?"

"He had no choice," Ira said. "Your barrier keeps him away."

The Grigori barked a derisive laugh. "For the moment. What was Jehovah's excuse for the last two thousand years?"

"We can't reason with him," Aaron said quietly to Ira. "No one can reason with these fools."

Ira frowned, wondering whether Barakel really was a fool. Certainly he had committed terrible crimes, but he had also made a sincere effort to make amends. He had taken action against his fellow Grigori and paid a horrific price for it. His wounds attested to that.

"But why, Aaron?" Ira asked, keeping his voice quiet. "Is it out of character for Jehovah? Sometimes it seems that way. He goes out of his way to forgive our transgressions. Forgiven, forgotten. Our Messiah's sacrifice—"

"Was dispatched for humanity alone," Aaron finished. "You know this. You know it very well."

This made it no less painful to see Barakel out in the cold. Facing Barakel with this difficult truth was even more difficult than it had been to face Mahaway, and that earlier experience had nearly broken Ira's heart. Mahaway's false hope had been almost more than he could bear.

Ira looked deep into Barakel's eyes. "You must understand why it has to be this way. You've seen what happens when our two species intermingle."

Species was the wrong word. Despite what the Grigori would have mankind believe, they were not some alien species from another part of the galaxy. Jehovah had made them. They bore more similarities to mankind than differences.

"All I understand is why you *think* it has to be this way," Barakel spat. "Jehovah is wrong, and it will come back to bite him."

"Where are the rest of the Grigori?" Brighton asked. "I saw at least a hundred of them inside the mansion, during the ritual. Did any of them escape?"

Barakel turned his bloody nose to stare at the young man. "The Grigori cannot be killed so easily. They have retreated."

That's all he'll say, despite what they did to him, Ira thought. "But once we lower the barrier, they'll be powerless to raise it again."

The Grigori conceded this with a single nod. "There may be other means of achieving their goals. Our goals, if they will have me." Barakel gazed out over the exposed mud of the riverbed. "Though it's no certainty you'll be able to lower the barrier. It may be too late."

It saddened Ira that Barakel would rejoin them after making strides on Jehovah's behalf, but this was the way Jehovah had ordained matters. Perhaps the Grigori could not be rehabilitated, their fates having been sealed long ago.

"Barakel, we bear you no ill will, but we advise you to give up the struggle," Aaron said. "This story can end just one way. We know it, and so do you. You and your kind were designed for one purpose, and the moment you abandoned that purpose you committed yourselves to the current outcome."

"And if we return to it?"

Aaron's lips pressed together. "In time, there could be peace."

Ira thought this was a bit disingenuous. Aaron's definition of peace probably looked very different than Barakel's. The look of consternation on Barakel's face told Ira that even he sensed Aaron's true meaning.

"I see this cannot be settled," Barakel said.

"No, it can't," Ira said, feeling a crushing weight of sadness. "I'm afraid we've come to an impasse."

Barakel turned his back on them and staged back into the forest. "I must deliver the bad news," he called over his shoulder. "Pray we never meet again."

Ira felt deep in his heart that it was over, that he would never be troubled by Barakel again—though only time would tell whether the same could be said for the entire human race. The Grigori could protest for all eternity and never achieve their desired outcome. They had to face the consequences of their actions.

And so must I, Ira reminded himself.

*   *   *

For Brighton, the meditation was old hat. Ira instructed them to form an unbroken line and wade into the brown, sludgy water, focusing their thoughts on bringing down the barrier. Once they had entered the shrunken river—and it only went up to their ankles—Brighton felt the current of possibility he had sensed before, and with the sensation came a vision of the barrier itself, a spherical field of crackling energy. He wondered whether it looked the same to all the others, or if their visions were as unique as fingerprints.

This barrier, though invisible to the naked eye, had a similar effect to the various metallic barriers he and his fellow adventurers had encountered. At Giza, at Tiahuanaco, at Khunjerab, they had all been precisely the same.

Prisons, he realized with a start. *They're prisons, and there may be many more of them, keeping at bay ancient evils from the past.*

No wonder Ira had felt so ill at ease when they'd crossed through the barrier in Egypt. He must have been able to sense the creatures inhabiting it. Creatures like Abranel and Ohia, searching for some weak-willed soul to carry them out of captivity.

Regardless of what they saw, every individual in the circle could probably feel the strength emanating from Ira and Aaron, filling them and galvanizing them. The barrier may have been strong enough to keep Jehovah out, but it proved relatively simple to dismantle from the inside. It had been created through the power of human intention, and the same power was its undoing. It dissipated under their spiritual assault.

The river and the forest vanished with the same abruptness.

Brighton drew deep breaths as he opened his physical eyes for the first time in thirty minutes and beheld the starlit mountainside.

"It's time to say goodbye," Ira said to him, drawing him aside.

Brighton didn't know how to reply. "Does it have to be right this instant?"

"I've finished what I came to do. I died, Sherwood. If I were to linger, I wouldn't be much different than the Nephilim spirits, would I?"

Brighton felt awkward about it, but he pulled Ira into a hug. The rabbi resisted at first, but then surrendered to the moment.

"Ira, I need to tell you—"

"Don't," Ira said. "We've both apologized. Let's not belabor it. The point is, we're ending on good terms."

"Is this really the end?"

"For now."

In another time and place, Brighton would have found that answer infuriating. Vague and blurry, so typical of Ira's endless equivocations. Today, however, he smiled.

"It gives me great pleasure to know that you don't change," Brighton said.

Ira pulled away from the hug. "If only that were true."

And like a wisp of smoke, Ira went away.

EPILOGUE

Somewhere Else

This time, when Ira passed out of this life into the next he held onto his memory of it. He landed in a world of darkness and immediately used his natural faculties to transform it into a paradise. The heavenly dimension erupted into flamboyant color. The sky and woodland looked exactly like he had always pictured Eden. The perfect garden, everything in proper balance, well-maintained and nothing overgrown.

Enoch awaited him, lazing against the trunk of a particularly broad tree. Swollen cherries strained its branches, a flood of the over-ripe fruit having spilled to the ground. Ira stepped carefully to avoid squishing them under his runners.

"Do you trust me now?" Enoch asked.

Ira sat down next to Enoch. Wind rustled the leaves and plopped a cherry down into Ira's open palm. He smiled and brought it to his lips, tasting it.

"Of course I trust you."

"You didn't last time we spoke," Enoch reminded him.

He guiltily remembered that conversation in Trevor's parlor. "I wasn't in my right mind. I thought you might be working against me."

"I'm glad you came around, Ira. Even if it came so late."

"Too late?"

"It depends," Enoch said. "You're here, after all. That's a good sign."

Ira took a second bite of the fruit, finishing it off. "Trevor said I damaged myself by overusing the power of the zohar."

"Just about any use is too much." Enoch reached up and picked a cherry for himself. "You and I are alike in a lot of ways. I, too, once paid the price for failing to abstain from exhibiting that power. And there aren't many people who have faced the Grigori as we have. We were both forced to deliver catastrophic messages. It can't have been easy for you."

Ira nodded. "It's hard to understand why there's no room in Jehovah's heart for the repented ones."

"Barakel is not repentant," Enoch said.

"What price did you pay for your failure?"

"For one thing, I was taken out of the world and not allowed to return for thousands of years. Until you came along."

Ira's eyes flared in surprise. "I assumed that was by choice."

"I loved every day I spent in the world. I would have stayed for all eternity, were I allowed."

"I'm not sure I feel the same way. I love the world, yes, but given the choice between here and there?"

"The world is imperfect," Enoch agreed. "A work in progress. It's a far better place now than it was in my time. Barely recognizable. But I wanted to play a part in the world's redemption. Instead I've had to watch from afar. I envy you, Ira."

"Even after everything I've done?"

"I envy the full life you've lived."

Ira swelled with pride, and simultaneously knew that was the wrong reaction. "Yet I know I will face a consequence."

Enoch stood up, then helped Ira to his feet. The two men walked away from the tree, avoiding the fallen cherries.

"The problem is your memory," Enoch explained. "Once something is in your memory, it is almost impossible to forget."

The wording was so close to something Ira had once said to Brighton. Ira wondered if the similarity had been intentional.

"You must forget," Enoch continued. "You have learned too much. The damage you've sustained is directly correlated to the knowledge you've accumulated."

This, too, was similar to a position Ira had often taken. As though to demonstrate Enoch's point, Ira's memory ventured in time to a sunny day off the coast of Tubuai. Ira and Wörtlich had rested at the back of a boat. Ira could recall Wörtlich's exact words: *"Ira, you could do so much good with the knowledge you possess, but you keep it to yourself. Is that not the epitome of selfishness? If the discovery of the Book allows us to share its knowledge with the world, do we not have an obligation to do so?"*

That had always been the temptation—to use the power of creation for the betterment of mankind. To use it for good. Whereas the only safe option was not to use it at all.

I had the best intentions, Ira thought, *and it still destroyed me. I didn't know where to draw the line, where and when to stop.*

"You're going to take my memory from me." Ira said this very quietly, fearing the answer. "My memory is my life. The people I loved… the places… everything I knew, everything that made my life worth living, everything I fought and died for? My memory is what makes me *me*."

"You knew there would be consequences."

"Please," Ira pleaded. "Let it be something else."

He remembered his mother and father, and his sister. The streets he had grown up along, on which he had played and rode his ramshackle bicycle which was forever breaking down. The synagogue where his father had taught him from the Torah. The long days at rabbinic school, days on which he had longed to be anywhere else. He remembered Aaron on the day they'd met, in that classroom, on the day of the snowstorm, on the day that triggered his fateful journey. His heart broke for the memories he had always wanted and never had, the most painful being his absent wife and children. It was worse than death to go on existing after you'd forgotten everyone and everything that had ever happened to you.

"I'm sorry, Ira. It's a terrible fate."

"You can't know."

Enoch steered him along a path that would lead them outside the trees and into a clearing. The sun shone brightly on the grass. It looked like a lovely place to spend a summer afternoon.

"Would you like to meet him?" Enoch asked.

Ira couldn't take his eyes off the sunlight, growing brighter and brighter as they approached. "Him?"

"Jehovah. He lives here, after all."

The all-consuming light blinded him—literally, Ira thought, as all the other details of this place disappeared.

"He will not be what you expect," he heard Enoch say from somewhere far off. "He is—"

"Don't tell me," Ira said. "I want to find out for myself."

*　　　*　　　*

The three-hundred-year-old Maison Chambois slanted over the River Lammat in central Zurich. Passersby strode over cobblestones next to the river's concrete embankment, and a string of red boats bobbed against the dock below it. Lagati barely spared them a glance.

It was a perfect day, and bound to get better once Lagati saw Antoinette again. He'd been able to think of nothing else on his day-long journey out of the mountains. At last free of the Grigori, he had a new lease on life, one so improbable that he couldn't account for it. For a while there, he hadn't been able to see past his own death. But here he stood, below a blue sky and surrounded by the comforts of his favorite city. Yes, it was a perfect day.

A young man in a bellhop's getup met him at the hotel's revolving door and took him inside, where the manager, a mustachioed native Swiss, greeted him.

"Good day, sir," the manager said, bowing low. "Your usual rooms have been prepared."

"Very well. Has the lady arrived?"

"The lady, sir?"

Lagati's heart sank. "I'm expecting Ms. Patenaude to join me. Please call up when she's here."

"Of course, sir." The manager offered an obsequious smile.

He entered the penthouse and closed door behind him. He then removed his jacket, freshly purchased earlier that morning so he could arrive looking presentable, and tossed it over one of two chaise lounges. His shoes clicked over the tiled floor.

Lagati slipped onto the balcony and admired the scenery. The Maison occupied the best slice of real estate in all of Zurich. The balcony boasted two enviable panoramas—the River Lammat wended through lushly urban hilltops, and the sparkling waters of Lake Zurich beckoned to the south.

He eased himself down into the cold embrace of a wrought-iron chair, relieving the pain so effectively disguised by his new suit. It would take weeks to recover, assuming he'd endured no damage beyond the superficial wounds scarring his once supple skin.

I'll be fine, he told himself. *I've been through worse.*

This was an outrageous lie, told reflexively. Of course he hadn't been through worse. He'd been through a literal form of hell.

He dozed off as the lake air rolled over him, aware only of the knock at the door that startled him awake.

"Antoinette!" he said as he darted back through the salon. He composed himself before unbolting the door, otherwise he might have thrust it open with the undisciplined exuberance of a pimply teenager.

Instead of Antoinette's lovely face, Lagati stared into the dull gray eyes of the hotel manager.

"What do you want?" Lagati demanded, not caring if he came off too aggressively.

The manager was stupefied. He collected himself quickly, however, and snapped a smile onto his face. "Your wine selection, sir."

Only then did Lagati notice the bottles in the manager's hands. Two selections, both exquisitely expensive. His usual order.

"Thank you." Lagati took the wine and retreated into the suite.

He placed both bottles on the fireplace's ornate mantel. He looked up at the clock as the minute hand finished another of its endless revolutions. Antoinette should have arrived by now. What could have delayed her? No explanation made sense—

—except for the one that did.

Lagati shook it off. No, she had gotten out. Of course she had. He had practically ordered her to flee, and she wouldn't have dared ignore his instructions. Besides, Wendell wouldn't have let her. Wendell would not have let him down in this matter.

As much as it had pained him to lose his home, to lose the Khunjerab base, to lose his status, none of those losses would compare to losing Antoinette.

Stop obsessing, he told himself. *She'll be here.*

He needed no more convincing. He moved into the bedroom and

smoothed the satin sheets, tucked as neatly as a candy bar wrapper. He was exhausted, and the bed proved quite a temptation. If he fell asleep, even for an hour or two, chances were that Antoinette would have arrived by the time he awoke. What better way to pass the time than by sleeping through it?

Lagati removed his shoes and lay down. The room was so quiet, but soon it would be filled with conversation. Antoinette was one of the best conversationalists he had ever known; it was one of the reasons he had grown so fond of her.

Soon, he reminded himself as he fell asleep. *She'll be here soon.*

*   *   *

The town of Ercolano, long ago subsumed by nearby Naples, hadn't changed in all the time Dario had been away. The air still smelled like salt and the roads remained dirty and congested. Vesuvius looked ready to belch up an apocalyptic cloud of death, but it barely troubled Dario's fellow citizens. They went about their business without the briefest look at the volcano. Dario had never gone a day here without staring at it for several minutes, but perhaps that's because he'd spent most of his time excavating the ruins at Herculaneum. Those ruins never let him forget what had happened two thousand years ago.

Dario hadn't been able to resist the lure of stopping here. When the train pulled into Naples, he'd gotten off without a second thought. He wouldn't be missed back home if he took a day to revisit his old worksite.

The narrow street housing the Herculaneum expedition's research office remained as unimpressive as ever. Dario instructed the taxi driver to stop along the curb outside the drab two-story building.

"Dario Katsulas? Could it be?" a voice asked.

As Dario paid the driver, he saw a stooped old man locking the front doors to the office. Dario would have recognized Sal Agostino anywhere; the professor had given Dario one of his first jobs.

"Good to see you, Professor," Dario said in Italian.

Agostino's eyes lit. "I heard what happened in South America."

"Rumors." In truth, Dario didn't know what kind of reports had gotten out about the events in Tiahuanaco, but it seemed safest to deny that anything extraordinary had happened. "I'm back in Italy. For good, hopefully."

"I don't suppose you're looking for work?" Agostino grinned. "We are still working closely with the Cairo Institute. There may be a position available."

"I appreciate that, but I think I'm ready to leave all that behind. I'm going back home."

"Somewhere in the south, is that right?"

"Palermo," Dario confirmed.

"Then why have you come?"

"For old time's sake." Dario took a deep breath as he looked toward the looming hulk of Vesuvius. From this angle, it was impossible to see the ruins of the villa. "Do you think I could access the site?"

"For you? Of course."

The professor only required a few minutes to prepare the necessary credentials to get Dario past security.

"I think I know the way," Dario said when Agostino offered to take him up the mountain personally. Not that Dario wouldn't have appreciated the professor's company; he simply wanted to take the journey alone.

Approaching the Villa of the Papyri was like travelling back in time. He entered the terrace and walked over its red paving stones. Vines and shrubs grew overtop just about every stone wall, column, and surface. Dario sat at the edge of a thirty-foot cliff and enjoyed the vista. Beyond the expansive city, dimmed by a trace of smog, lapped the ever-shifting waters of the sea.

The villa constituted a fascinating analog for the resilience of life. Every few hundred years, the volcano unleashed its fury, killing everything along its slope—and sometimes in more distant history, that destruction encompassed a wider area—but life invariably returned. Trees and foliage overtook the land again. The people returned. Perhaps foolishly, but they returned.

This line of thought brought up a reservoir of guilt for having killed Ohia—and Edie. Edie had done nothing wrong, and she might have been saved. He hadn't thought so at the time; he had believed that by killing her, he was saving her from a lifetime of torment.

But Brighton survived, he thought. *He was joined to one of the Nephilim, and he came through the experience whole and healthy. Who could say whether the same might have been true of Edie?*

The fact that he had barely known her only worsened his guilt. Would he have tried harder to save her had it been someone he was close with? Would he have brought himself to strangle the life out of Rhea with his bare hands?

He was forced to conclude that he wouldn't. Something he would have to live with.

At least he was home. In his worst moments, Dario hadn't believed he would ever see Italy again. He determined to never forget the horrors he'd seen, or the men and women who had died, but he would do his best to move on.

He owed it to Rhea to try.

*   *   *

The house was quieter than a mausoleum, and just as lonely. Gayle walked from room to room through her home of almost seven years. The furniture was covered in a fine layer of dust, a week's worth of accumulation that she normally wouldn't have abided in her other life, her normal life. The life she'd shared with Henry. She spent a few minutes in the bedroom, staring at the side of the bed where Henry had slept. Where he had died.

I won't be sleeping here tonight, she thought. She chose the fluffiest pillow and a folded comforter from the hall closet and carried them to the living room couch.

Pain throbbed in her palm and she turned her attention to the bandage. The doctor had said it would take a couple of months to heal, and even then she might live with occasional pain for the rest of her life. The long-term effects seemed appropriate somehow.

Night came, but she couldn't sleep. Instead she brought her laptop to the kitchen counter and sat on a stool. Once the screen flared to life, she went online and searched her contacts. Lots of them showed up, represented by green dots overlaid on a map. She could find no trace of Faisal, the only person she wanted to talk to. The only person besides Elisabeth who would understand what she was going through.

She began to type an email, stream-of-consciousness sentiments pouring out of her fingers like ink from a pen. She hoped he was all right, that he had managed to get home. Or maybe he remained in Gilgit, helping the survivors. God only knew how long it would take to restore order.

In the morning, an unexpected visitor showed up on her doorstep: the priestess Alice.

"Where have you been all week?" Alice asked when Gayle invited her inside. They sat across from each other at the kitchen table. "I sensed you were very troubled after we scattered Henry's ashes. You were asking about the Starseed people."

Gayle stood up without answering these loaded questions. She got a pair of teacups from the cupboard and began heating water in the kettle. She returned to the table.

"I needed to heal," Gayle said. No way was she going to tell Alice what had happened.

"Did you find any answers to the Starseed question?"

Gayle saw that Alice wanted an answer as badly as Gayle had a week ago. Alice would be better off with a convenient fiction.

"I'm afraid not," Gayle said. "I must have been wrong about what killed Henry."

Alice frowned. "I see."

The tea kettle whistled and Gayle got up to pour the steaming water into cups. She brought the cups to the table along with teabags.

Alice steeped the tea, raising and lowering the teabag with a slow, steady rhythm. "You had convinced me that the Starseed people were involved, Gayle. All of Henry's symptoms were consistent with energy burnout."

"It was a good theory," Gayle said. "But I was wrong."

Lying to Alice almost certainly meant Gayle wouldn't be able to continue their friendship. She wasn't up to the task of maintaining the lie.

Gayle felt crushing loneliness after Alice left. One by one, she was losing her friends as she decoupled herself from her former life.

I'll have to sell the house, Gayle realized.

Her head snapped up when she heard her laptop beep from its roost on the marble countertop. She hurried over and pried open the screen.

Gayle smiled, zeroing in on the bright green dot that blinked to life next to Faisal's name. Just like that, she didn't feel quite so lonely.

*   *   *

Brighton met Elisabeth on the sidewalk outside their hotel in Nuremberg. Together they drove twenty minutes east of the city to a hamlet situated along a winding stream.

"You're sure this is the place?" Brighton asked.

"He lived here as a child, yes."

Brighton parked the car and they stepped onto a shady lane lined with old houses on both sides.

"It feels strange to be here," Elisabeth said quietly. "What's a memorial without a body?"

"A memorial is about commemorating the dead. We don't need Wörtlich's body to remember him and celebrate his life."

She pointed to a house at the summit of a hill. The land around it was thickly forested except for a meadow on the northern slope.

"He was very fond of this land," Elisabeth told him as they hiked toward the meadow. "Emery brought me here once. He wanted to come back once he retired, after he finished teaching. Of course, we were no longer an item by that time."

They spent much of the afternoon wandering around the meadow as Elisabeth told Brighton about her and Wörtlich's time together. Brighton was amazed by the surprising details of the man. Wörtlich had struck Brighton as a deeply intelligent if stodgy old academic, but they hadn't gotten the chance to get to know each other. There hadn't been time for that.

"Are you going home after this?" Brighton asked after a lull in the conversation. "Back to the States?"

"Yes. Aren't you?"

Brighton ran his hand through the grass absently. "Not sure. I don't have a life to go back to. Most everyone thinks I'm dead, and I wouldn't even know how to begin explaining my absence. Perhaps it would be better to start fresh somewhere."

"Like where?"

"Oh, it doesn't matter."

"But surely there's people you would like to see again."

His first thought was Rachel, the girlfriend he'd left behind almost two years ago. He had looked her up and been pleased to discover that she'd gotten married and moved out west. What would be the point in dropping in on her? How might he expect her to react? She had moved on.

"Not really," he said, sighing. "It's better this way."

He saw Elisabeth back to Nuremberg, but didn't accompany her to the airport. It made more sense to stay put, at least until he had decided what to do with himself.

That evening, as he lay on his hotel bed, he was struck by the silence. Nobody was chasing him. He had nowhere to be, no crisis to avert. How bizarre that such peacefulness had once been his status quo!

His mind leapt from one disorienting dream to another. In the lucid moments between dreams, he clung to the knowledge of his present safety. It would be a long time before his dreams caught up to reality.

Amidst Brighton's nightmares, he briefly found himself on the edge of a broad river. He smiled as he watched the water flow downstream with almost overwhelming force. These waters, he believed, would never run dry.

"Ira, I'll never forget you," he whispered to himself.

Just as suddenly, the river was gone. With quiet confidence, he knew he would never see it again.

ABOUT THE
AUTHORS

EVAN BRAUN is an author and editor who has been writing books for the last two decades. *The Law of Radiance,* his third published novel, is the final volume in The Watchers Chronicle, the first two books being *The Book of Creation* and *The City of Darkness.* He lives in Winnipeg, Manitoba.

CLINT BYARS hails from Atlanta, Georgia, where he lives with his wife Sara and two children, Sydney and Reese. The author of *Devil Walk,* an autobiographical book chronicling his experiences with the demonic realm, Clint is also involved with Pokot Water, an international project aimed at providing clean water wells to remote regions of Kenya. He is the pastor of Forward Church.

9 781486 609130